FOR YO[...]
A SPECIAL INVITATION

**Come journey with us to the
wildest frontiers of the heart...**

Diamond
Wildflower
Romance

A breathtaking new line of
searing romance novels

...where destiny meets desire
in the untamed fury of the
American West.

...where passionate men
and women dare to embrace their
boldest dreams.

...where the heated rapture
of love runs free and wild
as the wind!

Prisoner of Passion

Captured in a whirling vortex, Elena gasped. What was wrong with her? She should be struggling, fighting to be free, but instead she had this terrible, wicked longing for she knew not what. She fought for breath as his palms cupped her buttocks and went still lower, drawing her pantalets down to her knees and over her ankles. His lips and fingers tickled a path upward, drawing tiny circles on the inside of her thighs. . . .

She gazed at the dark head bent over her and tried to concentrate on the heavens beyond but her body refused to ignore the sweet torment of his mouth and teasing fingers. "No, you can't!" she cried.

"But I can." His lips whispered against hers before lowering to suckle hungrily at her breast. Her barriers crumbled beneath the luring mouth and hands that drew her further and further down a path of no return. . . .

BANDIT'S KISS

MARY LOU RICH

DIAMOND BOOKS, NEW YORK

This book is a Diamond original edition, and has never been previously published.

BANDIT'S KISS

A Diamond Book / published by arrangement with the author

PRINTING HISTORY
Diamond edition / January 1993

ISBN: 1-55773-842-4

Diamond Books are published by The Berkley Publishing Group,
200 Madison Avenue, New York, New York 10016.
The name "DIAMOND" and its logo are trademarks belonging to Charter Communications, Inc.

PRINTED IN THE UNITED STATES OF AMERICA

10 9 8 7 6 5 4 3 2 1

To Raymond and Johnny, without whose love and support none of this would have been possible.

To my mother, Eunice Gammage, who shared with me her great love of reading and who encouraged me to write as far back as I can remember.

Thanks, Mom

BANDIT'S KISS

Chapter One

MARIA ELENA DE VEGA propped her head on her palm and watched the first rays of dawn creep silently across her floorboard. Sighing, she rose from her rumpled bed with sleep evading her again just as it had all week. Savoring the coolness of the floorboards against her bare feet, she walked to the window and opened the shutters. She gazed down on the courtyard, where a multitude of birds gathered for an early bath in the fountain. The peaceful scene below did nothing to quell the turmoil building inside her. Only a few hours from now she and her sister, Conception, would exchange places and Elena would be on her way to the convent.

Unable to still her anxiety, she went to the dresser and picked up her brush. Drawing it through her long black hair, she shook her head in disgust at the image in her mirror. "How could you let Cepi talk you into this madness?" The deeply shadowed topaz eyes staring back at her had no answer.

A soft tap at the door sent her heart into her throat. Had father discovered their plan already? She hurried forward and opened the door a crack. Her knees buckled with relief when she saw it was only her maid, Lupe.

"*Buenos dias, señorita,*" Lupe said with a bright smile. "I was across the patio and saw your shutters open. Would you like your bath now?"

1

"*Sí*, Lupe. And please send some powders along with a breakfast tray to my room. I have a headache." This was supposed to be her excuse for not dining below; her excuse for not riding as she usually did every morning. In truth her head *was* pounding, and she felt quite ill.

Later, after she'd bathed and choked down a portion of her breakfast, Elena stretched out on her bed and attempted to calm her jangled nerves. But before long she got up and smoothed the covers. She sighed. It was no use. If she was this undone, she wondered at her sister's state of mind.

Feeling a desperate need to keep busy, she rebraided her hair. Finally, after twisting it into a coronet on top of her head, she fastened it securely with her hairpins.

She walked around her comfortable but sparsely furnished room, straightening things, touching childhood treasures: a small brightly colored rock; a silver-framed daguerreotype of her mother. You're not leaving forever, she told herself, but still she shivered, feeling that after today nothing would ever be the same.

She jumped when a soft knock sounded on her door. "Elena, it's me," Conception called out. "I've come to say goodbye."

Swallowing down her fear, Elena took a deep breath, knowing she was as ready as she'd ever be. She placed a hand over her stomach. Her middle felt as if she'd been kicked by a horse. She hurried to the entry and ushered her older sister inside. She stared at Cepi's dark dress and thickly veiled hat. "You look like you're in mourning."

"How else do you think we could get away with it?" Conception whispered, already removing the hat. She tossed it on a chair and quickly slipped out of her deep blue traveling dress. "Are you ready?"

Elena noted ruefully that her sibling showed no sign of her own unrest. In fact, Conception's blue eyes fairly danced with excitement. "You act like you're going on a picnic."

"Even better, I'm eloping," Conception teased.

"Aren't you worried at all?"

"Not in the least. Now, hurry up and get dressed." Conception darted to Elena's closet and rummaged among the few hangers. "Ugh. Don't you have anything more stylish?"

"No, I don't," Elena said with disgust. "I didn't plan on your wearing my clothes."

Conception finally removed a dark cotton frock and put it on. She took a black wig from her traveling bag and held it up. "Remember this? I took it from the masquerade trunk in the old wing." After covering her silver-blond tresses, she eyed herself critically in the mirror. Her nose wrinkled in distaste. "Well, I won't have to wear it long. My own clothes are packed in the trunk I said you borrowed for your trip to Santa Fe."

"I know. Remember? Lupe and I had to move it down here last night," Elena said. "I think you stuffed your furniture in there, too. It weighs a ton."

"I wanted to be sure I have everything I might need," Conception said innocently.

The sounds of rattling harness and pounding hoofbeats in the courtyard outside drew Conception away from the mirror and sent her scurrying toward the open window. Cautiously parting the lace curtains, she peered out. "The coach is here."

Trying to calm her shaking hands, Elena frantically fastened the last of the buttons on the high-necked navy silk dress. "There. How do I look?"

"The hat—quickly." Conception grabbed the headgear and slapped it down on Elena's head. "Stoop down."

Elena bent so that the heavy veiled piece could be anchored to hide her dark hair. "Oww! You don't have to ram the hatpins through my scalp," she said wincing.

"We have to make sure it won't fall off. *Perfecto*. See for yourself," Conception said, shoving her toward the dresser mirror.

Elena gasped. "Oh, I can't believe it." The girl reflected in the mirror looked exactly like Cepi when she'd entered the room only minutes before. For the first time since she'd agreed to this charade, Elena actually believed they might get away with it.

"Do you remember what to do, little sister?" Conception asked, anchoring the veil with yet another hairpin. "I've already bid Father goodbye, so all you have to do is go to the carriage."

Elena nodded, remembering the "goodbye." The row had practically shaken the rafters in the hacienda the day before. It ended with their father shouting that Conception would do as she was told, and Cepi screaming back a vow that she would never speak to him again. Elena knew, unless he had changed his mind, she wouldn't have to worry about confronting him. The knock on the door sounded loud as a cannon.

"It is time, señorita," the guard called out from the hall.

Filled with icy apprehension, Elena walked to the window and looked out. Below, four matched horses pranced in front of a shiny black coach bearing the Spanish Angel crest. A dozen well-armed outriders accompanied the carriage. All of them waited for her. She sucked in a ragged breath.

"Don't forget these," Conception said.

Elena wiped her sweaty palms on her dress and took the long white gloves from her sibling's pale hands. She drew them on to hide her own darkly tanned skin. She glanced at her sister. "I guess I'm ready."

Conception gave her a hasty embrace, then pushed her toward the doorway. "Go quickly, Elena, before they come to see what is taking me so long. *Vaya con Dios,* my sister, until we meet once more."

"*Vaya con Dios,* Cepi. Be happy," she whispered. She waited until Conception, wearing the simple clothes and dark wig, took her seat by the window. After a farewell wave of her hand, Elena opened the door and stepped into the hall. "I'm ready, Francisco," she whispered to the waiting man.

"*Bueno,* señorita. Then we will go." He turned to lead the way down the stairs.

"*All you have to do is go to the carriage.*" Conception's instructions had sounded so simple. Elena took a deep breath to gather courage. Swallowing against the dryness in her throat, she slipped past the open door of the library—and her father seated behind his desk.

"Goodbye, my precious," he called out.

"Goodbye, Father," she croaked before she recalled Conception's vow never to speak to him again. *Please, God, don't let him follow me to the carriage.* She shivered, forcing her cowardly legs to increase their pace down the shadowy hallway toward the arched entry doors of the hacienda. By the time she'd reached the sunlit courtyard, she was running to the safety of the waiting coach.

When they were out of sight of the walled compound, relief and exhaustion overcame her, and rocked by the heavily springed coach, Elena drifted off to sleep. Sometime later a gnawing pang in her stomach awakened her.

Yawning, she sat up and tossed back the multitude of veils. She frowned, wishing she could remove the contraption but knew she dared not. Even though she'd closed the coach curtains to keep out the dust, a sudden stop could be her undoing. She'd never be able to get the hat on again before the door opened.

Patting her rumbling stomach, she glanced about the coach. *Cepi loves to eat. There has to be food somewhere.* She spied a large lump under a folded lap robe on the black leather seat opposite her. *A basket.* Lifting it to the seat beside her, she grinned at the weight. After removing her gloves, she poked among the contents, finding tortillas filled with shredded beef; goat cheese wrapped in corn husks; beans and rice in a covered pot so thick it was still warm; grapes, along with a rosy peach fresh from the orchard; and a bottle of chilled sangria.

As Elena sampled the fare, it occurred to her that after the sisters at the convent discovered who she really was and sent her back to her father, she might be on bread and gruel for the rest of her life. She took another bigger bite. *Well, at least today I won't starve.*

After devouring a good portion of the meal and a half bottle of the wine, Elena repacked the hamper. Now in better spirits, she chuckled, knowing if Conception had remembered the basket, she would have removed it to take later.

She lowered her veils and raised the coach curtain. Moving to the opposite seat so she could avoid most of the dust, she gazed out the window, nodding her head when a close-riding *vaquero* touched his hat in respect. She noticed the ammunition belts crisscrossing the man's chest and the rifle encased in his saddle sheath. The others she could see were likewise armed. Father might be sending Conception to the convent, but he appeared to be taking no chances with her safety.

Elena knew she owed her armed escort to the bandit that had plagued the gold shipments. *El Gato del Noche,* the cat of the night, people called him. Because like another mysterious black cat, the jaguar, he appeared out of nowhere and disappeared the same way—along with the Spanish Angel gold. Her father had placed a large bounty on the man's head, but no one had yet collected it.

Apparently the outlaw had a personal vendetta against her family's Spanish Angel ranch, for he robbed no one else. She'd heard the maids whisper excitedly, telling tales of his mysterious good looks and his daring deeds. They made him sound quite romantic. But romantic or not, Elena hoped he remained elsewhere. She would have enough trouble this trip without any bandit adding to it.

The coach wheels churned the red earth, filling the inside of the carriage with fine silt. Elena reluctantly lowered the curtain to avoid more of the dust that covered her clothing and the seats. The air grew stifling with the coach closed, and Elena envied the men outside, wishing she, too, could be on her horse. She considered asking if she might ride atop the carriage but immediately dismissed the idea. Conception, loathing the heat, would never ride outside, and since Elena was supposed to be Conception, she couldn't, either.

Realizing by the position of the sun that it was just past noon, Elena knew they wouldn't reach the convent until well after dark. Shut inside, the day would drag. Hoping the time would pass more quickly if she could manage another nap, she leaned back against the seat and closed her eyes.

The sound of gunfire jolted Elena from her sleep. She sat up puzzled. Leaning forward, she yanked at the window drape and stuck her head out the window. The flatland had disappeared, and sage and juniper-covered hills rolled into the distance. She twisted to see in the other direction. The coach was entering a narrow red rock canyon.

A gunshot cracked from above. Someone in the rocks had fired at them!

"Señorita, close the curtain! Get on the floor. Bandits!" the man riding beside the coach shouted at her.

Elena slid from her seat to her knees. "Bandits?" Unable to contain her curiosity, she lifted the edge of the shade and peeked out.

Zing! A ricocheting bullet penetrated the drape above her head. It plunked into the seat facing her.

"*Madre de Dios!*" Elena gasped. She dropped the covering and hugged the floor.

"After them!" a voice called out. Hoofbeats thundered away from the coach and faded into the distance.

A loud rumble filled the air.

Thunder? Impossible. A landslide!

The coach rocked. It teetered on edge.

She gripped the seat. *It's going over!* She screamed. Her fingers lost their hold. Her head rammed against the door.

The vehicle crashed down on its wheels and jolted to a stop. The door jerked open. Dazed from her bump, Elena looked up from the floor. Her eyes widened. The biggest man she had ever seen stood in front of her.

From under a massive, battered sombrero eyes as big and brown as a puppy's stared at her in amazement. "*Dios mío!* It is a woman!"

More angry than afraid, Elena hastily straightened her skirt, which in the tumble had risen above her thighs. She scrambled to the seat and tried to regain a portion of her dignity. Staring past the man, she saw that her father's "protectors," lured away from the coach, had been overpowered. She was surrounded by bandits.

The big man motioned to another until a series of bewildered eyes gazed at her. Clothed in rags, but armed to the teeth, the men milled around the carriage, arguing in hushed voices. They seemed unsure, uncertain of what to do. Apparently she was the last thing they'd expected.

Other hoofbeats raced toward them. The men backed away from the coach.

A man on a huge black stallion galloped up to the conveyance. He drew the prancing beast to a stop just outside the open door.

"*Qué pasa?*" he growled. "What is wrong? Why aren't you unloading the gold?"

"*Jefe*, there is no gold," the giant answered. He stooped to peer inside again, as if hoping to see something he had missed. His large fingers tugged at a thick, drooping mustache. "The coach, she carries only a woman."

"A woman?" The newcomer jumped from his horse. With a jangle of spurs, he strode to the open coach door.

Staring into the large barrel of the bandit's pistol, Elena was grateful for the heavy veil. She forced her eyes upward, past the gun to the gloved hand; up the sleeve of the silk shirt; across a broad shoulder to the scarf tied around a tanned neck. She raised her gaze to the thin, unsmiling lips above a strong chin. The rest of the man's face was hidden behind a mask. The bandit chief, from the top of his flat crowned sombrero to the toes of his shiny boots, was clothed completely in black.

Elena gasped, knowing him instantly. It wasn't just his clothing, nor his unusual height or the breadth of his shoulders that identified him. It was the watchful menacing stillness with which he regarded her, the lethal predatory awareness radiating from him.

Elena's heart beat with such frantic painful strokes she found it hard to breathe. She shrank back against the seat. No romantic figure this, the man was terrifying. "*El Gato del Noche,*" she whispered.

"I see you recognize me," the man purred in a dangerously silken voice.

Elena fought rising panic. She must remain calm; to do otherwise might incite him to further violence. She sat frozen, every nerve, every muscle, every fiber of her being distressingly aware of his tall, virile masculinity. The faint scent of horse, leather, and tobacco drifted through the open coach door to assail her nostrils. Sensual and sleek, like the cat he was named for, he had a restlessness, a barely leashed savagery, that she sensed could erupt at any time.

His features expressionless, he made no effort to ease her tension. He brazenly assessed her, going from the tip of her veil-covered hat, to insultingly linger on the agitated rise and fall of her breasts, before sliding down her dress to her booted feet. Uneasy, she watched, waited, wondering what his next move would be.

Slowly, deliberately, *El Gato* backed away from her and turned his gun toward the now unarmed men who had been yanked from the top of the coach. "What trick is this?" he asked so softly that the men appeared more frightened than if he had shouted.

Raising a hand, the driver touched his forehead, making the sign of the cross, as if hoping his hasty prayer would save him from the outlaw's wrath. He stammered an answer. "It is true, señor. There is no gold. We carry only Don Enrique de Vega's daughter." He pointed toward her.

A snarl of pure rage came from the bandit chief's throat. "Where do you take the bastard's spawn?"

"We travel to the Convent of the Virgin of Lasting Sorrows, señor. Señorita Conception is to become a nun," the driver whined.

El Gato again glanced inside the coach.

Elena trembled under his piercing gaze.

He tilted his head, studying her thoughtfully. "He must think highly of this daughter to offer her such protection."

The coachman twisted his hat nervously. "*Sí*, señor. She is the joy of his life."

"Then he would pay well to get her back," El Gato said.

Conflicting, turbulent emotions coursed wildly through Elena's veins, belying the icy perspiration that trailed down her back, making her shiver. He couldn't—he wouldn't. But she knew that was exactly what he intended.

"No, señor. You cannot do this," the coachman protested. "Señor, *por favor*. Let her go," he pleaded. "Don de Vega, he will be very angry if you do not."

The bandit's laugh was cold, without feeling. "He can have her back—after he pays the price."

"What price, señor?"

"One hundred thousand *dollars* . . . in gold."

The coachman gasped. "But that is a fortune."

The chief nodded. "Is she not worth it?"

"*Sí*, señor. But this is much money. What if *El Patrón*, he does not have it?"

"Then he will no longer have a daughter." The bandit chief gripped the top of the doorframe and bent his head to peer inside the coach. His gaze raked Elena's body, then his eyes locked on the veil. His lips drew back in a humorless smile, showing teeth, brilliant white against his dark skin.

Her heart fluttering like a trapped bird, Elena gasped, recognizing the smile for what it was. The joy of a tiger sighting its prey. Fighting the impulse to scream, she rubbed the gooseflesh prickling her arms.

As though sensing her fear, his smile widened. Through the slits of the mask, eyes of midnight blue glittered like frozen chips. The sun flashed off the bandit's guns as he straightened to motion to one of his men. His voice, chilling as a blast of winter wind, commanded, "Take her!"

Chapter Two

ELENA paced back and forth across the brightly patterned Indian rugs that covered the dirt floor of the dimly lit cave. The eerie shadows cast by a lone flickering candle on the table did nothing to reassure her troubled mind. "How much longer?" she cried. Her voice echoed back from the black depths, mocking her. Being confined in the chamber was driving her mad. Staying her restless movements, she peered down the narrow passage to where bright rays of sunshine filtered across the opening. She closed her eyes and listened to the childrens' laughter, mothers' scolding, and dogs' barking. Hearing the happy sounds, she might have imagined herself in any small rural village. She had only to open her eyes to know all was not as it seemed.

It had been three days since she'd been blindfolded and brought to this place. Three days she'd been held prisoner, isolated from everyone except the heavyset man with the drooping mustache who'd brought her there; the man the leader had called Emanuel. In that time she'd made several attempts to distract the lumbering, bearlike man, slipping past him, hoping to escape. Every time he'd caught her before she'd exited the cave entrance.

At least she hadn't been mistreated, she thought. The giant had been kind enough, providing her with fresh water and meals. She couldn't suppress a faint smile, remembering his embarrassment when he brought her a large covered vessel to use as a chamber pot.

Crossing her arms over her breasts, she shifted her gaze, tracing the tubelike passageway from the cave mouth to the large chamber room where she was being held. She'd never seen anything like it. It was frighteningly beautiful.

The ceiling high over her head dripped with long icicles of shining rock. Near the wall, two large pillar-shaped formations rose to touch the roof. Tracing their rough patterned ridges with her fingers, she wondered at their age. Amidst their grand splendor, the narrow rustic bunk between them seemed even more out of place. The bed had been made of poles lashed together with strips of rawhide. Wider strips woven across the frame formed a surprisingly comfortable support for the hay-stuffed mattress and pile of bright blankets.

After smoothing a wrinkle from the covers, she walked to a sturdy table set against the wall and picked up a heavy clay jug. She pulled the stopper, then poured water into a tin cup and took a sip, grimacing as she swallowed. The water was tepid and tasted of minerals, but it was all she had to ease her thirst.

Next to the jug, leaning from the top of an empty bottle, a sputtering candle scented the musty, damp air with burning tallow and beeswax. "All the comforts of home, if you don't mind living like a bat," she said ruefully. The cavern swallowed the sound of her voice, enforcing her uneasiness.

Again, she glanced toward the cave opening. What had become of the masked leader? she wondered. She hadn't seen him since she'd been brought to the outlaw camp. She shuddered, remembering the cold, unfeeling voice that had cut through her like a knife; the granite-blue eyes that promised he'd show no mercy if the ransom wasn't paid.

When she'd questioned Emanuel, the man simply told her *el jefe* wasn't on the mountain. Where had he gone? She blinked. *Por Dios! What will happen to me when he does return?*

Elena sat down on the woven leather chair seat and chewed a ragged fingernail. She wished she knew what was taking place at the hacienda. Had her father discovered it was she and not Conception that had been taken? A chill, not caused by the dampness, crawled up her spine. Now that she'd had time to consider her rash deception, she was terrified of her father's reaction.

He had sworn Conception must enter the convent, babbling something about the angel. She shivered. The angel. Angelina Sandoval, the wife of Don Luis Sandoval, who'd died when a tile had fallen from the roof and struck her on the head. The servants said *La Madama,* the Mistress, still roamed the halls of the hacienda as if searching for the husband and young son she'd left behind. Elena had never seen the apparition, but the spirit had haunted her father for as long as she could remember. He must have some mad idea that the angel had told him to do this. Otherwise he'd never have sent Conception away. Her nervousness making it impossible for her to sit still, Elena stood and once again began to pace the floor.

Elena knew Conception, the image of their blond mother, Soledad, had always been her father's favorite—petted, pampered, given the very best of everything. While she, Elena, with her dark skin, hair, and eyes, had been a constant reminder of the despised Indian blood he carried. Although not neglected, she had never been given more than the bare necessities.

Elena remembered other times, years ago, when she had incurred his wrath.

Once she and Conception had found an old storeroom in the unused wing of the house. They had been delighted with their discovery of the masquerade wigs, elaborate *mantillas,* fancy capes, and ball gowns packed among cedar chips in old brass-bound trunks. Against the wall they'd discovered a portrait of a dark-haired young woman dressed in an elegant blue satin gown. While rummaging in a trunk, Conception had unearthed the very gown in the painting and insisted Elena try on the dress. Together they had gone to show their father.

Conception had remained in the hallway, watching when Elena swept into the library. Elena remembered how she'd held her dark head high, wanting to show her father that she, too, could be beautiful like the lady in the picture. But when he'd looked up from his papers, his reaction hadn't at all been what she'd expected.

His eyes had widened. He'd gasped. The color had drained from his terror-stamped face.

Elena had been so confused, she hadn't known what to do. Then, giggling, Conception had bounced into the room and broken the spell. Their enraged father had sent both of them to their room without dinner, forbidding them to ever enter that section of the house again.

Elena had hidden the satin gown, but she had never discovered the identity of the woman in the portrait, or the reason for her father's reaction. After that, at times Elena could have sworn he'd seemed a little afraid of her. But that was ridiculous, as he'd never hesitated to punish her for the slightest misbehavior.

Cold fear wrenched her insides as she wondered what punishment he would mete out this time. Whatever he decides, she thought, Conception will be married and there won't be a thing he can do about that. Another thought stopped Elena in her tracks. *What if he makes* me *enter the convent instead?*

She believed in God and attended mass when the priest traveled to the small chapel on the hacienda grounds, but she didn't want to spend her whole life praying and being pious. Being held in the cave would be freedom compared to the confinement of a lifetime behind those cloistered, holy walls. That fate frightened her even more than the bandit. Panic-stricken, she whirled, staring toward the gleam of light at the cave entrance. "*Madre de Dios!* What have I done?"

"Thank you for a most excellent meal." Diego smiled across the table at his host, Don Enrique de Vega.

"Don't mention it, my friend. Come, Diego, join me in the library for some sherry." The stocky man raised a pudgy hand to wipe at bits of food clinging to the thick clump of whiskers that drooped over yellow-stained teeth.

Diego daintily dabbed the heavy linen napkin to his own bulky, but carefully trimmed, mustache. Pursing his mouth primly, he eased his chair back from the still heavily laden dinner table and got to his feet. He straightened his clothing, fastidiously flicking a tiny piece of lint from the tight purple velvet trousers with his manicured fingers, before turning to follow the older man into the paneled, book-lined room.

Enrique pulled the stopper from a crystal decanter, poured a measure of sherry into a glass, and handed it to Diego.

"*Gracias.*" Diego nodded. Taking the drink, he lowered himself gingerly to the edge of a brown leather sofa. He hid a smile behind a lavender monogrammed handkerchief as he watched Don Enrique pace the floor.

"I still find it hard to believe." The man ran a hand over his balding head. "To have my precious Conception snatched from under the noses of my *vaqueros*."

"Señorita Elena must be very upset about her sister," Diego said, just to make conversation. He'd only seen the younger girl once, and that was from a distance. He thought she must be disfigured or have some sort of infirmity, as she'd never been present on any of the many occasions when he'd dined with the family.

"Ha!" The man waved his pudgy hand. "She isn't even aware of it. She left three days ago to visit her aunt in Santa Fe."

"How long will she be gone?" Diego asked, trying not to yawn with boredom, his mind on other things.

"She didn't say. I wasn't even aware she was going so soon. When I came in from the range, I found a note telling me she had decided to leave early." He waved his hand again, as if dismissing the subject. "Enough of her. My mind is on more important matters. To think of my precious darling in the hands of those ruffians."

"The very thought of it makes me ill." Diego fanned his face with the scrap of linen. "What do you plan to do?"

Don Enrique paused at the desk. He pulled the stopper from a different gleaming decanter and slopped brandy into a crystal snifter. He tossed the drink back, swallowing it in one gulp. "I have to take the ransom to the old church ruins. Nothing is more important to me than having my daughter enter the convent."

"Oh, my. You don't suppose . . . ?" Diego allowed his voice to trail off.

"Suppose what?" the older man asked impatiently.

Diego fanned his face. "Oh, it would be too horrible to imagine."

"What are you babbling about, Diego?" Enrique snapped.

"You don't suppose the bandits . . . touched her?" Diego said faintly.

Don Enrique grew pale, as if that thought had not occurred to him. "No, they wouldn't dare." He shook his head. "I won't even think of it. Conception must enter the convent."

"My friend, why is this so important to you?" Diego asked, intrigued by the man's behavior.

Enrique walked to the chair behind the desk and flopped into it. After pouring another drink, he leaned forward. "Do you believe in ghosts, Diego?" he whispered hoarsely.

"Oh, my, yes. Although I would probably swoon if I should ever encounter one." Diego raised the back of his hand and pressed it to his forehead. He sagged against the back of the couch.

"I've seen one," Enrique whispered, looking about the room. "Right here in the hacienda."

"Here?" Diego squeaked, sitting up again.

"Have you heard of the angel?"

Widening his eyes, Diego nodded. "Yes, but I never considered it to be true."

Enrique drank the brandy in one gulp, then refilled the glass. "Well, you can believe it. She has tormented me for years. But lately it has grown even worse. She promised to condemn my soul to hell if Conception does not enter the convent."

The sip of sherry that Diego swallowed rose to choke him. Wiping tears from his eyes, he looked at the older man. "How do you know this? How does she speak to you?"

"She haunts my dreams. That's where she told me." He turned away, his shoulders bent. He placed his hands palms down on the heavy mahogany desk. "That's why I must get my daughter back." His eyes narrowed. "And I will." He slammed his fist down on the desktop, rattling the crystal with the force of his blow.

Diego leaned toward him. "What are you going to do?"

"Not what they think. I will take the ransom to the ruins as they want." A sly smile split the lined face. "But the thieves will never live to spend it."

"I don't understand," Diego said, mopping his face.

"I have a watch posted. When they come to retrieve the money we will capture them and make them lead us to their hideout."

"What will you do then?" Diego asked innocently. His insides twisted into knots.

"I have one hundred armed men in the hills. They will swarm over the bandits like locusts on a field." Enrique's lips parted over his teeth, his smile like that of a jackal. "Not one of them will be left alive."

"But what of the women and children in their camp?" Diego asked softly, his skin growing cold.

"Spawn of the devil. It matters not if they are one day or one hundred years old, they will be driven into the desert or they will all die."

Diego felt the blood drain from his face as he listened to his host speak of the slaughter of innocents. He knew the man would not hesitate to do what he said. In fact, he would relish it. Preoccupied with his thoughts, he started at the touch of a hand on his shoulder.

"Diego, are you all right? I'm afraid I have offended your delicate constitution with all this talk of bloodshed."

"I am feeling rather weak," Diego whispered. Gripping the couch back, he rose to his feet. "If you will excuse me, I must be going." Grateful that he was staying in the guest house instead of the main hacienda, Diego dabbed at the cold sweat dotting his brow. He did feel sick, realizing the men might at this very minute be riding into an ambush.

He had to warn them. Knowing firsthand of de Vega's cruelty, Diego had no doubt anyone captured would be tortured unmercifully.

He allowed his host to escort him to the wide entry doors and bid him goodbye. Knowing the man was still watching, Diego walked mincingly down the steps and allowed Carlos to help him into the waiting carriage. Cursing, he curbed his impatience until they were out of sight of the hacienda, then he leaned forward. "Whip them up, Carlos. We have a hard night's ride ahead of us." A vengeful smile crossing his face, he softly finished the sentence. "Then I intend to see what I can do to condemn a man's soul to hell—where it belongs."

Chapter Three

ELENA forced herself to swallow one more bite of the beans and rice that lay almost untouched on the pottery dish, hoping that by concentrating on her evening meal she could take her mind off whatever lay ahead. But it was no use; the food stuck in her throat. She placed her fork on the table and pushed her plate aside. Once again the gravity of her situation rushed in to confront her.

Three days. The time for her father to pay the ransom had passed, and still she'd heard nothing.

The softly spoken threat of the bandit chief returned to haunt her: *"He has three days to pay the gold. If he does not, he will no longer have a daughter."* She shivered and rubbed her arms, warming them against the chill creeping up her spine. The man's words had been deadly. So had the look on his face when he'd said them. She could expect no mercy from the man known as El Gato.

Drawing in an unsteady breath, she jumped to her feet and paced back and forth across the cave, unable to remove the bandit from her mind. She didn't know if she should feel grateful or apprehensive about El Gato's absence. Who was he? Why did he attempt to hide his identity? Her eyes narrowed thoughtfully. Was he afraid of being recognized? That would explain the mask.

21

His appearance had been so striking she knew if she had ever met him, masked or not, she wouldn't have forgotten. Taller than most. Strong and lean, his proud demeanor told her he was no ordinary thief. But the thing that added most to her disquiet was the feeling of danger that surrounded the man, the smoldering rage she sensed he fought to contain.

She turned toward the cavern entrance and watched the last slender rays of sunlight withdraw from the chamber floor as day surrendered to encroaching nightfall.

Her foreboding threatened to overcome her in the darkness. She hurried to the table, picked up a flint rock, and struck a spark to a sliver of wood. Carefully she carried it to the table and lit the cold remains of the half-burned candle. Holding her hands over the flickering flame, she savored its warmth, attempting to take comfort from the meager light and not notice the eerie shadows it cast on the cave walls.

Even from her prison chamber, she sensed the tension in the camp, as if others, too, waited for something to happen. Tonight there were no sounds of playing children, no barking dogs. The guitars that had strummed softly every night since her capture were quiet. The unnatural silence rasped on her nerves.

Her disquiet getting the best of her, she walked to the hard baked-clay ground around the circular rock firepit. Leaning forward, she peered up through a hole in the cave roof that acted like a natural chimney. Because the night was warm, there was no fire. Through the opening she saw bright stars twinkling in the ebony sky.

The soft dripping of water echoed from deep within the cave. Earlier in the day she had explored, hoping to find an exit farther in. Inky blackness and a faint fluttering overhead had sent her running back into the main chamber. She'd decided then that any escape she attempted would have to be made from the front entrance, even though she knew, from the way she was guarded, there would be scant chance of that.

A faint shuffling of footsteps warned her Emanuel was coming to pick up her dinner plate. Elena quickly readjusted the heavy veil, hiding her ebony locks in the thick folds. Once again her thoughts involuntarily went to the bandit chief. What dark secret did he hide behind his mask? Elena chewed on her lower lip, wishing for the millionth time that she hadn't been so eager to help her sister.

El Gato raced Diablo from the crest of the hill, sliding the horse to a stop in the midst of the camp. The beast had run like the wind, and he knew they had made good time. He jumped down, throwing the animal's reins to a young boy who'd run up at his arrival. "Is Rafael still here?" he asked anxiously, praying he had arrived before his friend left for the mission.

"No, señor. He rode out more than two hours ago."

"*Por Dios.*" Fear made him close his eyes. He was too late. "Damn Enrique de Vega! If he harms one hair on Rafael's head—" He spun on his heel and headed for a small group of men gathered around a campfire.

"*Jefe*, we did not expect you so soon," Emanuel said. "Is everything all right?"

"Things are not right, my friend. I came to stop Rafael, but I am too late." El Gato reached out and closed his unsteady hand around the tin cup full of coffee the stout man offered.

"*Qué pasa, amigo?*" Emanuel asked. The faint firelight etched the lines of concern written on his weathered face even deeper.

"I've learned that de Vega has a hundred men in the hills. He watches the mission, waiting for Rafael to come for the money. He plans to capture him." He took a painful breath.

"He will force Rafael to tell where the camp is."

"Don't worry, *Jefe*. Rafael will never tell." Emanuel's soulful eyes were as innocent as a child's above a large, slightly crooked nose. His heavy, drooping mustache nestled above a gently smiling mouth.

"I almost pray he does," El Gato said softly, walking away into the darkness. How could he explain the cruelty of Don Enrique to a generous, simple soul like Emanuel? El Gato followed a well-worn path to where a large outcropping of rock formed a natural outlook with a view for miles around. He sat down on a boulder, wishing he could see through the blackness of the night. But it was no use. His friend was out there somewhere, maybe in trouble, and there was not a damn thing he could do but wait.

He would never forgive himself if anything happened to Rafael. He should have known a man like de Vega had no honor; that he would risk even the life of his daughter rather than lose any of his ill-gotten gains.

He thought of his little ragtag band, mostly farmers whose land had been taken by the greedy de Vega. They would have little chance against gunmen. He would wait, see if Rafael made it back, then urge the people to leave the mesa when it became daylight. He knew most of them had relatives in other villages who would take them in. This was his fight, and they had made it theirs out of loyalty, but he could no longer endanger them and their families. He frowned. There had to be another way.

He thought of the strange conversation Don Enrique had had with Diego. Now he wished he'd paid more attention to the man's ramblings. He raised his hand to his eyes, trying to wipe away the fog clouding his brain. God, he was tired. Maybe if he got some sleep his mind would be clearer. He took one last look at the thick darkness in the valley, drained the dregs of the now cold coffee, then turned and walked back to the campfire.

"*Jefe! Jefe*, wake up!"

El Gato jerked back to consciousness at the touch of Emanuel's hand on his shoulder. "What is it?" he asked, automatically shaking out his high-topped boots before pulling them on.

"A horse, *Jefe*. Coming across the canyon. I think it is Rafael's." Emanuel crumpled the rim of his sombrero between his fingers. A worried frown wrinkled his plump face.

"Rafael? Thank God!" El Gato tucked his shirttail inside his pants and hurried toward the crest of rock where he'd waited the night before. He stood on the pinnacle, shading his eyes with his hand, shielding them from the slash of crimson that told of the coming dawn.

A lone gray horse walked slowly across the valley floor. The rider lay slumped against the animal's neck. When the gray stopped to crop grass, the man fell to the ground.

"Oh, God. No!" Aching inside, the bandit chief spun on his heel and ran to camp to get his stallion. Slamming his gear on the black, El Gato called to Pedro, a tall skinny man with a hooked nose, telling him to saddle up and follow.

His face grim, El Gato checked his twin Colt .44s, then slid them back into the black leather holsters. Not waiting for the other rider, he raced Diablo toward the head of the narrow rock trail that led to the valley. Eyes narrowed, he scanned each hill for de Vega's riders, afraid they might have trailed Rafael back to the hideout. But the only sign of life he saw was the gray gelding.

When he had traversed the steep, rocky path to the canyon floor, El Gato kicked the stallion into a gallop, swiftly covering the distance to his friend. He pulled the horse up, jumping off before the animal came to a stop. Rafael lay unmoving, facedown on the ground.

El Gato knelt and gently turned the young man over. He unbuttoned the front of Rafael's blood-covered shirt and pulled it away from the awful cavity in his chest. His trembling hand felt for a heartbeat. Faint, but it was there. He blinked, hiding the threatening moisture in his eyes.

Pedro rode up and jumped down to join him. "Is he alive?" the thin man asked softly.

"Barely. When I get on Diablo, hand him up to me. Cover the hoofprints in case he was followed, then bring his horse on to camp."

"*Sí, Jefe*." Pedro bent and lifted Rafael.

"Stand, Diablo," El Gato ordered.

The horse quivered, showing the whites of his eyes when he caught the scent of Rafael's blood, but didn't move when the wounded man was placed in his master's arms.

Cradling Rafael, El Gato guided the horse with his knees, heading him across the canyon and up the steep trail to the mountain stronghold.

"My brother!" a young woman cried out. Maria raced to the side of the horse, anxious to reach the unconscious man.

"He's been shot, but he's still alive," El Gato said. "Get Felipe!" he shouted to one of the gathering crowd.

"I am here, *Jefe*." The stoop-shouldered, gray-haired man who acted as the camp doctor hurried to his side.

Emanuel rushed to the stallion and took the bleeding boy in his massive arms. Carrying him as tenderly as a baby, the man walked quickly toward the hide tent, where Maria lifted the flap.

El Gato followed close behind.

Felipe, entering with his bag, pointed to a long rustic table. "Put him here. It will be easier to remove the bullet." He turned to El Gato. "Go, and take this one with you." He pointed to Emanuel, who blubbered noisily behind him. "Leave this to me and Maria."

El Gato reluctantly followed Emanuel out of the tent, try-ing to take comfort in the fact that Felipe was as competent as any doctor he'd ever seen. But a cold fist gripped his heart. Rafael's wound was bad—very bad.

He walked to the small campfire and poured a measure of scalding coffee into a battered tin cup. Looking around for Diablo, he saw the horse had already been cared for and now grazed with the rest of the ramuda in a fenced box canyon off to one side of the camp. Always on the alert, he scanned the rest of the village.

A row of primitive shelters hugged the edge of a bluff. Hides stretched over crude pole frames sheltered the people from the sun and rain, while the bluff blocked the wind. A bubbling spring at the edge of the canyon provided water for both people and animals. A trio of milk goats, tended by a small boy, grazed on scrub brush opposite the shelters. Hidden and easily defended, the whole camp rested in an oblong indentation on top of a large mesa. The only entrance was a steep narrow trail that wound precariously up the side of a cliff.

He marveled at the sight each time he entered the camp. Sipping his coffee, he thought back to the first time he'd seen it after he'd returned to New Mexico.

Riding alone, he'd tried to rob one of de Vega's gold shipments and had gotten nothing but a bullet in the arm for his trouble. After escaping the *vaqueros*, he'd stopped at Felipe's hut in search of water. The old Indian had taken him in and removed the bullet. Knowing the wounded bandit wouldn't be safe there, the elderly man had packed a cache of food and brought him to this mountain. In a few days Felipe and others joined him. All had grudges against Don Enrique and his band of *vaqueros* and wanted to join him in his fight.

With the people's help he'd stolen several sizable gold shipments. He'd also stolen sheep and cattle and generally harassed the greedy land baron, earning the name El Gato, along with the five thousand dollar price on his head. His glance strayed back to the tent. Guilt and remorse smote him anew. No matter how great his need for revenge, never before had his quest cost one of his men their lives. He prayed it hadn't now.

The late afternoon sun sank over the horizon, lighting the sky with crimson fire, but El Gato paid scant attention to the sight. His eyes were riveted on the man approaching him. Tears ran unashamed in twin furrows down Felipe's face telling him before the old man spoke that Rafael was dead.

Felipe confirmed his fears, then left him alone with his sorrow. He found it hard to realize that the handsome, joy-filled young man would never again ride like a brother by his side.

His heart twisting with pain, El Gato shook his fist toward the heavens. "Damn de Vega's soul," he cursed. "I swear upon Rafael's grave, if it takes the last breath I have, the bastard will pay dearly for his death."

Chapter Four

ELENA nervously chewed her fingernail as the shadows lengthened across the entrance to the cave. She dreaded the approaching darkness. This was the fourth day, and still there had been no word from her father. When she'd heard the arrival of a horseman last night, she'd dared to hope she'd soon be released, but her hopes had been dashed by the silence. The camp had grown so quiet it was as though even nature spoke in whispers. She rubbed the gooseflesh rising on her arms. Something was very wrong.

At dawn she'd heard horsemen leaving and then returning to the camp. After that . . . nothing. Emanuel had avoided her questions, bringing her food and departing quickly, his usually happy face wreathed in sorrow. Could it have something to do with me? she wondered. *Maybe Father refused to pay the ransom.* She shook her head. *No, he wouldn't have—unless he's discovered I'm not Conception.* She sucked in a breath. The thought filled her with terror.

Deciding to forgo the conceiling veil, she edged closer to the front of the cave, moving cautiously so as not to attract the guard's attention. Once there, she remained in the shadows, waiting until darkness fell. Taking a breath to calm her racing heart, she peeked out.

A small campfire flickered, sending a faint glow of light

on the area where the bearlike Emanuel could usually be found, but the spot was empty.

After slipping outside, Elena crouched behind a boulder and peered warily at the campsite. The guard wasn't there. In fact, she didn't see a soul anywhere. She glanced around, trying to orient herself. She sighed in despair. It was no use. The ground beyond the firelight was as black as the road to Hades. She had no idea which way to go.

She edged her way along the rough face of the bluff, traveling a good distance away from the cave before she was stopped by a protruding corner of rock. She peeped around it, then jerked back, her heart thundering like a drum. *Santa Maria!* She had almost walked right into the middle of the bandits. Wary, she leaned out again, straining to hear the hushed voices of the group of men crouched around a campfire. She frowned. Then, somewhere behind the gathering, she caught the faint sounds of women weeping. Scattered bits of conversation came to her . . . de Vega . . . Rafael . . . vengeance. A chill ran up her spine. Even if she couldn't make out all the words, she heard the anger in their voices. She bit her lower lip. What had happened to bring fury to the men, such sorrow to the women? Something bad—and it had to do with her father.

With her terror greater than it had been since her capture, Elena hugged the rocks, going back the way she'd come. She crept past the cave, wishing she could remember something about the way she'd been brought here, but she'd been blindfolded. She did recall the trail had been so narrow she'd bruised her leg on the rocks, and it had been steep— very steep. She'd almost slipped out of the saddle. Inching along in the inky darkness, she didn't find that memory comforting.

Praying she didn't step into eternity, she eased one foot in front of the other, reaching out to the dark with her hands. Now she knew what it was like to be blind. She noticed that the way under her feet appeared smoother, but if she wandered off the least bit, she stumbled over brush and stones. *A path?* Hope leapt in her breast. *The way out?* She felt her way along, until the trail wound through larger rocks, then boulders. She groped her way around one particularly large rock jutting up on the edge of the trail.

Reaching the other side, she stopped, scarcely daring to breathe. Even though she'd heard nothing, she sensed she wasn't alone. The fine hair on the back of her neck rose, making her scalp prickle. She clamped her teeth tightly together to keep back the terror rising in her throat. She strained to listen, but the only sound she could discern was the rapid drumming of her own heart. *I'm being silly. The darkness is causing me to imagine things.* But all of her senses told her different.

A slight trickling, a rustle of shifting sand and small gravel, came from in front of her. The faint sound broke her frozen trance. *Someone is there!* She whirled, fear overriding her need to be cautious. With her attention riveted on the blackness behind her, she didn't feel the small rock in the trail until too late. Stubbing her toe, she pitched straight into the dark shadow that now blocked her path.

Two hands reached out of the darkness and broke her fall. "No need to run into my arms, *querida*. We have the whole night," a voice said softly.

A firm mouth fastened on hers, cruelly silencing Elena's scream. She pulled away, recoiling from the biting taste of tequila. Curling her hands into fists, she beat at the strong arms that lifted her, carried her through the night.

Terrified, Elena stared at the face above hers. Even though it was too dark to make out his features, the raw, primeval essence of the man made recognition easy. She choked back a sob, knowing without a doubt she was at the mercy of El Gato del Noche.

He carried her only a short distance before he stopped and knelt to lower her onto a rough, woven blanket.

Wrenching herself out of his arms, Elena scrambled to her knees, frantic to escape. Before her feet could leave the blanket, a hand gripped the back of her silk dress. "Let me go!" she screamed. She twisted, clawing frantically at his arm.

Enraged, he muttered a drunken oath. "Stop it, you little fool. Do you want to run over the edge of the cliff?" he snarled.

"Yes!" she cried, anywhere to get away from him. She strained against the anchor that held her fast.

Cursing, he jerked her backward, ripping her dress as he tumbled her onto the cover.

A rush of cool night air brushed her skin. Terrified, she rolled, scooting away from the dark shadow that loomed over her.

"Woman, don't try my patience," he warned. His hand closed around her throat and pressed her back against the blanket. He straddled her, pinning her with his knees.

Elena cried out. *He's going to strangle me.* His hand left her throat to ease beneath her collar, slipping downward, sending shivers where he touched her skin. She heard the soft *pop, pop* of her buttons being undone. Her eyes grew wide. *Santa Maria!*

He ran cold fingers down her breastbone and parted the front of her dress. "Your skin is as soft as the feathers of a dove. But, *chica*, you wear too many clothes." He flicked a finger at the front of her lacy chemise.

Shuddering, Elena pushed at him, trying to get free.

Clasping her hands, he stood and pulled her upright beside him. Despite her struggles, he stripped the dress from her trembling body. Her skin and undergarments shone pale against the black of the night. He cupped her buttocks and pulled her toward him. "That's better," he murmured. "Don't you agree?"

"No!" she cried, trying to cover herself.

With a bitter laugh he shoved her down on the blanket. Lowering himself on top of her, his hands closed on the fullness of her heaving breasts. He bent his head, attacking her mouth with a fierce kiss.

Elena twisted, pushing upward, trying to free herself of the weight that relentlessly pressed her to the ground. Her heart fluttered erratically against her rib cage as his hands rubbed and stroked her virgin body.

She felt like a mouse caught under the claws of a marauding cat. She'd never been kissed before, never been held in a man's arms. Never known a man's embrace. She'd never had so much as a hug, not even from her own father.

His lips left hers, his breath tickling as he covered her neck with hot kisses. "No. No, please," she sobbed. "You can't do this," she pleaded, realizing with horror what he intended to do. "Please, I am innocent."

Hearing her words, he stiffened. Cursing softly, he relaxed his grip and rolled away.

Elena sat up and buried her face in her hands, unable to contain the sobs that racked her body. His arms closed around her. She tensed and tried to pull away.

He persisted, but this time his touch was gentle, comforting. "Shh. It's all right, *chica*." He raised a hand and smoothed her hair back from her forehead. He drew her to his muscular chest.

Undone by the tenderness of his touch, Elena cried like she'd never cried before. All the pent-up tension and fear of the past few days drained like the cascade from her eyes.

When the torrent stopped and became quiet sniffles, he put a finger under her chin and tilted her head. Taking the handkerchief from his neck, he wiped her tear-stained face. "I'm sorry I frightened you. You are not to blame for the sins of your father." His voice seemed so sad, so weary.

Elena raised her head, trying to see his face. But in the darkness of the night, she could only see the glitter of his eyes. "What do you mean?"

"It is none of your concern. Most of it happened a long time ago, before you were born." He lowered his head and kissed the tip of her nose, then her eyelids. His light touch sent strange quivers racing through her veins.

"Forgive me," he whispered. Uttering a soft sigh, he covered her lips with his own.

His lips were soft, his words gentle, his hands caressing. He nuzzled her neck, persuasively stroking her breast with a feathery touch. When he kissed her again and again, her senses left her to run rampant, confusing her, leading her down strange and unknown paths. Suddenly realizing what was happening, she gasped.

Seizing the opportunity, his tongue eased its way between her teeth, exploring, then advancing and retreating until she grew dizzy. Her head spinning, she found herself responding to his moist thrust with her own. He tasted of cigars and tequila, but she no longer found the sensation unpleasant, only strangely exciting. His mouth became more demanding, drawing her deeper within him. Her terror now vanquished, she trembled like a fall leaf under his touch. Her arms rose of their own volition to wrap around his neck, drawing him even closer.

He pulled the ribbons from her chemise and slowly eased it apart. She tensed when his palm slid up her bare skin to cup her breast. Love words whispered in her ear soothed away her uneasiness. His thumb stroked her nipple, bringing shivers of delight as it rose taut, thrusting upward, begging for more.

Her breath came in startled gulps when he nuzzled her neck and slipped still lower to take the sensitive peak between his teeth. He licked and teased the quivering tip with his tongue until she was overcome with an emotion she couldn't name.

Crumbling each of her barriers, his patient touch awakened something deep within her, something warm, intense, and foreign. Her breast tingled, swelling under his lips. His nibbling teeth sent waves of sharp sensations radiating from the rigid peak. He moved to the other tip to nibble and caress until it was the same. Her fingers fastened in his hair, urging more of the mound into his mouth. Under his spell, she hardly noticed when his fingers unfastened the buttons of her underdrawers.

Captured in a whirling vortex, Elena gasped. What was wrong with her? She should be struggling, fighting to be free, but instead she had this terrible, wicked longing for him to keep on with whatever he was doing. She fought for breath as his palms cupped her buttocks and went lower, drawing her pantalets down to her knees and over her ankles. Her senses reeled as his lips and fingers tickled a path upward, drawing tiny circles on the inside of her thighs.

She licked her swollen lips, savoring the faint tang of tequila and tobacco. She gazed at the dark head bent over her and tried to concentrate on the heavens beyond but her mind and body refused to ignore the sweet torment of his mouth and teasing fingers. A low moan echoed softly in her ears, and she realized with a shock the sound came from her. She shook her head, fighting too late this thing that taunted, beckoned her, tempting her with forbidden promises. "No, you can't!" she cried, all the while praying he would.

"But I can. And I will," his lips promised against hers. He lowered his head, nibbling until his mouth, warm and sensual, closed over her breast and drew her inside. He suckled hungrily until all she felt or wanted to feel was him.

Her hands slid over his shoulders, tracing sleek muscles under the silky black shirt. El Gato. The cat. She could almost swear she heard him purr.

He left one breast to claim the other until she squirmed like a thing possessed. His hand roamed her thighs and lower stomach, dissolving the last of her inhibitions, rushing her ever further down a path of no return.

Her blood roared like a wild thing in her ears while a strange aching tormented her lower region. Growing to a point where, no longer able to help herself, she surrendered. She sobbed, arching against him, seeking release for this thing taking her sanity. Her trembling hands clasped his neck. She tangled her fingers in his crisp dark hair and drew his mouth up to meet hers.

Leaving her breast, he seared her lips with a fiery kiss. His tongue insistently pushed between her teeth, plunging into her mouth, tasting, retreating, urging hers to do the same. His hand massaging, caressing the mound hidden by soft curls drove her to madness before his fingers parted and explored her innermost core.

She writhed, twisting her body to meet his, desperate to find release from this torture he'd created that held her helpless in his grasp.

He raised his head and uttered a bitter, mocking laugh. "I see you no longer struggle. You want me, hmm, *chica*?"

His words doused the fire as effectively as a bucket of ice-cold water. Want him? Want a bandit—a killer? *Madre de Dios! What am I doing?* Shame washed over her. "No-oo!" she cried, pushing at him.

"I think you lie," he said, lifting his weight from her. He got to his feet and disappeared into the darkness.

Praying he'd gone, Elena got to her knees. Patting the dark ground, she felt her way to the edge of the cover.

Behind her, he gave a soft chuckle. Giving no warning, he gripped her shoulders and lowered his body, flattening her backward onto the rough blanket.

She sucked in her breath. *Where are his clothes?* There was nothing between them except warm, naked flesh. Fear rose, choking her. She twisted beneath him, trying to shove him away. "No, don't—"

"Don't what, *querida*? Do this?" His lips covered hers, stifling her protests. "Or this?" Slowly, confidently, his hands and mouth beguiled her, seducing her in knowing, loving ways. Despite her determination to resist, she felt the fire ignite and creep insidiously through her veins, turning her will to mindless jelly. A voice screamed, *Fight him!* But her body refused to hear. The voice grew silent, drowned in a wave of rising desire.

His fingers went to the place between her thighs, advancing, retreating, bewitching her with their magic. Helpless in his grasp, she clung to him, craving still more. When she thought she would go mad with wanting, a sensation so sweet it robbed her of breath exploded within her.

"Do you want me to stop, *querida*?" he asked softly.

"Yes!" she cried, knowing what she was doing was sinful, wicked. But when he lifted himself above her, her mutinous body triumphed over her conscience. Feeling a sense of abandonment like she had never known, she raised her arms and drew him back. "No," she sobbed.

"No?"

Her heart beat so loudly, his voice seemed to come from far away, yet he was so close she felt his hot breath upon her cheek. She wanted—no, desperately needed something she couldn't even name. Something she sensed only he could give her.

"I will be gentle," he breathed softly, tracing the outline of her ear with his tongue. His fingers drew tantalizing circles on her lower stomach.

Releasing a sob, she lowered her arms, roaming his smoothly muscled chest with her hands, feeling the silky sprinkling of hair. Her palm slid lower to his stomach.

He gasped and lifted his head to kiss her swollen lips. He grasped her wrist, guiding her hand even lower, closing her fingers around something hard and hot. "See what you do to me?"

Elena felt herself flush with embarrassment. She tried to pull away, but his hand clamped over hers, staying her retreat, guiding hers up and down.

"That is one way to please a man, *querida*." He drew her hand back up to his lips and nibbled at her fingertips. "Now, will you let me please you?" he whispered against her earlobe. His breath sent delicious shivers of pleasure tickling up her spine.

She tried to say no, to close her ears against his luring voice, but the words wouldn't come. She wanted more.

"Tell me," he said, his fingers bewitching the part of her that cried out for him.

"Yes. Oh, yes," she whispered. She imagined him smiling at her wantonness, all the while enticing her, drawing her down forbidden paths.

He lifted himself above her. Gently parting her legs, he eased himself onto her quivering body, moving so slowly, so carefully, she sobbed aloud with frustration. She arched, raising her body to meet him.

Warm and hard, he pushed, entering the area between her thighs. She cupped his slim hips, pulling him further. He eased slowly forward, reaching a barrier, then plunged straight and true. His mouth swallowed her cry, while his body inched deeper and deeper into hers.

When she thought she would burst with the fullness of him, he slowly began to move. She forgot the pain as the roaring fire within her became an unstoppable inferno. Captured by the searing heat, she caught the rhythm of his movements. Matching him stroke for stroke, she strained with him to reach an unattainable summit.

He must be the devil, she thought as the flames he'd started flared so high they licked at her very soul until she was consumed by this outlaw, this bandit—this prince of the night. He led her through the inferno, ever upward, through the blackness, struggling toward a brilliant blinding light. Reaching the glory, she cried out and arched against him. He shuddered, raising her to explode with him into the millions of stars covering the velvety night sky.

Floating on a canopy of clouds, they drifted slowly back to earth. When he collapsed onto her love-swept body, she caressed his dark head. Filled with tenderness, Elena lay in openmouthed wonder at the thing she had just experienced. What she had done was incomprehensible, unforgivable. Yet, knowing the ecstasy she'd found with this unseen bandit on the dark side of a mountain, God help her, she would do it again.

How long they'd lain there, she didn't know, but when his crushing weight became too much for her, she attempted to move to one side.

Becoming aware of her discomfort, he raised himself on his elbows and gently kissed her lips. "Is that better, my love?"

When he shifted his weight, Elena was amazed to find they were still joined. "What do we do now?" she whispered.

He laughed. "This, *querida*." Smothering her face and

neck with tiny nibbling kisses, he began to move within
her.

Elena gasped in disbelief as the banked fire within her
began to rise. Her heart pounding against his, the two beats
merging into one as their consuming passion spiraled them
to still unknown heights, joining their life forces in a dance
as old as time.

After a while, obviously thinking her asleep, he rose from
the blanket. Elena heard him mutter an angry curse as he
rummaged about a short distance away. The pop of a cork
and the slosh of liquid told her he was drinking again. When
he returned to sit on the far side of the blanket, Elena grew
frightened. The gentle lover that had taught her such passion
was gone. Only El Gato, the bandit, remained. She heard the
splashing tilt of the bottle from time to time, until he tossed
it away in a clink of shattering glass.

When he sighed and stretched out beside her, Elena tensed,
waiting to see what he would do next, but in moments soft
snores told her he was in a drunken stupor. She sat up, staring
into the blackness. The cool wind sobered her, reminding her
where she was. She had to leave, get away before he woke up.
She shook her head. It was hopeless. In the dark she'd never
find her way to the cave. She didn't dare wander around the
camp naked. She might not be so lucky next time.

Lucky? She fastened her bitter gaze onto the still form
lying next to her. With her body still tingling from his
touch, Elena buried her head in her arms and silently sobbed
out her rage and humiliation. Later, exhausted from her
ordeal, she drifted off to sleep.

El Gato opened his eyes to the star-covered night. The
wind chilled his bare skin, and he reached out, half hoping
it had been a dream. When his hand touched the naked,

sleeping woman curled by his side, he knew it wasn't. He sat up and tried to clear his mind of the effects of the tequila. Clutching his head, he struggled to his feet, groaning when the pain threatened to split his skull.

He retrieved his scattered clothing and hurriedly dressed. Uttering a muffled curse, he gathered up the dress and underthings he had drunkenly ripped from the woman. He piled them on the blanket and carefully wrapped the cover around her. Praying she wouldn't awaken, he lifted her in his arms and strode toward the cave.

His stomach turned, sick at what he'd done. After she'd cried, he hadn't intended to do it. Then, when he'd attempted to comfort her, she responded to his touch with such sweetness he couldn't help himself. He knew his identity was safe. The night had been so dark, she couldn't have seen his face. Still he cursed himself for a fool, risking everything for a moment of passion with a woman he despised. Along with his guilt came wonder that the cold, haughty Conception de Vega could have such fire.

He carried her into the cave and laid her on the bed, covering her with another blanket he'd found at the foot.

Moaning softly in her sleep, she lifted her arms and fastened them around his neck.

He carefully freed himself but was unable to resist giving her one last kiss before he left. When his lips touched her love-swollen ones, he quivered. A bolt of fire lit his loins. "*Bruja,*" he whispered, jerking away. Shaken to his boots, he lurched out into the night, wondering if she truly could be a witch. He took in a sobering breath. Being the daughter of a devil like de Vega, anything was possible.

He walked to the pallet outside the cave and tossed a few more twigs on the embers of a small fire next to a sleeping man. "*Compadre,* wake up," he said, bending to shake the burly giant's shoulder.

Emanuel sat up, rubbing his eyes like a sleepy child. He peered up, his simple face lighting with a smile. "*Sí, Jefe*. What is it?"

El Gato knelt by his side. "Before daylight I want you to find some clothes for the woman. Then blindfold her and take her to the fork in the road. Give her a canteen and leave her there."

"Leave her there? All alone, *Jefe*?" The firelight deepened the worried frown on the big man's brow.

"It won't take de Vega long to find her," the bandit said bitterly. He took a thin cigar from his shirt pocket and lit it with a twig from the fire. "I want her out of here before daylight." He knew it was no longer safe for her here, and with Rafael's death on his conscience, he didn't want to add the girl's.

"But what about the money?" Emanuel asked.

"We'll find another way," El Gato assured softly. Straightening, he glanced toward the cave. In spite of his guilt, a sardonic smile twisted his face. He'd already taken the only thing *she* had of value . . . her virginity.

Chapter Five

A HAND gently shaking her shoulder woke Elena from her dream. "What is it, *querido*?" she murmured. She opened sleepy eyes to find Emanuel, not El Gato, bending over her. Gazing around, she blinked, surprised to find herself back in the cave. Realizing her state of undress, she quickly pulled the covers up to her chin.

"It is only I, señorita," the giant said apologetically. He held out a handful of clothes. "You must get dressed. We have to leave."

"Leave?" Her eyes narrowed, and she peered through the gloom of the candlelit cavern. "Where is El Gato?"

"Gone," he said. Meeting her gaze, he shrugged. "He will not be back." He placed the clothing on the bed, his soft eyes sympathetic and knowing. "There's water for you to wash. Please, we must hurry." Before she could question him further, he turned and shuffled out of the cave.

Gone! The words echoed in her mind. *Gone where?* Was she to be taken to him? Remembering Emanuel's shamefaced manner, she shook her head. Apparently the night had meant nothing to the bandit. The pain of betrayal pierced her heart as she realized El Gato had taken what he wanted from her and left. Now he was sending her away to face the consequences—and her father.

43

Sliding from beneath the blankets, she winced at the dull ache and thick stickiness between her legs. Hot tears trailed down her cheeks. She lifted the garments Emanuel had left, examining them in despair. If she'd had her own clothes she might have been able to hide her disgrace. But in these? She shook them out, finding only a loose white peasant blouse and a gathered skirt. No undergarments at all. She raised her head and stared toward the cave entrance. *Surely he doesn't expect me to wear only this?* Her lips quivered. She might as well wear a sign around her neck telling all the world what had happened.

Still, it didn't look as if she had any choice. Afraid Emanuel would enter before she was ready, she hurriedly washed and slipped into the clothing. After draping a blanket around her shoulders, she plopped the ridiculous hat and concealing veils on her head. In the darkness of the night she hadn't seen the bandit's face; that also meant he hadn't been able to recognize her. Maybe her father, believing her to be Conception, had paid the ransom. If so, maintaining her disguise might save her life.

After her "rescue," Elena sat astride her horse in the midst of the heavily armed men and brooded about her situation. Bitterness tightening her mouth, she tried to avoid the leering, knowing stares of the rough, crude band. Not the usual *vaqueros* these, most of them were *gringos*, strangers. *Pistoleros* hired by her father to hunt El Gato. Their lust hung thick and heavy in the air. Elena shivered, knowing if she weren't Enrique de Vega's daughter, they would be on her like a pack of dogs.

The garments she had on didn't help, either. In the heat the full peasant skirt and thin cotton blouse clung to her perspiring body, making it only too apparent she wore nothing underneath. They'd taken her blanket, and the hat had fallen from her head, leaving her open to the hot eyes that constantly drank their fill of her near nakedness.

During the long ride, she sat stiffly in the saddle, defiantly ignoring their suggestive whispers and invitations. But she could not help uttering a grateful sigh when the walls of the hacienda finally came into view.

Her relief was short-lived when she saw her father run from the courtyard to greet them. Recognizing her, the welcoming smile left his face, and his complexion grew livid with anger. Without a word he turned on his heel and walked stiffly back into the house. Trembling with fear, she was taken from her horse and escorted into the study to confront him.

After curtly dismissing the gunman, her father turned to face her. "Elena," he grated softly in a voice that chilled her blood. "I see you lied when you said you were going to your aunt's." His cold gaze raked her from head to foot, his eyes narrowing to slits as he took in her appearance. "Do you know what happened to your sister?"

Elena swallowed, trying to still her quivering knees. "No, Father."

He closed his eyes, grasping the desk for support. "On her way to the convent, she was kidnapped by bandits."

Intending to reassure him, Elena put out her hand. "No, Father. The bandits never had Cepi. I was the one taken."

His skin blanched. "You? You were the one on the stage?" He stepped around the desk. Reaching out, he gripped her arms so tightly she cried out from the pain. "If you were on the stage, then where is Conception?" he shouted, giving her a shake.

"Gone. We traded places. She and Ricardo eloped the day I left," she whispered.

The color rushed back into her father's face. "Liar!"

"It's true. By now she is married."

"No!" He buried his face in his hands for a moment, then dropped them to fix her with a bitter glare. "You tell me Conception has run off with Montoya—and you—" His voice choked, and he raked her with his gaze. Grabbing her arm, he dragged her into the main hall. He shoved her toward the tall gilt-framed mirror on the entry wall. "Look at yourself. *Puta*, whore. You have disgraced us!" He curled his lip in disgust.

Elena raised her eyes and looked into the mirror, scarcely recognizing the person before her. Her hair fell tangled and wild about her shoulders. The dusky darkness of her nipples showed plainly through the thin white blouse. The skirt ended at mid-calf, showing a good deal of bare leg. The girl she had been, the innocent virgin, had disappeared, and in her place stood a woman. A woman who had lain unashamed under the stars and learned of passion in the arms of a black-clad bandit.

She caught her father's forbidding image in the mirror. She'd had better treatment at the hands of the outlaws. *He acts as if I did it on purpose.* A rage like she'd never felt before filled her very being. She shifted her gaze and stared at her father, seeing the smallness of the man. How could she ever have been afraid of him?

Meeting her eyes, he took a step backward, flinching away from her accusing stare.

Her back ramrod straight, Elena left him and walked across to the stairway leading up to her room.

It was late afternoon when Miguel reached the small ranch he'd purchased when he first returned to New Mexico. It lay in an isolated canyon about two hours' ride from the Spanish Angel lands. Even though it took a good deal of riding back and forth, it was far enough off the main trail that he didn't have to be worried about being discovered. Nevertheless, he was cautious, keeping the carriage he used concealed in the barn. The great black stallion he rode as El Gato, along with a few mares, grazed in a well-hidden canyon.

He hurriedly washed and changed into the traveling clothes he'd worn when he'd left the Spanish Angel over a week ago. His firmly muscled torso padded with cotton-stuffed pillows sewn into a vest gave his body the appearance of portliness. The rose velvet breeches, skin tight and ornate with gold braid, encased his lean thighs and flared just past his knees over high-heeled patent-leather shoes. He pushed the thick fake mustache against his upper lip and stuffed his own hair under a grayish-brown wig. Standing back, he eyed himself in the mirror. His lip lifted in contempt when a resplendent Diego looked back. "*Caramba!* I look like an egg with legs." Unable to bear the sight, Miguel shuddered and turned away.

His thoughts left his alter ego and went to the woman. By now she would have reached the ranch. His triumph had a bitter edge as he remembered her sweet surrender and the fire with which she answered his passion. He shook his head, finding it hard to believe the way his body had responded to the haughty bitch. He snorted. Well, she wouldn't be so high and mighty now. He would have enjoyed seeing de Vega's reaction when his precious Conception reached the ranch, deflowered and dressed like a peasant, but he'd had obligations of his own on the mountaintop.

Remembering his friend, buried with only a simple wooden cross marking the high lonely grave, bitter pain clawed at his insides. He shook with silent rage. Nothing he could do to de Vega would be enough to revenge Rafael's death.

Miguel told himself it was his fault. He'd been too confident, and it had cost his young lieutenant his life. He'd known what the bastard de Vega was capable of. A memory of other graves flashed into his mind, the least of them marked Miguel Sandoval. He stared at himself in the mirror. A sardonic smile twisted his face. But, unknown to de Vega, he wasn't dead . . . not yet.

He tightened the string tie at his throat, grimacing at the rose velvet suit he now wore. He dabbed on the nauseating lavender scent favored by Diego and tucked a lace-trimmed linen handkerchief in his pocket. His mouth set in a determined line, he walked out the door to the waiting carriage.

It was after dark when Diego's coach drove up the long avenue to the brightly lit hacienda. As usual Carlos stopped in front of the huge house, and Miguel climbed out.

Although impatience chewed at him like a dog with a bone, he affected the pompous walk of Diego and walked casually across the courtyard. Stepping under the arches sheltering the veranda of the house, he lifted the gold-plated knocker and let it fall.

Immediately the door opened. A white-garbed houseboy smiled a greeting and ushered him inside. After a few words of conversation, Miguel followed the boy down the hall and into the main library, where Don Enrique sat behind his desk.

His face surly, the man looked up. Recognizing his visitor, his manner became more pleasant. "Ah, Diego. You have returned. Sit down," he said, waving a hand toward a chair opposite him. "Have a brandy with me." He mumbled the words as if he'd already had more than a few. He lifted a crystal decanter and slopped the liquor into a goblet. He shoved it across the desk.

"Oh, Don Enrique, you are too kind." Miguel flicked his lace handkerchief across the seat of a gold velvet chair, vanquishing any minute particles of dust that might cling to his elaborate suit of clothes. He settled in the seat and lifted the glass in his beringed hand. Pursing his lips, he took a tiny sip and peered across the desk at his host.

The years had not been kind to de Vega. His heavily lined face bore the florid complexion of a man who drank too much. The thick wavy hair he had had as a young man had receded to a thin grayish-yellow band ending just above his ears. His stocky figure had a decided paunch.

Miguel noted with satisfaction the man's slurred speech, red eyes, and unsteady hands. De Vega definitely looked as if he'd had a bad day. Pasting an innocent look on his face, he leaned closer. "My friend, you appear upset. Has something else happened while I was away?"

"Everything happened," de Vega growled. "My daughter betrayed me. She defied my wishes and eloped with that young bastard, Ricardo Montoya."

The sip of brandy slipped down Miguel's windpipe, strangling him. He coughed. "What?" he gasped in a most un-Diego-like voice. Catching himself, he added, "Oh, you poor man. Tell me what happened." His mind whirled. What the hell had happened? he wondered. He knew de Vega's men had found the girl. How could she have eloped so quickly?

"That bastard Montoya stole my daughter, my precious Conception. Now she can't enter the convent," he whined.

"How unfortunate. When did this come about?" Miguel asked, more confused than ever.

"Six days ago," the older man said, pouring himself another stiff drink.

"Six days ago?" Miguel narrowed his eyes, mentally counting backward. "But—that's impossible!" That was the day he'd kidnapped the girl off the coach. There had been no Ricardo with her.

He looked up to see de Vega eyeing him strangely. He removed the lace handkerchief and dabbed at his brow, trying to cover his slip of the tongue. "How impossible for you. Where is she now? The houseboy told me the señorita had returned."

"My men found *her* in the desert and brought her home," de Vega said harshly.

Miguel mopped his forehead. "I don't understand."

"Nor did I until *she* came riding in bold as can be, dressed like a whore." Spittle edged the corners of the man's mouth. Bitterness edged his words.

"Conception?" Miguel asked. The man's ramblings made no sense at all.

"No, you fool! Elena."

Miguel gaped in disbelief at the man behind the desk. "Elena? But how can that be?"

"She deceived me into thinking she was Conception by wearing her sister's clothes and taking her place on the coach."

Miguel, struck dumb by the announcement, realized with horror what he'd done. The girl in the coach hadn't been Conception. He'd kidnapped and ravished the young, innocent Elena. *Caramba!* No wonder the whole conversation confounded him. He looked up to see de Vega's face twist with fury. Miguel didn't understand the man's attitude. "Where is Elena now?" he asked softly.

"Upstairs."

"You told me she'd been kidnapped. What happened to her couldn't have been her fault."

De Vega slammed his glass down on the desk, slopping brandy over the rim. "Bah! Of course it was her fault. If it had been Conception on the coach, she wouldn't have been touched. *She* wouldn't have allowed it. *She* is a lady."

The man's reasoning infuriated him. Struggling to keep his emotions under control, Miguel asked, "What will Elena do now?"

Enrique shook his head. "My shame is that she bears my name. I almost wish they had never found her. It might have been better if she'd died in the desert."

His disguise forgotten, Miguel leapt to his feet, no longer able to control the rage burning in him. "I cannot believe what I am hearing. Elena is your daughter!"

"A daughter who even now carries the bandit's seed in her belly," de Vega said coldly.

"Por Dios!" Miguel felt the blood drain from his face as he realized the truth in the man's statement.

"To hide her disgrace I have to arrange a marriage and quickly. I have offered her to Guillermo, my majordomo," de Vega said. He raised his gaze to meet Diego's. "She has refused, but Guillermo will bring her into line. What do you think, my friend?"

Miguel stared at the man, appalled at his words. Guillermo's cruelty with both animals and women was well known. "Surely there is someone more suitable?" he gasped.

"Even if I had time to look, what other man would be fool enough to wed her?" de Vega chided.

"I will marry the girl," Miguel said, his rash words escaping before he could stop them.

De Vega looked up, startled. "Do you mean it?"

Miguel clenched his teeth and nodded.

"Oh, Diego, my *amigo*. You would do this?"

"I said so, didn't I?" Miguel growled.

The older man came from behind the desk and put his hands on Diego's shoulders. "You have saved the proud name of de Vega. Now you will truly be my son."

Miguel recoiled in horror as the reality of the man's words registered in his mind. *His son? Son to the bastard who murdered my family? Sangre de Cristo! What have I done?*

C̲hapter S̲ix

PACING the floor, Elena shredded her tear-stained hand-kerchief. She went to the balcony and raised her bitter gaze to the purple-hued, corrugated range of mountains. "Do you know what you have done to me? Do you even care?" she cried. She already knew the answer. He took the love she had so naively given and left, taunting her with the fact that now no decent man would want her.

She had dreamed of falling in love and marrying the man of her choice, of living together happily and having children. But now? A sob tore from her throat. She had a choice all right. She could marry Guillermo, who made her shiver with revulsion even being near him.

Or she could marry Don Diego Alvarado, whom she'd met only once when her father coldly announced she was to marry him. The man hadn't even spoken to her. She could tell by the look on his face he already regretted his offer.

And why shouldn't he? After all, even if she had been a virgin, she was no beauty like Conception. Tall and golden-skinned, with the straight black hair and brown eyes that bespoke of the Indian heritage her father had tried so hard to hide. Even if the high-born Spaniard could overlook her appearance, she was damaged goods. She bowed her head in shame. She didn't even have the excuse of being raped.

She had given herself eagerly, willingly, to a killer, a thief. She dabbed at her swollen eyes.

Well, Don Diego needn't worry. She wouldn't hold him to his offer. Her lips twisted in a bitter smile. She would go to the convent and spend her life in servitude helping others. She convinced herself it wouldn't be so terrible.

Almost a month later Elena thought ruefully of that vow as she tossed restlessly on her fleece-stuffed mattress. She sighed. Two days and three sleepless nights since she'd arrived home from the convent. Three weeks she'd been there. Three weeks! It had seemed like three centuries.

Instead of the servitude she'd expected, once she'd arrived at the convent, she'd been locked in a tiny windowless cell, a prisoner. Determined to break her spirit, Mother Superior had decreed Elena would remain there until the day she relented to her father's will—or the day she died. Shunned by the nuns and novitiates, of which she was neither, Elena had talked to herself to keep from going mad. Finally, realizing anything would be better than being locked up for the rest of her life, Elena had relented. Hysterically agreeing to the marriage, she'd begged permission to come home.

She fingered the soft cotton covers, comparing her bed at the hacienda to the crude, rough-blanketed one she'd had at the convent. Poor though it had been, she had managed to sleep, even if she had dreamed of *him* every night.

In disgust, she tossed back the covers and rose from her bed. She slipped on her robe and pulled a chair close to the window. Propping her arms on the sill, she stared into the star-dusted night, her gaze drifting toward the distant Pajaritos Mountains. "Damn you!" she cried, her emotions torn and confused. He was out there somewhere, hiding, his life exactly the same as it was before.

Maybe her father was right. Maybe she was a *puta*, a whore. Why else would that night still haunt her dreams? When El Gato had taken her innocence, he had awakened a passion that tormented her sleep. She choked on a sob. Now, because of that one night, her life would never be the same. She hugged her arms across her breasts and closed her eyes against the hot tears.

All too soon soft mauves and purples slivered up from the crests of the hills and invaded the quiet darkness. The delicate shades trembled, then surrendered to the attack of orange and crimson that slashed across the heavens heralding the approach of a new day.

Wiping her eyes, Elena looked across the courtyard toward the vacant wing of the house. The wing that, after today, she would share with her husband, Diego. Cold fear gripped Elena's heart, leaving her weak and trembling. Today would be her wedding day, but she felt as if she were going to her execution.

A vision of the simpering dandy she would marry came into her mind. The man had scarcely spoken to her. Why had he said he would marry her? Especially since he knew she wasn't a virgin. Most men of good birth would scorn her. Another vision, that of the black-clad bandit, flashed before her, mocking her with his smile.

She had always hoped that, like Conception, she would marry for love, even though she knew in most Spanish families marriages were arranged when female children were still in their cradles. Spanish girls of good blood were seldom without the company of their *duenna*, a maiden aunt or other unmarried or widowed female relative who chaperoned them with an eagle eye. But such had not been the case with her and Conception.

True, their Aunt Dorotea, their mother's only sister, had arrived after her mother's death and stayed for a while when they were younger, but even Dorotea could not put up with their father very long. After calling their father a crude ruffian, the good lady had departed in haste to Santa Fe.

A soft knock from the hall brought Elena out of her reverie. She rose from her chair and crossed the floor to open the door.

Consuela, her friend and middle-aged maid, smiled at her. She held out the gown of heavy satin, draped over her arm. "Look, Elena. I have pressed your dress," she said, bustling into the room. She hung the garment on the front of the closet. Her plump face beaming, she ran her hands down the front, smoothing out the folds. "Is it not beautiful?" She sighed, looking at Elena for confirmation.

"It is lovely," Elena said. A bittersweet smile crossed her face. Diego's manservant, Carlos, had delivered a carved wooden trunk to her room yesterday. Inside, after the old tradition, she'd discovered her wedding garments.

Instead of white, the gown was deep cream, which only added to its old-fashioned beauty. Lace rose from the heart-shaped neckline of the fitted bodice to a high collar, edged with tiny seed pearls. The sleeves puffed at the top, narrowing at the elbows to end in a vee at the back of her hands. Flaring gracefully over a multitude of petticoats, the skirt had a center panel of matching lace, while the back of the skirt puddled in a shimmering train. A long veil of delicate cream lace fitted gracefully over a high mother-of-pearl comb. Hearing little of the maid's happy chatter, Elena fingered the soft satin, touched by the thoughtfulness of the man she was to marry.

Consuela left the room but returned after a bit with a heavily laden tray. "I knew you would be too excited to eat later, so I prepared a fine breakfast for you." The maid spread the meal on a linen-covered table by the window.

A soft morning breeze lifted the fragrant aroma of ham, biscuits, fresh peaches, and coffee, filling the room with their savory goodness. But as their varied scents reached Elena's nostrils, her stomach lurched. Clamping her hand over her mouth, she dashed behind the screen to her commode, retching until she thought she would lose her insides.

Finally, weak and shaking, she allowed Consuela to help her into a chair. "My poor *niña*. With you it is only nerves, but I felt much the same when I carried Pablo," the maid said, brushing a lock of hair from Elena's eyes. "So sick, every morning, I thought I would die."

The maid chattered on, but Elena had stopped listening. She ran her palm over her uneasy middle. A baby? Mentally she counted the time since her last flow. She was late.

"Little one, do you want me to remove the tray?"

Numb, Elena nodded.

"I will leave the coffee and see to your bath," the maid said, setting the china pot and a cup to one side. In a few moments she left the room.

Elena lifted the pot with a shaking hand and filled the cup half full. Sipping the aromatic brew, she walked onto the balcony and sat down on a curved wicker bench. She raised her gaze to the heavens. A child? *Madre de Dios*, please, don't let it be true. A child should be conceived in love, not because of a bandit's lust. Unable to hold back the flood of tears, Elena bowed her head and sobbed.

In the guest house Miguel also rose before dawn to pace the floor in restless agitation. Today he would marry the daughter of his worst enemy; a woman who detested the sight of him. He paused to light a cigar, then blew a cloud of thick smoke into the air. Glancing toward the hacienda, he shook his head and sighed. In spite of himself his loins tightened as he remembered the night on top of the mountain when he'd taken her innocence, her beauty, and her fire, when she had surrendered to her passions in the arms of El Gato. Now, because of a mad impulse, she would become his bride.

Bride? His eyes widening, he stared down at his portly figure, padded to fit his role as Diego. *Caramba!* How could he have forgotten? As her husband, he would be expected to share her bed. He worried the end of the cigar with his teeth. "What in the hell am I going to do?" He sucked in a deep breath. "I have to come up with something—and quick."

Chapter Seven

HER skin as cold as a marble statue, Elena took her place beside the large, portly man resplendent in wine velvet. The pale gleam of candles gave an almost dreamlike quality to the small Spanish Angel chapel and to the sparse group captured in their wavering light. Through the ivory lace veil, Elena noticed the beaming look her father bestowed upon her and the Spaniard. Her mouth twisted in a bitter smile. Strange, after all the years of seeking her father's approval, now that she had gained it by marrying Diego, it no longer seemed to matter.

She shifted her gaze from her parent to her maid, Consuela, and Consuela's husband, Francisco, whom she'd asked to witness the ceremony. Behind them was Diego's manservant, Carlos, his face unsmiling, almost grim.

The only other person in the room stood in front of her, the elderly Father Dominic, who had heard her confessions all her life. Elena bit her lip. All her confessions but one, that is. How could she ever tell the saintly old man of the wicked rapture she had found in the arms of a bandit? She cast a sideways glance to the man by her side. Or that she might be entering into holy marriage with this man while carrying another's child?

Elena was startled out of her thoughts when Diego took her hand and enclosed it in his. Suddenly reality set in. She began to tremble. Afraid, she raised her head to meet intense blue eyes that stared solemnly down at her. Nervous, she lowered her gaze, thinking it odd she hadn't noticed before how tall Diego was. Maybe his rotund figure had made him appear shorter.

His voice low and serious, Diego repeated his vows after the priest. When he finished, an expectant silence filled the room. Diego squeezed her hand, and Elena raised her lashes to find every eye on her. Her heart slammed against her rib cage. Her turn had come. Fighting the impulse to bolt from the room like a frightened rabbit, Elena parroted the phrases, her voice faint and quavering. Finally the deed was done. For better or worse, until the day she drew her last breath, she was the wife of Don Diego Alvarado.

The priest motioned for them to kneel and receive the wedding mass. The tall candles on either side of them flickered, mocking her with their symbol of fertility. The mass was beautiful and reverent, with the rich sounds of the Father's voice, asking in Latin for God's blessing on the happy couple.

At one point Diego was enveloped in her veil to show that she would protect and care for his comfort. As the priest's voice droned on, Elena bitterly wondered if anyone would ever care if she was happy or comfortable. In her culture women were treated like cattle, bought and sold to the highest bidder with no say in the matter. But the man's every whim was to be granted, every wish immediately obeyed. He had the right to lock his wife away, beat and abuse her if she were disobedient, while he could do anything he wished and still be respected by his peers. She glanced sideways at Diego, fearfully wondering what kind of husband he would be.

At another point in the ritual, they were bound to each

other with a chain of fragrant flowers symbolizing their oath
to share a lifetime together.

A lifetime. She shivered, thinking of the future and all that
it entailed, tending to his every need, sharing his bed, having his children. *Madre de Dios, please help me to do it.*

Deep in her own thoughts, Elena didn't realize the mass
was over until strong arms drew her to her feet. She gasped
when Diego lifted her veil and bent to gently kiss her lips
and claim her as his wife. With her eyes closed, a vision
of another dark head and a ruthless mouth flashed before
her, his kiss branded in her memory. Choking back a sob,
she wrenched her mouth away.

Opening her eyes, she saw Diego's shocked reaction.
Mortified, she looked down, fighting tears, silently cursing
the bandit for intruding into the moment; for making a
mockery of what should have been the most important day
of her life. Forcing El Gato from her mind, she turned to the
man in front of her. "I'm sorry," she whispered. She raised
her lashes expecting censure, but saw only sympathy and
understanding in her husband's eyes.

Her hand clasped in his, they left the sanctuary to be
greeted by the well-wishers outside. As the gate bell tolled
announcing their union, Elena blinked in the bright sunlight.
She stared at the group around her.

The men had forgone their *calzónes*, the loose homemade
trousers of unbleached cotton, and their cotton shirts, straw
hats, and *huraches*. Instead they were clad in their finest.
Many wore charro costumes with high waisted dark trousers and short bolero jackets with rows of silver buttons
and braid. Frilled shirts, spurred boots and wide brimmed
sombreros finished their outfits.

The women wore embroidered white blouses, and full
red and green skirts with colorful embroidered trim that

flared over bright petticoats. Draped on their shoulders were *rebozos*, or shawls.

Around the fringes of the crowd, the *pistoleros* lounged, eyeing any señorita not in the company of her mother.

A shout welled up from the crowd of people. "Dona Elena!" Rose petals filled the air around them. Elena glanced up at Diego, surprised to see him smiling at her.

"They are cheering for you. They must love you very much," he said softly, before kissing her icy hand.

She gave him a timid smile, grateful for his kindness. He looped her arm through his, and together they walked to the courtyard, where a chorus of violins and guitars played and tables were set for the *fiesta* to celebrate their marriage.

Two whole sides of beef roasted over fiery coals, filling the air with their spicy fragrance. Iron and copper kettles brimming with rice, beans, and tamales simmered over smaller fires. Tortillas, along with great loaves of crusty bread, coffee and *mezcal* were served from a wagon bed. For the wedding party the finest wine from the Spanish Angel vineyards was poured. Long plank benches that had been made for the women remained unoccupied, for even the oldest woman was made to dance.

After the wedding toast the guitarists strummed a haunting melody. Smoothly, firmly, Diego slid his arm around her and swept her into the dance. Tense, at first Elena moved like a wooden puppet, but caught up by the music she began to relax. They danced in silence, as if each of them were reluctant to break the mood. Drawn against Diego's stout figure, she was amazed at the lightness with which he moved.

When the music died, Diego kissed her cheek and relinquished her to her father for the next dance. Then she was claimed in turn by each of the *vaqueros* whom she had known from childhood. She saw Diego's mouth tighten when Guillermo stepped up to take his turn. Not wanting to create a scene, she gave her new husband a hesitant smile, comforted by the fact that he was concerned for her.

She tried not to take offense when the majordomo held her closer than was necessary. It was only when he drew her closer still, and she became aware of his arousal, that she looked up in alarm. "Please," she whispered.

Guillermo's swarthy face grew dark and angry. "Please? You should be *my* wife. But you refused me, taking that *petimetre,* that dandy, instead." His eyes glittered with hate. "You will be sorry, Elena, because married or not, I intend to have you." When he saw Diego approaching, he left her and stalked away.

Elena fought to hide her panic when Diego drew her into his arms for the next dance. Frightened and relieved at being rescued from Guillermo, Elena moved even closer, almost clinging to her husband. After a few moments Diego seemed uncomfortable, almost distressed by her presence. So much so that, feeling embarrassed, she tried to ease away.

Removing them from the rest of the dancers, Diego gazed down at her. "Elena, are you all right?" He turned to stare after Guillermo. His eyes narrowed. "Did he say or do anything to upset you?"

"No. Nothing," she said hurriedly. "I am just a little tired."

He frowned. "And probably hungry?" he suggested.

Elena, seeing one of the *pistoleros* start toward her, quickly nodded, not wanting anything else to mar the day.

Diego, taking her cue, tucked her hand in his arm and swiftly whisked her away to eat.

The rest of the day he stayed close by her side, and late in the afternoon, when her shattered nerves and the tension of the last few weeks began to tell on her, he instinctively seemed to know. Drawing her to one side, he waved to the cheering crowd then escorted her inside the wing that housed their new suite of rooms.

Pausing in the hall outside her door, he bent toward her and gave her a gentle smile. "You look exhausted, my sweet. Why don't you take a nap?" When she nodded numbly, he gave her a kiss on the forehead and left.

It was dusk when Elena rose from her bed after a deep and welcomed sleep. Nightfall found her seated in front of the mirror in her new bedroom apartment. Trying to hide her anxiety from Consuela, Elena clasped her hands in her lap, but the gold band weighed heavy on her finger. She stared at her image, hardly recognizing the pale, marble-like face gazing unhappily back at her from the glass.

Chatting gaily, Consuela removed the pins from Elena's coronet of braids and brushed them into shining waves against the virginal white of her bridal nightdress. "You will be so beautiful for your husband, señora," the maid said.

Husband. Elena's heart thudded heavily in her breast. The term sounded as strange as the man. Envisioning his fussy manner, his outlandish clothes, his almost prissy walk, she sighed. Why couldn't he be more like . . . She shoved the thought from her mind, telling herself Diego was kind, gentle, everything a husband should be. She frowned, remembering that at times he'd seemed nervous to the point of agitation, especially when he'd been forced to hold her close to dance.

She sensed he'd had his own reasons for saving her honor by taking her for his wife. Because he had, regardless of the reasons, she was determined to fulfill her obligations.

"There." The maid sighed. "I will leave you now, little one, before your husband arrives to throw me out." Giving

Elena's shoulder a reassuring pat, Consuela quietly glided out of the room.

Left alone in the bedchamber, Elena nervously twisted a long lock of hair about her finger. The thought of the man who would soon be entering to share her bed sent her bolting from her chair.

Once standing, she was drawn to the balcony by the soft strumming of a guitar coming from the shadowy courtyard beneath her window. The beautiful melody seemed somehow familiar, though she couldn't remember where she had heard it. She leaned back against the rough adobe wall and closed her eyes, listening as a deep, rich voice began to sing.

The ballad told a tale of a man and woman, and a forbidden night of love. He sang of the man's sadness when the woman was forced to wed another and of the man's departure to the mountains, never to return.

When the song ended and the last strains of the guitar died on the flower-scented evening breeze, she opened her eyes to see a dark figure staring up at her. The man raised his hand and tossed something onto her balcony.

She bent and picked up a perfect white rose. "Gra—" she began, but the singer had vanished into the night. Thinking of the song, a deep sadness settled around her heart. She lifted the blossom to her mouth, drawing its soft petals against her lips. She inhaled its sweet perfume, wondering who the man had been. A sharp knock on her bedroom door jolted her out of her contemplation.

Diego! She whirled toward the entry. Her hand clutched the rose stem so tightly the thorns pierced her flesh. Her mouth dry, her heart thudding heavily in her breast, she walked forward and slowly twisted the knob. Expecting to see her husband, she stared in surprise at the man standing in the shadowy hallway.

"Señora," the man said tersely, giving her a small bow. "Don Diego asked me to deliver this to you." He handed her a small envelope sealed with wax and walked quickly away.

Elena stared at the note, bewildered at this turn of events. Going back inside her room, she closed the door and leaned against it. She drew in a slow breath, trying to calm her racing heart and still her wobbling knees. She raised her other hand and noticed the droplets of blood against the white flesh of her palm. The rose lay where she'd dropped it on the floor. She picked up the flower, then crossed to the washstand. Reluctant to open the envelope, she lay it to one side and wiped away the red stain. She closed her eyes and lifted the flower to her nose, drawing strength from the sweet fragrance once more before placing the bud in the crystal vase beside her bed.

Sighing, she returned to the stand and picked up the missive. She had expected anything but this. She tapped it against her chin. A strong scent of lavender wafted up her nose. She lowered it, recoiling from the odor and the memory it brought of the foppish, stout man now her husband.

Making an effort not to wrinkle her nose in distaste, she stared at the elegant crest imprinted on the red wax seal. She turned the envelope over and saw her name penned in a fastidiously neat scroll on the front. With a sense of dread, she ran her nail along the wax, breaking the seal. She opened the paper and scanned the message.

Shocked, Elena stared at the note in disbelief. Not knowing whether to be relieved or outraged, she raised her lashes and stared at the empty four-poster bed. The bed she would not be sharing this night with her husband. She turned slowly toward the door, wondering what kind of man she had married. What sort of man would wish for his wife to sleep alone on their wedding night?

*

Miguel paced the floor of his bedroom, waiting anxiously for Carlos to return. He ran a hand through his hair. "Delicate constitution? A headache? *Por Dios!* I sounded like an old woman." His lip curled in scorn, hating the image he was forced to present. He sighed, trying to think of another reason for avoiding her bed. He knew he had to think of something. Even Diego couldn't plead a headache every night.

He closed his eyes, recalling the way she'd looked in the moonlight, with her long hair blowing and her tempting curves revealed as the evening breeze pressed the filmy night garment against her body. His loins tightened. He smiled, feeling a certain satisfaction that only he knew the fire, the passion, hidden under the virginal white nightdress.

He sighed, forcing the image away from his mind. He almost wished he didn't. It made it that much harder to continue the charade. Knowing what he did, there was no way he could have entered her room without ending up in her bed.

"I was a fool for marrying her," he told himself. But still the idea of Guillermo, or any other man, putting his hands on her left him twisted with jealousy. A rueful smile crossed his face. "Now that she is my wife and I have every right to bed her, I can't, for then she would know I am El Gato."

He raised a hand to massage his temples. The worrisome train of thought truly had given him a headache. Hearing the door open, he raised his head, relieved to see Carlos entering the room. "Well, what did she say?"

Carlos shrugged his shoulders. "She said nothing."

Miguel raised a brow. "Nothing?"

"I handed her the note and I left. She went back into her room."

"Damn it!" Miguel took a cigar from the box on his nightstand. He viciously bit off the end and spit it into a silver cuspidor. Lifting a candle to light the smoke, he caught a worried look on Carlos's face. "What's the matter now?"

"Miguel, we have waited a long time, and always you have acted with caution." The old man shook his head. "But tonight you did a very foolish thing."

"What? Sending the note?"

"No, *niño*." Carlos stepped closer, his eyes full of anger. "Do you think I have not heard your voice often enough to know it was you who serenaded the girl?" He raised a finger to shake it at Miguel. "And to make matters worse, you were dressed as El Gato," Carlos scolded. "Do you want to get both of us hanged?"

Miguel, knowing the man was right, put his hand on Carlos's shoulder. "I'm sorry, old friend. I promise to be more careful."

Carlos grunted and gave him a dubious look.

"It's very late and I think we had both better go to bed," Miguel said, wanting to end the discussion.

Nodding, Carlos sighed. *"Buenas noches, chico."* Muttering under his breath, he went out the door.

Alone again Miguel walked onto his balcony and leaned against the shadowed stuccoed wall, his thoughts filled with the woman in the next room. The woman that, because of his rash impulse, was now his wife.

He frowned. All the years he'd waited, plotting his revenge, and now because of one moment of weakness, his plans could fall around him like a house of cards.

He raised his gaze toward the hills, thinking of the mesa and the band of people waiting there. They depended on him. He couldn't let them down. He lowered his eyes, focusing on the long wing of the house opposite him, where his old adversary slept. A vision of his mother's anguished face swam before him. "Promise me, Miguel, that you will never forget," she whispered.

Self-reproach smote him as the old hate swelled inside. He narrowed his eyes, switching his gaze to the balcony of the next room. He cursed himself for acting like a lovesick fool. Even though Elena was his wife, she was also the spawn of de Vega. That made her, too, his enemy. He couldn't afford to forget it. Too much was at stake. Too many lives hung in the balance. "I won't forget," he vowed softly to the night sky. He took the cigar from his mouth and threw it on the porch floor. After viciously grinding the butt under his heel, he stalked back inside his room.

Chapter Eight

ELENA, overwrought and tense from the wedding and the rest of the day's ordeal, had fallen into an exhausted slumber from the moment her head touched the pillow.

Now, opening her eyes to the first bright rays of the new day, she stretched, feeling remarkably refreshed. She breathed a grateful thanks for the headache that had kept Diego from her bed last night. She had another reason to give thanks. She wasn't pregnant. With the cramps she was experiencing this morning, she knew her monthly had arrived, thus giving her another reprieve.

But it also gave her time to dread the inevitable. In spite of the hate she bore El Gato for what he had done to her, she couldn't help comparing his slim, sleek body to Diego's paunchy figure. She'd taken her vows in the church and had promised to love, honor, and obey her husband. She sighed, wishing she could find more to admire about the man she'd married. Determined to be a good wife, she could only pray that in time she could come to care for him.

Later in the morning, cursing himself for a coward, Miguel pushed aside his untouched breakfast and finished his fifth cup of coffee. Setting down his cup, he got to his feet and checked his appearance in the mirror.

Diego, immaculately clad in dove-gray suede, looked back. He straightened the deep purple jabot on his blouse, then twisted the ends of his fat mustache. He pressed the lump of hair to his upper lip, making certain it was secure. He'd almost lost it yesterday at the *fiesta*.

Grimacing, he tucked a handkerchief into his pocket and turned away from the mirror. He opened the door and pranced down the hall, stopping in front of Elena's bedroom suite. Taking a breath, he raised his hand and knocked softly on the door.

"Come in," a woman's voice called.

Removing his handkerchief, Diego fluttered through the doorway, but, except for Consuela, the room was empty. Waving the lavender-scented kerchief, he peered down at her. "I'm looking for my wife."

Consuela straightened and patted her hair. "I think she is in *la sala*, the living room, señor." She gave him an apologetic look. "We had so little time, the only rooms ready in this wing are the bedrooms. The señora was anxious to get your house in order. Would you like me to get her for you?"

Diego sighed. "No. I will look for her there." He waved the handkerchief in front of his nose, then twirled and left the room. In the hall he stuffed the scrap of linen in his jacket pocket and went in search of his wife.

Damn! He had hoped to have this over with by now. He walked down the stairs leading to the main salon, dining, and kitchen areas. This end of the U-shaped hacienda was a complete house in itself. Old memories rose, tightening his mouth into a bitter line. He and his parents had shared this wing before his father died on the horns of the bull. After his death, unable to face the loneliness, Miguel and his mother had moved to the center wing to be closer to his grandfather. Even though he found it easier to live in this section, he found himself haunted by more than one ghost from his past.

Again he removed his handkerchief and paraded into the large main room. He wrinkled his brow, perplexed at finding not Elena, but yet another maid sitting on the floor under a large dining room table.

The girl, busily cleaning the massive hand-carved mahogany legs, seemed unaware of his presence.

"I do not wish to disturb you, señorita, but I can't seem to find my wife."

The maid gave a startled gasp and scooted back in such haste she bumped her head. A dirt-speckled face peeped from beneath the table. "Diego?"

Miguel blinked, scarcely recognizing the begrimed face. "Elena?" He leaned closer. "What are you doing?" he asked in horror.

She scrambled from beneath the piece of furniture and hastily brushed at her skirt, sending a cloud of dust and cobwebs into the air.

"Fahh!" He jumped back and bent to wipe a sooty web from his pants leg.

"Diego! I am so sorry!" she cried, reaching out to brush another off his jacket. Her fingers, blackened with grime and beeswax, only served to leave an even larger smudge in its place. "Oh," she said, fastening wide topaz eyes on him.

"Don't touch me." He backed to a safe distance and cast a disparaging eye over the furniture. "This stuff is filthy. Wherever did it come from?"

"I found it stored in one of the back rooms. I think it belonged to Don Luis Sandoval and his family. They all died here, you know. It was so lovely, I thought maybe we could use it."

Miguel felt the color drain from his face. He put out a hand to steady himself against the wall as a picture of a similar table, smeared with blood, flashed into his memory.

"Diego? Are you all right?" Elena asked, taking a step toward him. "You look quite ill. Maybe you should have remained in bed."

Miguel sucked in a breath, pushing the past into the far corners of his mind. He turned toward Elena, raking his eyes over her slender frame.

Her dirt-speckled brow wrinkling in concern, she stood before him dressed in a peasant skirt and blouse, her hair bound in a kerchief.

A surge of anger flowed through Miguel that his wife should demean herself doing this sort of work, or any work for that matter. "I am not ill, just shocked to find my wife groveling on the floor like a servant. I will not have it. You are mistress of the hacienda, and you will behave as such." He narrowed his eyes and waved his hand at the disarray surrounding them. "Find someone else to clean up this mess."

Surveying her disheveled appearance, he curled his lip in contempt. "After you make yourself presentable, I wish to have a word with you." He turned away from the shocked, hurt look on her face. "Now, I must go change my clothes." He spun on his heel and abruptly left the room.

He clenched his hands at his sides, furious with himself for being so harsh with her. Damn de Vega for permitting the girl to act like a servant in her own house! Seeing her dressed as such, he recalled other times when he had seen her working in the gardens and in the orchards, picking fruit, but hadn't recognized her as de Vega's daughter. Well, now that she was his wife, he'd see to it she never had to lift a finger again. It was the least he could do after all she'd been through.

He walked toward his bedroom, his long stride changing to the precise steps of Diego as he remembered his role.

Por Dios! The girl would be his undoing yet. He shook his head. She looked lovely, even with the large smudge across her nose. When her golden eyes filled with tears, he'd had to fight the urge to pull her into his arms. The soft swell of her breasts, rising and falling at the top of the low-cut blouse, brought back memories of the satin feel of her skin . . . and the way her body had responded to his touch. He quickened his pace.

Reaching his room, he hurried inside and closed the door. He stripped off his clothes and splashed cold water on his face, wishing he could cool other parts of his overheated body as well. He threw a disgusted look at his image in the mirror. "Well, *hombre*, you've certainly gotten yourself into a mess this time."

It was late afternoon and past the time for siesta when he once again rapped on Elena's door.

The door opened and Elena stood before him, immaculate from the top of her shining head to the tip of her toes. She wore a dress of white lawn embroidered with tiny yellow flowers. Matching yellow slippers encased her dainty feet. The front of her hair was piled high on her head with small curls edging her forehead and cheeks. The rest hung in a curtain of black silk down to her hips.

He stared at her, finding the vision so enchanting that for a moment he forgot his purpose in coming. Perplexed topaz met his before she blushed and dropped her gaze.

"Won't you come in, Diego?" she said, her voice so soft it sent shivers of desire up his spine.

Still not able to find his tongue, he cleared his throat, reminding himself of his role, and followed her into the room. The faint, light scent of flowers drifted to his nostrils. He inhaled, trying to trace its source, then realized with a start it came from her. He clumsily lowered himself to the chair she indicated and watched her gracefully settle in the one opposite.

She shyly raised her lashes and gazed questioningly up at him. "You mentioned you had something to discuss with me?"

"What?" Miguel answered, coming out of his trance. "Oh, yes. I—uh—" He pulled at the peach-colored cravat, finding it suddenly too tight. This was going to be much harder than he thought.

"Are you still feeling ill?" she asked.

Miguel swallowed. "I'm better, thank you." He forced his gaze away from the luscious rise of bosom as she leaned forward and placed her cool fingers upon his perspiring brow.

"You feel quite warm," she said, touching the back of her hand to his cheek.

"And you aren't helping the condition," he mumbled between clenched teeth.

"What?" she asked.

"Don't you think it is hot in here?" He got to his feet, careful to keep his back to her, and walked mincingly toward the window. He removed the lace-edged kerchief from his pocket and dabbed at his face. He had to get it said and get out of here before he gave himself away. Taking a deep breath, he gathered his emotions tightly under control. He turned back and retook his seat. "My dear, I have something to tell you. Something I find very difficult."

"What is it, my husband?"

"Oh, dear," he said, in his most Diego-like voice. "That's just it. I can never be a true husband to you." He paused, sneaking a sideways look at her.

"I don't understand," she said.

He pursed his lips and waved the scrap of lace. "It's because—I—oh, my—I don't know how to tell you."

She lowered her lashes. A tinge of pink flushed her cheeks. "It's—it's because I came to you not a virgin, isn't it?" she whispered.

Damn, how could she think that? He scowled at her. "No, that's not why."

"You aren't"—her cheeks flamed red—"how do I say it . . . ?" she whispered.

"Of course not!" Miguel straightened in his seat and glared at her, horrified that she could even think that. He took a breath and spat it out before he changed his mind. "I can't, you see." He sighed.

"You can't? Have you had an accident or something?"

"Yes." He stared at the floor. "I suffered an injury." That was the truth, he thought. He had been shot, but thank God the bullet hadn't come anywhere near there.

She uttered a shocked gasp. "You mean—?"

He frowned. She wasn't making this easy. "Yes. I'm impotent, so I'll never be joining you in your bed."

"Oh, poor Diego." Her eyes wide and sympathetic, she added, "I'm so sorry."

He squirmed uncomfortably under her scrutiny.

"Is it painful?" she asked, eyeing his lower region.

Blushing like a schoolgirl, he clasped his hands in his lap. "My manhood is not a proper subject for discussion."

She jerked her gaze away. "Forgive me," she whispered.

"As I was saying, I can never be a true husband to you, but if we are very discreet, no one will ever know." He reached over and took her hand. "I know you must be disappointed, my dear, and because I'm not able, I think you should take a lover. I could not expect you to do otherwise," he said magnanimously, knowing she'd never do it and that this outrageous suggestion would strengthen his lie.

"You expect me to take a lover?"

"Yes, my dear. After all, you are a young woman, and women do have certain needs."

"Certain needs?" She stood up and walked behind her chair. Turning, she gripped the back of it so tightly her knuckles whitened. She stared at him, as if she could not believe what she was hearing. "What if I did take a lover? What if there was a child? What would you do?"

With a quick intake of breath, he jerked his head up, surprised by her question. He narrowed his eyes and frowned. "Are you pregnant?" When she shook her head, he relaxed. She was testing him. She couldn't mean it. After a moment he smiled. "That's a wonderful idea. I would be delighted to have an heir."

Elena appeared more confused and angry than ever. "If you don't want me as a wife, then why did you marry me?"

He got to his feet and took a few precise steps toward the doorway. His hand on the knob, he turned. "It is expected of a man of my position"—he paused—"and then, of course, there is your dowry," he added with a laugh. "Good night, my dear." He exited the room and closed the door behind him.

Stunned, Elena stared after him. Her dowry—one third of the Spanish Angel Ranch. The other one-third went to Conception, and the remainder went to Don Enrique's first grandchild upon his death. *"Madre de Dios!* That's why he said I should take a lover."

She still found it hard to believe he was dysfunctional as a man, found it hard to believe he would never share her bed. He had even given her permission to take a lover.

A wild laugh tore from her throat as she remembered the vow she'd made to be a good wife to Diego, a wife he neither wanted or needed.

She rose to her feet and walked out onto the balcony. "A lover? *Santa Maria!* Never could I do that." Her eyes, as if they had a will of their own, raised to stare at the distant hills. In spite of herself, she remembered how she'd trembled beneath the touch of El Gato. Could she spend the rest of her life alone after once experiencing the rapture he'd taught her?

She touched her fingers to her mouth, remembering the bandit's ruthless lips on hers. Certain needs, Diego had said. Needs El Gato had awakened, needs that left her tossing in her sleep. Needs that would never be fulfilled.

"Damn him! Damn them all!" she cried. Sinking to her knees, she buried her face in her hands, her foolish girlish dreams dissolving into a woman's bitter tears.

Chapter **Nine**

A WEEK later Elena found she could cope, if not come to terms, with the arrangement she and Diego called marriage. In fact, she realized her situation hadn't changed much from the time before she'd spoken her vows, except now as Diego's wife, she had even less to occupy her time. Since the day he'd found her on her hands and knees, the servants had strict orders not to allow her to lift a finger. A battery of maids now had the wing shining clean and all the furniture in place. Because she'd had no part in its arrangement she felt like an intruder, a stranger in the rest of their vast apartment, and as a result she'd spent most of the hot summer day pacing the floor of her room. Bored and restless, with her husband away from the hacienda on business, she found she had absolutely nothing to do.

After a light dinner on her balcony, she wandered in the courtyard, examining each flower until she swore she knew them by name. She sat on the rock-rimmed edge of the fountain pool and lifted her hot, heavy hair off her perspiring neck. Watching small golden fish dart here and there, she envied them their watery state and wished she, too, could swim in the cool water.

Why not? She raised her head and gazed thoughtfully at the twilight sky. By the time she changed, it would be near dark. Did she dare? She pursed her lips. Diego would have apoplexy, as would her father—if they found out. But who was to tell them? She grinned. "Not I," she said, running for the stairway.

After quickly changing her pale lawn dress for her riding skirt and boots, she picked up her quirt and left the house by the back stairs. She hurried through the dusk and crept silently to the barns.

She slipped past a busy groom and edged her way into the shadowy stable. Inside, the stable man, Juan, turned in surprise. Not wanting to be discovered, she put a finger to her lips, motioning him to silence. She flashed a quick smile when he gave her a wink and nodded, then continued with his chores.

Ignoring the sidesaddle her father insisted she use, she chose a saddle used by the *vaqueros*. After putting the gear on her Arabian mare, Silver Moon, Elena led her to the rear stable entrance and through the back gate. She smiled. Since Juan had seen her, she knew the exit would remain unlocked until her return.

Once outside the thick adobe walls, she stuck her boot into the stirrup and swung her other leg over the saddle, to ride astride. Afraid of discovery, she rode cautiously until she reached the far side of a small rise. Pulling Silver Moon to a stop, she checked the territory around her. *Not a soul in sight.* Removing the narrow strip of rawhide from the end of her long braid, she ran her fingers through her hair, letting it blow in the soft breeze. Lifting her head, she inhaled the hot sage-scented air. "Ah, *Luna*," she cried, calling the horse by her pet name. "Freedom!" Urging her mare into a gallop, she raced across the desert, feeling at ease for the first time in weeks.

Hearing the sound of a running horse behind him, Miguel cursed and hurriedly pulled his stallion into the cover of a thick clump of brush. He slipped from the saddle and covered the horse's nose to silence any warning sound the animal might make. Blending into the shadows, he waited.

His eyes widened when the rider grew nearer. It was a woman, riding alone and obviously in a great hurry. The gray mare thundered past him. He stared in disbelief. *Elena!* He watched her disappear, leaving only a trail of dust. *Where could she be going?* A heavy frown creased his forehead. *Night is a strange—and dangerous—time to take a ride.*

He climbed back onto his saddle and craned his neck to trace her path. Every fiber in his body wanted to follow her—to see where she went. His eyes narrowed with jealousy. Or *whom* she rode to meet. "*Caramba!*" He glanced up at the darkening sky. He couldn't go after her. His men were waiting.

Shaking with anger, he gave the restless horse a kick, turning him away from the trail he wanted so badly to follow. If she did ride to meet someone, it was his own fault. He'd told her to take a lover. He glared back over his shoulder. "Damn it, I certainly didn't mean it."

Already late, and in a foul mood, he ran the stallion, his flying hooves covering miles. He finally reached the hilltop and joined his waiting men. Pulling the black to a stop, he glanced at the road below them. "Any sign yet?"

Pedro edged his horse closer, knowing how voices carried in the clear air. "No, *Jefe*. But José, he watched them leave the mine. Only four outriders guard the wagon."

"Good. That means they don't expect trouble," Miguel said softly. Impatient, he shifted his gaze to the dark sky. *I hope this doesn't take all night.* De Vega was sending the gold out late at night, hoping to slip it past the bandits, but the fool hadn't been able to resist boasting about the shipment. A wry smile twisted Miguel's face as he imagined de Vega's reaction to knowing the person he'd bragged to was El Gato.

Unable to keep his mind on the gold he'd planned to steal, Miguel twisted in the saddle and scowled at the trail behind him. *Where had she gone?* His tormented mind filled with visons of Elena in another's arms. Her lover tangling his fingers in her silky long black hair; discovering the secrets of her satiny curves. The man who would hear her cries of passion as he led her toward a fiery peak of ecstasy. Miguel muttered a curse.

Rigid with anger, he fought to control his rampaging emotions. Reaching into his pocket, he removed a thin cigar and viciously bit off the end. He flicked his thumbnail at the head of a match, sending sparks and an acrid smell into the air. In the soft glow of the lucifer's flame, he noticed every eye on him.

"What is the matter, *Jefe?*" Emanuel asked, his large brow crumpled in a worried frown.

"Nothing you can help, my friend," Miguel said. He lit the cigar and shook out the match. Would she be home yet? It was all he could do to keep from turning the stallion and racing toward the hacienda to find out. He wondered what she'd do if he confronted her with his suspicions.

Shaking his head, he sighed. What a scene that would be, he thought. A rueful smile twisted his mouth. El Gato charging into the hacienda, demanding to know why Elena, *Diego's* wife, rode out to meet a lover that *Diego* had told her to take.

If Elena didn't shoot him on sight, her father would have him hanged. He clenched his teeth on the cigar so hard, the muscles jumped in his cheek. Shot or hanged, it was a situation he didn't intend to stand for. He scowled into the darkness. He'd have to think of something.

"*Jefe*. They are coming," Pedro whispered.

"Get ready, *amigos*," Miguel called softly to the heavily armed band of men. Adjusting the mask over his face, he led the group toward the unsuspecting wagon.

Elena unerringly guided her mare into a deep cleft where tangles of trees and vines hid the spring from view. Penetrating the junglelike growth, she dismounted and tied her mare to a clump of brush. She took a cautious look around, not wanting to run into any bandits or *pistoleros* who might have the same idea. At least she didn't have to worry about Indians, unless they were renegades. Most of the tribes were too superstitious of the angel to come anywhere near the ranch. Finding the deep spring-fed pool inviting and empty, she smiled.

The place was a true oasis, almost fairylike, sheltered with alders, sycamores, and willows. She inhaled the fragrance of wild mint and verbena that covered the ground in a violet carpet.

Feeling like a truant schoolgirl, she quickly removed her boots and clothes and climbed to the top of the jutting rock that formed a natural diving platform. Raising her hands above her head, she leaned forward and plunged headfirst into the cool blackness. She surfaced, shaking her head, throwing droplets of water across the sleek surface of the pool. She swam back and forth, allowing the pent-up tension to flow from her body. At last, relaxed and exhausted, she climbed from the water. Stretching out on a slab of rock, she found it still warm from the day's sun.

The soft evening breeze caressed her, drying the water from her skin. The peaceful night sounds of deep-voiced frogs and chirping crickets told her all was well. She lay there for hours, watching the moon cross the ebony night sky, until she grew drowsy. Afraid she would fall asleep, she reluctantly slipped back into her clothing.

She walked slowly back to Silver Moon, untied her, and took her to the water to drink. After the mare slaked her thirst, Elena led her out of the shadowy growth into the bright moonlight. Seeing the mare hesitate and prick up her ears, Elena tensed.

A soft nicker came from the shadows of a nearby cotton-wood tree.

"Who's there?" she called, her voice quivering.

A slender figure stepped into the moonlight. "It is only me, Elena."

Elena put a hand over her breast in an attempt to calm her racing heart. She walked toward the smiling man. "Juan, you frightened me."

"I'm sorry, *amiga*. I wanted to make sure you were safe," he said softly. He took the reins of her horse and led both mounts back to a stand of thick green grass next to the pool. Leaving the horses to graze, he stepped away and came to stand by her side. He skipped a rock across water that was turned to silver by the bright moonlight. "Remember when we used to swim here as children?"

"Yes," Elena said. "And now, because of the bandits and father's hired guns, no one swims here anymore." Placing her hand on his arm, she peered up into liquid dark eyes. "How did you know I would come here?"

He smiled at her. "Because I know you are unhappy. When you were younger, you came here often to cry."

Elena looked up at him. "How did you know? There was never anyone here."

"You never saw me, *chica*. But I was always never far away," he said gently. "Tonight you did not cry. I think your hurt is too deep. Am I not right?"

She nodded, swallowing back a sob. "You know me too well." She leaned forward, laying her head against his shoulder. Juan, four years older, had been her friend since birth. He knew her better than she knew herself. She sighed, drawing comfort from the strong arms closing around her. Memories of other arms and passion-filled kisses rushed to confront her. She gazed up into his thin, bronzed face. "Juan, will you kiss me?"

His eyes widened in surprise. Seeming disturbed, he bent his head and gently kissed her cheek, avoiding the mouth she offered to him.

Nice, she thought, but like being kissed by a brother. She pulled away. "I'm sorry, my friend. I shouldn't have done that."

He sighed, giving her hair a playful tug. "Little one, any time you feel you need a kiss, remember I am here. Now I think we had better go before someone discovers you are missing." He brought her mare to her and went to mount his horse.

Elena stood for a moment, thoughtfully reflecting on another kiss, not at all like a brother's, but one that sent fire rushing through her veins.

"Are you going to daydream all night, Elena?" Juan said teasingly. "Come. I will race you to the juniper." He raised his hand and pointed to a group of stunted trees silhouetted in the moonlight.

Elena quickly swung into the saddle. Ordinarily she would never run the horse at night, but the moon made it bright as day. Nudging Silver Moon into a gallop, she raced toward the trees.

"Ha! I beat you," Juan crowed. "I think your mind was not on the race." He leaned toward her and peered into her face. "Maybe the night scares you, or maybe you dream of a certain tall *hombre* who sings love songs to you in the moonlight, eh?"

"Love songs?" she asked, then remembered the night of her wedding when the mysterious singer tossed her a rose and vanished. "Who was he, Juan?"

"No one from the hacienda, *amiga*. I saw him before he disappeared into the darkness. He wore a black mask."

"A mask?" Elena gasped, her eyes widening as she recalled where she'd heard the song. The melody had drifted to her on the night wind when she was held captive in the cave. "No wonder he seemed familiar," she murmured. She rode the rest of the way home in silence, angered, yet thrilled, by the audacity of the man called El Gato.

Chapter Ten

MIGUEL left his jubilant men and raced the stallion toward the ranch. He should be happy, but for the first time he found no joy in relieving de Vega of a gold shipment. He wrinkled his forehead into an angry frown, wondering if his roving wife had made it home.

Damn! Just married and he couldn't turn his back without her slipping off to meet someone in the dark. Moonlight silhouetted the hacienda walls looming in the distance. Slowing his horse, Miguel angled off to one side toward a hill covered with rocks and clumps of chamiso.

The stallion jumped when a man appeared out of the shadows and hurried toward them. "Is everything all right, Miguel?" Carlos whispered anxiously.

Miguel swung from the saddle, landing lightly before the older man. "Yes. All went well, my friend." He raised his hand and patted the horse's sweat-caked chest. "Better get Diablo under cover. We are not the only ones out this night," he muttered.

"Miguel, are you not going to your own ranch, then returning in the carriage as we had planned?"

"No, Carlos. You bring the carriage to the back entrance of our wing as if I were just arriving. Since it is late, I hope no one will notice that I am not in it."

"*Amigo*," Carlos hesitated, placing his hand on Miguel's sleeve. "Promise me you will not do anything foolish."

Miguel saw the deep frown lining the man's forehead. "Don't worry, old friend. I will be very careful."

He waited impatiently for Carlos and the horses to disappear from sight, then, slipping through the darkness, he made his way over the outer wall and into the grounds of the compound. Edging through the courtyard gate, he remained in the shadows until he'd scrutinized the area. Certain he was not being observed, he climbed the thick vines to his balcony and silently entered his room.

After locking the door, he stripped off his shirt and mask, then poured water from the silver pitcher into the matching basin and washed away the trail dust. Now clean, he shook out the garment and put it and the mask back on, knowing they would help him blend into the darkness. He went to his balcony and stared across at Elena's room. *Is she there?* He clenched his fists at his sides. *Or is she still out in the bushes somewhere with a lover?* Rage building, he closed his eyes. He could see her now, writhing beneath some man, her cat eyes filled with passion. *Por Dios!* His eyes flew open. One way or another he had to know, and there was only one way to find out.

Stepping onto the railing, he lifted his hands to the porch roof and swung lightly across to the floor of her balcony. From the shadows he peered into her room. Her bed loomed white—and empty—in the moonlight. A fresh surge of anger tore at him. He strode boldly inside and scanned the room, hoping she might have fallen asleep on the settee. She wasn't there. She hadn't returned home.

Running his hand through his hair, he prowled about the room. *She should be here by now. Where is she?* He stopped as another thought hit him. Maybe she'd run away with the man she had gone to meet. Maybe she had no intention of coming back. "*Mierda!*" he hissed. Ready to hunt them both down, he whirled. He'd barely reached her balcony when a soft click froze him in his tracks. Melting into the shadows, he watched Elena slip cautiously inside her room and close the door.

She threw her quirt on a chair. Uttering a soft sigh, she raised her arms over her head and stretched like a satisfied cat. She pulled off her boots, then removed her blouse and riding skirt and draped them over the back of the settee. Watching her underthings follow, Miguel sucked in his breath.

Standing like an ivory goddess before her dressing table, she lifted a hairbrush and drew it through her cloud of midnight-black hair. She continued until it lay in a shining ebony curtain to her hips. Moonlight slanting into the room played on her creamy white curves.

Miguel's fingers tightened on the iron railing. His loins filled with a sudden rush of heat.

He heard a clink of glass as she removed the stopper from a small crystal bottle and dabbed her bare neck and arms. The light floral fragrance drifted on the evening breeze, tantalizing his senses. His breath coming thick and fast, he closed his eyes, unable to move without giving himself away. Trembling with jealousy, he raised his lashes and raked her body with his hot gaze. *Where had she gone? Who else had made her moan with desire as he stroked those silky limbs?*

The idea filled him with a murderous rage. She was his. No man but him would ever touch her again. He'd see to that if he had to lock her in her room. He almost felt relieved when she pulled on a lacy nightgown and slipped into her bed. He watched until her quiet breathing assured him she had fallen asleep, then he jumped across to his own balcony.

Tormented by the night's happenings, Miguel tossed and

turned on his bed, unable to sleep. His own words came back to mock him. *"You may take a lover,"* he'd told her. He raised his fist and pounded his pillow into a lump. But damn, he never thought she'd do it. And now that she had, there wasn't a thing he could do about it . . . unless . . . He smiled in the darkness, a plan forming in his mind.

Elena rose from her bed shortly after dawn. Smiling, she stretched her arms above her head and greeted the new day. For the first time in weeks she'd been able to sleep without having her dreams interrupted by *him.* But walking out onto her porch, she found she could not so easily dismiss his presence, for there on the balcony floor lay a single perfect white rose.

She bent and snatched up the blossom, staring at it a moment before crushing the fragile petals, shredding them between her fingers. Her eyes narrowed. So he'd been here again. "How dare you?" she hissed, tossing the remains of the flower over the railing.

A sound in the hall, followed by a soft tap on her door, made her turn. Drawing her lips into an angry line, she went back into her bedroom. Quickly slipping into her robe, she answered her door.

Diego stood in the hallway. Fastidious even at this early hour, he wore a lime-green fitted suit and a pale yellow blouse. He beamed a bright smile at her. "Good morning, Elena. I heard you moving about and wondered if we might breakfast together."

Her morning already ruined, Elena looked uneasily at her husband, wondering when he'd returned. She nodded her head. "If you wish, Diego."

He clapped his hands together. "Excellent. I will have the cook prepare a tray and bring it to your terrace." He turned and pranced down the hall toward the stairway.

"Well, at least he's in a good mood," she said, closing the door. Knowing he would expect her to be dressed, she selected a morning gown of pale yellow batiste printed with tiny white flowers and quickly slipped it on. After she dressed, she ran a brush through her hair. Arranging it in a single thick braid down her back, she secured the end with a yellow ribbon.

She went to the bed and neatly smoothed the covers. She lifted her pillow, intending to fluff it before drawing the coverlet up. Something sharp pricked her finger. She jerked her hand back. Her eyes widened. There, by her pillow, lay a white rosebud.

She gasped, recoiling from the flower as if it were a snake. "*Madre de Dios!*" He'd been here in her room, watching her sleep. The image filled her mind. The tall, slim man standing by her bed, a mocking smile on his face as he bent and placed the blossom next to her. Thoroughly shaken, she picked up the rose and drew its silken petals over her lips. Closing her eyes, she inhaled its sweet fragrance. In spite of herself, her pulse quickened and a flame deep within her flickered to life. "No!" she cried, tossing the bloom away from her. She brought her hands up and covered her eyes. Trembling, fighting for control, she went to answer the soft knock on her door.

Diego, followed by a maid carrying their meal, entered the room. "I hope you're ready for breakfast, my dear."

After directing the placement of the tray on the terrace, Miguel pulled out a chair and seated Elena, then settled himself across from her. He eyed her critically.

Looking fresh and lovely, she smiled pleasantly and prepared his plate. She handed it to him.

Taking it, he scowled at his breakfast. He shoved the eggs around on his plate. *Damn it. Anyone staying out as late as she did should at least have shadows under her eyes.*

"Is anything wrong, Diego?" she asked innocently.

"I was thinking how rested you look, my dear. You must have retired early. When I returned last night, I knocked on your door, but you didn't answer," he said, waiting for her reaction.

She blinked, her eyes wide with surprise. "I took a headache powder," she said quickly, lowering her lashes. "I'm sorry I didn't hear you."

He chomped down on his toast. *No wonder, since you were halfway across the ranch.* "I thought you might have taken my suggestion and found a lover," he said smoothly, watching her like a cat watches a cornered mouse.

Elena's fork slid from her hand and clattered to the floor.

"Never mind, my dear. Here's another." He held out an extra fork, catching the slight tremble of her fingers as she took it.

"Did you?" he asked softly.

"Did I what?"

"Take a lover, damn it!"

Elena stared at him. He realized with a shock he'd forgotten to be Diego.

"No. I didn't," she said with a slight frown. She eyed him quizzically.

"By the way," he said in Diego's precise voice, "someone woke me last night, singing beneath your window. When I stepped onto the terrace, he disappeared."

She paled and took a quick sip of coffee.

"I don't suppose you know who it was?" he said.

"No." She hastily swallowed a mouthful of food and attempted to change the subject. "How was your trip, Diego? You look a bit tired."

"I accomplished quite a bit, but I do find business so exhausting. It will probably take a month to get my strength back." He sighed wearily. "I will be retiring early each night and will most likely have my dinner sent to my room." He reached out and touched her hand. "I do hope you don't mind my being such poor company, my dear."

She pulled her hand away and fiddled with her napkin. "No, Diego. It's quite all right. I'm sure I can find something to occupy my time," she said sweetly.

"That's good, my dear. I hate to think of you being bored." He picked up his knife and viciously attacked his ham. Spearing it with his fork, he raised his eyes to meet her guileless gaze. *Find something to occupy your time? I'll just bet you can, my lying little wife,* he thought. But the next time you leave, I'll make damn sure you're not alone.

So angry he couldn't trust himself to speak, Miguel ate the rest of his meal in silence. He scowled across the table at Elena, who serenely buttered her bread, obviously unaware of his displeasure.

How could she look so innocent after what she'd done? A sharp pain spread through his middle. He doubled over, clutching his abdomen.

"Diego, are you all right?"

Gritting his teeth, he got to his feet. "You'll have to excuse me. I'm afraid my breakfast has given me a terrible case of indigestion." Glowering, he threw down his napkin and strode across the floor, leaving Elena to finish her meal alone.

Once in his room he peered at his face in the mirror. His tired eyes were bloodshot and ringed by deep shadows. And the washed-out wig and mustache didn't help, either. He sighed in disgust and turned away. He looked like hell, and he'd done nothing but rob a coach.

Deep in thought, he rubbed his cheek. *What am I going to do about Elena?* Anger surged through him, making his indigestion worse. Groaning, he rubbed his middle.

He felt like beating her. *Why can't she be like any other wife and stay home and knit or something?* He paced the floor. This marriage was certainly not working out as he had planned.

Last night, when he'd placed the rose beside her pillow, he'd had to force himself to leave. She'd looked so sweet and innocent, with her mouth drawn into a tempting pout. She'd probably been dreaming about her lover. *Dreaming?* *"Caramba!"* He hadn't had a good night's sleep since he'd met the little witch.

So exhausted he could hardly stand, he shook his head. His gaze drifted to his bed. *Maybe I'll take a nap, then pay Don Enrique a visit. Then perhaps I'll take another nap.* He sighed, thinking he was getting worse than an old man. He eyed the bed again. Maybe it wasn't such a bad idea at that. He narrowed his eyes. A cynical smile twisted his mouth. Tonight he intended to see what she was up to, and he certainly didn't want to fall asleep and miss it.

Locking the door, he removed the wig and mustache, then took off his fancy suit of clothes. He closed the shutters, plunging the room into darkness. "Tonight," he promised. Heaving a weary groan, he stretched out on the bed.

Chapter Eleven

MIGUEL paced the floor as he had done most of the afternoon after the siesta he'd planned on hadn't materialized. He'd tossed restlessly on his bed, too keyed up to sleep. He couldn't forget Elena and her guilty behavior at breakfast. Even the pleasure of hearing Enrique de Vega's outrage at the loss of his gold had paled as Miguel waited impatiently for night to fall.

He poured himself a drink and watched the sun sink in a blaze of crimson behind the rose-colored hills. His lips curled in a smile. Darkness would not be far behind. He narrowed his eyes, recalling the vision of Elena the night before, of white limbs and long black hair when she'd stood naked in the darkness. "Tonight, my little white cat, when you leave to meet your lover, I will be close behind." Enraged by the idea of her running to another's arms, he tightened his fingers on the stem of the crystal brandy glass until it threatened to shatter in his hand. He frowned. What he intended to do once he caught her, he had no idea.

He cynically wondered what her reaction had been when she'd discovered the rose in her bed. He hoped she'd been as shaken as he'd been when he'd put it there. He hadn't expected her to affect him so. He'd intended to place the rose on her pillow and leave. But the sight of her had left him trembling with desire. He'd wanted to join her,

take her in his arms, and ignite the fire smoldering under
that innocent facade. His lips tightened to a thin line, certain that last night she'd shared that same passion with
another.

His heart racing with excitement and the need for vengeance, he quickly dressed in the black pants and shirt, then
strapped the silver revolvers onto his hips and jammed the
black mask into his pocket. He poured his third drink,
then, frowning, set it aside. He had no intention of getting drunk this night. He checked his appearance in the
mirror, satisfied when the lean figure and sardonic face of
El Gato looked back. Lighting a cigar, he leaned back into
the shadowy foliage of his balcony to wait.

Sometime after the last light in the house had been extinguished, he glimpsed Elena creeping across the courtyard.
He shoved his hat on his head and climbed down from the
balcony. He exited the courtyard and hurried toward the
thick outer wall. Finding the handholds he'd used since his
return, he scrambled over the top.

Outside the compound he ran some distance to the clump
of bushes where he'd told Carlos to meet him. Neither his
horse nor his servant was there. Furious at being detained,
he paced the ground, fuming with impatience. When he
heard the soft *plop, plop* of muffled hoofbeats, he left the
shadows and strode forward. "You're late."

"Miguel, this is nonsense. You take too many chances.
You are bound to get caught," Carlos said, his voice thick
with disapproval.

Miguel took the reins of the black and swung into the
saddle. "Nevertheless, it is something I must do. I will leave
the horse here when I return. He will not be spotted before
morning." He tied the mask into place.

"I'll take care of Diablo. You take care of yourself," the
old man grumbled.

"*Adios*, my friend." Miguel urged the black into the darkness and raced toward the patch of brush where he'd seen Elena the night before. Knowing she hadn't had time to beat him there, he dismounted. Standing close to the stallion's head, he watched and waited.

Diablo's ears twitched. Miguel put his gloved hand over the horse's nose to keep him silent. Elena, on the silver mare, galloped by. Miguel made ready to follow her when his keen ears picked up the sound of another horse. Silently, he again blended into the brush. A man rode past, trailing Elena in the darkness.

"Her lover," Miguel hissed between clenched teeth. Shaking with rage, he eased himself into the saddle and followed both of them from a distance.

Elena and the mare disappeared in a grove of trees at the base of a steep hill. The man didn't join her as Miguel had expected, but dismounted and crouched on the ground as if waiting.

Confused, Miguel frowned. *This doesn't make any sense . . . unless he isn't her lover, but is watching over her. But if that is the case, why didn't he ride with her instead of staying behind in the darkness? And if he isn't her lover, then where is the bastard?* He raised his eyes to the grove of trees where Elena had disappeared. *There, of course.*

Leaving the stallion out of sight, Miguel slipped from shadow to shadow until he was in the trees. He crept forward, careful not to make any sound that would betray his presence. Parting the branches, he sucked in a startled breath. There before him, naked as a wood nymph, stood Elena.

He scanned the surroundings for her lover, but she appeared to be alone. He watched fascinated as she dived into the moonlit water, scarcely causing a ripple on its silvery surface. A fierce joy leapt in his breast. Maybe she hadn't ridden to meet a lover. Maybe she only wanted to go swimming.

Unable to resist temptation, he threw caution to the wind and stripped off his clothes, leaving the mask in place. Waiting until her back was to him, he slipped into the water, then swam under its surface until he saw the pale gleam of her body ahead of him. Like a hungry fish after a morsel of choice bait, he circled.

Rising suddenly in front of her, he wrapped his arms around her and drew her beneath the water before she could cry out. She struggled, slippery as satin in his grasp. Wrapping his hand in her hair, he molded his body to hers, feeling her coolness next to his heat. Fastening his mouth on hers to silence her, he brought her to the surface.

Her eyes widened in shocked recognition. She twisted her mouth away, gasping for air. "You!" She opened her mouth to scream.

He pulled her to him and swallowed her cry. Her arms thrashed the water wildly as he once again took her down. He rose slowly, holding her close. One hand holding her head, the other cupping her round hip, he held her tightly against him. He pushed his tongue into her mouth, gently tasting her sweet nectar.

She fought like a wild thing, clawing his shoulder and back with razor-sharp nails.

Anger and pain surging through him, he grabbed her arms and pinned them to her sides.

Through water-spiked lashes, her tawny eyes narrowed. "Let me go, you bastard!" she hissed.

"Why are you so angry, *querida*?" he asked innocently, stroking her quivering flesh with his palm. "Didn't you miss me?"

"Miss you?" She shoved his hand away. "You took what you wanted from me. You ruined my life. Now let me be."

He smoothed a lock of wet hair from her eyes. She flinched away from his touch. He shook his head. "I took nothing you didn't give willingly." He rested his hands on her shoulders. His gaze locked on hers. "Ah, *querida*, remember how wonderful it was?" He waved a hand toward the sky. "We soared together with the stars." He slid his hand down and gently caressed her breast, drawing lazy circles around the nipple with his thumb until its pebbly surface hardened to a taut bud.

She slapped his hand away. "You didn't even know it was me. You thought I was Conception."

Miguel hesitated. He couldn't tell her that her father had told him. "My body knew the difference. It never would have responded to your sister like that." He brightened. "Besides, I know she is a blonde. When I took you back to the cave, I saw you had dark hair." He hadn't—he'd been too hungover to notice. "You were asleep, but I kissed you. I wanted to stay and make love to you again."

She tilted her head and gave him a dubious look. "If it was so wonderful, why did you leave me?"

He closed his eyes, once again forced to remember the aching loss. "Because of your father one of my men died that night. I had to send you away for your own safety."

"I'm sorry. I didn't know."

He lifted her chin and locked his gaze on hers. His fingers gently caressed her cheek. "Now do you understand why I had to let you go?"

She nodded, but still appeared wary.

Slowly pulling her into his arms, he held her head against his chest and kissed her hair. Even though his body craved release, when she stiffened he relaxed his hold. Ignoring the warning glare she fixed on him, he bent his head and claimed her cool, soft lips.

For a moment she swayed toward him, kissing him back, then jerked away. Her fists pounded his chest. She opened her mouth to protest.

"Remember how good it was, *querida*, when I held you like this?" Holding her fast, he eased his tongue into her mouth. Exploring her warm moist cavern, he teased her tongue with his own. His hands roamed her body, gently stroking her water-slicked flesh, making her respond to his knowing call. Slowly, surely, he felt her passion rise.

She moaned and ceased her struggle. Her arms lifted to tighten around his neck. Her eyes dreamy, she pressed against him. Pearly drops of water dotted her cheeks with a pale sheen. Her hair floated in a silken fan on the surface of the pool.

"I've missed you, little cat," he whispered. His fingers stroked the area between her inner thighs, until he felt her slick, warm heat. "*Querida,*" he groaned, his hunger rising to a fever pitch.

"Elena?" a man's voice called from the edge of the pool. "Elena? Are you all right?" he called again, more urgently this time.

Coming to her senses, Elena gasped and pushed her bandit lover away. He sank beneath the surface, sliding his mouth down her body to her navel. She quivered as he sank lower, kissing her nest of curls before the ripple of the water around her told that he'd swum away.

Her heart racing, she turned to the man on the bank, hoping he hadn't seen. "I'm fine, Juan," she called in a breathless voice. "I just had a cramp."

"It's time to leave, *amiga*," he urged, "before someone discovers you are gone."

"I'll get dressed," she promised. When Juan left, she searched the area around her. She was alone. El Gato had disappeared. She shuddered, realizing if Juan hadn't interrupted when he did, she would've surrendered to the bandit's passion . . . again. She dived, using the coolness of the water to calm her heated blood. Knowing she didn't dare tarry longer, she swam toward the bank.

After dressing, she left the shelter of the trees and ran toward the waiting horses. Avoiding Juan's brooding regard, she swung into the saddle.

They rode in silence until they reached the hacienda gate. When she dismounted, Juan put out a staying hand. "Elena, be careful. It is a dangerous game you play, little one. I would not like to see you get hurt."

She glanced up at him, not knowing what to say. "Good night, *amigo*," she whispered. Standing on her toes, she gave him a light kiss on the cheek.

Avoiding the bright moonlight, she hurried toward the wing she shared with her husband. She paused by the back staircase to remove her boots, then crept down the hallway toward her room. Feeling a twinge of guilt, she paused outside Diego's door. She pressed her ear against the panel. All was quiet. He was asleep.

Slipping inside her room, she closed the door. She sagged against the cold surface. Her heart pounded in relief. Moving quickly in the darkness, she removed her clothing and drew her nightdress over her head. She lifted her brush and stepped to the balcony intending to remove the snarls from her still-damp hair before she went to bed.

Her bare foot brushed something in the dark. She knew before she picked it up what she would find. She closed her eyes and hugged the fragrant white blossom to her breast. She took a deep breath, inhaling its sweet aroma, once again imagining herself enclosed in El Gato's strong arms.

She sighed. The arrogance, the boldness . . . the wonder of the man.

Horrified by her wicked thoughts, self-reproach washed over her, forcing her thoughts to Diego, her husband. Even though he'd encouraged her to take a lover, she couldn't forget her vows that easily. In the eyes of the church and God, she was his wife until the day she died, and as such, she'd promised to be faithful.

Keeping that promise in mind, she dutifully tossed the bloom away and concentrated on brushing her hair.

Determined to spend more time with her husband and be a better wife, she walked back into her room.

But even as she turned down her coverlet, she felt the edges of her resolve crumble. There on her pillow lay another white rose.

Chapter Twelve

AWAKENED by a commotion in the ranch yard, Elena rubbed her sleepy eyes and rose from her bed. At the window she drew back the curtain and peered out. A heavily laden coach was being unloaded by a flurry of bustling servants. She rubbed her eyes again, her spirits sinking as she recognized her sister clasped in their father's arms. She groaned. Her stomach tightened into a knot. *I should have known it was too good to last. Conception has come home.*

She barely had time to dress before a commanding knock sounded on her door.

"Elena! Let me in," an imperious voice called. "It's Conception."

Pasting a smile on her face, Elena swung the door open.

With a swirl of satins and lace and a torrent of perfumed air, her blond older sister swept regally into the room. Ignoring Elena's outstretched arms, she gave her a quick peck on the cheek before turning away to examine her surroundings. "Well, sister dear, I hear you are married." Conception idly picked up the silver-backed brush set that had been a present from Diego. "Looks as if you are doing all right for yourself." She scrutinized Elena from head to foot, noting her morning dress was of the latest design.

"Hello, Cepi," Elena said without enthusiasm. "I wondered when you intended to come back. Is Ricardo with you?"

Conception arched her brows. "Of course. I left him to supervise the unloading." She went to peer out the window. "I wouldn't want any of my new things to get broken."

The lump in Elena's middle sank to her toes. She frowned. "Are you moving in here, too?" she asked, praying the answer would be no.

Conception whirled around. "Where else would you expect me to live? I certainly couldn't consider living on Ricardo's small *estancia*. I thought perhaps we'd live in this wing, but I guess we'll have to make do with my old suite—until other arrangements can be made." She cast her eyes around the spacious room, as if already envisioning herself in residence.

Elena's mouth tightened in anger, reading her sister's thoughts. "It's quite lovely now, isn't it? Diego is very comfortable living here."

Conception laughed. "I heard about your experience with that bandit. I suppose you were lucky to get even Diego after that," she said, curling her lip in contempt.

"I consider myself very fortunate. Diego is a fine, generous man."

"It warms my heart to hear your praise, my dear," said a pompous voice from the doorway. Diego, dressed in pale peach and cream, strutted into the room. He raised his lace handkerchief to his nose and eyed his sister-in-law disdainfully. "Hello, Conception. I see we are blessed with your presence once again."

"Why shouldn't I be here? It's my home, too," Conception said with a pout.

Elena sucked in a breath, feeling the storm building. Seeking to ease the tension, she placed a hand on her sister's arm. "Of course, and we are delighted to see you looking so well. Won't you and Ricardo take breakfast with us?" she invited.

"Father expects us to take our meals with him. He has ordered Cook to prepare all my favorites," she purred. "Oh, by the way, Elena, would you be a dear and fetch some ripe peaches from the orchard? You know how I love them with fresh cream."

Elena's newfound self-confidence drained from her as it always had in the face of her sister's superior attitude. Despising herself for giving in to her sibling's demands, Elena reluctantly nodded. "All right, Conception," she said, wanting to avoid the tantrum her sister would throw if she refused.

Feeling a sudden need to protect her, Diego stepped forward and put his arm around Elena's shoulders. "I'm sorry, Conception, but from now on you will find a servant to do your bidding. I will not have my wife climbing trees. It would be most unseemly."

The blond sniffed. "She never minded before."

"I mind," Diego said imperiously.

"Well, I certainly wouldn't dream of upsetting *you*, Diego." Gathering her skirts, Conception swished out of the room.

Elena closed the door and sagged against it. Glancing up, she noticed the smug, satisfied smile on Diego's face. "I think Conception has finally met her match," she said. Thinking of her sister's hasty departure, she collapsed in a fit of nervous giggles.

A wavering, almost reluctant grin tugged at the corner of Diego's mouth. Then, as if no longer able to contain his mirth, he burst into hearty laughter.

Wiping her eyes, Elena peered up at her husband through tear-spiked lashes. "She was as mad as a wet cat," she said with a grin.

Diego chuckled. "She certainly appeared to have her fur ruffled."

"You know she won't rest until she gets even," Elena warned him. Sobered by the thought, she bit her lower lip, wondering what Conception would do.

Diego stepped closer and reached out to lift her chin. "That's what I'm here for."

Elena, surprised by the move, looked up. Mirth-filled sapphire eyes, edged with long sooty lashes, gazed warmly into hers. Despite the repugnance she felt for his foppish appearance, her racing heart pounded illogically in her breast.

He gripped her shoulders and slowly bent toward her.

Knowing he intended to kiss her, she closed her eyes and steeled herself not to flinch away. But when his lips and mustache brushed her forehead, irrationally another set of arms and lips flashed into her mind. Dazed, she opened her eyes. For a moment she could have sworn his blue eyes blazed with desire, then he released her and quickly left the room.

Confused by her contradictory emotions, she stared at the closed door. She raised an unsteady hand and touched the spot where he'd kissed her. She couldn't believe the way she'd responded to him. Instead of the revulsion she'd expected, she'd felt a strange attraction, almost a yearning. The same longing she'd felt with El Gato. Comparing the two, she uttered a shaky laugh. "*Madre de Dios*. I am imagining things." She sighed. "I probably didn't get enough sleep last night." Smothering a yawn, she gazed longingly at her bed, then reluctantly shook her head. With Conception in residence, no one was likely to get any sleep.

Miguel sagged against his closed door, finding it hard to believe what he'd almost done. His palms still tingled from contact with her shoulders; his fingers burned with the memory of her smooth cheek. His lips longed to kiss more of her satin skin. She'd looked so adorable with her golden eyes shining.

He clenched his fists, recalling the way that she-wolf of a sister had ordered her about. He narrowed his eyes. They'd soon learn he'd not stand for Elena being treated like an inferior. If he had his way, they'd all kneel at her feet.

He frowned. Why did he feel so protective of her? Why should he want to shield her from anything that might hurt her, including her own father and sister? He told himself that she also carried the de Vega blood in her veins and that made her the same as them. He sighed, knowing his heart felt differently.

From what he had seen, they had never treated her like part of the family but more like an indigent relative or a servant. Maybe that was why he couldn't resist anything that might add to her comfort. He remembered the wagonloads of furnishing and other things he'd bought from the freighters in Santa Fe. The bolts of silks and satins he'd purchased and had made into the lastest gowns. The colors he'd selected to set off her topaz eyes and golden skin.

He closed his eyes, reliving the memory of last night. Unable to contain his curiosity, he'd slipped back into her room. Asleep, she'd looked as innocent as an angel, her long hair spread in an inky fan over her pillow, her lips curved in a sweet smile. Seeing his rose clutched in her hand, he'd felt his heart leap, hoping she dreamed of him. Afraid she would wake to find him there, he'd returned to his room. Desire and an irrational joy flooded him, knowing she was his and his alone. Just the thought made him warm with passion.

He rubbed his back against the door facing. His wild little cat. The scratches she'd inflicted were beginning to itch. Sighing impatiently, he glanced at the bright morning sun, wishing he could hurry its fiery trek across the heavens. Thinking of his plans for the evening, he grinned. He couldn't wait for it to get dark.

Later in the day Miguel scowled at the note in his hand. "Tell him we'd be delighted," he said, not meaning a word of it. With a curt nod he dismissed the servant and closed the door. He wadded the missive into a tight ball and threw it in the trash. "So Enrique wants Diego and Elena to join the family for dinner." He shuddered with distaste, knowing they had no alternative.

He rubbed his temples beneath the wig. Maybe he could plead a headache. With Conception shrieking like a fishwife all day, he truly did. He rejected the idea. To do so would leave Elena at their mercy, and that he would never do. He'd seen how just a word from them could destroy her self-esteem. He wished he could help, give her the courage she needed to stand up to them, but knew she'd have to find it on her own. He could only imagine what she'd endured her whole life. Damn them anyhow! How she could be related to that pair, he'd never understand.

Knowing it was time for *siesta* and not wanting to disturb her, he went to his desk and penned a note, informing her of the dinner plans. He sensed she'd be as thrilled by the affair as he was. He grinned, adding another line to the paper. Satisfied, he closed the letter with a drop of wax and sealed it with his ring. Going into the hall, he slipped the note under her door.

Dressed for dinner, resplendent in a deep gold velvet suit that set off the pale cream of his silk and lace shirt, Miguel preened before his mirror. "Diego, you look quite grand tonight, if I do say so." He anchored his perfectly tied cravat into place with a topaz and diamond stickpin. A matching ring adorned his hand. Buckles with the glittering stones topped his high-heeled gold suede shoes. Tucking a fat velvet bag inside his jacket, he left his suite. Outside Elena's room he knocked softly.

Opening the door, Elena seemed awed. "Diego, you look splendid this evening." She swept a hand down her dress. "Is this the gown you wanted me to wear?" she asked shyly, motioning him inside.

Entering the room, he nodded, unable to find his voice. He stared at the vision before him. The gown of shimmering pale gold dipped scandalously low in front, baring the tops of her creamy breasts. The sleeves puffed at the shoulders and narrowed at the elbows to sheath her slender arms. A snug-fitting bodice accentuated her tiny waist, while the full skirt flared over trim hips. She wore the front of her hair in a shining coronet of braids, leaving the rest to cascade down her back.

"Diego, is something wrong? Do I look all right?" she asked anxiously.

Gathering his rampaging emotions in a tight grip, he nodded. "Lovely, my dear wife. Just lovely." He pursed his lips, cocking his head sideways. "Perhaps I can provide a few finishing touches. Turn around, my sweet, and close your eyes." He removed the bag from his coat and emptied the contents on her dressing table.

He smiled, watching Elena's wondering expression as he fastened a necklace of filigree gold dripping with topaz and diamond teardrops around her slender neck. He leaned close to tuck three glittering jewel-encrusted stars into her hair. Unnerved by her nearness, he clenched his teeth, struggling with an urge to draw her into his arms. Taking her hand, he slid an oblong topaz ring on her finger and clasped a matching bracelet on her slender wrist. Not able to resist, he lifted her palm to his mouth and gently kissed the spot where her life and heartlines crossed. The last of the jewels, a pair of cascading topaz and diamond eardrops, he placed in her hand, too shaken to try to fasten them onto her shell-like ears.

"I'm afraid you'll have to do the rest, my dear. I fear I'm far too clumsy." In truth, just being near her, smelling her flowerlike scent, made him tremble.

Elena opened her eyes, widening them in amazed delight when she saw the jewels. "Oh, Diego, I've never dreamed of wearing anything so beautiful." She spun toward him, her eyes bright with unshed tears. "Thank you, my husband," she whispered. She lifted her arms and pulled his head down, her lips warm on his as she gave him a tremulous kiss.

Miguel sucked in his breath, feeling his body swell with passion. Grateful for the padding in his breeches, he pulled away from her grasp, fighting to control his hunger. He cleared his throat and straightened his neck piece. "Put the earrings on, Elena. We wouldn't want to be late," he said more harshly than he'd intended.

She hastened to fasten the slender, glittering strings into her ears. Finished, she turned shyly toward him. "Do I look all right, Diego?"

"Absolutely breathtaking," he murmured softly.

When he'd seen one of the pieces at the assayer's office in Santa Fe, he couldn't resist asking about it and learned an elderly widow had more pieces for sale. He'd purchased the lot, knowing the golden tones of Elena's skin and eyes would set off the deep amber stones to perfection.

When she slid her hand into the crook of his arm, pride swelled his already abundant person. Closing his hand over hers, he escorted her down to dinner.

Miguel, matching his steps to Elena's, swept her into the salon where Don Enrique, Conception, and Ricardo were having a sherry. "Oh, dear, I hope we haven't kept you waiting," Miguel said to the trio. "I surprised my wife with a few trinkets I picked up in Santa Fe. I think they are most becoming. Don't you agree, Conception?" he said innocently to the blonde, finding it hard to suppress a grin when her mouth dropped open in shock.

"Trinkets, Diego?" Enrique said. "Those stones are fit for a queen."

Miguel lifted his blushing bride's hand to his mouth and kissed it. "It is my wife's beauty that makes them appear so."

"I agree, Diego." Ricardo, with an admiring leer, stepped forward to give Elena a lingering kiss on the cheek.

Miguel narrowed his eyes. Jealousy infused his veins.

"Thank you, Ricardo. My husband is very generous," Elena said, turning her warm smile toward Diego.

"Well, do we intend to eat, or shall we just stand around and admire Elena all night?" Conception snapped. Tightening her lips into a pout, she flounced, unescorted, into the dining room.

De Vega shrugged and followed his daughter.

"Dear me. Conception seems a bit upset about something," Miguel said. He looked into his wife's dancing golden eyes, glad he'd been the one to spark the happiness there.

Ricardo sighed. "Pay her no mind, Diego. Conception is always upset about something."

Thanking his lucky stars he wasn't tied to the witch, Miguel cast a sympathetic glance toward his brother-in-law. Looping Elena's arm through his, Miguel squeezed her hand and led her into dinner.

After the meal, when the women departed for the salon, de Vega invited the men into the study for cigars and drinks.

Sitting on the leather couch, Diego swished the last swallow of brandy around the bottom of his glass before finishing it. His bored glance took in the stout figure of the man sitting behind the desk. The man busy plotting the downfall of El Gato del Noche. "And how do you propose to catch this bandit, Enrique?"

The man leaned toward him, his black eyes glittering with hatred. "With bait he can't refuse," he hissed. "Somehow he has managed to stop every shipment leaving the ranch. So from now on the gold will not be sent to Santa Fe. It will be brought here."

No longer bored, Miguel listened intently.

"Where?" Ricardo asked.

"I am building a vault of iron and stone. No bandit will be able to penetrate its walls. It will be guarded day and night, and when it is full, an army of men will escort the shipment to the bank." He smiled and poured himself another drink. "Even El Gato cannot get his hands on this gold."

"What if he tries?" Miguel asked, intrigued by the idea.

"He will meet his death," de Vega said with an evil smile. "The ground around the vault is layered with explosives. If the thief is spotted, we will let him get near, then . . . *poof!* Nothing will be left of him."

"Won't the gold be blown up, too?" Ricardo asked.

"No. The gold will be underground, easily recovered and removed. It does not matter if the vault is damaged. Once El Gato is dead, it will not be needed." He threw back his drink, swallowing it in one noisy gulp. "Then I will be revenged for his trying to kidnap Conception and stealing my gold."

Miguel's eyes narrowed. "He didn't take Conception. It was Elena he kidnapped." To hide his anger, he swished his lace-edged handkerchief at a spot of dust on the couch.

Enrique looked up at him. "Of course, Diego. After her disgrace, let us thank God she does not carry the ruffian's child."

Miguel clenched the stem of the brandy glass so tightly it snapped in his grasp. *Remember you are Diego,* a voice inside warned as he fought to contain the fury raging through his body. Finally getting himself under control, he rose to his feet. Placing the broken glass on the desk, he stared down at his host. "You will have to excuse me. I am going to bed."

De Vega stared at the glass, then raised an astonished gaze to Diego. Seeing his son-in-law's scowl, he hurried from behind the desk. He rushed to Diego's side and clutched his sleeve. "Please forgive me, my son. You did me a great favor by marrying the girl. It was terrible of me to remind you of that unfortunate incident."

Miguel fixed him with a cold stare. Reminding himself of his role, he forced a smile. "It was Elena who did the favor by marrying me. Now you must excuse me. I have a headache." Brushing off the man's hand, he swiftly left the room.

Trembling with rage, Miguel cursed de Vega under his breath. It was all he could do to keep from tearing the man apart with his bare hands. Concern for Elena filled his mind. He frowned, worrying how she had fared being left alone with her witch of a sister. Nearing their suite of rooms, he paused outside her door. Had she retired for the night? Hearing Conception's voice, he sighed. After knocking once, he stepped into the room.

Elena, looking a bit pale, flashed him a look of gratitude.

He turned toward the blonde admiring herself in the mirror. "Conception, I am surprised to see you here at this late hour. I expected to find Elena asleep."

"We had much to catch up on, Diego," Conception said defensively. "But since you are ready to retire, I guess I will go to bed." She rose from her spot in front of the dressing table and started toward the door.

Miguel put out a staying hand. "One moment, my dear sister-in-law. You've forgotten something," he said, motioning to the glittering topaz stones around her neck.

"I just wanted to borrow them, but if you object . . ." she said, making no motion to take them off.

"I do object. Return them at once," he said sharply.

Her eyes narrowing with naked hate and jealousy, Conception ripped the jewelry off. "Here, take her stupid necklace. I wouldn't be caught dead in the gaudy thing." Shoving it into his hand, she flounced out of the room, slamming the door behind her.

He handed the necklace to Elena, noting her dismay when she examined the fragile clasp Conception had broken in spite. She raised stricken eyes. "Oh, Diego, I am so sorry."

Wanting to ease her sorrow, he lifted her to her feet and wiped the tears from her eyes. "There's nothing to be sorry for, my dear. It can easily be repaired." He gently kissed the top of her shining hair. "Now I think we should go to bed and try to get some sleep—while we can," he teased. When she nodded, he reluctantly released her.

"Good night, Diego. I hope you have pleasant dreams."

He gave her a warm smile, wishing it could be more. "Good night, Elena. May yours be pleasant, also," he said softly, exiting her room. Entering his own, he took care to lock the door behind him. He frowned. Now that he had incurred Conception's wrath, he would have to be doubly careful. If she discovered his identity, not only he, but Elena, would suffer the consequences. Damning the blond bitch to perdition, he removed his clothes and lay naked on his bed. Pushing her from his mind, his thoughts switched to de Vega's plan to keep his gold. Miguel smiled. He never could resist a challenge.

Chapter Thirteen

CONCEPTION'S voice rose in a high-pitched screech that reverberated through the house.

"*Mierda!*" Gritting his teeth, Miguel quickly made his escape down the back stairway and left the walled courtyard of the hacienda. Reaching the main compound area of the ranch, he slowed his pace. "*Caramba!* The woman has a voice that would drive nails," he muttered.

Now that he was out of earshot, he wondered what to do with himself. He stared thoughtfully at a long cluster of buildings, then regretfully shook his head. No. Diego would never be caught in the stables. Everyone knew he was terrified of horses. Besides, they were dirty and smelled, both things his alter ego was supposed to detest.

Turning in the opposite direction, at the far end of the walled grounds he spotted a grove of trees. *The orchard.* He smiled, recalling earlier days when he and Benito, Carlos's young son, had played there as children. Strolling toward the shade of the trees, he brushed at a smudge of dirt on his fussy pale blue embroidered jacket.

As he did so, another similar jacket came into mind; a jacket he had traded to Benito on that fateful day long ago in exchange for a mongrel pup. Because of that trade, Benito, wearing the garment, had been mistaken for Miguel and murdered along with the rest of the Sandoval family.

115

Carlos's son now lay in the Spanish Angel graveyard under the headstone marked Miguel Sandoval.

Deep in bitter reverie, Miguel was startled when a not-yet-ripe peach fell from the tree and hit him on the shoulder. "What the—?" He stared up into the higher branches.

Fear-filled wide brown eyes stared back.

Miguel, trying to keep a solemn face, arched his brow. "What is it I see? Could it be a squirrel?"

The child, a boy about five, giggled. "I'm not a squirrel."

"Well, if you aren't a squirrel, what are you doing up there?"

"I was trying to get that peach." The child stretched toward a choice red-tinged fruit that was just out of reach. Losing his grip on the branch he was holding, he desperately grabbed for another. "Ohh!"

"*Por Dios!* Don't move!" Miguel, silently cursing the outlandish outfit he wore, scrambled up the tree, praying he could make it before the little boy tumbled to the ground. His heart in his mouth, Miguel precariously balanced himself, his feet on one lofty limb, one arm wrapped around another. He stretched his other arm toward the child who dangled overhead. "Take my hand."

"I can't, señor. I'm stuck," the little boy wailed.

"Stuck? Where?" Miguel's gaze followed the child's leg backward, to where it was wedged between two branches. If the child fell, his leg would surely break. "It's all right, *niño*. I'm coming." He pulled himself up the limbs until he reached the sobbing child. After freeing the youngster's hand from where it was fastened in a death grip on a small branch, he placed him in a more secure position. He then freed the child's foot. "Now, *niño*, wrap your arms around me and hold tight. I'll see if I can get us down without breaking both our necks."

"But the peach, señor!"

Miguel grinned. He'd forgotten how single-minded small boys were. He plucked the peach and handed it to the child. Carefully making his way down the tree, he'd almost made it to the bottom when the seat of his pants caught on a sharp branch. He twisted to get free and heard a loud rip. "No," he groaned. A second later he and the boy were on the ground.

"Oh, señor, your beautiful suit!" the child cried in dismay, pointing to the tear.

Miguel shook his head. "The suit is of no importance, but that cut is." He examined a long, bloody welt that ran up the back of the boy's leg. "I think we'd better get it taken care of." Lifting the child, Miguel strode to the back gate of the courtyard and entered his wing. Reaching the top of the stairs, a startled gasp made him look up to see Elena standing there.

"Diego, what has happened to Paco?" she cried, running to his side.

"He had a small accident, huh, *amigo*?" Miguel said.

"Bring him into my room." Elena hurried ahead to open the door.

"Señor, I can't—*Mi madre*. I will get into trouble."

"Shh. Dona Elena is the boss around here." He nodded toward Elena. "We'll both be in trouble if we don't do what she says." He placed the child on the settee where Elena indicated and turned to see her staring at his backside. Meeting his eyes, her face flamed red. Running a hand down his hip, he discovered a large expanse of bare skin. "My pants!"

"The señor tore his beautiful suit climbing the tree," the child explained.

"Climbing the tree?" She gave Miguel a questioning smile.

"Uhh, if you can tend to the boy, I'll change clothes."
When she nodded, he backed through the exit and went
into his own room. *Por Dios!* Had she seen the padding?
He examined his rear view in the mirror. Maybe she hadn't
noticed. After washing, he quickly changed into a dove-
gray suit and went back into Elena's room.

His heart raced at the sight of Elena on her knees tenderly
applying salve to the small boy's cut. He knelt beside her,
happy to discover the boy's wound wasn't as bad as he'd
thought. "How is he?"

"Very brave," she said with a smile. "As were you,
Diego. He told me what you did."

"Well, I couldn't very well let the child dangle in midair.
I had to do something." Uncomfortable under her scrutiny,
he switched his attention to the boy. "Did she let you keep
the peach?" he teased.

The youngster tucked his head. His lip quivered. He
handed the peach to Elena. "I'm sorry, señora."

"What the devil?" Miguel took the fruit and returned it
to the child. "Paco, I was joking. The peach is yours."

Seeing the fear on the little boy's face, Miguel frowned
at Elena. "What is wrong with him?"

She sighed. "The orchard is forbidden to the children.
The choicest fruit is reserved for the house, and only the
bruised or overripe fruit is sent to the village. It is my
father's orders."

Outraged by her statement, Miguel got to his feet and
scowled across at de Vega's wing. "That is ridiculous. If
we ate nothing but peaches, we couldn't begin to eat the
crop of even one tree, let alone an orchard full."

Elena nodded. "I know, but it is the custom."

"Custom be damned!" He knelt by the boy. "Paco, any
time you want a peach, or for that matter a bushel of

peaches, you come to me. I'll see to it you get so many peaches you are sick of them."

The boy's face split in a wide smile. "Sí, Señor Alvarado."

Miguel frowned. "I thought we were friends. Call me Diego." He glanced up at Elena, giving her a mischievous smile. "Say, Paco, does your mama like peaches, too?"

"*Sí*, Diego," the boy said excitedly.

"Elena, how are you at picking fruit?"

"Better than you, Diego," she said with a laugh.

"I'll take that as a challenge." He held out his hand. "Come on, Paco."

Giving Diego a conspiratorial wink, Elena grasped the child's other hand. "Let's go find a basket."

Chapter Fourteen

ANGRY voices rang through the hacienda shattering the peace of the afternoon *siesta*. Grimacing, Elena pulled her pillow over her head. She had to admire her sister for stamina. Not many people could arise early in the morning screeching and go to bed late the same way. It had been a week since Conception returned, but it seemed more like an eternity. Elena sighed, longing for the former tranquillity. Tension in the household had become unbearable, and tempers flared with little provocation—even Diego's.

Since the raid on the orchard, he had remained closeted in his room, his blue eyes taking on an almost desperate look. Elena knew the only reason he hadn't fled to Santa Fe was because he was loath to leave her at her sister's mercy.

Angry because Diego would not give up the wing he now occupied with Elena, Conception threw daily tantrums, apparently believing her behavior would make everyone so miserable he would be forced to relent.

But Elena knew Diego had no intention of inconveniencing himself for her sister's whims. She hoped Cepi would soon come to terms with the situation and settle down before she drove all of them crazy.

Conception, like a bad habit, showed up at Elena's door every night after dinner and remained until either Elena went to bed or Diego arrived to throw her out. She'd tried to convince Cepi that Diego did what he pleased, and even if she did ask him to give up the rooms, she was certain he would not change his mind. She sighed, longing for the days and nights when she could roam the house and gardens at will. Now she couldn't leave her room without running into Conception. She felt like a trapped animal.

The tap of high heels echoed in the hall, and a sharp knock sounded on the door.

Groaning, Elena rose from her bed. Clad only in her underwear, she opened the door. "What do you want now, Cepi?" she asked wearily.

The blonde swished into the room. "I wish to wear one of your gowns tonight. My own wardrobe is not nearly as extensive, and besides you never dress for dinner anyway."

"I'd think you could manage with what you've already taken," Elena said tersely. Preparing to shut the door, she saw Diego standing in the hall.

His brow dark as a thundercloud, he brushed past her and entered the room. He strode to the closet and slammed the door, almost catching her sister's grasping hand in the process. "Conception, you will no longer be permitted to 'borrow' my wife's things."

Conception, her lips in a pout, gave him a mutinous look. "Elena doesn't care."

"Well, I do. Yesterday you ruined her favorite dress." He glowered at her. "In fact, you have intruded in our lives long enough. From this day forward you will not enter this wing without an invitation."

"That is ridiculous. This is my house."

"No, it isn't. When I married Elena, one-third of the house *and* the ranch became mine."

"Oh, really?" A cold gleam in her eye, Conception turned to Elena. "Are you pregnant yet?"

Elena shook her head.

Raking Diego with her gaze, Conception curled her lip in contempt. "I don't wonder." She turned to Elena. "Do you remember the terms of Father's will?"

Closing her eyes, Elena nodded.

At the door Conception gave them a sly smile. "If I were you, I wouldn't make any plans just yet." The door closed. The click of her heels echoed in the hall as she hurried away.

Diego frowned at her. "What is she talking about?"

"I thought you knew. According to Father's will, the remaining one-third of the ranch goes to the first grandchild."

"The first grandchild? *Caramba!*" Diego hit his brow with the flat of his hand. "My anger may have just cost us the ranch." Raising his head, he studied her. "Unless . . ."

She stepped closer, staring trustingly up at her husband. "Unless what, Diego?"

"Unless you get pregnant."

Elena giggled. "We both know there's not much chance of that."

Scowling, he paced the floor. "We must find a way." Raising a brow, he walked around her. "Hmm." He eyed her up and down. His scrutiny reminded her she wore nothing but her underwear. She snatched up a robe and put it on.

He stroked his chin, then nodded. "Yes. That's the answer." He met her puzzled gaze. "Do you have any preferences, my dear?"

"For what?"

"A lover."

"Diego!" she gasped.

He shrugged. "I just thought maybe I could find someone not too objectionable to do the deed."

Elena closed her gaping mouth, outrage replacing her astonishment. "Do the deed? I'm not a cow or a brood mare to be brought to a stud!"

"Forgive me, my dear. I'm only trying to help."

She spun away from him. "I can't believe we are having this conversation."

"I'm sorry, Elena. It's just that the ranch is so important to me." He sighed. "It's too bad El Gato wasn't more of a man."

"El Gato?" Elena cried, appalled at his words.

"Yes," he said, picking a piece of lint from the lapel of his sapphire-blue jacket. He preened before the mirror, patting his wig and his fat mustache. "If he had made you pregnant, all of our troubles would be over." He pursed his lips as if deep in thought. After a few moments he flashed her an excited smile. "I must go to Santa Fe." He walked toward her and took her hand in his. "Don't worry about it, my dear. I'll handle everything." He gave her hand a pat and went to the door. "Have the maids prepare the extra room. I may be returning with a guest." He gave her a wink and left the room.

Elena stared after him, her eyes widening in horror. He wouldn't—he couldn't mean . . . But the words he'd uttered came back to mock her.

Tossing in her bed, unable to sleep, Elena rose at dawn the next morning. She glanced out the window and saw Diego's coach leave the ranch yard. A sinking dread washed over her. How long would he be gone? When—and with whom—would he return? Unable to bear the thought, she dropped the curtain and turned back to the room.

She couldn't believe this was happening. Her marriage had turned into a mockery, a nightmare from which she couldn't awaken. Even though Diego was the most pompous, arrogant man she'd ever met, she had seen another side of him that was kind and sympathetic. But now . . .

She shook her head. He couldn't have meant it, but, remembering the look on his face, she knew he had. She stared at her bed. The bed he was unable to share with her. How could he coldly expect her to mate with another, a virtual stranger?

She tried to imagine herself in a stranger's arms with no love, no gentleness, allowing the man to take her until she conceived a child. She buried her face in her hands. Even the idea made her shiver in horror.

"I won't do it!" she cried. But Diego had made it clear that was exactly what he wanted. She knew he'd married her for her share of the ranch. Surely it couldn't be so important that he would expect her to give birth to another's child in order to get it? A chill ran up her spine. A husband ruled his wife. He could force her to bend to his will. He was expected to punish her, even beat her if she did not obey his wishes. "But this?"

Tormented by the previous night's events, Elena sought to ease her tenseness in the calmness of the garden. She had barely sat down when she heard Conception calling her. She closed her eyes. What else could happen? Heaving a disparaging sigh, she watched her sister hurry across the courtyard toward her. "Hello, Conception."

"I heard your husband leave this morning. I wanted to see you, but that man wouldn't let me pass."

Elena frowned. "What man? Whatever are you talking about?"

"I can't believe you didn't know. Diego posted a guard. The man refused to let me enter your wing."

"Well, I didn't know." Diego had said he'd make sure she wasn't bothered. That must be what he meant. "Why did you want to see me?" She was almost afraid to ask.

Conception smiled. "I want to invite you to dinner. You must be lonely with your husband gone."

Elena peered warily up at her sister. Dining with Conception was the last thing she wanted to do, but she didn't know how to gracefully refuse. "All right, Cepi. Thank you for the invitation."

"Good. See you tonight." Conception whirled and hurried toward the house.

In spite of her sister's manner, Elena sensed dinner would not be what she hoped for. Her stomach tightened in knots. Conception was up to something, but what?

That evening, dressed in a simple, pale green gown, Elena entered the salon.

Her father looked up from the drink he'd been pouring. "Ah, Elena. Come, sit with me while we wait for the lovebirds."

"Lovebirds?" Elena asked, taking the glass of wine he held out to her.

"Conception and Ricardo. I have never seen a happier couple." He sighed. "You know how opposed I was to the match, but I was mistaken."

"Mistaken?"

"In what the angel wanted."

"The angel?" Elena asked, confused. This whole conversation made no sense to her.

He sighed. "Yes, Elena. I thought the angel wanted Conception to enter the convent." He leaned closer. "I must have been mistaken, for I haven't seen her since."

"Who? Conception?"

"No, the angel," her father said, shaking his head. "Elena, if I didn't know better, I'd think you were simpleminded."

"I'm sorry, Father. I guess I am overly tired."

He leaned forward and patted her hand. "That's quite all

right, my child. I've never seen Diego in such a foul mood. Why, he even snapped at me."

"He's been upset by the turmoil since Conception's arrival," Elena said defensively.

"She's so high strung. Just like Soledad, her mother."

Elena looked at him, biting her tongue to keep from adding that Soledad had been her mother, too.

"Ah, yes." He smiled, cocking his head to one side. "Here comes my precious now."

Conception and Ricardo swept into the room. The blonde, dressed in an elaborate gown of pale blue satin, hung on her husband's arm and gazed adoringly into his dark eyes. She turned to greet her father, raising her brows when she saw Elena at his side. "Oh, Elena, I'd forgotten." She gave her a smug look. "I'm sorry we kept you waiting. We were— ah—otherwise occupied and forgot the time. Didn't we, darling?"

"It's all right, Cepi," Elena said, realizing her sister was flaunting the fact she and Ricardo had just made love.

Ricardo, seeming embarrassed by the remark, disengaged himself from his wife's clutches. Taking his father-in-law's cue, he poured himself a stiff brandy from the crystal decanter on the table. He downed it in one gulp and poured another.

"You can bring that one into dinner, my pet," Conception purred. "The sooner we eat, the sooner we can retire," she whispered, loud enough for Elena to hear.

Ricardo groaned, rolling his eyes toward the ceiling.

Elena would have thought the whole thing funny, if she wasn't aware of the consequences. She slid her trembling hand into the crook of her father's arm and followed the couple into the dining room.

After the meal Conception hurried her reluctant husband off to their suite.

Elena, knowing her father preferred his books to her company, excused herself and went to her room.

Uncomfortable in the hot, sticky night, Elena removed her dress and stretched out on the bed. Her thoughts went to Conception and Ricardo. She felt a strange kinship with the man, knowing how relentless her sister could be when she set her mind on something. And right now, Conception wanted to get pregnant. Elena shook her head. Poor Ricardo already looked a little ragged around the edges, but at least he loved Conception. She closed her eyes against hot tears. *He* hadn't gone off to fetch his wife a lover.

Depression settled over her like a heavy, damp blanket. She thought longingly of the pool, but immediately rejected the idea. *He* might be there.

She rose from the bed to walk restlessly around the room. Her tortured musings contemplated the purpose of her husband's trip. Cold fear sluiced down her back. When would Diego return . . . and who would accompany him? A feeling of being trapped made her throat tighten. She gasped for air. Her steps quickened until she paced about like a caged animal. Panting for breath, she stopped. Whether El Gato was there or not, she couldn't stand another minute in this room.

She scrambled into her riding clothes and ran down the back staircase. Cautious, she made her way to the stables, relieved to find Juan wasn't there. This night she didn't want him with her. This night she had to be alone.

After removing one of the keys to the back gate from a nail in the tackroom, she tucked it in her pocket. She hurriedly saddled Silver Moon, then led her through the gate and locked it behind her.

Out of sight of the hacienda, she gave the mare her head, allowing her to race across the desert. She shook her braid loose. The hot desert wind buffeted her face, tangling her hair as it whipped out behind her. Tonight she wouldn't be followed. Tonight she would cast her fate to the winds.

On a rocky knoll Miguel squatted on his bootheels and watched the copse of trees. Hearing the drumming of hoofbeats, he smiled. His heart quickened as a dark-haired figure on a gray horse raced into view. "Elena," he murmured.

Lighting a cigar, he resumed his seat, waiting for Juan to follow. When a period of time elapsed and no rider appeared, he frowned, thinking of the danger. She shouldn't ride unprotected so far from the ranch. A thrill accompanied the fear. He tied on his mask. Tonight he wouldn't be interrupted. Tonight she was alone.

Tossing the cigar away, he led Diablo down the hill, ground-tying him in the cover of the trees. His heart racing with excitement, he stayed in the shadows, scanning the pool for her pale form. She'd had ample time to get into the water, but the pool was empty. His gut tightened. *Por Dios,* had she drowned? He yanked his boots off and raced toward the spring. Muffled sobs jerked him to a halt. He spun toward the sound, stumbling frantically through the darkness.

A sliver of moonlight showed her amongst the shadows, stretched out on the ground. Sobs shook her slender body.

Thinking she might have been thrown, he rushed forward and knelt beside her. He ran trembling hands over her body in search of broken bones.

Gasping, she jerked upright. "Get away!" she cried, pushing at his hands. She scrambled to her feet. "Don't you touch me," she warned, grabbing up a stick. "Who are you?" Her voice choked as she peered up at him. Her tears glimmered like small pearls on her face.

"It is I, *querida*," he said softly.

"El Gato! I should have known," she said bitterly. "Go

away. Leave me alone." She slumped back to the ground.

Miguel stared down at her. His body ached, on fire with wanting her. He knew he could take her. Alone and helpless, she couldn't refuse him. But he knew he could never live with himself if he did. After a moment he turned and walked slowly into the darkness, her tears piercing him like a hot knife.

Damn Conception and de Vega! He couldn't lose the ranch, but the terms of de Vega's will put him in a terrible position. And he, in turn, had pressured Elena. He had to tell her what he did, knowing the growing sense of loyalty she'd felt for Diego wouldn't have permitted her to be with El Gato. Now he hated himself for doing it.

He'd never forget the shock and horror on her face when he told her he intended to fetch back a lover. He clenched his hands at his sides. He'd kill anyone who dared to touch her. But she didn't know that, didn't know that he, El Gato, was also Diego her husband. Her sobs tore at him. He felt sick. Knowing he was the cause of her misery made the pain even worse.

Retrieving his boots, he put them on and went to fetch the stallion. He rode back to the rocks and waited. A long time later he saw Elena mount the mare and ride toward him.

He urged the black from cover. Not wanting to frighten her, he stayed where he was until she recognized him. Then afraid to intrude, he followed from a distance, making sure she reached home safely.

Dismounting to unlock the hacienda gate, Elena turned, watching until the bandit waved his hat and galloped back the way he'd come.

Her emotions in tatters, she stared after the man they called El Gato, feeling a strange sense of sadness as he disappeared from sight. At the pool she'd been frightened, then angered, to find it was him. Even though his touch had been gentle, she knew he'd wanted her. She'd felt it between them, like the constant pull of a white river current. Being stronger, he could have taken her. But he hadn't. He'd left, only to see her safely home. He was the cause of all her problems, but try as she might, she could not hate him.

Her mind troubled, she quietly closed and locked the gate. She led the mare into the barn and removed the saddle gear, hanging it over the gate of an empty stall. Grateful to find the stable quiet, she brushed the horse in the darkness, removing sweat and dust from the mare's silvery coat.

Knowing she shouldn't tarry longer, Elena left the barn and cautiously made her way to the house.

Once in her room she removed her clothes. She wiped her face. She was still hot and sticky and now dusty as well. Sighing, she lifted the silver pitcher and poured water into the basin. After going all that way to the pool, she hadn't even gotten wet.

Chapter Fifteen

THE next day dawned even hotter than the one before, with every living thing seeking whatever shade it could find. Those who could stayed within the thick walls of the hacienda, hoping to obtain relief from the heat. There tempers flared, with occasional voices rising in anger as patience grew short in the suffocating stillness.

By afternoon clouds gathered, stacking ominously over the Sangre de Cristo Mountains, while the earth in the valley scorched and shimmered under a sun that sucked every vestige of moisture from the atmosphere.

Finding her bedroom unbearable, Elena spent most of the day downstairs in her salon reading, taking light meals in the shade of the terrace instead of the stuffy dining area. Not until twilight did she leave the north wing to venture out in search of a breath of air.

To avoid being waylaid by her sister, Elena shunned the courtyard and walked instead toward the village in the far corner of the walled grounds. Unlike Conception, Elena liked to come here, counting her only friends among these simple people. Feeling a kinship with them, because of her Indian blood, she did what she could to help in times of sickness or trouble.

The ranch proper was built like a small town. For protection of the Spanish Angel and its people an outer wall twelve to fifteen feet tall enclosed about twenty acres around the main ranch house. All of the buildings, barns, vineyards, orchards and wells, as well as the village where the ranch workers lived, were contained in this area. The huge U-shaped hacienda, a fortress in itself, sat in the middle, separated from the rest of the compound by the courtyard whose bell tower and wall provided an added measure of safety as well as privacy to the residents.

The splendor and extravagance of the hacienda contrasted sharply with the poverty of its people. Here, in the village, there were no elaborate paved courtyards filled with multi-tudes of blossoming flowers and flowing fountains. Here, she saw only bare earth crowded with small adobe huts. The only greenery was tiny, carefully tended individual garden plots, laboriously watered by buckets carried from the com-munal well. Behind corn, squash, and beans hung washlines strung with traditional white cotton clothing, worn to reflect the desert heat.

Now that the sun had gone down, the ranch children crept from their homes and filled the dusty yards with joyous laughter and squeals. Mothers sat on their doorsteps, fanning themselves and keeping a sharp eye on a multitude of offspring.

Elena made her way toward one of the houses. She stopped to chat with a girl barely in her teens, who sat on the threshold suckling an infant at her breast. Smiling, Elena sat down on the step beside her. "Hello, Rosita. How is the little one?"

The girl smiled, touching the baby's cheek. "She is much better now, señora." She removed her nipple from the baby's mouth and pulled up the top of her low-cut white blouse. "Would you like to hold her?"

"I'd love to," Elena said, taking the child in her arms.

The babe's bright dark eyes gazed innocently up at her.

Her lips, round and red as a small rosebud, nuzzled Elena as if hoping for more dinner.

What will life hold in store for you, precious one? Elena wondered. Breathing in the sweet baby smell, she brushed a gentle kiss on the soft forehead. After a while she reluctantly handed the child back to her mother. "She's so beautiful."

Troubled, Elena looked at the thin-faced girl. "If you need anything else—anything at all—tell Juan. He will see that I get the message," she told the girl.

"Thank you, señora, but you have done much already, and things are better now. Rodolfo has asked to marry me. He watches over us." A small, dark man came to stand behind her in the doorway. He nodded respectfully before turning adoring eyes to the mother and infant in his care.

"I'm very happy for you. I wish you both much happiness." After saying goodbye, Elena left the couple and walked slowly back toward the hacienda.

Her mouth tightened, remembering how the majordomo, Guillermo, had savagely raped and beaten the girl, leaving her to almost bleed to death in the barn. Discovering her naked and broken body, Elena had sent for the midwife who served as a doctor for all of the workers. Together they saved her life, but Rosita's small body swelled with the seed of that brutal act, delivering the child a bare eight months later.

In spite of the heat, she shivered, knowing her father would have forced her to marry Guillermo. Diego, for whatever reason, had saved her. In spite of his strange quirks, she owed him a large debt of gratitude. She sucked in a breath, remembering the purpose of his trip to Santa Fe. She knew her sense of obligation would never be enough to give him a stranger's child.

The memory of the tiny babe flooded her, making her

ache with emptiness. She would love a child, regardless of who fathered it. It was what she would be required to do to have one that filled her with terror. If only there was some other way.

A guitar strummed softly as a young man serenaded the girl of his choice—under the watchful eye of her mother.

Elena's pulse quickened, remembering another serenade when El Gato sang to her from beneath her balcony. She turned her eyes toward the distant mountains, watching heat lightning dance and flicker over the top of the peaks. Was he there tonight?

Avoiding the courtyard, she slipped up the back stairs and entered her room. Finding it hotter than ever, she went onto her terrace. She lifted her heavy hair from the back of her neck, but tonight no breeze came to cool her. Even the frogs and crickets remained silent, as though, in the heat, their song took too much effort.

In the shadows she leaned back against the sweet-smelling vines. The splash of the courtyard fountain brought images of cool water in a desert pool. She could almost feel it washing over her hot, sweat-drenched body. She shook her head, rejecting the idea. *No, he might be there again.*

She sank reluctantly into a wicker chair and pulled her damp blouse away from where it was plastered to her skin. Again visions of the spring-fed pool beckoned. Thoughtful, Elena bit her lip. *He might not be anywhere near.* A trail of sticky perspiration trickled between her breasts. She sighed. As miserable as she felt, it would be worth the risk.

Her decision made, she scrambled into her riding clothes and slipped swiftly through the shadows to the barn. Bridle in hand, she edged toward the dark stall. When Silver Moon nickered a soft welcome, Elena glanced around and felt in her skirt pocket for a lump of hard brown sugar to keep the horse quiet. Her fingers touched something. *The gate key.* She'd forgotten to replace it last night. She smiled. Well, it would make things easier this evening.

A single lantern burned at the far end of the barn, leaving the area where she stood in semidarkness. After bridling the mare, Elena peered around for the saddle she'd hung over the stall gate. It wasn't there. Juan probably put it away.

She tiptoed down the corridor to the tack room. Her hand on the door, she froze. *Voices!* Placing her ear against the door, she heard Juan and a woman murmuring soft words of love in the darkness. Elena grinned. So that's why he hadn't followed her last night. She sobered. It also left her with a problem. She couldn't get her saddle.

She eased back down the hallway, hoping Silver Moon wouldn't nicker. Frowning, she stopped outside the stall and rubbed the mare's nose. *I either have to stay home or ride bareback—and I don't intend to stay home.* She opened the stall and led the mare to the rear exit.

Silently taking the horse outside the compound walls, Elena found a good-sized rock and used it as a step to climb astride. Although she'd ridden bareback many times as a child, she definitely preferred a saddle now, she thought, shifting her weight to avoid the mare's backbone. Urging the horse into a smooth canter, Elena pointed her in the direction of the pool.

As Elena rode, she noticed the unnatural silence of the night. Even the sound of Silver Moon's hooves seemed muffled by the soft sand. She breathed a sigh of relief when the outline of the cottonwood trees surrounding the pond loomed in front of her.

A feeling she wasn't alone made her halt the mare. Was it El Gato? She peered into the darkness. She had the eerie feeling that someone, or something, was watching her, but seeing nothing, she shrugged. *Probably imagining it . . .*

Silver Moon snorted and danced sideways.

Elena tightened her grip on the reins. If the mare sensed a presence, too, it couldn't be her imagination. "Who's there?" she called, straining to see. The black night closed like a suffocating cloak around her. A shiver crawled up her spine. This wasn't the smartest thing she'd ever done. A band of renegade Apache could be just out of reach, and she wouldn't know until it was too late.

Stomping her feet, the mare blew nervously through her nostrils.

"Easy, Luna." Feeling she had nothing to gain by running, Elena touched her heels to the mare's sides, urging her forward. The horse took one trembling step, then another.

The scream of a big cat split the darkness.

The terrified mare reared, spinning on her hind legs.

Unseated by the sudden move, Elena crashed to the ground. The horse raced away, leaving her alone. Elena lay on her side, fighting for the breath knocked from her by the fall.

In front of her, a sleek black shape moved out of the shadows. It hissed and spat, sending hot, putrid breath onto her face.

Elena froze. Her pounding heart sent her blood roaring into her ears. She tried to swallow, but fear made her mouth so dry her tongue stuck to the roof.

Lightning flared in the distance, silhouetting the jaguar. It crouched, ready to leap.

Knowing the cat would tear her to bits, Elena screamed.

Hoofbeats raced toward her, vibrating the ground. "Elena?" a voice called.

"Here!" she cried.

A shot rang out. The jaguar leapt over her and disappeared into the night.

El Gato slid from his horse and gathered her to his chest. Almost frantically he kissed her hair, her forehead, her eyelids.

Elena clung to him, taking sanctuary in his strong arms. He held her trembling body and smoothed her hair away from her eyes. "It's all right now, *querida*. You are safe. The cat is probably halfway back to Mexico by now."

"I've never seen a jaguar before," she said, staring into the darkness.

"They are not usually this far north, but sometimes they follow the river in search of food."

"He thought I was his dinner." Elena gave a quivering laugh.

Gripping her shoulders, El Gato pulled away and stared down into her face. "You are all right? The cat did not hurt you?"

"No," she said, her voice shaky. "I'm fine, just bruised and frightened."

He drew her close again, wrapping his arms tightly around her. "Oh, *querida*, when I think of what could have happened."

As his reassurance calmed her fear, other senses took their place. With her head on his chest, she became aware of the pounding of his own heart against her ear, of his clean masculine scent, blended with leather and tobacco. When his words registered, she lifted her head, gazing at him in wonder. "You really do care."

Not answering, through the mask his dark eyes fastened hungrily on hers. Standing there in the midst of the approaching storm, with the wind lifting his hair from his forehead, he looked like she imagined the devil would look—dark, wickedly handsome, and dangerous. Yet, in his arms she was not afraid, for to her he looked as if he could conquer the world, make even the elements bend to his will.

He cupped her head between his palms and gently covered her lips with his. He kissed her slowly, thoroughly, leaving her dizzy and yearning for more. His heart pounded against her palm, like the steady beat of a pagan drum. Answering its call, she sighed and swayed toward him. He kissed her as though he would devour her, then taking a deep breath he drew away. "*Mierda*, Elena. What you do to me."

He nuzzled her cheek, then lifting her as if she were a feather, he carried her toward the tree-shrouded pond. "Silver Moon!" Elena cried, remembering her mare.

"She's right behind us. That's how I found you," he murmured. Heat lightning flickered, showing the bandit's face. "Diablo will take care of your mare," he said softly. He smiled, showing a flash of white teeth. He kissed the tip of her nose. "And I will take care of you."

The promise in his words sent Elena's heart fluttering wildly against her rib cage. Lowered to a patch of lush grass beside the pool, she reluctantly removed her arms from around his neck. Her forearm brushed the ground. Pain shot through her elbow. "Oh," she gasped.

"What's wrong, *querida*?"

"I must have skinned my arm when I fell." Finding a large rip in her blouse sleeve, she gingerly touched her bleeding forearm and elbow. "It's full of dirt."

"Here. Let me see." He drew a match from his pocket, struck it, and carefully examined the tender area. He left her and went to the pond. Returning with a wet handkerchief, he patted it over the wound, repeating the process until the scrape was clean. He rinsed the cloth and carefully wrapped it around her arm. "Is that better?"

"Yes. Thank you," she said, marveling at how the man could appear so savage and yet be so gentle.

He sat down across from her and leaned back against a boulder. A flash of lightning showed his frown as he stared up at the sky. A rumble of thunder followed. "The storm will be here soon. There is no time to get you back to the hacienda. We will have to find shelter."

"Where?" she asked.

"Come." He took her hand and drew her to her feet.

The rising wind whipped her hair, blowing it wildly around them.

El Gato gave a shrill whistle. The stallion, trailed by the mare, trotted out of the cover of the trees.

El Gato lifted Elena onto his saddle and swiftly mounted behind her. Leaving the pond, he pointed the black toward a cliff that rose steep and forbidding in the distance.

The howling wind lifted sand and dirt, stinging their skin and eyes. Lightning lit the landscape with an awesome glare, showing Silver Moon, her eyes wide with fright, running beside them. The roll of thunder followed. Crashing and growling like an angry beast, it shook the ground. Beneath her, Elena felt the strength of the powerful stallion as he raced through the night.

The first drops of cool water pelted them, filling the air with the scent of freshly dampened earth. The droplets quickened to a driving rain that drenched them, plastering their clothing to their skin.

El Gato bent toward her, his voice torn away by the wind. "Hang on, *querida*. We are almost there."

The stallion slowed when he reached the base of the cliff. Picking his way carefully among the rocks, he inched up the steep, rubble-strewn hill.

The wind howled around them like a tormented demon. Thunder pealed even louder. El Gato leaned forward,

hunching his shoulders. Cordlike muscles drew her into
the protective curve, warming her with the heat of his
body. Secure in his arms even in the face of the storm,
Elena felt no terror. Her heart pounded with a strange, wild
exhilaration that filled her very being, making her part of
the fierceness around her.

Reaching a broad ledge, El Gato guided the horse under
the lip of an overhanging cliff. Sheltered from the brunt
of the storm, he turned the stallion toward the valley and
waited for the mare to struggle up the rocky slope and
join them.

A bolt of jagged lightning lit the sky and valley below.
The deafening crash of thunder shook the ground. Elena
wiped the water from her forehead and shivered against
El Gato, siphoning the warmth from his body where it
touched hers.

Silver Moon scrambled over the ledge and stood trembling next to Diablo. The stud nudged her gently.

El Gato held Elena close for a moment, then threw his
leg over the back of the horse and stepped to the ground.
He closed his hands around her waist and lifted her down
beside him. "You, too, tremble, little one. We'd better get
you out of these wet clothes."

He lifted a dripping strand of hair back from her face.
At the touch of his fingers, another quiver shook her, one
she knew was not caused by the cold. Lightning lit the sky
again, but she didn't see. Her eyes were on the tall, dark
bandit.

Roguishly handsome, his dark hair plastered slickly to
his head, he gazed down at her. "Are you afraid of the
storm?"

"No," she whispered, her heart racing. Thunder crashed,
surrounding them, reverberating off the canyon walls. Her
gaze locked on his, and she felt herself being drawn under

his spell. Her mind told her to break away, to run while she could, but her body refused to leave. She swayed toward him, sighing when his arms welcomed her home. She melted against his long lean frame.

"Oh, Elena," he moaned, bending his head. His lips, fierce and demanding, fastened on hers. Though his kisses bruised her, her mouth parted, allowing his searching tongue to enter. She responded eagerly with her own.

Lost in the magic of his kiss, she clung to him, wildly, desperately, as if fearing he might leave her if she didn't hold him fast. His warm palms cupped her breasts, making them throb with delight. Her nipples rose into sharp peaks questing for the heat of his hand through the wet blouse.

"So sweet," he murmured, pressing her lips again.

When the kiss ended, she lifted her lashes to meet midnight eyes. Undoing her buttons one by one, he slid his fingers over her collarbone and stripped the clinging blouse from her body.

Elena raised shaking hands and unfastened his wet shirt. Parting it, she buried her face in his neck. Reveling in the taste, the slight musky scent, the feel of him, she trailed her fingers through his soft chest hair.

Gasping, he quickly shrugged out of the garment. "I'll be back, my angel." He brushed her forehead with a lingering kiss, then walked swiftly to the horse. A moment later he returned with a bedroll in his hands. Shaking it out, he spread it in a patch of soft, dry sand.

His eyes on hers, he offered his hand, drawing her to him like a moth to a flame. Closed in his arms, his deep, passionate kiss took her breath. Murmuring words of love, he nibbled at her earlobe, then, fluttering kisses down her throat, he claimed the bend of her neck.

Undoing the ribbon of her chemise, he eased it over her head and pulled her to him. Elena closed her eyes, savoring the feel of his flesh against hers. His hair tickled her cheek as she leaned her head against his bare chest. His heart pounded strong and quick against her ear.

Raining soft kisses on the top of her head, he encased her breasts with his palms, squeezing them gently. The thumbs circling her nipples sent shards of hot sensations radiating from the taut peaks.

Drawn against the hardness of his passion, Elena trembled, suddenly afraid, but his gentle touch soothed her, eased her fear. Lost in his searing kiss, a shiver of a different kind took its place.

After a moment he put his hands on her shoulders and held her away from him. "Elena?" he asked, his voice ragged with emotion.

In the flash of lightning she gazed into his face, seeing the question in his eyes. Suddenly she knew he wouldn't force her. No was all she had to say. But the word wouldn't come. The wistfulness in his eyes crumbled the last shred of her resistance. She gave him a tremulous smile. "Yes. Oh, yes," she whispered, giving herself freely, expecting nothing but his passion in return.

With a glad cry, he pulled her into his arms.

Tears of joy flooded her eyes, and she lifted her arms to welcome his embrace. Drawing his mouth down to meet her own, she surrendered to the intoxication of his kiss.

Hurriedly shedding the rest of their clothes, they stood for a moment gazing at each other. Elena scarcely noticed the tempest raging about them, or the fierce gust of wind that drove rain under the cliff, peppering her body with icy drops. She was only aware of the storm building inside her.

A flash of lightning illuminated El Gato's body, turning it into a sleek, dark figure of aroused masculinity. A strand of black hair drooped on his forehead. The smile he flashed was wickedly dangerous, but the look in his eyes would have melted stone.

Gently lowering her to the blanket, he covered her flesh with his own. "*Querida*," he murmured. "You'll never know how much I've missed you." He smothered her mouth, her face, her neck with hot kisses. Whispering words of sex and love, he traced the outline of her ear with his tongue. Tremors of excitement raced up her spine, arousing her sleeping passion.

Feeling warm, safe, wanted, Elena looped her arms around him, pulling him to her so her breasts cradled his head. Her fingers kneaded his back, tracing the muscles that twisted like rope. His skin was damp and silky and smelled of soap and woodsmoke. She inhaled his scent, wanting to remember it for the times she'd be alone. The idea that he would leave made her cling to him even more. She took his earlobe in her teeth and teased it with her tongue, savoring the faint salty taste.

He bent his head and lapped at her nipple. The roughness of his tongue drew it into exquisite hardness. She fastened her hands in his crisp dark hair, urging more of the taut peak into his mouth. He nibbled and sucked, sending bursts of sharp pulsations vibrating through her very core. She pressed against him, her body quivering like a guitar being fine-tuned by a master's fingers.

She moaned, wishing he had two mouths when he left one breast to tease the other into submission. Whispering soft love words in her ear, he slid his hand down her belly to tangle in the tight curls below. She tightened at the intrusion, but his fingers stroked her sensitive nub until she arched against him, her veins filling with a heat only he could quench. She writhed beneath him, tossing her head from side to side as he drew her higher and higher.

His fiery kisses robbed her of breath and turned her bones to mush. His hands made her body sing with joy.

His head lowered, following the path of his hands to her moist nest. "No," she gasped, trying to squirm away. Gently, but firmly, he forced her thighs apart, seeking her innermost being. His tongue probed, rasping the bud of her womanhood with his hot, moist heat. Coaxed into a flaming torment, she tightened with an ache so exquisite she thought she would die. Unable to help herself, she cried out and arched to meet him, exploding in wave after wave of liquid fire.

When the spasms subsided, leaving her weak and filled with wonder, he kissed his way back up her stomach, again suckling at each breast before coming to claim her lips. "Elena, *mi vida, mi corazón*," he whispered, nuzzling her ear and neck. His hands explored her body, searching out sensitive places that she hadn't known existed until he found them, touching them to rekindle her desire. When she quivered, again reaching that perfect pitch, he rose above her and entered slowly. Impatient, she pulled him to her, needing him to fill her with his throbbing manhood, drawing him deeper and deeper to reach her very soul.

He waited, giving her time to adjust to the fullness before he began to move, advancing and retreating, making her crazy with wanting. She caught his rhythm, matching him stroke for stroke, the tempo increasing until at last, frantic to find release, she clasped his slim hips and raised herself to meet him. Whimpering, she strained for a peak so high she thought she would die before attaining its crested top. Not letting her stop, he drew her higher still, driving, pounding her, melding their bodies with a fury that matched the raging storm.

Lightning crackled across the sky, piercing the earth with a white hot fork, drowning Elena's cry of ecstasy.

Exploding into wave after wave of rapture, she left her body to soar above and beyond the white-capped peak.

El Gato cupped her buttocks, drawing Elena even closer. His cries lost in the roar of thunder, he joined her as a fierce shudder shook his sweat-sheened body. After a moment of eternity, his passion spent, he collapsed in her arms.

Filled with the wonder of what they'd shared, Elena held him close, running her loving palms over his back, memorizing the ropelike muscles under her fingertips. She buried her face in his neck, rubbing her cheek against the faint scratch of his whiskers, her body still tingling with the thrill and damp, musky fragrance of his passion.

She knew he was a bandit, her father's enemy and as such hers, also. But here in the heat of his arms she'd learned of love and become a woman, his woman, although in the eyes of God and the church she belonged to another. She'd committed an unpardonable sin, but she felt no guilt, only a strange, satisfying completeness. Confused by her emotions, she wondered how something so extraordinary could be wicked.

He raised his dark head and kissed the end of her nose before raising himself off of her. Rolling onto his side, he lifted his arm and encircled her shoulders. He drew her close, curving his body around hers. "Elena, my love," he murmured in her ear, "you are so beautiful, so perfect."

"And you, El Gato, take my breath away," she whispered. Twisting in his arms, she frowned up at him. She drew her finger across the silky mask, down the bridge of his nose and traced the outline of his lips, smiling as he nibbled playfully at her fingertips. "I've just realized I've lain in your arms two times like this, and I don't even know your name."

He stiffened, hesitating. Then he bent toward her, brushing her lips with a soft kiss. He nuzzled his way to her ear. "My name is Miguel, *querida*."

"Miguel." She sighed, rubbing her cheek against his. "Miguel." A rush of hot tears filled her eyes, knowing he was beginning to trust her.

She raised herself on her elbow and stared down into his face. Although the mask made it impossible to clearly see his features, she knew he was waiting to see what she would do.

"I will never betray you, El Gato," she whispered. Even though she longed to remove the scrap of silk, she didn't. Instead she bent toward him, feeling the soft brush of the cloth against her upper lip. She lowered her mouth to his and eased her tongue between his teeth, boldly exploring its moist recesses.

Finally, breathless, her heart pounding, she gave him a deep kiss and lay back against his arm. She looked around, surprised to see the velvety night sky sprinkled with millions of diamondlike stars. "The storm is over," she said sadly. A sharp pain rent her, knowing their time together must come to an end. She already felt the loneliness.

Tears blurring her vision, she gazed up into his eyes. "Love me, Miguel," she whispered, feeling a fierce, almost desperate longing to have him inside her. She drew his head down to hers, surrendering her life, her soul, to the man called El Gato.

His manhood throbbed to life, stiff and hot against her thigh. His dark eyes glittering in the moonlight, he lifted himself over her. Smiling, he covered her body with his own. Their loving sighs filled the air as he once again plunged into the excited warmth of her, making them into one. With a slow tormenting pleasure, he began to move in her, and as his movements quickened, so did hers until she met him with a growing, flaming urgency. He kissed her tears away and nuzzled her neck, whispering into her ear. "Don't be sad, *querida*, the night is long. Our storm has just begun."

Chapter Sixteen

IT was the wee hours of the morning when Miguel raised himself on his elbow and gazed at the sleeping woman curled at his side. His Elena. His lover. His wife. He traced her jawline with his finger and again felt a warmth building in his loins. *Mierda*! He couldn't look at her without wanting to take her in his arms and make love to her.

Last night they'd soared among the stars, each time touching earth only briefly before rising to ever higher planes. And every time, to his amazement, her passion had matched his own. What a rare jewel she was. A woman possessing both beauty and fire. And yet she remained sweetly innocent, but eager to learn all he had to teach her.

He heaved a reluctant sigh and rose from the bed, knowing they must leave very soon to reach the hacienda before daybreak. He couldn't risk someone discovering her absence.

He went to the rocks where he'd spread their clothing after she'd gone to sleep. Finding the garments dry, he dressed, then gathered her things and placed them beside her on the blanket.

He knelt beside her and touched her shoulder. The satin feel of her flesh beneath his hand sent a ripple of desire coursing through him. Studying her face, he thought she was the most beautiful woman he'd ever seen. Long sooty lashes lying against high cheekbones showed her Indian ancestry. Her nose, long and straight, came from old Spain. Her skin, naturally golden brown, had the texture and feel of a rose petal. But with all of this it was beauty of soul that made her so extraordinary. Kind, generous to a fault, he'd never heard her say a harsh or unkind word about anyone. She gave unceasingly of herself without asking anything in return.

Miguel realized in that moment that he loved her, and he would wish for nothing else in the world if he could spend a lifetime at her side. It wasn't her looks or her fire, but her pure goodness that claimed his heart and his love. Now he understood why the people of the hacienda had strewn her path with rose petals on the day of their wedding. She, not Angelina Sandoval, was the true Spanish Angel.

He gazed down at lips, full and generous, ripe and swollen with his love. Unable to resist, he bent and claimed them once again.

She opened her eyes and gazed sleepily up at him. "Miguel."

"*Querida*, time to wake up. We must get you home before daylight."

Smiling, she lifted her arms from beneath the covers, her fingers reaching out for him, coaxing him to rejoin her in the bed.

"No, you don't!" He laughed, fighting the temptation. He caught her hands and pulled her to her feet, devouring her body with his hungry gaze. The pale moonlight turned her figure to gleaming marble. Like an Aztec princess, regal and proud, she stood naked and unashamed before him. Her long hair rippled like ebony silk in the cool breeze. "Miguel," she coaxed, holding out her arms.

Unable to resist, he groaned and pulled her close, covering her face with kisses. "My sweet, I long to lower you to the blanket and spend the rest of the night making love to you, but I must think of your safety." Drawing in a ragged breath, he set her away from him and gave her a gentle swat on her shapely bottom. "Be a good girl and stop tempting my sanity. Get dressed, *querida*. We must ride." Already hardened with passion and afraid he would lose the battle he so desperately fought, he stepped away from her and went to saddle his horse. Giving his heated blood time to cool, he returned to find she had dressed and rolled up his bedding.

She walked to his side and handed him the bedroll. "I never knew the air could be so clean and fresh. Um, smell the sage?"

"After the storm last night, the whole world seems new," he said, gazing at her. "We'd better get started, my love."

Nodding, she started toward the silver mare.

Flashing her a wicked grin, he reached out and pulled her back, lifting her onto the stallion instead. "I may not be able to make love to you as I want, but I do intend to hold you close for as long as possible."

He looped the mare's reins so she wouldn't stumble and left her free, knowing she would follow Diablo. Miguel went to the stallion and mounted behind Elena. Wrapping her in his arms, he urged the horse down the trail.

"Miguel, I wish we never had to go back." She raised her hand to caress his cheek.

"So do I, my love, but I fear we must." He sighed, kissing her palm.

On the valley floor he nudged Diablo into an easy gallop. Too soon the high walls of the Spanish Angel came into view. Wheeling Diablo, he guided him to the mound of rocks where he'd previously met Carlos. He halted the stallion and waited for the mare to join them.

Miguel dismounted. His eyes on Elena's, he lifted her down. Holding her close, loath to let her go, he bent his head and gave her one last lingering kiss, before placing her on the mare's back.

"Goodbye, El Gato, my love. When will I see you again?" she asked, her dark eyes warm in the predawn light.

"Tonight," he said, wishing the sun were going down instead of coming up. "Not even your father's *pistoleros* can keep me away. I will wait for you by the pool." He frowned at her. "Be careful, *querida*. I will understand if you do not come. Go now." He swatted the mare on the rump and sent her on her way. He climbed to the top of the knoll and waited until Elena was safely inside the gate before he mounted Diablo and rode away.

Elena led Silver Moon toward the barn, grimacing every time the mare's hooves rang out against a stone. Breathing a sigh of relief when they entered the stable, she froze when a figure rose from the fresh straw of the mare's stall.

Juan's accusing voice cut through the stillness. "Elena, are you all right? I've been crazy with worry. When I found the mare gone and you didn't come home, I rode to the pond." He pinned her with his furious gaze. "I searched everywhere. Just where were you, Elena?"

Elena stiffened, angered by his tone of voice. She relaxed, realizing he had only been concerned for her safety. She found it hard to lie to him, but she couldn't tell him the truth. Shifting her gaze to a piece of straw, she moved it around the floor with the toe of her boot. Picking her words carefully, she began. "I had an accident. A jaguar frightened the mare and she threw me."

He gripped her arms. "Are you all right?"

"I'm fine. Lightning scared the cat away. After I caught Silver Moon, I took shelter from the storm under a cliff. I fell asleep. When I woke up, I came home." She held her breath, hoping he wouldn't question her explanation.

He gave her a dubious look. "I think more happened than you are saying, little one. Now, you had better get into the house before someone else finds you missing." He took the reins from her hand and led the mare into the stall.

"Thank you, Juan. Good night." Leaving the barn, she took the back path toward the hacienda.

To save time, she cut across the courtyard. Catching a glimpse of white under the arcade, she held her breath and backed into the shadows, praying she hadn't been seen.

Leaving the arches, a woman glanced furtively around, then hurried into the darkness and sat on a secluded bench.

Conception? Elena wrinkled her forehead into a frown, wondering what her sister could be doing.

Stealthy footsteps crunched in the gravel. A man entered the courtyard and slipped toward Conception.

Elena clamped her hand over her mouth, stifling a startled gasp. Guillermo! She stepped from cover to call out a warning. The cry died soundlessly on her lips when Conception rose from her seat and motioned to the man.

Elena pushed back into the shrubbery and watched the majordomo approach the bench and sit next to Conception. Leaning close to each other, they spoke in muffled voices.

Elena wished she could hear what they were saying, but afraid they would see her, she remained in hiding.

A short time later the pair rose to their feet. Elena gasped when Guillermo pulled Conception into his arms. After a long embrace and a passionate kiss, the two separated, giving a furtive look around before going their separate ways. When the foreman was out of sight, Conception entered the salon and closed the door.

Frightened and confused by what she had seen, Elena skirted the courtyard and ran to her room. Her heart pounding, she leaned against the safety of her closed door.

A shiver crept up her spine. Conception and Guillermo? It didn't make sense. Elena knew her class-conscious sister wouldn't lower herself to consort with the man unless she desperately wanted something from him. Elena rubbed the goosebumps rising on her skin. She had the awful feeling their meeting had something to do with her.

Exhausted and troubled, she quickly shed her clothes and pulled her nightgown over her head. As she slid into her bed and closed her eyes, she longed to feel the strength of Miguel's arms around her, loving her, protecting her from the danger she sensed was near.

Heading the horse toward the pond, Miguel sighed, wishing he had the power to be in three places at once.

As El Gato, he needed to be on the mountain with his men. The angry band grew restless. Only a strong leader could keep them from doing something foolish on their own.

As Miguel, he couldn't resist the temptation of Elena. He found himself unable to think, weak with wanting, needing to lose himself in her silken flesh. He smiled ruefully. Seeking revenge against de Vega, he'd taken her virginity and lost his own soul to her sweet innocence. He didn't know what wild impulse had made him say he'd marry her, but a desire for revenge made him go through with the act. Now thoroughly entangled in his own deception, he had to make her pregnant in order to regain the ranch.

And as her husband, Diego, he couldn't touch her without putting his real identity and the lives of his people in jeopardy. He shook his head, wishing he could tell her the truth. But could she forgive him, after discovering he'd lied to her and used her and the child he would give her to destroy her own father?

Now, knowing he loved her, he grew afraid for all of them. If he became careless, if de Vega discovered his ruse, not only he but Elena would be made to suffer. No one would believe she didn't know her own husband was El Gato.

He worried about her safety when he had to be away from the hacienda. Carlos, as Diego's manservant, was required to be with him, and he needed the man to carry his orders to and from the mountain. From other servants Carlos had learned that Guillermo had made threats toward Elena. Apparently the man bore her a grudge because she had rejected him for Diego. Miguel frowned. He needed someone there at the hacienda. Someone he could trust to watch over her. But who? Pondering the question, he rode back to the cliff to wait and watch for the coming night.

In her bedroom Conception took off her heavy robe, then, holding her breath, she silently resumed her place in the bed. She turned on her side and stared at the back of her sleeping husband. She grimaced, wiping her mouth with the back of her hand. Her skin felt raw where she'd scrubbed it, trying to remove the stench of Guillermo. She shuddered; the man made her skin crawl. If only she didn't need him.

She gently traced her husband's backbone with her finger and inhaled his clean masculine scent. She wished Ricardo wasn't so angry with her. Why couldn't he be rich? Then having the ranch wouldn't be so important. She blinked back tears. But he wasn't rich, and she couldn't live without the comforts and extravagances she'd always known. They could have everything. Why was he being so unreasonable? All he had to do was get her pregnant.

She sighed, admitting she'd gone about it all wrong. Why had she behaved so stupidly? Ricardo had been flattered and obliging at first, believing he had inspired her sudden passion. When he begged exhaustion, she'd railed at him, telling him she had to get pregnant before Elena or lose the ranch. She'd never forget the coldness in his eyes when he informed her he wasn't a stallion to perform on demand.

Now, because of her tantrums, he not only wouldn't make love to her, he wouldn't even speak to her. She narrowed her eyes. She refused to give up the ranch and all the wealth and power it represented. If Ricardo wouldn't help her, she'd find another way.

She drew her lips into a pout. It wasn't fair that Elena, who could live happily like a peasant, should have it all. If she couldn't get pregnant, she had to make sure Elena didn't, either.

She'd never been close to her younger sister. They'd been as different as night and day. Still, she didn't intend for Elena to be hurt . . . but Diego was another matter.

She twisted her mouth into a crooked smile. It shouldn't be hard to persuade Guillermo to do her bidding, especially since he blamed Diego for stealing Elena from him. She'd use Guillermo's anger to fan his resentment against Diego. She'd be doing Elena a favor by getting rid of the pompous fool. And if Guillermo got caught in the process, so much the better—as long as he didn't involve her. Conception thought of how she planned to flatter Guillermo, let him steal a few kisses, if in giving them she got what she wanted in return. If she was clever enough, Guillermo would think the whole scheme was his idea.

And when the ranch was hers, she'd still allow Elena to live here, not in the new wing she had now of course, but maybe here in this section. They could fix up the rest of these rooms for the nursery. She smiled. Elena would make an excellent *duenna* for the children she and Ricardo would have.

Exhausted from her late-night plotting, Conception closed her eyes. Ignoring the crow of the cock announcing the arriving dawn, she drifted into a deep sleep.

Chapter Seventeen

THE sun slanting through her bedroom window woke Elena from a fitful sleep. Groaning, she rose from her bed and slipped on her robe. Every bone in her body ached from the fall she'd taken the night before. Stifling a yawn, she smiled. She'd gladly suffer a hundred falls to have Miguel rescue her and hold her as he had last night. The knowledge that she would see him again tonight sent her pulse racing. Now fully awake, she went into the hall and called the maid, instructing her to prepare her bath.

A short time later, when the brass tub had been filled, Elena eased herself into the warm floral-scented water, allowing it to wash away her aches and pains. As she lifted the cloth to lathe the soothing liquid over her skin, she frowned, her thoughts troubled by what she'd seen in the courtyard. Conception and Guillermo. It didn't seem plausible. Whatever Conception was up to this time, Elena feared her sister was headed for real trouble.

In spite of the warmth of the water, she shivered. Half Mexican, half Anglo, Guillermo represented the worst of both worlds. He was not the kind of man Conception could put in his place by a disdainful look. Not even fear of her father would stop the man if he wanted something. Elena frowned, remembering other confrontations when her father

had been the one to back down, almost as if the man had
some sort of hold on him.

The majordomo had no morals, no conscience. He was
a bully who enjoyed terrorizing those weaker than himself.
Large and strong, handsome in a crude way, he fancied
himself a ladies' man, bragging about his conquests to
anyone who would listen. Any woman unlucky enough to
catch his eye had to be careful never to be alone. Not even
the sanctity of the chapel had proved safe. Truly evil, the
man had forced himself on a young woman in front of the
very altar where she'd gone to pray.

It angered her that her father had done nothing about it,
but she knew that, like most of those of Spanish blood, he
feared to draw attention to himself in the Anglo courts.
He'd seen their justice turn against other *hacendados* when
knowledge of their wealth fanned the white man's greed.
But even if he had turned Guillermo over to the authorities,
the girl would have been too terrified to testify.

Elena knew Conception had no idea what kind of monster
she was dealing with. Somehow she had to warn Cepi, make
her see the danger of the game she played.

Shaking her head, Elena knew she couldn't. How could
she explain her own presence in the garden at that time of
the morning? Cepi would only accuse her of spying. Or
worse, Conception might discover she left the hacienda
at night to be with El Gato. With their father offering a
reward of five thousand dollars for the bandit's capture,
she couldn't afford to arouse Conception's suspicion. Elena
knew she'd never let the love she had for the outlaw be the
cause of his destruction.

The love? Elena closed her eyes, imagining herself in
his embrace. The memory sent her heart racing, her body
tingling with longing. She smiled in wonder, knowing she
truly did love him, with her heart, her soul, every fiber of

her being. And no matter what happened, she would die rather than let harm come to him.

But her love carried with it a strong burden of guilt. By loving the bandit chief she betrayed everything she held dear, her family honor, her husband, her marriage, even her faith. She sighed, pushing it from her thoughts. However wicked, none of it seemed to matter. She would sacrifice everything for a night in El Gato's arms.

"Señora? Señora?"

"What?" she asked. Startled from her reverie, Elena saw her young maid, Lupe, standing by her tub.

"Would you like me to rinse your hair and help you to dress before I bring your breakfast?"

Elena smiled up at her. "Thank you, Lupe, but I can manage. And instead of a large meal, I think I would prefer fruit, toast, and coffee."

When the girl left the room, Elena quickly rinsed the soap from her hair and climbed from the tub. Drying herself, she winced, discovering the purplish bruise on her right hip. She examined her scraped arm, thankful to find it didn't look as bad as she had feared it might, although it still showed a telltale redness. Hoping it would escape comment, she broke a piece from an aloe plant and rubbed the sticky juice over the area. She smiled, thinking it strange that the black cat threatening to eat her had been frightened away by another dark cat of the night, El Gato.

After hastily donning her slim pantalets and chemise, she picked up her brush and attempted to smooth the tangles from her hair. Catching her reflection in the mirror, she halted the brush in midair and stared. Blinking, she peered closer. She looked different, older and almost pretty. A girl no longer, but a woman; a woman who'd tasted the fruit of passion; a woman who glowed with the bloom of love.

Praying no one else would notice the change, she finished her hair, fashioning it into a neat bun at the back of her neck. She had just slipped into a demure light yellow morning dress with loose long sleeves to hide her arm when the maid entered with her breakfast.

Later in the morning Elena strolled in the courtyard, only vaguely aware of the fresh-washed fragrance of the flowers. She nodded absently to one of several gardeners, who bid her a polite good morning while he busily cleaned up leaves and debris left from the night's storm. But her mind wasn't on the men or the yard they so carefully tended. She knew she had to talk to Conception, to warn her about Guillermo, and she had to do it in such a way that she wouldn't become suspicious. Praying the right words would come to her, she set off in search of her sister.

Entering the central wing, she caught sight of her brother-in-law and quickened her steps. "Ricardo?"

He turned. "Elena." Smiling warmly, he took her hands and kissed her on the cheek. Retaining his hold, he stood back and gave her an admiring glance. "You look lovely this morning. Positively radiant in fact."

Feeling her face flush with warmth, she shyly tucked her head. "Thank you, Ricardo. It must be the weather. It's wonderful outside. I've been walking in the garden." Remembering her mission, she gazed up at him. "I wanted to see Cepi. Is she still in her room?"

His smile turned into a scowl. "Oh, yes. She is still there . . . in bed."

Elena frowned, never knowing her sister to sleep overly late, even when they'd had a *fiesta* and she had danced all night. "Is she sick?"

He sighed, shaking his head. "No. Not at all. She's pouting." He ran a hand through his neatly cropped dark hair, his face troubled. "Elena, I love Conception, but I swear I do not understand her. Sometimes I wish we had never returned to the Spanish Angel."

"What is the problem, Ricardo?" she asked gently. "Can I do anything to help?"

"Not unless you can convince her that being a small rancher's wife isn't so bad. My *estancia* provides a comfortable living, but I fear she will never be happy there. She believes she is worth nothing without the wealth and position she has here."

Elena frowned, listening intently. Could it be true? Elena's father had made her feel inferior by denying her everything but her basic needs. But she had found contentment, discovering she didn't need or want the things he'd lavished on Conception. Had Conception become so dependent on material things to make her happy that she believed herself unworthy of being loved, incapable of returning love herself, without them?

She raised her head, feeling a great sadness for both her brother-in-law and Conception. "I'm sorry, Ricardo. I know she does love you." Elena only prayed Conception loved him enough to change before it was too late. Ricardo was a proud man. He would never forgive his wife, regardless of her misguided motives, if he ever found her with Guillermo.

She patted his arm. "I'm sure she'll come around in time," she said with more conviction than she felt. "Would you tell her I'd like to see her when she gets up?"

When he nodded, Elena left the wing, happy to return to the clean air. For some strange reason, she'd always felt uneasy in that section of the house. Shrugging off the feeling, she returned to her own set of rooms.

Her stomach growled, making her aware of a sudden ravenous hunger. She'd been so upset about Conception she'd only picked at her breakfast tray. She sniffed the aroma of fresh-baked bread drifting from the tiny walled section of yard in back of the kitchen. In summer the cooks baked the crusty loaves outside in round conelike ovens, filling the whole courtyard with their delicious smell.

She smiled, wondering if Miguel liked fresh-baked bread as much as she did. Her heart raced; a warm glow of anticipation filled her, knowing she'd see him tonight. "Maybe I could surprise him with a picnic," she murmured. With that thought, she headed for the kitchen.

Chapter Eighteen

ELENA paced the floor, impatiently waiting for the house-hold to retire to their respective rooms. Finally every light but the one in her father's study had been extinguished. That one didn't concern her. She knew her father would be so involved in his reading, a herd of bulls could stampede through the house and he wouldn't notice.

She looked out her window and sighed. Although it neared midnight, a few couples remained, strolling arm in arm on the grounds. *I can't wait any longer. If I do, he may not be there.* Hoping the lovers were so wrapped up in each other they wouldn't pay any attention to her, she tucked the woven basket of food and wine she'd snuck from the kitchen under her arm, then crept from her room. Hurriedly, slipping from shadow to shadow, she made her way to the stable.

She placed her bundle on the cleanly swept barn floor next to the mare's stall. Feeling her way through the darkness to the tack room, she pressed her ear against the door and listened for any telltale sounds. The room was silent. She eased the door open, breathing a prayer of thanksgiving that Juan and the woman were not there.

After removing her gear, she carried it back to the stall and quickly saddled her Arabian. Something rustled the hay in the stall behind her. She froze, holding her breath. Trem-

bling, she stared into the darkness, watching for movement.
When no other sound followed the first, she closed her eyes
and sagged against the horse. Just a mouse, she thought. But
nevertheless, when she'd led the mare through the gates and
mounted to leave the hacienda in the distance, she breathed
a sigh of relief.

She hurried Silver Moon, taking a slightly different path
so she wouldn't leave a definite trail to mark her passing. Halfway to the pond she frowned and slowed the
horse. Even though she'd heard nothing, the short hairs
prickling on the back of her neck told her she wasn't alone.
Easing the gray behind a clump of brush, she waited and
watched.

Out of the darkness a figure dressed in white followed on
a dark horse. *Juan.* She closed her eyes and silently cursed
the man. She told herself she should be glad it was a friend
and not one of the *pistoleros.* She frowned, watching him
grow nearer. *Now what am I going to do? I can't lead him to
El Gato.* Considering her plans for the evening, she neither
needed nor wanted any witnesses.

Urging the Arabian out of the brush, she recklessly raced
across the desert, luring Juan away from the trail to the
spring. She pulled her horse to a stop on the crest of a hill,
knowing he would spot her in the silvery moonlight. When
he turned toward her, she dipped below into an arroyo and
hid in the shadows. She smiled, certain she'd lost him when
he passed by her and continued down the hill. Walking the
mare, she backtracked until she was out of earshot. After a
few more minutes she felt safe enough to race Silver Moon
toward the pond.

When she reached the trees, she guided the mare into
their thick cover and dismounted. She peered into the silent
shadows, praying Miguel was still there. Hearing the stallion nicker, her heart thundered joyfully in her breast. He'd

waited. Her hands trembled as she removed her bundle. She gave the mare a pat and watched her trot into the darkness to join Diablo.

Before she could turn, strong arms closed around her and a warm voice whispered huskily beside her ear. "*Querida,* you are late. I was afraid you weren't coming."

She turned in his embrace and smiled. "Not even my father's *pistoleros* could keep me away," she said, remembering his vow.

Through the holes in his mask, his eyes widened in alarm. "They didn't—"

"No, no." She shook her head. Raising her hand to his cheek, she eased the lines of concern from his face. "It was only Juan. He followed me, but I left him chasing shadows in the hills."

"Who is this Juan, and why does he follow you, Elena?" he said, his voice filled with jealousy.

She snuggled closer. "Only a very dear friend. We grew up together. Juan has always seemed like a big brother. Since I was small he has watched over me." She sighed. "He is afraid I'll get into trouble."

"As well he might," he growled, bending his head to smother her with fierce kisses, "especially if he knew my intentions tonight." He lifted her into his arms, the basket dangling from her fingers, and strode to a moonlit, grassy area. Kissing her again, he set her on her feet.

"I brought a picnic," she told him, holding out her prize. "Fresh bread, cheese, apples, and wine."

"Sounds delicious." He removed the bundle from her hands and placed it to one side. "But, *querida*, right at the moment I hunger and thirst only for you." He drew her into his arms. His hands stroked her body. His touch ignited her blood, making her quiver with anticipation.

Not to be outdone, she fumbled with his buttons. Sliding

her hands inside his shirt, she trailed her fingers over his bare chest. Her hand dipped lower and tugged the shirttail from his pants. Removing the garment from his body, she heard him gasp with pleasure. "I, too, am ravenous for other things, my love," she told him.

They quickly shed their clothing and came together in a swift embrace, each eagerly molding their naked flesh to the other. He fastened his hands in her hair and brought her lips up to meet his own, claiming them in a searing kiss. Drawing the pins from her hair, he threaded his fingers through it until it fell, brushing against her hips.

"Oh, Miguel"—she sighed, snuggling her head against his chest—"I thought the day would never end."

"I, too, my love." Gripping her shoulders, he held her away from him. His dark lashes lowered seductively. His lips parted, showing a flash of white teeth below his mask as he gave her a tender smile. "You are so very lovely."

Her own gaze slowly caressed him, igniting her passion as she feasted on his slim, virile strength. Her pulse racing, she locked her eyes on his. Slowly, tentatively, she reached up to untie his mask.

Miguel gently grasped her wrist. "No, my love. I would trust you with my life, but knowing my identity would put you in danger. And this I will not do."

Reminded of the price her father had put on the bandit's head, Elena sighed and tried to hide her disappointment. Not wanting to spoil one of their rare times together, she laid her head against his chest and held him close. "I'm sorry, Miguel," she whispered. "I know you are right. It's only that I wanted to memorize your face for the times we can't be together."

Echoing her thoughts, he swept her up in his arms and carried her to the blanket. The fragrant white blossoms of clematis and crushed wild mint scented the air around them.

A chorus of frogs and crickets added their serenade.

Miguel lowered himself beside her and, murmuring soft words of love, drew her close. His feather-light touch traced the path of her spine, before drawing lazy circles on her hips. He kissed her eyelids, her nose, her mouth, then claimed the base of her throat, where her pulse beat a rapid tattoo. His hands trailed around her waist and rose to cup her breasts, gently kneading until they tingled and the nipples rose into tight, firm buds. His head dipped and he took one tip between his teeth, teasing it with his tongue.

She fastened her fingers in his hair, urging him closer.

He closed his mouth over her breast, suckling the sensitive peak, making every nerve ending come alive. His hand slipped down, drawing tantalizing circles on her lower stomach before caressing the heated mound of her womanhood.

He stroked the sensitive nub until she gasped and arched against him, quivering like a candle in the midst of a white-hot flame. A hollow ache between her legs throbbed into a writhing torment, but still he urged her onward until a flood of molten desire exploded within her and carried her over a dizzying crest.

Wanting to pleasure him, she slid her hand down his hard flat stomach and clasped his thick rod, palming its heated length, until he cried out and closed his hand over hers, stilling the motion. He raised his head, pressing his lips to hers. His tongue lashed hers in a frantic mating, his hands again bringing her to the peak of desire.

She pulled him tight against her, desperately needing him to fill her and ease the exquisite agony threatening to tear her apart. Finally, when she thought she could wait no longer, he slowly eased inside her. When he entered, she raised her questing body to meet his. Sobbing with relief, she wrapped her legs around his firm hips, drawing his long shaft ever farther into her simmering tightness.

With frustrating slowness, he penetrated deep within her, retreating and thrusting upward as she arched to meet him. She matched his strokes in an ever-increasing fury, striving for a distant brightness that threatened to take her sanity before she attained it. He carried her with him, bringing the elusive reward ever nearer until his own fiery passion brought her to the brilliance. She cried out, her body shattering into a thousand pieces of glimmering, far-reaching points of light.

When she'd achieved the splendor, he quickened his pace, pounding her welcoming flesh. Reaching his own climax, he gasped. Cupping her buttocks, he lifted her to meet his explosion. A quivering shudder ran through his sweat-sheened body as he pulsated, filling her very soul with his vibrant life force. Finally drained by his release, he collapsed breathlessly against her. She cradled his head in her arms, holding him near, content to languish in the golden aftermath of their love.

After a few moments he rolled onto his side and pulled her close to him. Propping his head on his palm, his mood dreamy, he gazed into her eyes. "*Querida,* again we have soared amongst the stars." He sighed and gently caressed her lips with his own.

She ran her fingers through his thick black hair. "Oh, Miguel. I never would have believed such feelings existed. I must be truly wicked, for you have shown me such joy that now I feel I can't live without you."

"Elena, my sweet, tonight I was so afraid you weren't coming. I wanted you so badly, I almost rode to the hacienda to get you," he said, tasting the hollow of her throat.

She raised her lashes in alarm. Fear that he might be so foolhardy made her tremble. "You must never do that. I couldn't bear it if I were the cause of anything happening to you."

He placed her hand on his chest. "Feel what is happening to me now?"

She felt his heart pounding wildly against her palm. She moved his hand to cover her breast. "Mine, too." At his touch, her nipple pouted for his attention. Pushing him back against the blanket, she stretched out on top of him, nibbling at his lips, his neck, the lobes of his ears.

His arms closed around her, his breath quickening against the hollow of her throat. "I am like a man starving. I can't get enough of you," he murmured.

She felt him harden against her leg. Her own desire rose eagerly, matching his as he again led her to unconquered heights.

After a fierce, wild joining, her fires temporarily banked, Elena raised herself on her elbow and studied the shadowed face of her bandit lover. As she watched the moon play over his features, she wished just once she could see him without the mask, in the full light of day. Would he be as handsome as she imagined? Whether he was or not, she knew it wouldn't matter. She loved the man he was inside, not the man he appeared to be.

She trailed her fingers through a light sprinkling of silky chest hair, feeling the steady rise and fall beneath her fingertips. Her gaze took in the rest of him. Tall, slender, but powerfully built with a trim waist and lean hips and— very masculine. When he walked, he moved with a silent untamed grace, reminding her of his namesake, the jaguar, the cat of the night.

Interrupting her train of thought, he gave her a wicked smile and rose to his feet. He pulled her to him, molding her flesh to his for a long kiss. Giving her a swat on her bare bottom, he grinned. "Now for a swim, and then we will have our picnic. Race you to the water," he said, turning toward the pond.

Uttering a delighted laugh, she sprinted past him and dived headfirst into the deep pool. Rising to the surface, she saw him cut the water, hardly raising a ripple. She waited for him to come up beside her. When he didn't, she frowned. Where was he? He should have come up for air by now. Frightened, she called out, "Miguel?"

"Here, love," he called from behind her.

Heaving a sharp sigh of relief, she spun toward him. A lock of black hair drooping into his eyes, he gave her a mischievous grin. Determined to punish him for scaring her, she raised her hands to the top of his head and pushed him under. Knowing he'd be after her, she swam swiftly away toward the shadowy cliff.

He rose, spluttering. He reached out, grasping nothing but air. Hearing her laugh, he turned toward her. "Want to play, do you?" he growled, diving beneath the surface.

Elena treaded water, watching for telltale ripples, but there were none. His hand clasping her ankle gave the first clue to his nearness. She sucked in a deep breath before he pulled her under. Only when he had her firmly in his grasp did he allow her to surface.

His eyes wicked, he gazed at her, holding her helpless and immobile in his arms. "It seems I've found a mermaid." He ran a hand down her body, making her quiver beneath his touch. "Hmm, no scales." He nibbled her ear. He placed his hands under her arms and raised her above him. He closed his mouth over the tip of her breast, gently teasing her nipple with his teeth. After doing the same with the other, he gazed up at her in mock surprise. "This part's woman." He cupped her bottom, drawing her close to him. "And no tail." He sighed. "No mermaid after all."

He cocked his head, giving her a quizzical look. "You're not a fish, so I can't eat you. What shall I do with you?"

"I'll help you think of something." She slid down his body and pulled his lips to meet her own. Her eyes widened as she felt him rise with rekindled desire.

"I think you have at that." He lifted her, parting her thighs, then brought her slowly down, impaling her with his long length.

Pulling him closer, she encased him in her throbbing heat, joining them together, filling her body with his presence.

"Was this what you had in mind?" he asked. He began to move inside her, his slippery body rubbing slowly against hers, creating a friction so delicious, so exciting, she could hardly breathe.

"Almost," she said with a gasp, joining his watery dance.

He increased the pace, sending rippling circles sloshing softly against the rocky sides of the pond. He cried out. Shuddering, he drew her tightly to him.

She arched against him, her own body echoing his thundering climax. She grew dizzy as wave after wave washed over her as though he'd permeated all barriers and claimed her very soul. Drawing the fruit of his loins deep within her, she sank with him beneath the water.

"Elena?"

She raised her eyelids, surprised to find herself lying on the grass. Miguel knelt over her. "Are you all right?"

She smiled. "Yes, my love."

"*Por Dios*! I was afraid I'd drowned you," he said with a shaky laugh.

"Miguel, is it always going to be like this?" she asked, filled with the wonder of his loving.

"Like what?"

"I can't explain. It's almost like dying and going to heaven."

He drew her into his arms. "Only with you, *querida*. Only with you." He kissed her forehead. "Now my delightful water nymph, you'd better get dressed. Otherwise we'll never have our picnic and you'll die of pneumonia."

"It's summer, silly." She laughed. Shrieking, she shrank away from his hands as he grabbed up his shirt and began to wipe her dry. Discovering she was ticklish, he tormented her with fiendish fingers until she found he also suffered from the same malady. Teasing and tumbling on the grass like children, they finally collapsed in a heap.

Then, with Miguel in his underdrawers and she in his shirt, they opened the parcel and had their feast. After they'd devoured the loaf of fresh bread, apples, and cheese, they shared the sangria, drinking from the bottle because Elena had forgotten the glasses.

Happy, contented, and slightly tipsy from the wine, Elena lay back on the grass, her head on El Gato's shoulder. She marveled at the brilliance of the star-studded sky. Never had it seemed so bright. The moon bathed them with silver beams, turning the world around them aglow with light and shadows. The very air seemed scented with a special fragrance. Feeling the magic, Elena whispered to the man at her side. "I wish this night would never end. I wish I never had to return to the hacienda, that I could stay here always with you."

He turned his head and gave her a gentle kiss. "I wish it, too, *querida*." He sighed. "But I am afraid our wishes do not make it so." He lifted her hand and kissed her palm. "Now, my sweet, as much as I hate to see anything covering your beautiful body, you'd better get dressed." He rose from the grass and pulled her to her feet, holding her close for a moment before he released her.

"But—"

Miguel tensed. He placed his finger to her lips, warning her to silence. He peered past her into the darkness. He'd heard nothing, yet his senses told him someone was out there just beyond the trees, waiting. Whoever it was, he couldn't let them find them like this.

"Miguel?"

Raising his hand, he shook his head, then motioned for her to get dressed. Placing himself between her and the intruder, he quickly slid his legs into his pants and pulled on his high leather boots. He took the shirt she'd removed and shrugged it on. Stuffing the tail inside his pants, he looked around for his guns. Uttering a silent oath, he remembered he'd removed them and hung the gunbelt over his saddle horn.

He cursed himself for a lovesick fool for allowing himself to be distracted; for forgetting those who would like to see him dead. Now, because of carelessness, he'd been caught unarmed and had put Elena in danger as well.

When Elena had dressed, he led her deep into the shadows. Bending close, he whispered into her ear. "Stay here. Don't move and don't say a word. We are not alone." Praying she would obey, he slipped away from her and went back to the grassy area. Knowing he had to keep them from finding Elena, he squared his shoulders and left the trees. He walked boldly into the open.

A man in white on a dark horse sat facing him. "That is far enough, El Gato," he said, biting out each word. "Where is Elena?" The man edged his mount closer. The moon gleamed ominously off the barrel of his rifle.

Miguel didn't answer. His sharp eyes focused on the gun pointed at his chest.

"No, Juan!" Elena cried. Bolting out of the shadows, she ran toward the intruder.

Miguel whirled, but he was too far away to stop her. "Elena, come back!" He started toward her.

"Stop or I'll kill you," the man in white warned. The sharp click of a hammer being drawn back echoed in the tension-filled air.

"Juan, no! Juan, you can't! Please, I love him," she sobbed, tugging at the man's pant leg.

Juan looked down at her. "And I love you, *amiga.* But I will not stand by and see this *ladrón,* this thief, put you in danger."

"He hasn't. Juan, you don't understand."

"I understand more than you know. Now, get on your horse and ride out, little one," he ordered. He turned toward Miguel. "El Gato and I have unfinished business."

Wary, Miguel watched the man, uncertain of what he should do. As far as he could see, Juan was alone. But not knowing who else might be hidden, he didn't want to take a chance on Elena getting caught in a crossfire. Even without his pistols, Miguel was certain he would be the victor. It would only take a second to throw the slender knife tucked in his boot. But still he hesitated. Knowing how much Elena cared for the man, Miguel felt reluctant to hurt him.

Elena stepped between them, shielding Miguel from the gun. "I will go, but only if each of you gives me your word you will not harm the other." She turned to him. "El Gato?"

"I promise, *querida.* Now, please go."

She looked up at the horseman. "Juan?"

Juan sighed and lowered the rifle. "All right, Elena. Wait for me by the rocks."

Miguel, tense and uneasy, watched Elena fetch her horse. When she had mounted and was out of sight, Juan slid from the saddle and walked toward him.

"Now, El Gato, Miguel Sandoval, Diego Alvarado . . . whoever you are, I will tell you exactly what you have done."

Miguel sucked in his breath and stared at him. "How did you know?"

Juan glanced around, then motioning for Miguel to follow, he strode into the cover of the trees.

"Are you alone?" Miguel asked, sensing an uneasiness about the man.

Juan stopped and peered around. "*Por Dios*, I hope so. If not, we are all in trouble." He crossed the grassy area and sat cross-legged on a large slab of rock. He motioned for Miguel to sit beside him.

His back to the pond, Miguel lowered himself to the rock. Troubled, he stared intently into the young man's face. "How did you know?" he repeated softly.

"I've known since the day you came back to the hacienda and asked Elena to marry you."

"But how can that be? I don't know you. You weren't even born when I left," Miguel said in disbelief.

"Remember the walk you took through the village?"

Miguel nodded. After Elena had refused to marry him and entered the convent, he'd been restless and bored. One night, as Diego, he'd strolled through the grounds. He'd been enraged at the condition and poverty of the people.

"You talked to *El Viejo*, the old one, my grandfather. Blind since the raid, he still sees more than most men. He knew you. He felt your hate and your anger. He sensed you had returned to seek revenge. He told me, so that I could watch out for Elena." Juan shook his head. "But even knowing what I did, I couldn't stop her from marrying you."

"She said you were like a brother to her," Miguel said, jealous of the man's concern for his wife.

Juan laughed bitterly. "I am her brother. But you must never tell her. It would put her in an awkward position, and as things are now she has enough to deal with." His face twisted in anguish. "You are not the only one to hate de Vega. Soon after he'd claimed possession of the ranch, he took my mother into his bed. She was barely fifteen. To help her family, she had gotten a job in the kitchen. *'El Patron'* forced her to warm his bed each night until her belly grew big." His voice shaking with emotion, he paused to take a deep breath. "When he sent her away, Father Dominic took her to San Miguel where she stayed with her sister Consuela and her brother-in-law Francisco, until I was born. My mother died from childbirth fever. Consuela gave birth about the same time, but her son was stillborn. She took me to her breast and raised me as her own son. To hide the truth and to protect me, she buried her child beside my mother." He raised his head and stared at Miguel. "So you see, you are not the only one with reason to hate. But I do not take out my revenge on Elena!" he hissed.

"I would do nothing to harm Elena," Miguel said, shaken by Juan's words.

"Then why do you lie to her and let her torture herself with guilt? Making her so desperate to see you that she puts her own life in danger?"

"What danger?" Miguel said sharply.

"Guillermo."

"Guillermo?" Miguel leaned forward, clutching Juan by the arm. "I know he's made threats, but if that bastard has come near her—if he has touched her . . ."

Juan shook off his grasp. "He hasn't—yet. But he is suspicious. Since her rejection and your marriage, he watches her when she doesn't know he is looking. He wants her." Juan leaned closer. "What do you think would happen if he saw her ride out and followed? She would never reach here. He would be on her like a jackal after a wounded rabbit. She would be helpless against him."

Miguel shuddered, horrified by the vision. "*Mierda!* You are right. She must never be allowed to ride out alone again. But how can we stop her?"

"By giving her no way—and no reason—to leave."

Miguel frowned. "How?"

"I will move the mare. Put her into the stall next to the room where I sleep. Elena will not ride any other."

Miguel nodded. "You've taken care of the way—but the reason?"

Juan stabbed a finger at Miguel's chest. "That part is up to you, my friend."

Miguel sighed. "I would tell her the truth if I could, but you know Elena can't lie. It's not in her nature. I care not for myself, but the men, the people who trust me—I cannot risk their lives."

Juan sighed. "You are right." He shrugged. "I do not know the answer."

Miguel, worried about Elena, got to his feet. He held out his hand. "Juan, I hope our quarrel has come to an end. I, too, care for your sister. Maybe between the two of us we can keep her safe."

Juan got to his feet and shook Miguel's hand, cementing the truce. "I only hope we are men enough to do it. She can be very stubborn when she puts her mind to it."

Miguel laughed softly. "How well I know. Now let's go show the little imp we haven't killed each other and see her safely home."

Chapter Nineteen

TOO restless to settle anywhere, Elena prowled her room like a caged cat. Even though it had only been a week, it seemed an eternity since Miguel had held her in his arms and made her drunk with passion; an eternity since Miguel and Juan had escorted her home from the pond. She scowled. Now that she'd made that ridiculous promise, it probably would be an eternity before she saw him again.

Her pace increased, her agitation made worse by knowing that any day Diego and "his guest" would return to the hacienda. Even though she was determined not to give in to her husband's demands, she still didn't know how she could avoid them. She rubbed her temples. Boxed in like this, she couldn't think.

On edge, she'd been so ill-tempered she snapped at every one, even Consuela, whom she loved like a mother. Poor Lupe ran from the sound of her voice.

She picked up a book and impatiently thumbed through the pages, then, muttering an uncustomary oath, she threw the volume across the room. Her eyes narrowed as she stepped onto her terrace and watched the twilight fade into dusky dark. She clenched her fists and raised her defiant gaze to the mountains. *I don't care what I promised. I cannot live like this.*

She ripped off her dress in such haste she sent the but-

tons bouncing across the floor. Then she yanked on her
riding clothes. "I'll go for a long ride. Then I'll go to the
pond," she said, breathless with the thought that El Gato
might be there. "Maybe a swim will relax me. It certainly
couldn't make things worse." Snatching up her quirt, she
left the room.

When she reached the stable, she slipped inside and
went to Silver Moon's stall. When no glad nicker met her
call, Elena peered over the gate. *Nothing but clean straw.
Where's Luna?* Confused and fearful, she glanced around.
Has something happened to her?

She made her way through the barn, hastily checking
every occupied stall. A bolt of relief shot through her when
she finally spotted the familiar silver head at the very end.
Juan must have moved her. Cautiously Elena moved toward
her, sucking in a breath when the mare recognized her and
nickered. "Hush, girl," she whispered, hurriedly reaching
out to open the gate.

A hand clamped over Elena's shoulder.

She froze.

"Going somewhere, *amiga*?"

Elena turned mutinous eyes to Juan. "Yes. I am."

"No. I don't think so," Juan said quietly. "You gave us
your word, remember?"

"That was before I discovered it was impossible to keep,"
she muttered. She placed her hands on his shoulders and
smiled sweetly up at him. "Please, Juan. I'll be careful."

His face stern, he removed her hands. "No. You can't
go."

"You could go with me if you are so worried," she
said.

"I have other plans for my evening."

"Well, I have plans, too. I'm going riding, and you can't
stop me. Now, saddle the horse," she ordered.

His lips thinned, but he made no move to do as she said.

Desperate anger surged through her. "It's my ranch. I am the boss. You are only a stablehand. You have to obey me," she said, trying to ignore the hurt in his eyes. "Very well, I'll do it myself." She stepped around him and reached for the gear.

He gripped her arm. "No. I will not let you go," he said, his voice determined.

"But I must see him," she pleaded.

"He won't be there," Juan said.

"How do you know?"

"He told me. He also told me not to let you leave the ranch. He told me to tie you up if I had to."

Elena drew in an outraged breath. "You wouldn't dare."

"Only if you make it necessary, señora."

She gritted her teeth. "All right, Juan. You win—this time. But sooner or later I will go. You wait and see. You can't watch me all the time."

"I hope that won't be necessary. You did give your word, remember?"

"How can I forget since you keep reminding me?" she snapped.

Furious with both Juan and Miguel, Elena turned on her heel and left the stable. Distraught, her mind on the domineering pair, she stormed toward the house. *How dare they tell me I'm not to leave the grounds?* No one had told her that since she was eight years old. Now, at eighteen, she had no intention of obeying. *Juan and his idea that I am in danger. Danger from what? Certainly not El Gato.*

But he was just as bad, agreeing with every word Juan said. She slapped her quirt against her skirt. If she couldn't leave, how could they ever be together? She frowned. Maybe Miguel didn't want to be with her anymore. He certainly seemed anxious to get rid of her.

She shook her head. *No, he loves me. I'm sure of that. But he can't come here and I can't go to him. What will we do?* Without him she would be like a flower without water. She'd shrivel and die. She needed him for her very existence. At the thought of never being with him again, tears filled her eyes and spilled down her cheeks. "I'll run away. I'll find him. I'll leave here and never return," she vowed.

Diego's face loomed in front of her. Her steps slowed. She couldn't. She could disgrace herself, but not Diego. She might not be willing to obey him, but she owed him too much to desert him. Sobbing, she broke into a run and collided with a man that suddenly appeared in front of her.

Brutal hands gripped her arms. "Where do you go in such a hurry, Elena?"

Terrified, Elena blinked away her tears. She stared up at the huge man looming over her, a twisted grin on his face. "Guillermo!" She struggled, trying to break his grip. "Release me at once!"

He laughed. "And so late at night, too. Did you ride to meet a lover? El Gato, maybe?" His hot eyes raked her body.

Elena inhaled, trying to quell the fear in her voice. "Where I go is none of your business. Let me go!"

"Not yet, pretty one." He wrapped his arms around her and pulled her against him. He bent his head, pressing his mouth to hers in a slobbering kiss. Reeking of tequila and onions, his tongue forced its way between her clenched teeth. Helpless, lifted to where her feet no longer touched the ground, she dangled like a captive doll, her arms pinned to her sides. Praying for strength, she drew back her boot and kicked him as hard as she could on the shins.

"Ow!" he cried, releasing her arms.

Elena, her heart pounding, ducked around his upraised hand and raced toward the stairway. Reaching the safety of her room, she quickly bolted the door. She raised a trembling hand to wipe her mouth. *Does Guillermo suspect—* her eyes widened—*or does he know?* Her legs too weak to support her weight, she collapsed in a heap against the door. "*Madre de Dios,* now what will I do?"

El Gato, accompanied by Carlos, left the mountain stronghold just after sunup. Worried about Elena, he'd been tense and anxious, unable to concentrate on the matter at hand.

He'd spent a week in Santa Fe and an additional two weeks on the mountain—three weeks away from Elena. He'd hoped by spending time with his men he could curb their impatience, but his own restlessness had made matters even worse. They'd accused him of abandoning their cause, of preferring the luxurious life of the hacienda, of forgetting the people who'd supported him.

He'd tried to explain there hadn't been any shipments, tried to tell them the gold was being kept at the mine. He'd said that when it was moved it would be accompanied by a regiment of armed men and impossible to steal.

They'd scoffed at him, accusing him of losing his nerve. He shifted his glance to the elder man at his side. Even Carlos looked at him with doubt in his eyes.

He sighed. Maybe they were right. Since he'd been with Elena, life had become very precious, too much so to risk losing it. Had loving her made him weak and cowardly? Not sure of the answer, he sighed. If he doubted himself, how could he expect his men not to.

"Miguel." Carlos pointed to an approaching cloud of dust.

"Quickly, my friend, follow me." Miguel wheeled Diablo, heading him toward the *pajaritas*, a series of fingerlike, steep-sided gorges. Only one who knew them well could keep from getting lost. He grinned. El Gato knew them very well.

Slowing the stallion's pace so he wouldn't lose Carlos, Miguel entered one canyon only to exit and enter another. "Stay here, out of sight, while I lose our friends," he told the older man. Leaving the ravine, Miguel rode boldly in the open.

Spotting him, the riders turned their horses. Bullets plowed the dust in front of Diablo.

Miguel wheeled his horse, heading him back into the maze. He made tracks in the soft dust, dodging from one canyon to another. Finally entering one very narrow L-shaped crevice, he backed Diablo a distance out, then pointed the horse up an almost perpendicular trail that ran up the rocky wall. After a fierce struggle, the heaving stallion reached the top. From his lofty perch, Miguel laughed at the confusion below.

Men and horses crowded the narrow canyons, leaving one only to dead-end in another. Finally they entered the last, going single file into a crevice too narrow to turn a horse. There, not realizing the trap until too late, they stood end to end like cattle loaded in a chute.

"Que pasa, compadres?" he shouted down to them. "Did you get stuck trying to follow El Gato? Too bad. You'll have to forgive me for not waiting for you. *Adiós!*" He doffed his hat at the screaming, cursing men. Feeling better than he had in days, he rode to join Carlos.

Reaching the canyon, he called out to his friend. "You can come out now, *amigo*. The jackals will not bother us again."

The old man shook his head. "One day, Miguel, you will not be so lucky."

Miguel grinned. "Luck had nothing to do with it. Even a rabbit, when trapped by a coyote, has more than one exit to his hole."

Carlos shook a gnarled finger at him. "Don't be too sure of yourself. The wise rabbit, when chased by a pack of coyotes, knows when to lie low," he scolded.

Miguel laughed. "All this talk of rabbits is making me hungry. Let's go home, old friend."

Late that evening Diego and Carlos returned to the Spanish Angel. Eager to see his wife, Miguel directed Carlos to drive directly to the north wing instead of letting him out at the main entrance as he usually did.

Fluttering a creamy lace handkerchief, Miguel brushed dust from his apricot suit and stepped inside the salon. His heart quickened when he caught sight of a familiar dark head bent over a piece of embroidery. "Elena."

She looked up. "Diego." She got to her feet and came to him, greeting him with a kiss on the cheek.

Fighting to keep a tight rein on his emotions, Miguel crushed the scrap of lace in his hand. Reminding himself he was Diego, not El Gato, he brushed his lips across her forehead. Her light perfume rose to tantalize him, as did the creamy swell of her breasts rising above the square neckline of her emerald green gown. "My dear, you look lovely this evening."

"Thank you." She peered around him, anxiously watching the doorway. "Did you have a good trip, Diego?"

"Very tiring, I'm afraid." He frowned, watching her fidget. "Elena, whatever is the matter?"

"Did—do we—have a guest?" she asked, her eyes bright and anxious.

With a start, he remembered the "guest" he had promised to bring home. He'd forgotten all about it. He took one of her hands and sighed. "No, my dear. I'm afraid we don't." Watching the tension leave her face, he felt guilty for ever mentioning such a thing. "I'm afraid I don't know many people that well. When I broached the subject to the few I do know, they looked at me as though I'd gone *loco*."

She gave a very audible sigh of relief. "Are you hungry? The cook prepared chicken and rice for dinner. Even though we didn't expect you, I'm sure there will be plenty," she said with a smile.

"I'm positively famished. Let me freshen up a bit and then I'll join you." Unable to resist giving her another quick kiss, he abruptly left the room.

The *click, click* of his black-patent high-heeled shoes echoed on the polished floors as he made his way upstairs. In his room he sagged against the door, wondering if he had the endurance to continue this charade. Just being near her drove him insane.

She'd looked so tempting, so delectable, he didn't know how he'd kept from dragging her into his arms and kissing her senseless. He closed his eyes, still smelling the light floral fragrance she wore. "*Mierda!* Why did I say I'd have dinner with her?"

He strode to the liquor cabinet and poured himself a brandy. Examining his shaking hand, he shook his head. If he didn't control himself, he'd end up taking her on the floor under the table. "Most un-Diego-like behavior," he muttered.

He stripped off his dust-caked clothes and sponged himself down with the cold water from the pitcher, hoping it would cool his overheated blood. He stared at himself in the mirror. "You are Diego. Diego has an injury. He is incapable. Elena doesn't even appeal to you." He turned away in disgust. He could talk to himself all night. No matter what he told the face in the mirror, the message definitely wasn't getting through to the lower half of his body. It remembered Elena's charms too well to be convinced otherwise.

Sighing in despair, he sat down on the bed and buried his face in his hands. "Maybe I ought to shoot myself and be done with it. At least I'd save de Vega the trouble." Raising his head, he stared at the wall dividing their rooms. His heart increased its beat. His mouth grew dry. He groaned, knowing as sure as he sat there, he'd never be able to stay out of Elena's bed.

A good while later Miguel lay on top of his covers congratulating himself on his fortitude. Somehow he'd managed to make it through dinner. His mouth lifted in a rueful smile. Never mind the fact that he'd stuffed himself like a ravenous wolf to keep his mind off making love to Elena. But he'd made it, surviving the meal with nothing more than an acute case of indigestion. He groaned, rubbing his aching stomach. "If I eat many more meals like that, I won't need the padding for my disguise."

Wishing he hadn't sent Carlos to talk to Juan, he got up and paced the floor. The old man would know what to do for his misery. *Mierda!* He felt like he would explode.

He walked out onto his balcony, hoping he'd see Carlos headed back. Catching a glimpse of white, he narrowed his eyes. *A woman?* He frowned.

Swathed in a *rebozo*, the woman hurried toward a dark figure who emerged from the shadows to meet her. Uttering an oath, Miguel recognized the man. "Guillermo." In spite of the warmth of the night, he shivered. The majordomo clasped the woman in his arms and kissed her, before drawing her further into the darkness.

Watching the pair below, Miguel's eyes narrowed. Something about the midnight embrace didn't ring true. If he was right, what was Guillermo up to? And who was the woman? A maid, perhaps? Whoever she was, it was certain she didn't want to be recognized. If Guillermo was involved with a woman, then why had he been watching Elena? Was it just anger because she'd chosen Diego over him? Or was he after the reward? Did he suspect Elena could lead him to El Gato? Miguel's blood chilled.

After a few moments he watched them part, each to go his own way. His frown deepened. Something was definitely in the wind. He wondered if Juan might know what it was. His indigestion forgotten, Miguel returned to bed and an uneasy sleep.

Chapter Twenty

MIGUEL pushed back his breakfast tray and poured another cup of coffee. He frowned, listening intently to what Carlos had to say. "So," Miguel said, "Juan has seen Guillermo prowling about the hacienda. Did he mention seeing anyone with him?"

"No." Carlos's brow wrinkled in a frown. "Why?"

"Last night I saw him in the garden with a woman."

Carlos leaned closer. "Who?"

"She wore a shawl, but I assumed it was one of the maids. Whoever she was, she didn't want to be recognized." Miguel took a sip of his coffee. "Keep this between us, old friend. We don't want the fox to know he's been caught prowling around the henhouse until we can set the trap. In the meantime, keep your eyes and ears open. Let me know if anything unusual happens."

When the servant picked up the tray and left the room, Miguel walked onto his balcony and stared thoughtfully at the opposite wing. He hadn't told Enrique that he'd returned. Maybe it was time for Diego to pay a morning visit to his father-in-law.

Diego stood before the cheval mirror and checked his appearance. After adjusting the neckpiece of his pink blouse, he tucked a matching handkerchief into the jacket pocket of his gray linen suit and left the room. Humming softly, he ambled downstairs and crossed the courtyard.

A crash of breaking glass and raised angry voices told him Ricardo and Conception were at it again. His mouth tightened into a thin line. The woman needed a firm hand—applied to her backside—but easygoing Ricardo would never give it to her.

An angry masculine roar came from the upstairs room.

Miguel smiled, hearing Ricardo yell at her. Maybe there was hope for his brother-in-law yet.

Spying Enrique in the salon, Diego strode toward the open doorway.

"Diego! I'm glad to see you've returned," Enrique called, motioning him in. "Please, come, join me. I've just had the cook bring me a fresh pot of coffee."

"Good morning, Enrique. That would be delightful," Miguel said, entering the room. He lowered himself onto the gold velvet settee and took the cup of steaming, fragrant brew.

"How was your trip to Santa Fe?"

"Tedious and boring, I'm afraid." Miguel sighed. "I do wish these trips weren't necessary, but my business interests are becoming so vast, my solicitor simply can't handle them."

Enrique's eyes glittered. "You've certainly done very well, considering your previous circumstances. I wish I might say the same." He added a lump of hard brown sugar and stirred his coffee. "You say your interests are vast? What sort of things are you involved in?"

"Oh, cattle and some mining, mostly gold. I spend most of my time transferring assets from one hand to another." *From your hand to mine,* he added silently. Finding it hard to keep a straight face, Miguel sighed again. "I find I must cover a lot of ground to take care of everything."

"You do look rather tired," Enrique said sympathetically.

"I wish I had someone I could trust to run it all." He raised his head, watching the older man's expression. "Like your Guillermo."

"Ah, yes. Guillermo." De Vega scowled. "You do not know what you wish for, my son."

Miguel eyed him thoughtfully. "Why do you say that? Has he displeased you?"

"He does his job." De Vega waved his hand. "It's his manner. Sometimes he behaves as if I'm working for him." He inhaled. "But let us discuss more pleasant things."

Miguel smiled. "Is there any more news of the bandit— El Gato?"

"That one! My men spotted him, and just when they thought they had him, he escaped." De Vega shook his finger. "But I have patience. I'll catch him yet." He leaned back in his chair. "The *pistoleros* are as bad as the bandit. Now they demand more money. With the *ladróns* stealing my gold shipments, I am short of cash." He smiled, leaning toward Diego. "I don't suppose—?"

Miguel arched his brow. "How much?"

"Only five thousand dollars?" Enrique looked at him hopefully.

Miguel gasped. "Isn't that the price you put on the bandit's head?"

Enrique nodded. "I don't know which band of thieves is worse—El Gato's or Guillermo's."

"I would be happy to let you have the money, but I have recently reinvested most of my funds." He gave the older man a sad smile. "Maybe you should try another shipment. With the gunmen guarding it, perhaps it would get through."

"Do you think so, Diego?"

"At least you would see if the men you hired are worth their keep."

Enrique narrowed his eyes thoughtfully. "If they aren't, I'll fire the scoundrels and hire some who can do the job. So far all they've done is eat my beef and drink my wine."

"Father," Conception said, sweeping into the room, "you simply must—" She broke off and stared at Diego. "Oh." She frowned. "I didn't know you had returned."

"Hello, Conception."

"What is the matter, my pet?" de Vega asked.

"The maids are impossible. They refuse to clean the upstairs rooms."

"Why?" de Vega asked.

"The silly fools claim to have seen a ghost or something."

"A ghost?" Enrique paled. "The angel!" he gasped.

"Well, aren't you going to do something?" Conception snapped. "The place is a mess. Who's going to make the beds and gather laundry?"

Diego glared at her. "Why don't you do it? It might give you something to do besides scream at your husband."

Conception burst into tears and left the room.

Enrique cradled his head in his hands. "*Por Dios!* I am besieged with troubles—and now the angel has returned."

He raised his head and looked at Diego. "Long ago, because of my love for a woman, I did a terrible thing." He added softly, as if talking to himself, "And I have paid for it every day of my life since."

Miguel narrowed his eyes. *You bastard,* he thought, *you haven't even begun to pay.*

Enrique waved his hand apologetically. "I'm afraid I'll have to ask you to excuse me, Diego. Right now I am not very good company."

"Of course, Enrique. I understand," Miguel said, getting to his feet. "I only wish I could help." *Send you to perdition,* he added silently.

"No one can help me, *amigo*. I am doomed." Shaking his head, Enrique reached for the brandy.

Showing himself out, Miguel fought to contain his glee until he reached his own room. As he closed the door, he burst into laughter. Even though he thought the business about the angel was a bunch of superstitious nonsense, Miguel was delighted to find Enrique in such a quandary. Things couldn't be better if he'd planned it himself. He sobered. Now if he only knew what Guillermo was up to.

A large bag in his hand, a silly grin on his face, Diego waited for Elena to answer his knock.

The door opened and Elena, fresh as a breath of spring in a buttercup-yellow dress, smiled at him. "Diego. Come in." When he entered the room, she tilted her head, her expression puzzled. "What is all of this?"

"Before I went to Santa Fe, you mentioned Paco's birthday," he said, placing the bag on the floor by the settee.

Elena's eyes widened in dismay. "It's tomorrow. I forgot."

"I didn't." Miguel reached into the bag and removed a large candy-filled *piñata*. "Sit down and I will show you."

"Oh!" Elena squealed with delight. "It looks like a donkey." She raised excited eyes to his. "Is it—?"

He nodded. "To the brim." Reaching farther into the sack, he removed a large package and handed it to her. "Open it."

Elena untied the bundle and removed a small sapphire-blue velvet Charro jacket and pants, decorated with scrolls of silver braid. "They're beautiful."

"There's more," he urged, setting a pair of shiny, high-topped boots, socks, and underwear by the outfit.

Elena parted a layer of paper to find a pale blue embroidered shirt and silver string tie. She gazed up at him, her eyes glassy with unshed tears.

Miguel's heart plummeted. "It's too fussy, isn't it?" He'd hated stuff like that when he was small. Whatever made him think Paco would be any different? Dejected, he dropped the sack and started toward the door.

"Diego?" Elena leapt to her feet and ran to him. Before he could move, she wrapped her arms around his neck and gave him an exuberant hug. She rubbed her cheek against his before touching his lips in a tender kiss. She gazed into his eyes. "It's perfect. Paco will love it."

Lost in topaz depths, his senses reeling, Miguel clasped her to him in a passionate embrace. Overcome with longing, he bent his head, ready to claim her lips, when a muffled laugh jolted him back to reality. He jerked around and saw an embarrassed Consuela standing in the doorway.

"Caramba!" he cried, releasing Elena so suddenly she staggered backward. Blushing like a schoolboy, Miguel stammered an excuse and rushed out of the room.

Elena gasped, her eyes wide with amazement as she watched Diego's hasty retreat.

"I'm so sorry, señora. Do you want me to come back later?"

Bemused, Elena shook her head. "Come in, Consuela. We have a party to plan."

When the maid left, Elena folded the small garments and put them back in the package. She stared thoughtfully at the doorway, reflecting on Diego's embrace. Even though she was no expert on the matter, she recognized the feel of a man's arousal, especially at those close quarters. And his eyes . . . they'd fairly blazed with desire. *But he said he couldn't, that he was incapable.* Her eyes widened. "He lied to me!" she said with amazement. "But, why—?"

*

Elena smiled, watching her usually fastidious husband kneel in the dirt in the midst of the laughing children. Apparently engrossed in a game of tag, Diego seemed unaware of her scrutiny as he allowed Benito to catch him. *He's having more fun than the children.* She found it hard to believe the pompous Diego and the disheveled, dusty man chasing the shrieking youngsters could be the same person.

With the children eluding him, the panting Diego staggered close, then suddenly pulled Elena into his arms. "You're it, my love," he said with a breathless laugh.

Seeing the mischief dancing in his blue eyes, Elena giggled. "You cheated."

After she and most of the young ones had taken a turn, Elena and Paco's mother unveiled the cake. The young partygoers, wide-eyed and silent, watched Paco blow out the candles and open his presents.

Elena had a lump in her throat when the small boy reverently examined his boots and finery.

"You must thank Don Diego and Dona Elena, Paco," his mother gently chided.

Happy tears streaking his face, Paco approached the bench where they were sitting and murmured a shy thank-you to Elena. Ignoring his outstretched hand, the boy launched himself at Diego and gave him a fierce hug. "Thank you, Diego. I love you, *amigo*," Elena heard him whisper.

"*De nada*, my friend, don't mention it," Diego said, ruffling the boy's hair. "I love you too."

Elena thought Diego's own eyes looked suspiciously moist when he raised his head to give her a smile.

"And now the *piñata!*" Diego cried.

Paco nominated the youngest child to do the honors. Blindfolded and given a long stick, Jorge swatted the paper donkey until it split, spilling a great variety of candy onto the small yard. Excited children shrieked and squealed as they scrambled for the treats.

Finally, so that the other youngsters could also have a gift, Diego provided a large assortment of tops for the boys, bright beads or combs for the girls. After each claimed a treasure, the party was declared at an end and the youngsters left Paco's yard to go home.

Exhausted by the day's festivities, Elena looped her arm through Diego's and walked slowly toward the hacienda.

"I see your father's bandit trap is almost finished." Diego pointed to a squat, square building under construction some distance away from the rest of the village.

"Bandit trap?" Elena stared at the structure.

"Enrique intends to lure El Gato here. When he is captured, that will be his prison. I think it will be very interesting—if it works."

"Madre de Dios!" Elena gasped, crossing herself. "Let's pray he never comes here."

"El Gato might think the reward would be worth taking a chance," Diego said softly, gazing intently at her.

"The reward?" Elena asked, suddenly finding it hard to get her breath. She felt her face grow warm.

He grinned. "The gold."

"Oh, yes. Of course, the gold." Elena sighed her relief.

That evening Diego sat at the dining table alone. Elena, pleading a headache, had retired early. He frowned, recalling how pale and withdrawn she'd seemed. The day's activities had been exhausting; he just hoped she wasn't ill. He rose from the table and went upstairs to see.

He knocked softly, not wanting to disturb her if she was asleep.

"Yes?" answered a faint voice.

"Elena? It's Diego."

The door opened, and Elena, in her nightgown and robe, looked up at him.

"I was worried about you, my dear. Are you feeling better?"

She gave him a wistful, sad smile. "I'm fine now, Diego. Won't you come in?"

He frowned. She didn't look fine to him. "Are you sure you're up to it?"

She stepped aside. "Please, I would be grateful for the company."

After closing the door behind him, he followed her across the room to the balcony.

She looked up at him. "I hope you don't mind if we sit out here. It's so stuffy inside."

"Not at all." When he settled into a wicker chair, something poked him. Squirming uncomfortably, he felt beneath him and removed her brush. He offered it to her.

"Oh, I am sorry, Diego. I was trying to brush my hair to relieve this headache. Consuela usually does it for me, but tonight she is busy."

"Perhaps I could do the job," he said softly.

"I wouldn't want to trouble you."

"No trouble at all. I'd be delighted." Taking the brush, he reached across. "This is awkward. Maybe if we sat there?" They moved to the couch. He had her sit sideways and rest her back against his leg.

He drew the brush through her long locks, savoring the feel of them against his hand. Memory of the black shining curtain falling to her trim bare hips flashed into his mind. Disconcerted by her nearness, his strokes grew slower. His hand shook and his heart pounded. He gritted his teeth, fighting the urge to take her into his arms.

When the temptation became unbearable, he laid the brush aside, not daring to continue. "There, my dear," he said, his voice thick with passion.

She sat up and gave him a grateful smile. "Thank you, Diego."

She looked so lovely, so desirable. He wanted to crush her in his arms and carry her to the bed. *Get hold of yourself. Remember, you fool. You are Diego.*

Releasing a ragged sigh, he got to his feet, then remembering the necklace, he reached into his pocket. "I had this repaired in Santa Fe." He handed it to her.

"Oh, thank you." Her eyes bright, she examined the new catch.

"Now, my dear, I, too, am feeling rather fatigued, so I will say good night."

"Of course, Diego," she said, rising from the seat.

Her special scent rose with her to wrap around his senses, making him drunk with longing as he followed her to the door.

The creamy satin of her nightdress molded to her body, accentuating, rather than hiding, her soft curves, bringing back the memory of how she'd looked wearing nothing but moonlight.

He gazed into long-lashed golden eyes. His heart thudded wildly against his ribs. He fought for breath.

She stood on tiptoe and gently kissed his cheek. Her arms wrapped around him.

Feeling himself losing control, he desperately pushed her away. "No!" he croaked, putting even more distance between them. Bewildered wide topaz eyes locked on his. As if hypnotized, he swayed toward her.

"Diego?" she said, breaking the spell.

Diego. He stopped. *Mierda! I've got to get out of here.* He groped behind him for the doorknob.

She took a hesitant step toward him. "I'm sorry, Diego. I only wished to thank you."

"That's quite all right, my dear. Now I must be going," he said, retreating through the doorway.

Reaching his quarters, Miguel reached out a shaking hand and slid the bolt shut on the door. Lurching across the room, he reached for the brandy and poured the glass half full, downed it, and poured another. He sagged into a chair. "That was too close. One more second . . ." He shook his head.

Heaving a weary sigh, he rose to remove the hated wig, mustache, and clothes. After slipping on his robe, he paused by the desk and lit a cigar, almost burning the end of his nose in the process. *Dios!* He was a quivering wreck. He tossed down the brandy. He refilled his drink for the third time, then stepped onto his balcony and gazed up at the night stars. *What am I going to do?*

A faint, muffled sound caught his attention. He frowned. A woman weeping. He turned toward the adjoining balcony. *Oh, Elena, querida!* Her sobs tore through him, shredding his resolve. Unable to bear her sorrow, he swallowed his drink, ground the cigar under his boot, and returned to his room.

Feeling the effects of the brandy, he peered at himself in the mirror. The tortured face of El Gato looked back. He sighed, remembering the nights they had spent together. His body throbbed with unfulfilled desire. It had been over three weeks since he'd held her in his arms, but in the state he was in, it felt more like three years.

"Even a saint could not live like this!" he cried in frustration.

A grim smile crossed his face. He stripped off his robe. "And God knows I am no saint."

Chapter Twenty-one

ELENA, confused by her own emotions and Diego's behavior, fell across her bed and burst into tears. Diego had plainly been shocked by her boldness. He'd told her when he'd married her it had been for the ranch and to hide his infirmity. *But he doesn't have an infirmity!* If she was unsure before, she was certain now that his body wanted her even if he didn't.

She'd seen the expression of horror on his face when she'd kissed him. She frowned, remembering he'd always seemed uncomfortable when she'd touched him. But tonight he'd behaved as if she had a contagious disease.

Madre de Dios! What is wrong with me? Am I becoming so desperate for a man's embrace that I would try to seduce one who clearly finds me repulsive? Seduce? I only wanted to thank him, she thought defensively. She rejected the idea that if he had given her the slightest encouragement, she would have surrendered to his embrace.

But he is my husband. I am supposed to love him. She jolted upright. *Love Diego? No. I love El Gato.* Her head spinning, she covered her eyes. "*Por Dios!* Something must be wrong with me," she murmured. She had felt very moody and strange lately. "That's it. I'm losing my mind."

Confused and lonely, she wished she could talk to Juan, but, because of her sharp tongue, he was still so furious he wouldn't speak to her. She sniffed, knowing if she apologized he would relent. Her mouth drew into a pout. She wouldn't do it. She, too, was still angry at him for confining her to the hacienda.

The ranch had become worse than the convent. She couldn't even take a walk safely. Since her encounter with Guillermo, she scarcely dared to leave her room. "I can't live like this," she wailed. "I need to be free or I'll die."

Her thoughts went to Miguel. Would he be at the pond? She closed her eyes, imagining he was with her, holding out his arms, his eyes warm with love. "Oh, El Gato," she sobbed. "Where are you tonight when I need you so?"

"I am here, *querida*," a voice said softly.

Elena raised her head and stared toward her balcony. The rising moon silhouetted a tall, dark figure. "It can't be true. I am dreaming!" she cried.

He held out his arms. "Come, Elena. See if I'm a dream."

Her heart filled with wonder, she rose from the bed and slowly walked toward him. Raising her hand, she hesitated, afraid to touch him. Afraid he would vanish and she would be alone.

He reached out and closed his hand over hers. He placed her palm against his cheek. "See, *querida*. I am here."

Tears streamed down her face. She threw herself into his arms. "Oh, El Gato, my love. I thought I would never see you again." Cupping his beloved face between her palms, her fingers brushing the silk of his mask, she stood on tiptoe to kiss his lips, savoring the taste of brandy and cigars. Involuntarily she wrinkled her nose, vaguely noticing a faint hint of lavender.

His arms tightened around her. He lifted her feet off the floor, returning her kiss with fiery passion.

Dizzy with joy, she raised her head to look into his eyes. She brushed a lock of black hair back from his forehead.

"You are crazy to come here. You must leave. They will find you." As much as she loved and needed him, she couldn't risk his life. "Please, my love. Go quickly!"

He grinned down at her. "And I thought you were glad to see me." Shaking his head, he slowly unbuttoned his shirt and tossed it aside. He sat on the bed and pulled off his boots. "Not even your father's *pistoleros* could make me leave this night." Giving her a wicked smile, he padded across the room and bolted the door.

Elena's heart fluttered against her rib cage. Blood roared in her ears as he unbuttoned his pants and slid them over lean hips. He stepped free.

Following his cue, she hastily stripped the nightgown from her body, leaving it in a heap on the floor. She raised her head to see him smiling.

He crooked a finger, beckoning to her.

Trembling with anticipation, she ran into his outstretched arms.

Elena sighed and stretched lazily. She reluctantly opened her eyes, afraid it had been a dream, but her body, nude beneath the bedcovers, told her it hadn't. She lowered her lashes, reliving the ecstasy they'd shared. If only it would be possible to wake up in his arms. She ran her hand across the sheets. The bed felt cold and empty without him. Turning toward his indented pillow, she smiled through a sudden rush of tears. There beside her lay a single white rose. She lifted it to her lips. "Oh, El Gato, Miguel, my wonderful, foolish love."

Miguel lay in his own bed, his arms crossed behind his head. He smiled, his thoughts going to the woman in the next room. "*Por Dios!* I am like a rutting stag." But he knew it wasn't mere lust that made him want her. He loved her to distraction. He wished for nothing more than to be able to spend his life at her side, loving her, protecting her and his children.

He frowned. How could he hope to do that? In his situation the worst thing he could do would be to get her with child. A chill washed over him. He remembered the passion they'd shared and knew she might already be carrying his babe.

And what if he was caught? His luck had been phenomenal, but even a cat had only nine lives. What would happen to her and the child without him to protect them?

A picture of Guillermo flashed into his mind, sending a shiver up his spine. If El Gato was captured, Elena would be at Guillermo's mercy. His mouth tightened. Somehow he had to make sure that didn't happen. He had to find a way to get rid of the majordomo. Troubled, Miguel rose from the bed. If only he knew what the man was plotting.

Juan's words came back to him. *El Viejo, the old one, sees more than most sighted men.* Maybe Diego could pay him a visit. *El Viejo* might know what the bastard was up to.

He hurriedly bathed and tied his padding into place, covering it with a peach-colored blouse and pale green suit. He carefully tucked his own dark hair beneath the brownish gray wig and stuck the matching mustache above his upper lip. He scowled, wishing for the hundredth time that he hadn't made the wig part of his disguise. The damn thing made his head sweat and itch. Well, there was no hope for it now. Snorting with disgust, he left the room.

Reaching Elena's door, he knocked softly, hoping she might join him for breakfast. When he received no response, he sighed and made his way to the dining room.

A faint smile crossed his face. After last night she would probably sleep until noon. His heart raced, imagining her asleep, naked, her lips swollen from his kisses, her hair spreading like a silken fan across the pillows. Heat rushed to his loins, making his clothing uncomfortably tight. *Hombre, he scolded, if you intend to protect her, you'd better concentrate on the matters at hand—like Guillermo.* The thought sobered him, turning his blood cold.

He entered the dining room, poured himself a steaming cup of coffee, then sat down at the end of the long table. Brooding over his situation, his mind and stomach rebelled at the thought of food. He finished the coffee and stood, ready to leave for the village, when his gaze landed on a large basket of fresh-picked fruit. Maybe he'd take some to the old blind man. He picked out the choicest and piled them high in a pottery bowl. Then he covered them with a linen napkin and left the house.

Outside the courtyard Miguel strode through thick dust and headed for the old man's hut. El Viejo sat outside his door, eyes closed, apparently dozing in the warm sun.

Miguel stopped by his side and waited for the aged man to acknowledge his presence.

"Buenos dias, mi patrón. What brings you to my humble *casa?"*

Unable to suppress a grin, Miguel squatted on his heels beside him. "You probably already know. Could we go inside where we can talk?"

"If you wish." El Viejo held out a clawlike hand, stiffened and crippled from age.

Miguel gently helped him to his feet and followed him inside. The dwelling, though poor, was scrupulously clean.

"Please, sit down, Diego." The old man waved a hand toward a table and two benches.

"Juan told you?" Miguel asked, noticing the man had called him by his assumed name.

"Juan and I discuss many things." He raised his head and sniffed the air. "Do I smell peaches? And plums, too."

Miguel uncovered the bowl and pushed it forward. "I thought you might enjoy them, Santiago." He watched a sly smile spread across the ancient face. "I remember, too, how you used to lift me high in the air so that I might find the choicest fruit." Bitterness edged his words. He wished he could make things easier for the people whose labors and loyalty went unrewarded.

The old man touched his hand. "Miguel, I know your heart. I also know of your need for revenge. Be careful, my son. Danger trails your footsteps. I fear this time even the angel will not be able to protect you."

Miguel stared at him, wanting to ask what he meant, but the old one had closed his eyes. He was asleep. Miguel frowned and quietly left the hut with none of his questions answered. Remembering the old man's words, a chill crept up his spine. He, too, sensed the danger that made him want to hurry his footsteps and watch his back.

He nodded to various people who greeted him politely, but guardedly, as if surprised to find him again in their village. He knew Elena was the only one of the de Vegas who ever visited them. Thinking of his father-in-law, Miguel wondered what he had decided about the gold. He raised a brow. Why not ask him? He turned his steps toward the hacienda.

A shrill scream shattered the early morning quiet, freezing his hand on the door knocker. Not waiting for an invitation, Miguel jerked the door open and stepped inside.

A maid, her eyes wide with terror, ran up to him. "Señor, come quick. It is *La Madama*. The angel!" She grabbed his hand and pulled him toward the stairwell. She raised a shaking finger to point. "See?"

At the top of the landing a pale figure in blue hovered for a moment then vanished.

Miguel sucked in his breath. He wasn't sure it was the angel, but something had been there. He turned to the hysterical woman at his side. "She's gone now. And even if she wasn't, I'm sure she means you no harm."

The woman buried her face in her hands. "You don't understand, *señor. La Madama,* the Mistress, she comes as a warning." Her brown eyes fastened on his. "Someone on the hacienda is going to die." Crossing herself, she hurried away, beseeching the Virgin of Guadalupe for mercy.

The fine hairs on the back of Miguel's neck bristled. The old man's warning and now this. Icy perspiration trickled down his spine. Even as he tried to deny it, he felt the woman had spoken the truth.

He forced the thought from his mind and went in search of Enrique. Finding the study door shut, he knocked.

"Who's there?" a voice slurred.

"Diego."

"Come in. Hurry, shut the door."

Miguel entered the room, closing the door behind him. The air was foul with smoke, liquor, and the stench of fear. Wrinkling his nose, he noticed the ashtray overflowing with half-smoked cigars. His gaze went to the man slouched over the desk. "*Por Dios!* What has happened to you?" De Vega's face was gray and deeply lined. His bloodshot eyes stared, unseeing. His clothes were wrinkled and soiled. The man had aged ten years since they'd spoken yesterday.

Enrique slopped brandy into a glass and shoved it toward him. "She has come for me. I am going to die." Tears rolled down his face. "It would almost be worth it, if I could convince her it wasn't my fault." He shook his head. "But now it is too late."

Miguel sighed. The angel again. In spite of his hatred he almost felt sorry for the man. "Let me bring you some coffee." When Enrique nodded, Miguel left the room and went to fetch a tray.

A few moments later he returned and poured two cups, both strong and black. He placed one before his father-in-law. He lifted his own and took a swallow. His shaking hand told him Enrique wasn't the only one unnerved by the day's events. He waited until de Vega finished the cup. "Will you permit me to open the shutters? You might feel better with some fresh air."

"Whatever you wish, Diego. Just don't open the door."

Miguel unfastened the shutters and flung them wide, letting clean air and sunlight stream into the room. "There. It's a beautiful day outside, Enrique." He refilled the man's cup. "Have some more coffee."

He refilled his own cup and resumed his seat on the couch. "Have you thought any more about the gold shipment, or have the *pistoleros* ceased to be a problem?"

De Vega waved his hand. "Bah, who cares about them? I don't care what they threaten to do." He shrugged. "What can they do to a dead man?"

Miguel frowned. "You are not going to die. It distresses me to hear you talk that way." He removed his handkerchief to first blot his forehead, then a drop of coffee he'd spilled on his jacket. The man seemed obsessed with the notion. "You will be here a long time, doddling grandchildren on your knee."

The elder man lifted his head. His face lit with joy. "Oh, Diego. Are you telling me I'm going to be a grandfather?"

"No!" Miguel shook his head. "No," he repeated more softly. "I was referring to the future."

Enrique looked crestfallen. "I'm afraid I will never see it. Ricardo won't share the same room with Conception, let alone the same bed." He shook his head. "I really can't blame him. Before, I thought he was not good enough for my daughter, but since I have come to know him, I don't know why he would want her. I love Conception, but if I were Ricardo, I swear I would beat her."

Miguel lifted his eyebrows, trying to stifle a grin.

"Does Elena give you any trouble?"

Miguel chuckled. "Oh, yes. But not that kind." He wondered what the man would think if he knew the truth. *He'd have you shot, you fool.* "Enrique, you need some rest. I'll help you to your room and have the maid prepare a bath."

"All right, Diego." The man struggled to his feet. His eyes filled with tears. "I always wanted a son. I thought once I might have one, but things did not turn out."

Miguel frowned. Even sober the man's ramblings made no sense. He helped the elder man to his room, instructed the maid, and left. With his own head spinning in confusion, Miguel, too, decided a nap might be in order.

Entering the opposite wing, he eased up the stairway toward his room, his thoughts preoccupied by his problem with Guillermo. He still was no closer to a solution.

A slight noise made him glance up to see Elena leaving his room. He started to call out, but hesitated. Something in her manner told him she didn't wish to be seen. Staying in the shadows, he watched her take a quick look around, then slip back into her own quarters.

What had she wanted? Had she been looking for him? Maybe she'd left a note. Not knowing why he did it, he removed his high-heeled shoes and crept down the hall. Once in his room, he searched the table and dresser top. He frowned. No note. Should he ask her what she wanted? He paused, his hand on the knob. No. Something about her visit bothered him. He released the knob. His thoughts troubled, he clicked the lock shut on his door.

Catching sight of himself in the mirror, he shook his head. "You're getting as bad as Enrique." He sighed and looked longingly at the bed. After noon already. Time for *siesta.* He removed his clothes and hung them on a hanger. Stretching, he strode toward the bed and tossed back his spread, preferring to lie on the cool cotton sheets. He started to sit down when he remembered he still wore the wig. Lifting it, he placed the hunk of hair on the dresser.

Now fully prepared to enjoy his nap, he approached the bed. A slight movement at the edge of the turned-back covers caught his eye. *What the devil?* He frowned and carefully lifted the blanket. There, on his sheet, a scorpion lifted its tail, ready to strike.

"Mierda!" Snatching a towel, he wrapped it around the insect and removed it from his bed. Placing the cloth on the floor, he carefully unfolded it to expose his prey. When the elongated, reddish-brown body came into view, he crushed it with the heel of his shoe.

Shaken, he stripped the bed, searching for any others. Finding none, he collapsed in a chair, all desire for a nap forgotten. How could the scorpion have found its way into his bed? It would be impossible. Someone had put it there.

A chill crawled up his spine. If it had been night, he would have climbed into bed and been bitten. In the darkness he wouldn't have seen it. He knew the scorpion's bite was rarely fatal. But if someone wasn't trying to kill him, they intended to make him very sick. But who?

Carlos attended to all of his needs. The maids weren't even allowed in his quarters. Who else—?

The memory of a slender woman creeping from his room came unbidden to his mind. An icy hand twisted his anguished heart. His horrified gaze rose to the room next to his. "Elena!"

Chapter Twenty-two

MIGUEL spent the night walking the floor, his thoughts too troubled for any attempt at sleep. Earlier he and Carlos had torn the room apart to see if he had any more unwelcome guests. Even though they hadn't found anything else, he was still reluctant to lie down on the bed. The scorpion didn't worry him as much as it was the idea that Elena could do such a thing. A frown creased his brow as he remembered how she had avoided him since the incident. She'd even rejected his offer to dine together. As far as he knew she hadn't left her room, pleading a headache when he'd inquired after her well-being.

Why would she do it? She told me she loves me. He shook his head. *No, you fool, it's El Gato she loves.* Could that be it? Frowning, he went to the cabinet and poured himself a brandy. Could she be trying to get rid of Diego so that she could be with El Gato? It was the only reason he could think of.

Realizing the need for a clear head, he set the drink aside and forced himself to lie down. Soon exhaustion claimed him, and as the cock crowed, announcing the coming dawn, he drifted off into sleep.

Elena lay in bed, staring up at the lace canopy covering her four-poster, her mind troubled by the conversation she'd had with Conception. Why wouldn't Cepi listen? She'd tried to find some way to tell her sister about Guillermo without revealing that she'd seen them together in the garden. Conception, ignoring her warning, had poohed the idea the majordomo could be dangerous. Surely Conception couldn't be stupid enough to think she could handle the man?

Elena sighed. Nothing her sister had done lately seemed overly bright. What was the matter with her? Didn't she realize if she continued to meet Guillermo on the sly, Ricardo would surely find out?

She frowned, haunted by a remark Conception had made. "I know you can't be content with that ninny, Diego. Who could? Maybe someday soon you won't have to pretend," Conception had said, a smug smile on her face.

Elena chewed her lower lip, wishing she could have coaxed her sister into revealing more. But Conception, apparently realizing she'd already said too much, refused to continue the conversation and had made an excuse to leave.

Thinking her sister and the foreman were plotting against her, Elena had been on her guard, but Diego had no idea he might be in danger. Somehow she had to warn him. She frowned, wondering who had been in his room yesterday. She'd heard a loud thud and then footsteps running away. When she'd gone to investigate she'd found nothing. She told herself it had probably been the maid, but knew Carlos attended all of Diego's needs. Fussy beyond belief, Diego allowed no one else in his room. She'd even felt guilty entering without his knowledge.

She plucked nervously at the ties of her nightgown. How could she warn Diego when she didn't know what to warn him about? She couldn't tell him what she knew. He'd wonder why she'd been slipping around in the dark.

Since Miguel's appearance in her room, she'd felt uneasy around Diego. *Probably because you have a guilty conscience,* a little voice inside her whispered. She sighed. Everything was becoming a terrible tangle. *If only I had someone to talk to.*

Later in the morning Diego, determined to see his wife, tapped on her door.

Elena, her eyes haunted by deep shadows, answered his knock and invited him in.

He frowned at her. "Shall we sit on the terrace, my dear? I was disturbed at not being able to see you yesterday. I trust you are feeling better?"

Avoiding his eyes, she nodded. Leading the way to the balcony, she sat on one of the seats. "What did you want to see me about, Diego?"

He settled himself in the chair opposite her. "I wanted to know what you were doing in my room yesterday." He heard her gasp.

"I—I thought I heard something," she stammered. She raised her head and stared at him. "How did you know?"

He lifted his lips in a faint smile. "I smelled your perfume." He hadn't, but he didn't want her to know he'd seen her. "What was it you thought you heard?"

"I'm not sure. It was probably nothing." She shifted her gaze. "Diego?"

"What?"

"Did you find anything?" she asked hesitantly.

He narrowed his eyes. "Like what?"

She bit her lip before answering. "I don't know. Forget I asked," she said with a sigh.

"A scorpion in my bed would be hard to forget," he said sharply.

She jerked. Her eyes widened. "A scorpion!"

"Somehow a scorpion found its way into my bed."

"But how?"

"I hoped you could tell me."

"Diego, surely you don't think that I—" She shook her head.

"Of course not, my dear wife. Why would you?" he said smoothly, watching her grow pale. "You wouldn't have any reason for wanting me out of the way. Would you?"

She glanced up at him, a slow flush stealing over her face. "No!"

He locked his gaze on hers. She shifted uneasily in her seat. He hadn't wanted to believe it, but her behavior had given her away. She looked guilty as hell! She wanted to get rid of him so she could be with the bandit. Damn the unfaithful little witch! Trying to do away with her husband so she could be with her lover. He fumed, consumed with jealousy. Outraged, he clenched his trembling hands at his side to keep from shaking her. Unable to remain near her any longer for fear he'd yield to his impulses, he stood up. "I think I'd better leave."

"W-what?" she asked.

"I said I'm leaving."

"Oh. Goodbye, Diego," she murmured absently, her attention on something below.

"Goodbye!" He spun on his heel and stalked out of the room. After entering his own chamber, he sank into a chair and buried his head in his hands. Damn it! He couldn't believe how she'd behaved. She'd been so guilty, she hadn't even been able to meet his eyes. And after he'd confronted her with his suspicions, she'd practically ignored him.

He jumped to his feet. Rage filling his veins, he paced the floor. "She wants to get rid of me. Probably planning on running away with her bandit lover." He narrowed his eyes, imagining the vision of her pale body gleaming in the moonlight; of her being clasped in another's arms; her cries of ecstasy as the man made her his own. "Damn them both!"

Diego stared into the mirror. The blue eyes of the bandit stared back. He shook his head. He couldn't believe his own thoughts. "*Mierda!* She's driving me *loco!* I'm jealous of El Gato!" He groaned, rolling his eyes at the ceiling. "*I* am El Gato!"

Elena waited uneasily for night to fall, her troubled thoughts on the envelope she'd seen a maid hand Conception in the garden. She frowned, almost sure the note had been from Guillermo. A chill crawled up her spine. She was certain either he or Conception had been responsible for the scorpion in Diego's bed.

She closed her eyes, thanking God he'd found it before he'd been stung. Tears welled, knowing Diego believed she had done it. Why did he think she would have reason to do such a thing? A guilty thought made her gasp. Did he know about El Gato? She shook her head. Impossible.

She rubbed her cheek, recalling his actions. He had behaved as if he were jealous. She shook her head again. That *would* be ridiculous. But regardless of what Diego believed, she had to find out what her sister and Guillermo were up to in order to protect him. She glanced down at her navy blue dress. El Gato wore black so he could disappear in the darkness; she only hoped her garment would help her do the same.

Wearing soft-soled shoes, she slipped from her room and edged down the hall. Her petticoats rustled in the stillness. She'd never thought to remove them. She hesitated, then turned toward her room, freezing when she heard footsteps on the front stairwell. Knowing she'd be seen any minute, she threw caution aside and raced toward the back staircase.

When she reached the bottom of the stairs, she jerked the heavy door open and stepped outside. Her heart pounding, knees trembling, she sagged against the panel, fighting to regain control of her emotions. All the lights inside the house, except the one in her father's study, had been extinguished. Gloomy darkness shrouded the gardens. She scanned the courtyard, searching for movement.

Satisfied she was alone, she hurried silently toward the bench where she'd seen Conception and Guillermo meet. Relieved to find it vacant, she scooted past and hid in the thick shrubbery. She sucked in a deep breath and tried to calm her racing heart. She wiped her clammy hands on her gown. She'd made it here. Now all she had to do was wait.

A tall shadow crept toward the meeting place. The man's bulk and faint jingle of spurs told her it was Guillermo. He seemed restless, uneasy. He stared at the house, cursing softly under his breath.

Something brushed against Elena's ankle. She gasped before realizing it was only a cat.

The foreman whirled, peering in her direction.

Paralyzed with fear, Elena shrank farther into the bushes. She swallowed, shuddering with relief when he turned away from her and resumed his watch on the house. The cat purred and rubbed against her ankles. She closed her eyes, praying Guillermo couldn't hear. After a considerable length of time passed and Conception hadn't arrived, the man silently left the area.

Letting out a long sigh, Elena followed a path going the opposite way. It was longer, but at least she would avoid being seen. She ducked under an overhanging branch and tripped over the cat. The animal yowled.

An arm snaked out of the darkness and yanked her firmly against a muscled chest. "Just where are you going, Elena?"

Elena opened her mouth to scream, but before she could utter a sound, his mouth ground down on hers. His whiskeyed tongue forced her lips apart and lashed the inside of her mouth. She twisted, struggling to be free.

One massive arm held her firmly against him. The other squeezed her breast. His thighs, like tree trunks, closed tightly on each side of her legs, holding her captive.

Her heart pounded. Blood roared in her ears. She couldn't breathe. No matter how hard she tried, she couldn't get free. Light-headed from lack of oxygen, she sagged helplessly against him.

Releasing her mouth, he forced her backward, shoving her down onto the soft ground. Straddling her, he tugged at her skirt, pulling it up around her waist.

Elena gulped air, fighting the whirling darkness. Her head cleared. Aware of his intentions, she clawed at his groping hands. "No!" she croaked, renewing her struggle. "Let me go!"

He laughed. Holding her hands, he lowered himself, pressing her into the dirt with his attempt to penetrate her body.

Unable to free herself, Elena sobbed, knowing she had no chance against his suffocating strength.

Suddenly he raised his head and cursed, stiffening against her. He jumped to his feet. Grabbing her arm, he jerked her upright. "You won't say a word if you know what's good for you." Holding her close, he cruelly clutched the area between her thighs. "You'll be mine soon enough. I can wait." Cupping the back of her head with his palm, he bruised her mouth with a slobbering kiss, then shoved her backward onto the ground. Avoiding the paved walks, he muffled his footsteps in the soft earth and hurried toward the barns.

Shaken by her narrow escape, Elena drew a trembling hand to her mouth and tried to wipe away the stench of Guillermo's kiss. She felt like retching. She shuddered, closing her eyes.

A softly whistled ballad drifted on the fragrant night air. She froze, then gave silent thanks to the whistler, knowing he had scared Guillermo away.

Getting to her feet, she brushed the dirt and leaves from her clothing. She parted the bushes then cautiously stepped back onto the path. When she was certain she was alone, she lifted her skirts and raced for the safety of the house.

From the shadowed darkness, Miguel trailed behind her. When she'd gone inside, he'd climbed the vines to his balcony, fighting the urge to vomit. He'd seen her leave the wing and watched her hide in the shadows. He knew she'd been waiting for someone. He couldn't believe his eyes when Guillermo took the same path to join her.

He stalked to his door and opened it a crack, listening for her return. He heard her footsteps hurry down the hall and the soft click when she locked her door.

He eased his door shut and walked to the liquor cabinet. Cursing, he lifted an embossed brown bottle and poured a stiff drink. Downing it, he recalled the other time he'd seen the pair meet. Then he'd thought the woman was a maid. Anguish tortured his soul. He never would have believed it was Elena. He poured another drink hoping it would numb the hurt. He stared into the amber liquor, the same liquid gold as her eyes.

"Damn her!" Tightening his fingers around the glass, he hurled it against the wall. The glass shattered. Sparkling shards of crystal littered the floor. A large brown blotch covered the pale woven wall hanging and dribbled in slender fingers down to the baseboard below.

Grabbing the bottle he strode to the balcony and slumped into a chair. A bitter emptiness sapped his strength. "Why, Elena—why?" He'd believed her so gentle, so innocent. He'd risked capture just to be near her. He'd loved her.

He closed his eyes. He should have known better. After all, she was de Vega's daughter. The treacherous bitch. Not only was she unfaithful to her husband, but to her lover as well.

Damning her soul to hell, he turned up the bottle and tried to drown his pain.

Chapter Twenty-three

ELENA ran for her room as if the hounds of hell were on her heels. After locking her door, she slid to the floor, collapsing in a crumpled heap. She buried her face in her hands. Her teeth chattered from the aftermath of her fear. Uncontrollable tremors shook her body. Her breath came in ragged gasps.

She'd been a fool to take such a chance. Oh, God, what if Guillermo hadn't been frightened away? He would have raped her right there in her own garden. She felt unclean. She wiped her mouth with the back of her hand, trying to remove his taste. She shuddered at the memory.

Pulling herself upright, she staggered across the room. Frantically she yanked at her clothes, stripping them from her body. She wadded them into a bundle and shoved them under her bed out of sight. Tomorrow she'd burn them. Even if they were scrubbed until they were threadbare, she knew she'd never be able to wear them again. She couldn't stand to have anything near her that Guillermo had touched.

Wishing she had a tub full of bathwater, she lifted the china pitcher from her washstand and filled the small basin. She dipped a cloth into the cold liquid and lathered it with soap; she scrubbed her body, rubbing her skin until it hurt, then scoured her mouth and teeth. Hot tears stung her eyelids. She wished she could remove him from her mind as well.

The words he'd uttered haunted her. He claimed she'd be his before long. A spasm of fear shook her body, and she closed her eyes. She knew she'd die first.

She blinked her eyes open. *Por Dios!* In order for Guillermo to make good his threat, he'd first have to get rid of Diego. The image of her dandified husband pitted against the foreman came into her mind. She shook her head. Diego wouldn't have a chance. A deep frown creased her brow. Somehow she had to protect her husband. But how?

I need a weapon. A knife? No. She rejected the idea, remembering Guillermo's strength. She shuddered. *I don't want to get that close to him.* She chewed at her lower lip. *A gun? Yes!* She nodded thoughtfully. But it would have to be small enough to be concealed on her person.

Her decision made, she pulled on her nightgown and robe, then walked to her balcony and stared across at her father's wing. The light no longer glowed from his study. He must have gone to bed.

She scanned the courtyard, wondering if the man who whistled still roamed the grounds. The undisturbed chirping of the crickets and croaking frogs told her no one was about.

She walked swiftly to the entry and eased the lock back. Opening the door a crack, she peeped into the hall. Empty. She slipped through and pulled the panel shut behind her. The polished floorboards chilled her bare feet as she crept through the darkness to the staircase. Gripping the banister, she felt her way to the first floor.

There she hesitated. To avoid Conception's central wing and the main passageway, she'd have to leave the safety of the house and follow the dark covered veranda that ran the width of the U-shaped dwelling to her father's apartments.

She paused, her hand on the door. Her heart pounded. She couldn't do it. The idea of going outside terrified her. She swallowed. She had no choice if Diego was to be saved. Taking a deep calming breath, she opened the door and stepped through, clicking it shut behind her before she could change her mind.

She peered into the thick blackness. Fear rose in her throat, choking her. Forcing her feet to move, she hugged the wall of the house to avoid bumping into the many potted plants.

After what seemed like hours she reached the long extension marking her father's quarters. Trying to slow her racing heart, she closed her clammy hand over the knob of the salon door. Locked! She bit her lip to keep from sobbing aloud with frustration. *Now what am I going to do?*

Her gaze swept the long wall. A shadowed protrusion showed the study shutters still open. Her pulse thudded wildly. Leaving the cover of the terrace, she edged quickly across the rough flagstones. When she reached the window outside the room, she sighed with relief. Before she changed her mind, she ducked her head, parted the curtains, and slid through the opening. She landed in a heap on the floor inside.

Quivering with relief, she sat there for a moment to accustom herself to the darkness. She frowned. The room was so cluttered she'd be sure to fall over something and alert the household if she didn't light a candle. Slowly she got to her feet and closed the shutters, hoping they would block out any light. She slid her bare feet across the floor until her toe banged painfully into the side of the desk. She inched her hand forward, patting the objects on the polished top until she located the candlestick and matches. She struck the lucifer, sending a bright shower of sparks and acrid sulphur smoke into the room. Her eyes watering, she touched the trembling flame to the wick of a slender taper, then extinguished the match.

With the aid of the flickering candle, she removed a key from the desk drawer and opened the gun closet. She scanned the rows of weapons, discarding each in her mind. They were all too big. She'd never be able to carry one undetected. She sighed, ready to close the door, when she spotted a small wooden case.

She snapped the container open. Her heart leapt with excitement. Inside, gleaming against dark red velvet, lay a pearl-handled derringer. Picking it up, she read the brass plate inside the case. *Colt Model 41.* She sorted through the other items in the kit—a small silver powder case, papers, bullet mold, and caps. Knowing she'd never be able to assemble any herself, she sighed with relief when she found four complete bullets. She hurriedly slipped them and the weapon into her robe pocket, replaced the case, and locked the cabinet.

After returning the key to the drawer, she scanned the room. When everything was as she'd found it, she blew out the candle. She opened the shutters, grimacing when one squeaked, then, holding her breath, she scrambled out the window and raced for the shadowy terrace.

Although her legs felt like unset jelly when she finally reached her room, a sense of exhilaration filled her. Her mouth grim, she removed the small gun from her pocket. She curled her finger around the cold steel of the trigger, wishing she'd had it earlier. She opened the drawer of her dresser, wrapped the derringer and shells in a heavy scarf, and tucked it under her clothing. A disturbing thought knitted her brow into a frown. Now that she had it, she realized she didn't even know how to load the weapon, let alone shoot it.

*

Miguel groaned and pulled the pillow over his head to block out the bright morning sunlight. Certain if he moved his head would shatter into a million pieces, he moistened his lips and grimaced at the furry taste of his tongue. *"Mierda!"* he moaned, wincing from pain. He'd had hangovers before, but none like this.

A sharp knock sounded on his door.

"Go away!" Miguel whispered.

"Diego? It's Carlos. Open the door."

Easing to the edge of the bed, Miguel tumbled off onto the floor. He leaned against the bedpost, puzzled to see he still wore his boots. Rubbing his forehead, he stared down at the rest of his dark outfit. "What the hell?"

"Diego. Open the door!"

Grasping the bedpost, he hoisted himself to his feet and staggered across the room to draw the bolt. The move made his stomach roll. Eyes closed, he sagged against the wall. The door opened and closed.

Cursing, Carlos slid the bolt shut. "Miguel, what is wrong with you?"

Miguel opened one eye and raised a finger to his lips. "Shhh."

"Don't shush me." Carlos stepped closer and sniffed. "You're drunk!"

Drunk? Even the word hurt. Shuddering, Miguel lurched across the room and fell on the bed. He drew the pillow over his head to drown out the old man's outraged voice.

"What if I had been someone else—your wife—or de Vega? Imagine his surprise to find El Gato under his own roof, drunk and sleeping in his son-in-law's bed!" Carlos stomped across the floor. "Bah! I don't know why I bother. You don't listen. In your present condition maybe I should shoot you and save de Vega the trouble."

Miguel struggled to sit up. He moaned, clutching his head. "If you can do it quietly, go ahead. Otherwise, would you settle for getting me some coffee?"

Grumbling, Carlos stalked out of the room and slammed the door behind him.

Miguel sat on the edge of his bed and stripped off the clothes that marked him as El Gato. Easing to the closet to fetch his robe, something sharp pierced his heel. Lifting his foot, he pulled a shiny sliver from his callused flesh. Bewildered, he noticed the glass littering his floor. "What the devil?"

He traced the shards to the dark stain on the tapestry. The memory of the night before came back with a jolt. Guillermo—and Elena. The ache in his heart surpassing the pain of the hangover, he raised anguished eyes to stare out at the new day.

Elena, exhausted after a restless night, slept until mid-morning. Still clad in her nightgown and robe, although it neared noon, she sat on the settee and gratefully sipped coffee brought by her maid. Hearing a knock, she set her cup aside. "Who is it?"

"Diego."

She opened the door. "Good morn—"

Diego pushed past her and stalked into the room.

Shrugging, Elena resumed her seat and waved a hand to the chair opposite hers. "Please, sit down." When he remained standing, she raised her head to peer up at him. He looked terrible. Dark shadows ringed his eyes. His misbuttoned shirt gaped at the neck, and his wrinkled cravat hung untied. A light growth of beard showed on his cheeks. Even his mustache looked crooked. She frowned. "Diego, are you all right?"

His stance rigid, he glared at her, his blue eyes flinty and cold. "I have a headache. Do you have any powders?"

The ice in his voice cut her like a knife. Puzzled, she gaped at him. He didn't even sound like himself. Getting to her feet, she walked to her dressing table and opened the drawer. Returning, she held out the remedy he'd requested. "I hope this will help. You truly do look dreadful."

He snatched the tissue-wrapped powder from her hand. His eyes locked on hers. A glimmer of pain washed over his face, only to be replaced by a look of naked hate. Without a word he spun on his heel and left the room.

Utterly confounded by his behavior, Elena stared at the closing door. Her hand trembled, spilling the coffee she attempted to lift to her mouth. *A headache?* She shook her head, certain that whatever bothered him was far more serious than a simple headache. Could he have found another scorpion? Shaken by his visit, she locked her door and hurriedly dressed.

Going to her bureau, she removed the gun and examined it. She pressed a tiny latch. The barrel broke open, swinging sideways to reveal two small chambers. She inserted a pair of bullets and clicked the weapon shut. She sighed, feeling a small measure of satisfaction that at least she'd figured how to load it. Hoping it wouldn't go off on its own, she slipped it into her pocket. If, or when, it became necessary, she prayed she'd be able to shoot it.

Chapter Twenty-four

AFTER finishing her evening meal, Elena stepped onto her balcony to watch the sun set. She slumped onto her chair and rubbed her aching temples, hoping to relieve the tension she'd felt all day. Her troubled thoughts went to Diego and his strange behavior that morning. She couldn't forget the look in his eyes, the hurt and then the anger. What could she have done to make him act that way? Surely he didn't still believe she'd put the scorpion in his bed?

Remembering his appearance, she frowned. She'd never seen him so unkempt. It disturbed her. His headache must have been terrible to keep him in his room all day.

She twisted a lock of hair around her finger. Should she check on him? She rose to her feet. Of course she should. He was her husband. Maybe she could find out what was bothering him. Leaving her room, she knocked softly on his door. "Diego? It's Elena."

The door opened only a crack. Carlos, a hostile look on his face, barred her from entering. "The señor is sleeping." He shut the door firmly in her face.

Stunned by his actions, Elena returned to her room. She knew the man didn't like her. He'd never been more than barely civil, but tonight he behaved as if he truly hated her. Why? The question sent a bolt of pain through her already throbbing head.

Deciding to make an early night of it, Elena donned her nightclothes and retired to her bed. Lulled by the soft chorus of crickets and frogs, she drifted off to sleep.

After spending the day in bed, Miguel could contain his restless spirit no longer. He felt considerably better after a bath and had no trouble devouring the huge meal of tortillas stuffed with shredded beef and seasoned rice that Carlos brought to the room.

Remembering how cross Carlos had been with him all day, his lips lifted in a faint smile. If Miguel had been younger, the old man would have punished him. As it was, Carlos's scowls and mutterings convinced him how stupid his behavior had been. He sighed. Maybe everything had worked out for the best. At least now he could carry out his plan without feeling the least bit guilty. His eyes narrowed. In fact, he relished the idea of dispossessing all of the de Vegas, including Elena, his treacherous wife.

Recalling their morning meeting, rage flooded him again. How could she look so innocent after what she had done? And tonight, coming to see if he was all right. Probably checking to make sure he was sick enough that he couldn't intrude on her plans for the evening. He scowled. Come to think of it, he'd heard no sound from her room after she'd tapped on his door. The idea that she might be with Guillermo drew his mouth into a grim line.

He got to his feet and prowled about the room. Frustrated, and not knowing what to do with himself, he poured a glass of tequila. Feeling a sudden need for fresh air, he carried the drink to the balcony.

The soft summer breeze, fragrant with the scent of many garden flowers, wrapped around him. The refreshing splash of the fountain mingled with the croaking of frogs and chirping of crickets. The romantic scents and sounds brought back painful memories of another flower-scented night. A night of ecstasy and passion spent by a desert pool. He cursed.

In spite of his intentions to have nothing more to do with her, his gaze went to Elena's terrace. Jealousy flared. Was she in her room? Or was she with Guillermo, plotting how to be rid of him? Damn her! He gritted his teeth. The idea of her wanting another man made him crazy. He stared at her open balcony shutters. One way or another, he had to know.

His lip curled in a thin smile. Knowing Carlos had retired to his own quarters, Miguel swallowed his drink, then strode across the room and locked the door. After swiftly changing into dark clothing and mask, he scanned the courtyard. Not seeing Elena or her lover, he stepped from his balcony and dropped silently to the floor of her terrace. Standing in the shadows, he peered into her room.

The sight of her stretched out on the bed sent his pulse racing. A quick infusion of heat made him harden with passion. Cursing his traitorous body, he eased into the room and approached the bed.

Elena lay on her side, one hand under her cheek.

Even in the darkness he could see the expression on her face. It made him even more furious. She had no right to look so angelic. She should look like the whore she was.

She moaned softly and turned onto her back. Her breasts rose and fell softly under the thin, low-cut nightdress.

He sucked in a breath. Even knowing what she'd done, he wanted her. Unable to tear his gaze away, he remembered the first time she'd been his. Overcome by hunger and jealousy, he clenched his fists at his sides. His aching loins taunted him. He wanted to fill her, pound himself into her, teach her whom she belonged to. His hot gaze raked her, imagining her naked beneath him. His blood boiled with desire. Well, why not? Who had more right?

Filled with need, he drew off his high-topped boots. He ripped open the studs of his ebony shirt and tossed it aside. A grim smile on his face, he slid the tight-fitting pants down over his hips and kicked them into a pile with the rest.

Silently he padded to the edge of the bed. His eyes narrowing to slits, he yanked the sheet down, exposing the rest of her body. He leapt on top of her.

Her eyes flew open. She opened her mouth to scream.

Straddling her, he pinned her flailing arms and lowered his head, ruthlessly swallowing her protesting cries with a bruising kiss.

When she recognized him, and stopped struggling, he raised his head and glared at her. Topaz eyes wide and frightened, stared back.

"Miguel, what are you doing?"

"What's the matter, *querida*? Aren't you glad to see me?" His mouth twisted in a sneer. Ignoring the shock in her eyes, he slid his hand under the narrow shoulder ribbon of her gown and snapped it, exposing her heaving breast. He tweaked the tender tip between his fingers, making it rise rigidly under his rough caress.

She twisted beneath him, pushing at him with her hands. "No! Let me go!"

"Never." He fastened his hand in her hair. Holding her still, he ravaged her mouth with a bitter kiss. She had no right to taste so sweet, to be so soft, so warm. His hand closed on the soft mound of her breast, kneading it to firmness. His lips left hers, traveling to her throat, where her pulse pounded frantically against his tongue.

She lashed out, pounding his chest with determined fists, beating and clawing wildly before he gathered her wrists into his hand and raised them above her head. For a moment he held her there, taking in her disheveled beauty. Her tawny eyes gleaming like an enraged tigress only served to make him want to conquer her, to make her want him as she had no other man, to drive her mad with passion as she had him. His gaze went from her mutinous mouth to her heaving breast. Holding her immobile, he gave her a mocking smile and bent his head to torment her dusky nipple with his tongue. He smiled cynically when Elena moaned softly.

Leaving one nipple, he ripped the strap, exposing the other. Enclosing the bud with his mouth, he lapped at it with his tongue. Drawing it into a tight peak, he sucked at it greedily.

When his knee forced her thighs apart, she stiffened, her golden eyes pleading.

More gently he lowered his head to hers and tasted the saltiness of her tears. His hand left her mouth to slip between her legs, taunting her with his fingers, caressing her, making her warm and wet, in spite of her struggles. He teased her, arousing her to a fever pitch until she arched against him. Satisfied, he removed his hand, leaving her wanting.

Her lips were warm and swollen under his as he plundered her mouth, claiming her nectar for his own. His gaze locked on hers. "You are mine, Elena. Mine! Never forget it." He slid down her body and tasted the sweet honeycombed core of her, his tongue flicking the swollen bud, torturing her, proving his mastery. Then he withdrew, leaving her panting and unfulfilled.

He raised his head to gaze at her. Outrage and desire blazed in her eyes. His relentless fingers teased her, again bringing her to the brink before withdrawing. She trembled violently under his savage, yet tender, lovemaking. "Please," she whispered.

Aroused to a point he never thought possible, he still held back, ignoring the misery of his raging body, the need to castigate greater than his craving for fulfillment.

"Damn you, Miguel," she sobbed.

Hearing her cry of frustration, he raised his head and gave her a cold smile. "And now since you're so eager, I will show you whom you belong to."

Parting her legs, he plunged into her, burrowing himself into her soft satin warmth. He moved slowly, deliberately, each time withdrawing before he impaled her again. Her arms clutched him closer. Wrapping her legs around his back, she arched her hips to receive him.

"Is this what you want, Elena?" His lips crushing hers, he thrust upward faster and faster, each time stopping just before she attained her release. He throbbed achingly inside her, his agony as great as her own.

"I hate you!" she cried when he left her lips.

Unable to delay any longer, he sneered, mocking her, while he furiously drove into her, strongly, deeply, leading her ever upward on waves of passion.

She cried out, arching toward him, at last reaching the peak of her desire.

Dizzy, he clasped her hips, lifting her to meet his thrust, swept along on an undulating fiery crest until he shuddered, exploding, filling her body with his molten seed.

When the tide spent itself, washing him back to gentle golden sands, he collapsed on top on her, his body covered with the wet sheen of their joining. His breathing ragged, he finally withdrew to lay beside her.

Now, with his blood and anger cooled, he noticed the tears staining her cheeks. Reason returned, along with the horror of what he'd done. He told himself he didn't care if he'd hurt her. Hadn't she deserved it? But her muffled sobs tore at his soul. Feeling sick at heart, he raised a shaking hand to her cheek to wipe away her tears.

She flinched away. Topaz eyes, which had held only love and trust for him, now filled with bitter anguish and sorrow. "Why, Miguel? What have I done that you should treat me so?" she whispered.

He stared, shocked by the wounded look in her eyes. He'd intended to punish her, torture her for being with Guillermo, but his own heart grieved, appalled by his brutal actions. Then remembering Elena and Guillermo together, he pushed his feelings aside.

"Why, Miguel? Why do you treat me like—like a whore?"

He couldn't believe she'd asked. The woman must be a witch! A devil inside an angel's body determined to torment him into madness. Unable to answer, he rose from the bed and slipped into his clothes.

"You bastard. You filthy bandit." She spoke each word distinctly, scornfully, fury radiating from her slender body. She slid from the bed and walked to him. Her eyes blazing, she lifted her hand and slapped his face.

The sharp crack of her palm on his cheek sounded like a gunshot in the quiet of the room. For a moment shock held him motionless, then a white-hot rage took its place. He grabbed a handful of silky, black hair and yanked her to him. He drew back an open hand.

"What do you intend to do now, beat me?" she hissed, her voice filled with contempt.

Tempted, Miguel closed his eyes. Trembling, he slowly raised his lashes. He released his grip. "We aren't finished yet, *querida*."

"Get out! And don't come back. I don't want to see you again. Not ever." She tossed her hair out of her eyes. "If you show up here again, I won't need to call my father. I'll shoot you myself."

His mocking gaze scanned her nude body. He laughed.

A knock sounded on the door.

"Elena?" a voice called softly. "It's Conception. Let me in."

Miguel grabbed his boots and retreated to the balcony, uneasily wondering what Elena would do. Hurriedly yanking his footwear on, he melted into the shadow of the vines.

Elena shook her head. *What else could go wrong?* She wiped the tears from her face and stared into the darkness.

Hastily wadding the torn nightgown, she stuffed it beneath the covers. She jerked another gown from her drawer and pulled it over her head. Slipping on her robe, she released a ragged sigh and went to answer her sister's summons.

When she released the lock, Conception shoved the door open and entered the room. "It certainly took you long enough."

"I was asleep," Elena said. "What do you want?"

"Light a lamp," Conception said, flouncing over to plop down on the settee. "We need to talk."

Hearing the angry tone of her sister's voice, Elena sighed. Diego, Carlos, Miguel, and now Conception. She shook her head in despair, wondering how much more she would be forced to endure. Her hand shaking, she lit the small lamp and turned it to a low steady glow. She sat on the chair opposite her sister. "All right. What is it?" she asked, anxious to get it over with.

Conception's eyes narrowed. "I think you already know. I've talked with Guillermo. He told me how he found you hiding in the bushes. You intended to spy on us, didn't you?"

"I wanted to save you from yourself. You wouldn't listen to me. The man is dangerous."

Conception sniffed. "Is that why you threw yourself into his arms?"

Elena stared at her sister, unable to comprehend what she was saying. "What?"

Conception tilted her head. Her scornful gaze swept over Elena. "He told me how you attempted to seduce him. And would have succeeded, but he came to his senses and pushed you away."

"Sangre de Cristo!" Elena gasped. "Surely you don't believe him?"

"Why shouldn't I?"

"I admit I did go there to spy on you. I wanted to protect you. I stepped on the cat and Guillermo found me." Elena shuddered as the memory of his hands on her flooded back. "He threw me to the ground." She closed her eyes. "He tried to rape me."

"Oh? Then why didn't he?" Conception scoffed. "If that had been his intention, you couldn't have stopped him."

Elena drew in a ragged breath. "Someone else was in the garden. He was whistling. That's what scared Guillermo away."

"Really? I doubt anything would frighten him."

Elena, frustrated and angry, jumped to her feet. "Conception, you are a fool. Why else would you risk everything to meet with scum like Guillermo?" She halted in front of her sister. "What do you think Ricardo would do if he found out? Is being with that bastard worth risking your marriage?"

Conception rose to confront her. "Ricardo will never find out—unless you tell him. And if you know what is good for you, you won't." She pushed past Elena and left the room, slamming the door behind her.

Shaking her head, Elena clicked the lock. She hurried outside but found the balcony empty. El Gato was gone. She rubbed her pounding temples. Her headache had returned with a vengeance.

Today she'd felt pushed and pulled in every direction, as if she were in the midst of a whirlwind. A bleak smile crossed her face as she wondered if she'd still be in one piece when it was over.

Miguel sat on his balcony, pondering the conversation he overheard. Had he misjudged Elena? Had his jealousy made him see things that weren't there? He frowned, thinking back to that night. If what Elena said was true, it would explain what she was doing in the bushes. The woman he had seen with Guillermo must have been Conception. The blond bitch hadn't even tried to deny she'd met with him.

A chill crawled up his back. Elena said the man tried to rape her. My God! How could he have believed they were making love? He closed his eyes, shaking with outrage that the foreman dared touch her. Ironically, he and Juan had stopped her from leaving the hacienda in order to protect her, and now he'd discovered she'd been attacked in her own garden. He clenched his fists at his sides, wanting to kill the bastard.

Elena must have seen Guillermo and Conception together, too. That's why she was spying. He rubbed his chin thoughtfully. What could the majordomo and Conception be up to?

He stared into the darkness, wondering if Juan knew anything. He sighed. It was too late to see him tonight.

He frowned, suddenly remembering the incident with the scorpion. Elena claimed she'd heard something. Had she? Was she innocent of that as well? A glimmer of hope loosened the band constricting his heart. He'd never dared to love before. Maybe that's why the idea of her being unfaithful had hurt so much. Overwhelming shame washed over him at the ruthless way he'd treated her. He shook his head. She must think him worse than Guillermo.

If she was truly guiltless, he had a lot to make up for. He'd kneel on bended knee and beg her to forgive him. And when she did, he'd take her in his arms and cover her with kisses, tenderly showing her how much he cared as he made her his own.

The wounded look in her eyes haunted him. She'd never forgive him. And why should she, after the way he'd taken her? He cradled his head in his hands. *"Por Dios,* what have I done?" He turned his gaze toward her room. Maybe if he apologized? He shook his head, recalling her words. How could he apologize for that? She hated him. His own brutal actions had destroyed the fragile love they'd shared. *Oh, querida, what have I done?* The realization that she was forever lost to him came as a shock. A part of him withered and died, leaving him empty and hollow inside.

He slumped in the chair and tried to convince himself it was for the best. It might save her more hurt later when she found out who he was. His mouth thinned in a bitter line. But until that time he'd see that neither Guillermo, nor anyone else, including himself, ever hurt her again.

The bleakness of his life without Elena loomed before him. Anguished tears filled his eyes and overflowed down his cheeks. He knew he would give anything, even the ranch he had so long coveted, just to have her love again. Feeling more alone than he ever had before, he sat in the darkness and waited for the coming dawn.

Chapter Twenty-five

IN her bed Elena turned bleak eyes toward the bright new day. She hoped to awaken and find it had all been a bad dream, but the ache in her heart told her different. El Gato had come to her last night. But the bitter man that had taken her was not the one she'd grown to know and love. He'd been a ruthless stranger, one that sought to punish her for some unknown transgression. Outrage growing, her mouth tightened, remembering he'd almost struck her.

How dare he treat her like a whore? Last night he'd used her, tormented her before satisfying his lust. Then he'd left without so much as a word of explanation, as if she should know why he'd behaved as he had.

In spite of her resentment, tears welled in her eyes and trailed down her cheeks. She felt betrayed. He'd taken the love, which with tenderness, she would have given him freely, eagerly. Possessing her in such a way that he'd made her feel dirty.

She'd sensed the anger and frustration in his voice when he'd told her she belonged to him. She'd also seen the pain, the suffering in his eyes.

Could he be jealous of Diego? Strange, when he'd never mentioned her husband before. Why had he treated her that way? "Why, Miguel? Why?" she whispered to the empty room.

*

The day after El Gato's nocturnal visit, Diego, leaving
only a note, left on another trip. Although his departure
eased Elena's concern for his safety, she felt frightened to
be alone. During his absence, she stayed in her quarters.
The one time she did visit the village, she made certain she
was locked safely inside her room before dark.

Her nights were plagued by dreams of El Gato. She told
herself she hated him, yet she couldn't get him out of her
mind. How would she survive, never again knowing the
heat of his body pressed to hers; the safety of his strong
arms encasing her, holding her next to him as he murmured
soft words of love in her ear? The feel of his lips on hers,
searing her, branding her as his own? How could she live,
never again experiencing the passion when he drew her with
him to such fiery heights?

Something twisted inside her, torturing her with the
knowledge that she'd never see him again. What she'd
feared so long ago had come to pass. He was gone, never
to return, and she was only half alive without him.

Three weeks had passed since that fateful night, and
although it was past time for breakfast, Elena lingered in
her bath, hoping the flower-scented warmth would ease her
troubled spirit. Diego had returned yesterday, but he still
had not come to see her. She had no idea why he'd made
the sudden trip or if his attitude toward her had changed.
With Conception not speaking to her and Juan treating her
coolly, the only people she'd talked to in almost a month
were Lupe and Consuela.

Feeling a bit sorry for herself, she reluctantly climbed
out of the now-cool water. Drying, she winced when she
patted the towel over her breasts. They seemed swollen,
tender. Slipping on her underclothes, she frowned. Her

chemise barely fit. Had she gained weight? She stared at herself in the mirror. Her waist was trim as ever but her top was definitely larger. How could that be? Maybe she'd been eating too much. She rejected the idea. Lately everything she'd eaten had churned in her middle and, after a few bites, she'd pushed it away. She eyed herself again. Could it be because she was now a woman? That must be it. After trying on three gowns, she finally found a garment that would button.

She'd just finished dressing when Lupe called from outside the door. Bidding the girl to enter, Elena picked up her brush and walked to the terrace, waiting while the maid summoned two men from the hall to empty the tub.

By the time she'd dried her hair, Lupe appeared again, this time with her breakfast. Elena sat on the settee, instructing the girl to put the tray on the table in front of her. Even though she felt wretchedly unhappy, her stomach growled hungrily. She lifted the domed silver lid. The fragrant aroma of ham, eggs, and hot biscuits rose in a mass of steam, assaulting her nose. Her stomach lurched. She gagged. Gasping, she slapped the cover over the food.

"Is something wrong, señora?" Lupe asked, lifting the lid to examine the meal. Again, the odor invaded the room.

"Oh—" Elena choked, reeling away. Clamping her hand over her mouth, she ran for the chamber pot. Over and over she heaved while Lupe held her trembling body and wiped her face and lips with a wet cloth until her nausea passed. When Lupe helped her to the couch, Elena, weak and faint, slumped against the cushions and closed her eyes. Raising her lashes, she gave Lupe a grateful smile when the maid placed a cold, wet cloth on her forehead. "I don't know what is the matter with me," Elena said faintly. "I felt fine until I smelled the food."

Lupe's mouth split in a broad grin. She giggled.

Elena frowned at her. "What is so funny?"

"Maybe the señora is *encinta?*"

"Madre de Dios!" Elena swallowed, her eyes widening. She stared at her middle in horror. Mentally she counted back to the time when she'd had her last flow. Over two months. Tears filled her eyes and rolled down her cheeks. *Santa Maria! It can't be true.* But she knew as sure as apple trees had blossoms, she was pregnant with El Gato's child.

Unable to stay in his room, knowing Elena was so near, Miguel donned his costume, carefully checking his appearance in the mirror. The deep violet suit did nothing to disguise the shadows under his eyes. The lavender blouse only made him look more sallow. But still, as Diego was known to suffer from various illnesses, real or imaginary, nobody could possibly suspect what was really wrong.

After his unfortunate visit as El Gato, unable to face Elena, he'd left the Spanish Angel and gone to his own small ranch. Sending Carlos to the mesa, Miguel stayed in seclusion and tried to find an answer to his dilemma. He'd considered his choices. He could either stay on the Spanish Angel as Diego and be tortured with Elena's nearness, knowing he could never again claim her as his own. Or he could give up his quest for revenge and return to Colorado, never to see her again. Neither gave him any comfort.

Heaving a weary sigh, he went downstairs and crossed the courtyard, making his way to Enrique's wing. Since it was nearly noon, he knew he'd find the man in his study.

Escorted into the room by the houseboy, he greeted his father-in-law. Taking a seat, he appraised the elder man's appearance. "You are looking much better, Enrique. I take it the spirits are no longer roaming the halls?"

Enrique gave him a startled look. "*Por favor,* Diego. Do not jest about such things." He narrowed his eyes, peering at him. "I may look better, but you, Diego, look terrible."

Miguel sighed. "I have suffered from headaches lately. It might be the weather." He drew his handkerchief from his pocket and mopped his face. The damned wig was stifling and itched. He felt like a one-legged dog with fleas, longing to scratch but unable to do so.

He looked at the man across from him. "Have you found a way out of your predicament yet?"

Enrique leaned closer. "Yes, my friend. I have decided to take your advice."

His attention piqued, Miguel listened intently. "You mean—?"

De Vega raised a finger to his lips. He nodded. "This time it will be kept such a secret that even I will not know when the gold is to leave the mine."

Miguel frowned. "Why?"

"Every time the shipment is planned, the gold has been stolen. If it is loaded and hauled away on the spur of the moment, no one will know when it is leaving." He waved his hand. "So no one will be able to steal it."

Miguel pursed his lips. The old fool made sense even if Miguel did hate to admit it. He frowned. It would complicate things, however. "Well, *amigo,* I am glad to see you in such high spirits." He shook his head. "I wish my own problems could be solved as easily."

"Why, Diego, what is the matter?"

"I fear things aren't going well with my recent investments. I find myself losing money daily. If I intend to save anything, I must come up with some quick cash."

"If a loan would help, Diego, I do expect to have the money from the gold within a couple of months."

Diego brightened, then gave Enrique his most woeful look. "Thank you for your kind offer, but I am afraid that will be too late." He held his breath, waiting.

Enrique frowned. "Leave it to me. Would three or four weeks be too long?"

Miguel smiled hopefully. "I think I can hold out that long. I don't know how to thank you." He raised a hand to massage his temples. "I hate to leave you so soon, but I am afraid my headache has returned. Will you excuse me?"

"Of course. I do hope a rest will have you feeling better."

Miguel got to his feet. Dabbing his face, he pranced out of the room. He grinned. In truth, except for the damned wig, he felt like kicking his heels together. The old fool had fallen for his sad tale. Now knowing an approximate date, he could make plans to steal the shipment.

As he left the house, his gaze lifted to Elena's window. He forced his eyes away, unable to bear the ache in his heart. In spite of his elation, weariness settled heavily on his shoulders. He headed for his room, hoping this time he could lose himself in sleep.

By afternoon Elena's nausea had passed. In fact, she felt wonderful. She cautioned Lupe not to say anything about her pregnancy, saying she wanted to make sure. But Elena knew she didn't need to wait; she was certain. Still numb from the idea, she sat in the shade of her terrace and idly twisted a lock of hair. She rubbed her middle with a sense of wonder. *A child.* Sadness washed over her. *El Gato's child.* The only problem was what to do about it.

Should she tell Diego? Remembering the party, she knew he'd make a wonderful father, and he had wanted her to become pregnant. She frowned, knowing it wasn't so much that he wanted a child. To him, it was only another means of obtaining more of the ranch. A child should be loved for itself. She remembered how she'd felt holding Rosita's baby and the emptiness when she'd handed it back. Elena knew she would love the little one. But how could she bear to see a miniature of Miguel every day for the rest of her life without feeling his loss even more keenly?

She closed her eyes, imagining a sturdy little boy with black hair, deep blue eyes, and a mischievous grin, an exact replica of his father. *Oh, Miguel, what would you do if you knew we were going to have a baby?* Tears welled under her eyelids as she remembered his last visit. *Would you even care?*

Miguel rose from his nap rested. His mind clearer, he knew he had to make preparations for his departure from the hacienda. Concern for Elena's safety filled his thoughts. What would happen to her if he was caught—or killed? He shuddered, remembering her close call in the garden. He'd felt guilty leaving last time, knowing she wasn't safe with Guillermo around. He had a desperate need to see her.

After donning his disguise, he knocked at her door. A few moments later it opened.

Elena, a wary look on her face, greeted him. "Hello, Diego. Won't you come in?"

He stared at her, suddenly feeling awkward and afraid. "Would you have dinner with me?" he blurted. He saw her hesitate. "Please."

She gave him a gentle smile and nodded. "Of course." She frowned down at her dress. "Should I change?"

He swept his gaze over her. In the simple white gown with her hair down, she looked incredibly beautiful. "Never," he murmured softly. Catching himself, he shook his head. "You look fine, my dear." He offered her his arm. "Shall we go down now?"

She closed her door and slipped her hand through the crook of his arm. Her light perfume tantalized his senses, making him dizzy. He lifted his other hand and placed his palm over her fingers. Too soon, they reached the bottom of the stairs and the dining room.

When she paused at the end of the long table, he shook his head. "Please, will you sit there, next to me?" He waved his hand toward the head of the table. When she nodded, he motioned the maid to move her place setting. He drew out her chair and seated her, then sat at his usual place. "Would you like wine?" he asked, lifting the decanter.

"No." She smiled. "But I would like a glass of milk."

Milk? He shrugged. "Milk it is." After sending the servant to fetch it, he turned to her. "I want to apologize for my recent behavior. I have not been myself lately." That was certainly the truth. He picked up her hand, encasing it between his palms. "Will you forgive me?" he pleaded, his voice husky.

She stared at him. "Of course, Diego," she said slowly, a puzzled frown on her face.

"You will?" he asked. His heart soared, only to thud to earth when he realized with a start that it was Diego she was forgiving, not El Gato. Still, he could not let go of her hand. Not speaking, he gazed at her. She looked different somehow. Softer, with a kind of glow about her. He watched a slow flush turn her face pink. "You're blushing."

"You are staring at me." She tucked her head.

"Am I?" He grinned. "If I am it is because I find you so lovely."

She raised her eyebrow. "Diego, are you all right?"

He nodded, memorizing every line of her face, her long graceful neck, dwelling on the creamy swell of her breasts brimming above her low-cut neckline. He sighed, longing to caress them.

"Señor?"

"Hmm?"

"May I serve *la comida* now?"

"What?" He glanced up, surprised to see a servant beside him, holding a heavy tray of food. "Oh, yes." Feeling Elena's fingers wiggle under his, he realized with a shock he still held her hand. Reluctantly he freed her.

After the servant finished filling their plates, Miguel's eyes seldom left Elena. He stifled a grin, watching her devour her meal, eating almost a whole chicken by herself, two helpings of the savory rice, tamales stuffed with spiced shredded meat and chilies, along with fresh greens, squash, and three glasses of milk.

He raised a brow. He'd been hungry and only managed a quarter of what she'd consumed. He saw her push a bite of bread around to sop up the last of the gravy before popping it into her mouth.

She glanced up, embarrassed to catch him watching her.

He grinned. "You must have been starving."

She tucked her head and peeped at him from under long, sooty lashes. "I guess I was."

"Do you have room for dessert?" he asked as the maid cleared the dishes away. A second servant appeared with a tray of peach tarts, fresh fruit, and bowls of rich, creamy *panocha*, a pudding.

She nodded.

He managed one small tart while she amazed him by eating three, along with a little of everything else. He rubbed his chin thoughtfully. Apparently her anger at El Gato hadn't affected her appetite. After the meal he sipped a fragrant cup of rich coffee while she drank yet another glass of milk.

She sighed and raised her napkin to blot a white mustache from her upper lip. "Delicious."

He shook his head, incredulous. "Would you like to walk in the garden? The night is warm."

"That would be delightful, Diego."

He rose and stood behind her to help her from her chair. Rising, she turned toward him. Suddenly the smile left her face. She swayed unsteadily.

Alarmed, he reached out to catch her. "Elena, are you all right?"

She sagged against him, resting her head against his chest. After a moment she lifted her head. "I'm all right now. It was only a dizzy spell."

A dizzy spell? Probably from all that food, he thought. His heart pounding, he held her close and gently kissed the top of her shining locks. His senses reeling, he placed his hand under her chin, tilting her head. "Are you feeling better now, *querida*?"

Nodding, she sighed, her full red lips slightly parting. "Diego, I have something—" She paused, raising warm topaz eyes to meet his.

Mesmerized by her nearness, he slowly bent toward her.

"Diego!" a sharp voice said behind him.

Miguel blinked. He stared at the woman in his arms, horrified at what he'd almost done. Giving her a quick peck on the forehead, he forced a smile. "You probably ate too much," he said primly. "Maybe we should forget the walk."

The dreamy look left her face. Her mouth drooped in disappointment. She sighed. "Yes. That must be it." She stepped away from him. "Good night, Diego."

Miguel reluctantly watched her leave the room, then turned to face Carlos's anger. But the old man was gone. Feeling sad and more depressed than ever, Miguel slowly went upstairs to his room.

Chapter Twenty-six

JUST after dusk a week later, Miguel paced the floor of his room, his mind occupied with plans to steal the gold. The day before, Carlos had left to alert his men. When the old man returned, he and Diego would take a "business" trip, then Carlos and El Gato would go to the mesa to wait.

A rueful smile twisted Miguel's lips, imagining de Vega's outrage if he knew a member of El Gato's band was one of the men guarding the mine. Another, old Felipe, delivered goat's milk twice a week to the workers' families and would receive word of any unusual activity.

Miguel frowned. He had everything set, except for Elena. This morning, from his terrace, he heard her retching. Several times in a row she'd been violently ill, but later in the day she seemed fine. When he inquired about his wife's welfare, Consuela told him she was asleep. The woman had smiled at his concern and told him not to worry.

Even though the maid didn't seem the least bit troubled, he felt uneasy, but it was probably some kind of woman thing. Being an orphan, raised in a household of men, Miguel hadn't been around many women. Maybe that was why Elena confused him so much.

His frown deepened. Even though he hadn't spoken to her, he'd seen her walking in the gardens two days ago. He noticed she'd stayed in plain sight of the house and returned to her room before dark. If Carlos hadn't been with him, he would have joined her. But considering what had almost happened after dinner the other night, he thought it was just as well the elder man had been present.

He was miserable knowing he couldn't take her in his arms and love her. Just being near drove him out of his mind. He longed to go to her and beg her forgiveness. He wondered, if El Gato did appear in her bedroom, would she truly shoot him as she'd promised? He snorted. After the way he'd behaved, he couldn't blame her if she did.

He hated to be away from the hacienda for so long. How could he concentrate on the job at hand when he was so worried? What if she was seriously ill? What if Guillermo caught her again? He ran his hand through his hair. "*Mierda!* These thoughts are making me crazy." He decided to confide in Juan. Maybe he'd have a solution.

He wrinkled his nose and stared at the hank of hair on his dresser. Heaving a disgusted sigh, he slapped the mop on top of his head and tucked his own dark fringe in around the edges. While Diego could wander about the grounds unnoticed, El Gato, regretfully, could not. He adjusted the padding under his coat, stuck his mustache into place, then headed for the back staircase and the stable.

Gripping the railing of her terrace, Elena squinted at the figure hurriedly crossing the flagstone courtyard. "Diego?" She leaned over the balcony. It had to be. No one else would wear an apricot suit. *He's heading for the barn....* Her brow wrinkled into a puzzled frown. *That is strange, considering how he feels about horses.*

Uneasy, she glanced up at the fast-falling darkness. *Madre de Dios, what if he runs into Guillermo? Diego would be helpless. He doesn't know he's in danger. I have to do something.*

She ran to her dresser and took out the derringer. Grimacing, she closed her hand around the pearl butt. At least it was loaded. Hoping she could figure out how to fire it if need be, she stuffed it into the pocket of her rust-colored dress and ran down the stairs.

Nearing the barn where she'd seen Diego disappear, she glimpsed a bulky figure slipping in ahead of her. *Guillermo!* Her heart pounding, her mouth dry, she closed her sweating palm around the handle of the gun. *Madre de Dios, please don't make me have to use it.*

Miguel crept through the gloomy building. Only vaguely aware of the pungent smell of horses, manure, and sweet hay, he passed stall after stall until he reached the room where Juan slept. Seeing a light over the open half door, he knocked softly.

Juan peered out. His eyes widened. "Diego?"

"We need to talk." Miguel scanned the dim hallways.

"Not here," Juan said. "It's not safe. Someone might get suspicious."

Miguel grinned. "Especially since Diego is terrified of horses. Can you meet me tomorrow night at the pond?"

Juan nodded. "Now get out of here."

"All right, *amigo. Buenas noches.*" Miguel backed out of the light and melted into the shadows. His mind on Elena, he hurried through the dark corridor. He stumbled over something in his path and fell to his knees.

A small caliber gun cracked. A bullet whined past his head and thudded into the wall behind him.

Cursing, Miguel flattened himself and rolled to one side. He reached out, groping for whatever had tripped him. His hand closed over the handle of a pitchfork. Lifting the weapon, he peered through the gloom.

"Diego!" Crying hysterically, Elena ran toward him.

"Get down!" he shouted. He grabbed her, pulling her down beside him in the hay. Something gleamed in her hand. *Por Dios, she has a gun!* Dodging to one side, he yanked the weapon away. Horrified, he stared at her. "It was you?" he gasped. "You shot at me?"

"No!" Sobbing, she sat up and frantically patted his body. "Are you all right?"

"Yes," he hissed. Grabbing her fluttering hand, he pushed her flat. He sniffed the barrel of the small gun. It hadn't been fired. Holding her down, he shielded her with his body. "What are you doing out here?" he whispered angrily, squinting into the darkness for his assailant.

"I saw you leave the house. I felt you were in danger, so I followed. When you entered the barn, someone went in after you. I think it was Guillermo." Her voice died on a sob. "When I heard the gun, I thought he'd killed you."

A lantern bobbed through the darkness, then Juan knelt beside them. He stared at Miguel, his eyes widening when he noticed Elena. "I heard a gunshot. What happened?"

"Somebody target practicing in the dark. He missed," Miguel said tersely. "Did you see anything?"

"No, but I heard someone running away."

"We don't want to attract any more attention," Miguel told him. "Maybe you'd better go back to bed."

"You're right. Good night," Juan whispered. He blew out the lantern and disappeared in the darkness.

Miguel turned to the woman lying beside him in the hay. Shaken by the chance she'd taken, he gathered her into his arms. "*Por Dios*, Elena, you could have been killed." He felt her shiver. Even fearing Guillermo as she did, she'd run into the barn to protect him. Trembling, he held her closer. God, if anything had happened to her— He stared down, sensing her eyes on him. "Oh, *querida*, don't ever do anything like that again."

Her warm, irresistible scent wrapped around him, robbing him of reason. He bent his head and gently kissed her forehead, her eyelids, her lips. His kiss deepened. His tongue eased inside her mouth, savoring her sweetness. His hand caressed her breast, feeling the fullness as he circled her nipple with his thumb. Overcome with love, he lowered her to the hay and nuzzled her neck with hot kisses.

"Diego?" she gasped.

Diego! The name cooled him as effectively as a bucket of ice water. He sucked in his breath and drew quickly away. "Forgive me, little one. This whole unpleasant business has me quite undone. The idea that you, whom I love like a sister, could have been injured . . ." He quickly straightened his wig. *A sister? My God! If she believes that, she'll believe anything. Another minute and I would have taken her right here in the hay.*

Afraid he might yet yield to temptation, he struggled to his feet. His ankle throbbed with pain. Discovering the bruised joint would bear his weight, he held out an unsteady hand, clasped Elena's fingers, and drew her to her feet. "I think we'd better go to the house," he said hoarsely.

She stared up at him, her forehead wrinkled in concern. "Are you all right, Diego?"

"I hurt my leg. It is nothing." Even with the discomfort, he knew he was lucky. If he hadn't fallen, the bullet would have parted his skull.

Holding her hand, he hobbled to their wing. He paused in the dim light of the hall outside her room. Weak with longing, he gazed at the smudge on her cheek, her rumpled dress, her tousled locks. She'd never looked more beautiful. Smiling, he removed a wisp of hay from her hair.

He lifted her hand and placed the derringer in her palm. "Keep this with you, but for God's sake, don't go outside after dark again."

Tilting her head, she gave him a strange look. "All right."

He frowned. "Do you know how to use it?"

She shook her head.

He hesitated, afraid she might shoot herself. But still he would feel better knowing she had protection. He took the gun and removed the bullets, then showed her how to cock and fire it. When he felt she understood, he put the bullets into the chambers and handed it back to her.

He gently gripped her shoulders and stared down into her eyes. "I must leave tomorrow on business. I'm not sure when I'll be back. I asked Juan to watch out for you."

"You did?"

"That's why I went to the barn. Elena, you mean a great deal to me. I worry about your safety." He hesitated. "I want you to promise me something."

"What?"

"If that bastard Guillermo comes near you, shoot him."

She gasped. "How did you know?"

"I know a lot more than you think, *querida*." He smiled at the bewildered look on her face. "You look exhausted, my sweet. I think it's time you went to bed." Turning her doorknob, he eased her inside her room. Unable to resist, he cupped his fingers under her chin and brushed her lips with a lingering kiss. Afraid of what might happen if he tarried longer, he backed through the door and closed it.

Still tingling from his kiss, Elena stared at the closed door and touched her lips. Her heart pounded, leaving her breathless. She shook her head, confused by his strange behavior and her own reaction to it. She closed her eyes remembering his caress—his kisses—his deep voice. The way he'd called her *querida*. If she hadn't known it was Diego, she wouldn't have believed it.

She stared at the derringer in her hand. For someone who'd claimed to be afraid of guns, Diego appeared to know a lot about them. Sighing, she walked to the dresser and put the weapon away. Maybe exhaustion had distorted her ability to think, for nothing that had happened the whole evening made any sense.

Elena woke just after dawn, intending to tell Diego good-bye before he left. After hurriedly throwing on a robe and running a brush through her hair, she knocked at his door. "Diego?" Receiving no answer, she entered to find his bed made and the room empty. The strange combination of cigar smoke and lavender hung in the air. Oddly disappointed, she returned to her own quarters.

Taking off her robe, she slipped back into bed. She'd slept fitfully the night before, unable to put Diego's peculiar behavior out of her mind. When she did sleep, her dreams were confused, mixed versions of her husband and El Gato. She didn't understand her response to Diego's kisses and caresses the night before. Admittedly, she was fond of him. After all, he was her husband. But why had his kiss, his touch, lit her veins with the same thrilling passion she'd felt in the arms of El Gato? She shook her head, not knowing the answer.

She rubbed her middle. Maybe it was her pregnancy. She certainly felt different, going from tears to hysterical laughter over the silliest things. And after being so sick every morning that even the faintest scent of food sent her running for the chamber pot, by afternoon she wanted to devour everything in sight.

Lately, always exhausted, she'd spent most of each day sleeping or doing needlework, something that had bored her before. Evenings, she'd spent on the terrace in dreamy anticipation of the new life growing inside her. So far she'd managed to keep her secret. Only Lupe and Consuela knew. She ran a hand over her enlarged bosom to her still slim waistline. Soon her figure would thicken, blossoming with the growing babe, making it impossible to hide.

Her thoughts drifted to Miguel. She closed her eyes, sad that her baby would never know its true father. Their love had been so impossible—she, wife to another man—he, a bandit with a price on his head. If only things had been different. Her lip quivered, remembering the last time he'd been here. Would she ever see him again? And if she did, how would he react finding she carried his child? She wiped away the tears trailing down her cheeks.

And there was Diego. She knew when he returned, he would have to be told. He had already questioned Consuela about her illness. She knew the maid wondered why Elena hadn't been eager to tell him he was to be a father.

She frowned. After he'd returned alone from Santa Fe, Diego hadn't said anything further about wanting a child. Maybe he'd changed his mind. If so, how would he react to the news? Her spirits sank.

She uneasily remembered he hadn't mentioned anything more about her taking a lover, either. Now she not only had to tell him she'd been unfaithful, but that she was pregnant as well. How could she tell him about the baby without revealing El Gato was the father?

A queasiness rose in her middle. She was grateful no one knew what the bandit looked like. With Diego's blue eyes and her own dark looks, the child could easily pass for theirs. She tried to tell herself that, because Diego was a kind man and he cared for her, he would also love the baby.

Still not convinced, she was suddenly glad he was away. She wouldn't have to worry about his safety. And perhaps now, before he returned, she could find a way to break the news.

Chapter Twenty-seven

FINDING it hard to concentrate on the upcoming mission, Miguel left the jubilant men gathered around the campfire and strolled toward the ramada. Passing the cluster of shacks, he smiled when a group of half-naked children and a trio of barking dogs darted by.

At the high altitude a light sprinkling of frost glittered like diamonds on the sage and chemiso. The pungent scent of greasewood and cedar filled the clean, clear air. Taking a puff on his cigar, Miguel watched the smoke and his breath drift upward. His eye caught a glimpse of a dark-winged hawk as it sailed downward to land in the top of a squat piñon pine. His attention on the bird, Miguel stepped in a slight depression and retwisted his sore ankle. He cursed at his carelessness.

He hobbled to the corral and checked on the stallion, finding Diablo fit and full of high spirits. At loose ends, Miguel rejected the idea of returning to the village. Instead, feeling a need to be alone, he limped to the edge of the mesa and sat on a ledge of rock. His eyes swept the basin below. Scanning the surrounding mountains, his gaze lingered on the pass that led to the Spanish Angel and Elena.

A sad smile crossed his face. Before he'd left, he'd slipped into her room and stood by her bed, watching her toss in a restless sleep. Knowing that Carlos waited impatiently in the carriage, it still had taken every ounce of self-control he'd possessed to keep from gathering her into his arms, even though he'd known if he did, he might never leave. Now, here on the mountain, he felt regret and a strange foreboding that he might never see her again.

He sighed. He wasn't afraid of dying. He'd lived with that prospect for a long time. But never to see Elena again, never to hear her voice, her laugh . . . Never to hold her in his arms and lose himself in her sweetness, that he couldn't bear.

He picked up a small rock and tossed it away, watching it plummet a thousand feet to the valley below. A deep frown creased his forehead. His meeting with Juan at the pond last night troubled him, too. He'd told Juan about Elena's strange illness and his fear that something might be seriously wrong.

Juan had grinned and told him not to worry, he had a feeling nature would take care of everything. Miguel shook his head. What the hell nature had to do with Elena being sick, he had no idea.

He'd asked the young man to sleep in Diego's room until he returned. He didn't want Elena alone in that wing, and who would take better care of her than her brother? Elena, not knowing she and Juan were related, might have a problem understanding his presence, but the servants' rooms downstairs were too far away in the event she needed help.

The incident with the scorpion still bothered him. He knew Diego had been the target, but he wasn't sure why. He had a feeling Conception had a part in it. Her secret meetings with Guillermo left him uneasy. Not taking any chances, he'd arranged to have both entrances to the wing guarded, allowing only Juan to enter and exit after dark.

The young man knew the importance of keeping his presence in the house a secret, realizing he would find it difficult to explain to de Vega why a stable hand would be occupying Diego's room. But Miguel felt more at ease knowing Elena would be protected until he returned.

And if anything happened to him, Miguel had told Juan to contact a lawyer in Santa Fe, who would put a large sum of money at his disposal. He'd made Juan promise that if it became necessary, he would secrete Elena away from the ranch and take her to the McBrides in Colorado. From there Nick would see that she reached Billy Storm's safely. Miguel knew that the old rancher, who'd taken the orphaned Miguel Sandoval and raised him, would welcome Elena. He would protect her and treat her like a beloved daughter, something her own father had never done. A bitter smile twisted Miguel's face. Once there, Billy could tell her of the raid so long ago. He and Juan could explain why Miguel Sandoval had become both Diego and El Gato. He only hoped that when she knew the reasons, she'd understand and forgive him.

Feeling confused and a bit lonely, Elena released a wistful sigh. Thoughts of El Gato always sent her pulse racing. And no matter how badly he'd behaved she would always love him. Yet she discovered she missed Diego.

Across from her, Consuela looked up from her sewing. "Are you all right, *niña*?"

Elena gave her a smile. "I'm fine." Although her feelings for Diego had none of the passion she felt for Miguel, she'd grown very fond of her husband. She missed his pompous ways, his ridiculous outfits, his gentleness, even if she found his behavior a little disconcerting, especially that last night in the barn. She still hadn't figured that out.

Setting aside the tiny garment she'd been hemming, she stood up to stretch, trying to relieve the ache in her back.

"Oh!" Feeling a faint fluttering sensation, Elena clasped her hand over her middle.

Frowning, Consuela rose from her chair. "What is the matter, Elena?"

Elena smiled. "Nothing. My stomach feels funny, like I swallowed a butterfly."

A wide smile spread over Consuela's face. "That is the baby, little one. That is his way of telling you he's there."

An overwhelming sense of love washed over Elena, along with sadness that Miguel could not be there, to share this with her. Even though she'd threatened to shoot him, she yearned to have him hold her. Last night she'd awakened from a nightmare. She hadn't remembered the dream when she awoke, but it left her with a strong sense of unease, as if he was in danger. Praying it wasn't so, she'd pushed the feeling aside and tried to stay busy.

Patting her middle when the babe moved again, she smiled at Consuela. She sat down and resumed her hemming. *Little one, if you are anything like your father, you will be a handful.*

Time passed slowly for Miguel. More than three weeks had elapsed since he'd reached the mesa, and still he had none of the anticipation he'd experienced before previous raids. He dreaded the coming expedition. A messenger, sent by Felipe, had arrived earlier in the day, bringing news of the upcoming shipment. His report hadn't helped Miguel's sense of impending doom.

The gold would take a different route through open country. The number of outriders were doubled, with *pistoleros* taking the place of the *vaqueros* who had previously ridden with the shipments. Even though his men were eager, already planning how to spend their portion of the take, Miguel knew it would not be that easy.

From what he'd heard, it would be almost impossible. Instead of a wagon, the gold would be placed on mules— three strings of them—with only one carrying the gold. The others would be decoys loaded with worthless ore. In order to get the gold, he'd either have to get through the outriders and steal all three, or else find out which ones carried the actual gold bars.

Inside the cave, by candlelight he studied the crudely drawn maps spread before him on the tabletop. If the messenger had been right about the route, there was only one place where the pack train would be vulnerable. His finger traced the path through a narrow canyon between a range of conelike hills. Miguel sighed. Even if he was lucky enough to guess which mules carried the gold, how on earth could they outrun the gunmen and reach the safety of the mesa? He shook his head. They couldn't. Shoving the maps aside, he blew out the candle. He rolled his shoulders to remove the kinks, then left the cave.

Outside, he filled a battered tin cup from the coffeepot simmering at the edge of Emanuel's fire. Not seeing the man anywhere, Miguel strolled down the narrow path to the lookout point. It had become a habit to come here, to the place where he'd felt comforted by her presence, as though in spirit she'd come to the mountain to be with him.

Lowering himself to the soft sand, he leaned back against a boulder. Sipping the bitter, dark brew, he gazed up at the heavy clouds hovering over the mesa. Weary beyond words, he ran a hand through his hair. "Ah, Elena, what am I to do?" he said aloud, as if she were there to listen. "If I try to call off the raid, my men will be angry. They will think I have become a coward. As eager as they are to steal the gold, I am afraid they will try to do it without me. And yet if I go, I fear I may never return." He closed his eyes, regretting he hadn't asked her to forgive him.

A soft breeze lifted the edges of his hair. As thunder rumbled, shaking the ground, Miguel lifted his head. The first cool drops of rain hit his face and coursed down his cheeks to blend with his tears. Remembering another storm, he swallowed against the pain, realizing she might never know how much he loved her.

A crash of thunder woke Elena and sent her flying to her balcony to close the shutters. Instead, she stepped onto the terrace, letting the wind whip her night garment, tangling it about her legs. She took a deep breath, savoring the freshness of the cool raindrops pelting her face. A bitter pain twisted her heart, bringing back the memory of another cloudburst where at the edge of a cliff, in the midst of lightning and thunder, she and a black-clad bandit had come together and created a child.

"Oh, El Gato, my love, where are you tonight?" She faced the mountains and closed her eyes, bringing his image before her. Tall, dark, dangerously handsome, he smiled at her, but his smile held no joy, only incredible sadness.

"Miguel," she whispered. A blast of cold wind hit her. She shivered, only vaguely aware of the rain soaking her nightgown. He seemed close, his presence real. Longing to comfort him, she raised her hand to touch his cheek, but her caress met only empty air. The vision vanished, leaving her with an unbearable sense of loss. "Miguel," she sobbed. Overwhelmed by grief, she sank to the balcony floor.

Shutters banged, waking Juan from a deep sleep. Frowning, he sat up in bed, hearing the sound even through the pouring rain. It came from Elena's room. Could she be sleeping so soundly she couldn't hear it? After hurriedly slipping into one of Diego's robes, he left his room and tapped softly on her door. "Elena." No answer. He tried the knob. Locked. "Something is wrong," he muttered.

He rushed back to his room and opened the terrace doors. A wave of rain, driven by an icy wind, hit him, plastering his clothing to his skin. Gasping, he wiped strings of hair from his face and peered across to her balcony. Even in the darkness he saw the open doors clattering noisily against the iron railings. Why hadn't she closed them? Fear drew his mouth into a grim line.

Using the wet slippery vines for support, he climbed to the top rail of the balcony and jumped across. Landing lightly, he spun toward her bedroom, stubbing his toe against something lying at the edge of the porch. His eyes widened in horror. "Oh, my God! Elena!"

Scooping her in his arms, he carried her into the room and laid her on the settee. He closed and locked the terrace doors and quickly lit the lamp. Fear choking him, he turned to his sister. Was she dead? He knelt beside her and rubbed her icy hands between his. He touched a spot on her neck. She felt frozen, but she still breathed.

Realizing he had to get her out of the wet clothes, he ran to her dresser and tossed things aside until he found a nightgown. Yanking a handful of towels from a rack beside her bathtub, he ran back to the couch.

Supporting her with one arm, he stripped the sodden nightdress from her body with the other. After hastily drying her frozen flesh, he slipped the dry nightgown over her head.

"Elena!" he cried, massaging her legs and feet between the folds of the towel. He wrapped another around her wet hair and carried her to the bed. He tucked the blankets up to her chin. "Elena, wake up." He heard her moan.

"Elena, open your eyes." He breathed a sigh of relief

when she blinked, then raised her lashes.

"Juan?" She stared at him, confused. She shivered. Her teeth chattered. "I'm so cold."

"I know, little one." He looked around the room. "I'll be right back." He went to her door and peered out. He sprinted into Diego's room and picked up an armload of wood. He carried it into her room and built a fire in the raised adobe fireplace. When it blazed, he shielded it with the small metal screen and stepped back to the bed. Even though warmth filled the room, she still shook beneath the blankets. Somehow he had to get her warm.

Shivering himself, he hurried to Diego's room, and he quickly changed into a dry pair of pajamas and another robe. Then he grabbed the brandy and two glasses from the liquor cabinet and took them to Elena's room. After locking the door, he carried the bottle to the table by her bed. He poured a small amount into a glass and held it to her pale lips. She raised a hand to push it away. "Drink it, Elena," he insisted.

"I don't like it," she whispered between shivers.

"I know, but you have to get warm." He gave her an understanding look. "This little bit will do the baby and his mama a lot of good."

Her eyes widened. "How did you know?"

He grinned. "Drink it." He held the glass to her lips until the liquor was gone. "Better?"

She nodded.

After downing his own drink, Juan scooted onto the bed beside her. Propping her head against his knees, he unwrapped the towel from her head. "Let's get this mop dry before you get pneumonia." Using another towel he'd snared from the end of the bed, he rubbed her hair to remove the moisture.

Through a curtain of tangled ebony, she peered up at him. "What happened? How did you get here?"

He leaned close and whispered, teasingly, "It's supposed to be a secret, but Diego asked me to stay in his room while he's gone. He was worried about you." He frowned at her. "It appears he was right. What were you doing on the terrace in the rain?"

"I intended to close the shutters." Her eyes darkened. "I sensed Miguel. He seemed so sad I couldn't bear to leave him. When he was gone, I guess I fainted."

He took her hand, holding it between his palms. "I wish I could ease your pain, *chica*. You love him, don't you?"

She nodded. Her hand went to her middle. "I am going to have his baby, and he doesn't even know. I can't keep it a secret much longer.

"When Diego returns, he will have to be told. I don't know how he will react to the news." She bit her lip, but a small sob still escaped. "Oh, Juan. I am so afraid. What if Diego rejects the little one because it is El Gato's?"

Her eyes widened. "And what will El Gato do if he discovers another man is to raise his child?"

Juan pulled her against his chest and smiled into the firelight, wishing he had the right to tell her the truth. "Elena, you worry too much. Just take care of yourself and the baby." He lifted her chin and gently kissed the tip of her nose. "I have a feeling everything will work out just fine."

Chapter Twenty-eight

AFTER leaving the mesa at dawn, El Gato and his band huddled around a small campfire in the rocks above the canyon and watched for the signal telling of the mule train's approach. Shivering in an icy drizzle, the men talked in excited, but hushed, voices.

Pulling his poncho closer, Miguel listened to the hiss of the rain on the flames. He didn't mind the wet or the cold, knowing that for them the storm was a stroke of luck. Flash floods in the high country forced the gold shipment to take a longer and more perilous route. He counted on the mule drivers and *pistoleros* being so preoccupied with their own misery they would be less wary of being attacked.

Sighing, he lit his cigar with a small flaming twig and stared down at the trail, wanting only to get it over with so he could return to the hacienda and Elena.

"*Jefe*, the mules, they are coming," Pedro said, his black eyes bright with excitement in his long, lean face.

Miguel spoke softly, going over the plan again to make sure they understood. "We will attack from the front and the rear on horseback. While you"—he waved his hand to four marksmen he'd selected—"pick them off from the rocks. The gunfire should stampede the mules up the draw where Emanuel is waiting." He pointed across the canyon. "Pedro, you cover him in case any gunmen get by the rest of us."

Miguel's gaze swept the small band, knowing he might never see some of them again. "*Vaya con Dios, amigos.*"

He gave orders to douse the fire, and told the rest of his men to get mounted. With his band outnumbered, less than thirty of them against more than fifty hardened gunmen, he prayed the element of surprise would give them the edge they needed.

His cigar clenched between his teeth, Miguel swung aboard Diablo and checked his silver-plated revolvers. He found the weight of the guns familiar and comforting. Like old friends, he knew they wouldn't fail him. As before every gun battle, he felt intensely alive, his senses honed to a keen edge. His nostrils flared, inhaling juniper and sage; mud and manure; wet leather, wool and horseflesh; and the strongest scent of all—danger.

When the pack mules strung out through the middle of the canyon, Miguel signaled the attack. He charged Diablo at the front of the train while the remainder of his band cut off the retreat. Drawing his gun, reflex took over. Miguel's eyes narrowed, turning the men before him into faceless targets that would kill him unless he killed them first. His left hand fanned the hammer as fast as his right pulled the trigger, the deadly staccato downing as many men as he had bullets.

Rain, smoke, and flying mud mixed with screams of men and horses and the percussions of gunfire. Braying in panic, the terrified mules bucked, kicking at the horses of the men trying to hold them. The pack animals broke free and bolted up the draw toward Emanuel.

His first gun empty, Miguel shoved it into his holster and drew the other. He snapped a shot at a gunman who'd drawn a bead on Pedro.

"*Jefe,* look out!" a man called from above.

Whirling the prancing stallion, Miguel fired at the gun leveled toward him.

The man, lifted from the saddle by the shot, crashed backward into the mud, getting off another shot as he fell.

Diablo reared. A blaze of fiery pain sliced through Miguel's shoulder. Sheer effort kept him in the saddle. He gritted his teeth, firing the gun so rapidly the trio of shots seemed as one. Three more of de Vega's men went down in front of him.

"The hell with this—let's get out of here!" a man screamed. The gunmen that were able raced in panic back the way they had come.

Miguel signaled his men to let them go. He had what he'd come for—the gold.

"We did it, *Jefe*!" a jubilant man close by him shouted.

Miguel, turning the stallion toward the voice, blinked, trying to bring the man's face into focus. Blood, warm and wet, made a sticky trail down his chest and puddled in his navel. The last thing he noticed before he hit the ground was that the rain had stopped.

"Miguel," a voice called through the darkness.

Miguel struggled to open his eyelids.

Carlos loomed over him, his forehead creased in a worried frown. "It's about time you woke up," he growled.

Miguel tried to lift his head, but the old man pushed him back. Heavy pain thudded through his chest, making him reject any further impulse to rise. He stared up at his old friend. "What happened?" he whispered.

"You were shot." Carlos shook his head, holding up his thumb and forefinger. "An inch lower, *Miguelito*, and you wouldn't be here."

"The men?" Miguel asked, noticing for the first time he was in the cave.

"A few bullet holes, but they will recover." Carlos grinned. "De Vega's fine *pistoleros* were so confused that they shot each other. All we had to do was help them."

"Really?" Miguel raised his eyebrow.

Carlos nodded. "The others ran so fast they are probably halfway across Colorado by now. They won't bother us again."

"The gold?"

Carlos waved his hand toward a mountain of small golden bars. "The men have recast all of it except that bunch." He pointed to a sack. "By tonight they will be finished."

"Tonight?" He frowned up at Carlos. "How long have I been here?"

"Two days."

"When did I get shot?" He didn't remember a thing.

"Four days ago. We rigged up a travois to bring you back. You lost so much blood, we were afraid you wouldn't make it. Felipe removed the bullet and cleaned the wound."

Miguel gave him a weak smile. "It looks as if El Gato has a few lives left after all." Exhausted by the effort to speak and unable to keep his eyes open, he drifted back into oblivion.

Two days later, waking to find himself alone, Miguel rose from his bed and shakily made his way to the mouth of the cave. Drenched with cold perspiration, he sagged helplessly against a large boulder. Fighting for breath, he closed his eyes, too weak to take another step. "Damn," he whispered, hoping he didn't pass out.

"*Jefe*, you should not be up." Emanuel, his round face crumpled in a frown, hurried to his side.

"Just get me over there." Miguel pointed to a bedroll stretched out by the fire. He had barely lain down when another urgency made itself known. Cursing under his breath, he stared in disgust at the big man bending over him. "Emanuel, help me up," he whispered. How in the hell could he ever hope to get home to Elena? He couldn't even stand up long enough to relieve himself.

A week later, against Carlo's protests, Miguel insisted on being taken back to the hacienda. Arriving late at night, he gritted his teeth against the pain and allowed Carlos to help him up the stairs and into bed.

"Miguel, this is foolishness. I shouldn't have let you talk me into this. You are still too weak."

Miguel shook his head. "After a little rest, I'll be fine." He took the old man's hand. "Please understand, I have to know how she is. She's been sick."

"And you're not, I suppose," Carlos growled.

A soft tap sounded on the door. Miguel, catching Carlos's worried gaze, pulled the sheets up and motioned for the man to open the door. When Juan's dark head peered in at him, Miguel sighed with relief and waved him inside. Again Carlos locked the door.

Juan approached the bed and frowned at him. "You look terrible. Are you sick, *amigo?*"

"He's been shot, and he's too stupid to take care of himself. He insisted on coming back here." Carlos threw up his hands. "What am I to do?"

"Shot?" Juan knelt beside him.

"I'm all right. How is Elena?" he asked weakly.

"She's fine." Juan grinned. "Cranky, but fine."

"I couldn't stay away. I felt she needed me."

"I think you need each other." Juan sighed. "Are you going to tell her about your wound?"

"No! I will let her think Diego has taken to his bed to recover from a cold. For once I'm glad the man is such a weakling." He placed his hand on the young man's shoulder. "How can I ever thank you for watching over her?"

"You forget. She is my sister."

Carlos approached the bed and placed his palm on Miguel's head. "You feel a little hot. Juan?"

Miguel groaned when Juan, too, felt his head and nodded. "Just what I need, two worriers."

"Let me stay here with you," Carlos pleaded. "The gold can wait. A week or two won't matter."

"No. Tomorrow I want you to leave. This was our last raid. We have more gold than we'll ever need. Now I will continue my fight another way. The people have grown weary of fighting and hiding. They long to till the land and raise their children in peace. Give the men their share and take the remainder to Santa Fe. I will rest easier knowing it is safely in the bank."

"Well, I won't rest at all until you are back on your feet." Carlos shook his head. "Look at you. Who will take care of you?"

"I can stay here at night," Juan offered. "Elena can watch over him in the daytime."

Miguel frowned. "Remember, I don't want her to know."

"I'll tell her you have a bad chest cold." He looked at the door. "In fact, I'll go tell her now."

"Now? She knows you've been staying here?" Miguel asked. "It was supposed to be a secret. Did something happen when I was gone?"

Juan looked at him a moment, then shook his head. "No. One night we had a storm, and I went to close her shutters. I think she felt better knowing I was near."

Miguel had the uneasy feeling Juan wasn't telling him everything, but at the moment he didn't feel up to pushing the matter. Sighing wearily, he lay back on the pillows.

"I think we had better let you get some rest, *amigo*," Juan said, getting to his feet. "I will see you tomorrow night." He turned to the older man. "Have a good trip, Carlos. I'll try to keep him out of trouble."

"A hopeless task," Carlos chided fondly as he ushered the younger man out of the room and locked the door.

After taking a dose of bitter herbs that Carlos mixed with a glass of water, Miguel closed his eyes, only too glad to welcome sleep.

Awakened by noise in the next room, Elena quickly answered Juan's knock. "Is anything wrong?" she asked, closing the door as soon as Juan stepped inside.

"Your husband's back," Juan said quietly. "He is very sick. He said to tell you it is only a chest cold, but he is running a fever. I think we need to watch him carefully for a few days. Carlos must leave tomorrow on business, and I told him we would take care of Mi—Diego while he is gone."

"Of course." Elena glanced at the door. "Maybe I should go see him."

"Not tonight. Anyway I think he's sleeping." Juan touched her arm. "Elena, I think it would be best if you kept the maids out of there. They might—disturb him."

Elena frowned at him. She had a feeling Juan was trying to warn her about something. But what? "All right, Juan, if you think that is best."

"I do, little one. Now I think you had better get back to bed. One sick person at a time is all I can handle." He bent and kissed her forehead, then left the room.

After locking her door, Elena crossed the floor and eased herself back under covers. Her thoughts went to the man in the next room. He'd been gone much longer than she'd expected, and now suddenly told that he was home, she didn't know what to do. She had avoided the rest of the household, especially Conception and Father. But she couldn't avoid her own husband, especially since he was sick and needed her.

She placed her palm over her middle, feeling the baby move beneath her hand. Would Diego notice her thickening figure? She bit her lip. Maybe she could wait until he was well, but how much longer could she keep it a secret?

Chapter Twenty-nine

FEELING guilty for sleeping longer than she'd intended, Elena hurriedly completed her toilette and dressed. Critically examining her appearance in the mirror, she sighed. The full cut of the gown hid her blossoming figure—as long as she didn't stand sideways. Well, if Diego noticed, she'd have to tell him sooner rather than later. The thought filled her with dread.

She exited her room and tapped softly on his door. When he didn't answer, she stepped inside. "Diego?"

Cheeks flushed with fever, Diego glanced up from his bed. "Elena," he said, attempting a feeble smile.

Concerned, she hastened to his bedside and placed her palm against his forehead. Her brow wrinkled into a frown as the heat of his parchment-dry skin seared her fingertips. "I had no idea you were so ill," she murmured.

"My sweet, I am better now that you're here," he said weakly, gazing up with shadowed blue eyes.

Lifting the silver pitcher, Elena splashed cold water into the basin and dampened a washcloth. Taking a seat beside him, she sponged Diego's face. Even with the cool cloths, his flesh grew warmer. Alarmed, Elena laid the rag aside. "Diego, we must do something for your fever." She started to rise. "I'm going after Consuela."

"No!" he croaked, clutching her arm. "Tell no one.

Medicine—on the dresser. Mix—a spoonful—in a glass of water."

Tell no one? Wondering at his words, she swiftly prepared the potion. She slid her arm behind him to support him and held the liquid to his lips until he drank it down. When she gently lowered his head and removed her arm, she gasped. His hair slipped sideways! Amazed, she leaned closer. *It looks like a wig!* She picked up the wet cloth and slid her fingers along the edge of his hairline, pretending to wipe his brow. *It is!* The edge of the wig lifted easily. *Could he be bald? Is that why he wears a hairpiece?* No. A rim of crisp, dark hair met her questing fingertips.

"What's wrong, Elena?"

"Nothing, Diego," she said quickly. She studied him. Why hadn't she realized before that the hair was false? Maybe because the fusty wig matched the rest of his ridiculous appearance? Something else seemed different. Her eyes narrowed thoughtfully as she traced the outline of his body under the covers. Was it her imagination—or had he lost weight?

"Elena?"

"Yes, Diego?" She smiled sweetly. "Would you like some breakfast?" She leaned closer. Placing her hands on each side of his body, she gave him a kiss on the cheek. Yes, he was definitely thinner. Slender in fact. It would be impossible to lose that much weight . . . unless his portly build had also been a ruse.

Pushing the paunchy body, the grayish-brown hair, and fat mustache from her memory, she imagined him slimmer, with dark hair. *No! It couldn't be!* Narrowing her eyes, she scanned him again, mentally adding a suit of dark clothes and a mask. *Madre de Dios!* Her eyes widened. Her heart skipped a beat.

"I could use some coffee," he said with a frown. The

fever-bright blue eyes locked on hers.

Her senses reeling, she forced herself to smile. "I'll see to your coffee and a bit of food, too." Whirling away, she rushed from the room.

In the hall she sagged against the door, her mind a mass of conflicting emotions. Love, amazement, and confusion warred with outrage and resentment. Impossible—but true. Diego and Miguel the bandit were the same person. She clamped a hand over her mouth to smother a startled cry. *Por Dios! El Gato is my husband!*

"Señora? Are you all right?"

Elena glanced up to see Lupe hurrying toward her. Drawing in a breath to hide her discomposure, Elena told the maid to bring up a breakfast tray, but instructed her not to enter the room because Don Diego was ill.

Watching the servant leave, Elena thought of all the months past. The months he'd filled with lies and treachery. Her rage grew as she recalled everything he'd put her through, especially his shameful treatment of her that last night in her bedroom. Her lips thinned into a vengeful line. *He might be sick, but he'll feel even worse when I'm through with him.* She stepped inside and leaned against the door, eyeing the sleeping man. *Yes, my deceitful bandit husband, I'll take care of you—all by myself.* She walked slowly toward him.

Pausing by the edge of his mattress, she pressed her palm against his forehead, strangely glad to find him cooler. The medicine must be working, she thought.

She stared at the wig. The masquerade certainly explained a lot of his strange behavior. Why he hadn't made love to her on their wedding night. Why he claimed to be injured. She grinned, now understanding what she had believed at the time to be an aversion to her kiss. Knowing his passionate nature, he hadn't dared let her get that close. Her gaze lingered on the familiar profile. Even with the disguise, how could she not have known? And why hadn't he told her? She frowned. He didn't trust her!

Taking the rag from the basin, she squeezed it out and wiped his face. "Poor Diego," she murmured. When his eyes blinked open, she lowered her lashes seductively and leaned toward him. Watching his eyes grow large, she gave him a long sensual kiss—on the lips. Then slowly, passionately kissed his cheeks, his chin, the tip of his nose.

"Elena?"

She raised a brow and looked down at him. "Hmm?" She moistened her lips. He closed his eyes, anticipating her kiss. She lovingly trailed her hand down his cheek. "You don't need this anymore," she said, straightening.

"Oow!" he yelped, clamping a hand over his mouth.

Waving his thick mustache between her thumb and forefinger, she glared at his shocked expression.

He rubbed his upper lip. "*Querida?*"

"*Querida?*" She locked accusing eyes on his. "I think you owe me an explanation, Diego—or is it El Gato?"

He drew in a breath. "How did you find out?"

"When I wiped your forehead, you almost lost your hair."

He patted his head. Finding the wig still in place, he gave her a wary look. "What are you going to do?"

"What do you think I should do? If I had any sense, I'd call my father," she said, whirling toward the door.

Taking her at her word, he heaved himself off the bed and lurched forward, grabbing her arm.

"Don't touch me!" Furious, she shoved him away. His face blanched deathly pale. Groaning, he clutched his chest and sank to the floor. Frightened and anxious in spite of her anger, Elena fell to her knees by his side. "Miguel, what's wrong?"

"I'm sorry, Elena," he croaked. Pain twisted his face. A dull sheen of perspiration dotted his forehead. "I never meant to hurt you. Will you forgive me?" he whispered weakly. Sagging against her arm, he closed his eyes.

"Miguel?" Cradling him in her arms, Elena became aware of something bulky under his night garment. *What's that?* Trembling, she carefully undid a few buttons. Her eyes focused on the thick red-stained bandage swathing his chest and widened in horror. Dear God! She brought one fluttering hand to her mouth to stifle her tortured cry. Miguel didn't have a cold. He was hurt!

Opening his eyes, Miguel followed her stricken gaze to his chest. He reached out to take her hand. *"Querida?"*

Her tear-filled eyes met his. "Why didn't you tell me you were injured?" she cried.

"I didn't want you to worry. Look at you. Do you think I wanted to see you like this?" He struggled to his feet. Reeling unsteadily, he held out his hand. Seeing his plight, Elena leapt to his side and helped him to the bed. Exhausted, he sank back on the pillows, pulling her down with him. He raised his hand and wiped away the tears coursing down her cheeks. *"Querida,* please don't cry. It's only a little bullet wound. I'll be fine."

"A *little* bullet wound?" She gave him a sorrow-filled look. "I know why you didn't tell me—why you never told me anything. You didn't—you don't trust me." She shook her head, her sobs increasing.

"It's not that I don't trust you. But, *querida,* knowing your goodness, your honesty, how could I expect you to keep a secret like that? I love you, Elena. When I was shot, my only regret was that I hadn't been able to beg you to forgive me." He kissed her palm. "Now whatever happens, at least you know the truth. I risked all by coming back, but I had to see you. If you can't forgive me—if you feel you have to tell your father, I'll try to understand."

Seeing the stricken look on his pale face, all desire to punish him disappeared. A warm rush of love took its place. She slid her hand over his head and removed the wig. Caressing his cheek, she gave him a tender smile. "I'd never betray you. Miguel, don't you know I love you?"

Blinking back his own tears, he didn't answer, but instead lifted his arm and pulled her down to his chest. He pressed his lips to hers. "Oh, *querida*, what did I ever do to deserve you?"

She nuzzled his neck. "You kidnapped me, ravished me, then sent me home to my father in disgrace. Then, disguised as Diego, you married me. As my husband, you avoided my bed, pretending to be impotent, and urged me to take a lover." She raised her head and gently lifted a lock of hair from his eyes. "Then you, as El Gato, became that lover, filling my life with love and my nights with passion. What more could a woman ask?" she said softly.

"Elena, you'll never know how very much I love you," he whispered, holding her close.

Awhile later, hearing a knock, Elena eased away from her sleeping husband. She crossed the floor and opened the door a crack to see Lupe with their breakfast. Motioning for silence, Elena stepped into the hall and pulled the door closed behind her. She reached for the tray. "I'll take it," she told the maid. "You can go downstairs now."

When Lupe left, Elena reentered the room and carried the server to a bedside table. She went back to close and lock the door, then leaned against it, her thoughts troubled. Miguel still hadn't told her the reason for his charade. It couldn't have been only to find out about the gold shipments. A spy in the mining camp could have done that. Why had he concocted the disguise of Diego?

She sighed. For whatever reason, Miguel was here and he was hurt. It was now up to her to protect him.

He moaned and opened his eyes. "Elena?"

"I'm here, my love."

When she came back to the bed, he pulled her close, savoring the feeling of just having her near. He nuzzled her neck. "I wish I had the strength to make love to you, my sweet."

"Don't you even think about it." She pulled away from him and sat up. "First, I've got to get you well. I'll start by giving you breakfast."

"You're the only food I need, *querida*. Would you take off all of this"—he raised a hand and motioned to her clothing—"and just lay here beside me?"

"Are you sure I won't hurt you?" she asked shyly.

He shook his head, smiling as she modestly turned her back to remove her clothes. He lifted the edge of the cover in invitation when, still wearing her chemise and drawers, she raised her eyelashes to peep at him.

She joined him under the sheets and snuggled close, careful not to touch his injury.

He cupped his hand under her breast, feeling it overflow his palm. Was it his imagination or was she bigger? He traced its ample contour with his thumb. *Definitely larger. Could it be?* He slid his hand down her softly rounding stomach. His heart racing, he locked his gaze on hers. "Elena, I think I am not the only one who's been keeping secrets. Tell me, *querida,* is what I suspect true?"

She gave him a tremulous smile and nodded. "Yes, Miguel. I am with child."

He carefully pulled her to him. Holding her close, his hand caressed her middle. "A child," he whispered in wonder. "Elena, we are going to have a baby!"

But in spite of his elation, a shiver of fear crawled up his spine. Here he, El Gato, lay badly wounded in the home of a man who hated him and wanted him dead.

He kissed Elena. The woman he loved more than life itself lay beside him, their child growing in her belly.

Another terrible truth hit him. The heat and the swelling below his shoulder told him all was not as it should be with his wound. With Carlos gone, he was helpless to do anything about it, even though if he didn't get help he might lose his life. He didn't know what to do. He couldn't take the chance on anyone else learning his secret. If the gunshot didn't kill him, de Vega would—once he discovered Diego was also El Gato.

He squeezed Elena closer. Dear God, he couldn't die now. Not when he had so much to live for. A different pain washed through him, as he realized he might never see his unborn child. And without him to protect them, what would happen to the baby and Elena? *Por Dios!* He closed his eyes, no longer able to contain the tears seeping beneath his lashes. By returning to the Spanish Angel, he had put all of them in mortal danger.

Chapter Thirty

IT was late morning when Elena woke to find it hadn't been a dream. Miguel, her love, her husband, the father of her child, lay sleeping beside her. She snuggled as close as she dared without touching his injury. She frowned. He felt even hotter and his breathing sounded ragged, labored. Raising her head to look at him, she stiffened. Icy fear clutched her heart. *Santa Maria!* Miguel wasn't asleep—he was unconscious!

Her agonized gaze riveted on her husband, Elena scrambled from the bed and into her dress. *I have to get help. But who?* She twisted her tousled hair into a knot and anchored it with a hairpin. *Juan! He will know what to do.* After closing the door, she hurried down the back stairs and ran toward the barn.

Conception gazed down at the needlework she'd been doing, examining the puckered stitches and the uneven pattern. Shaking her head in disgust, she tossed the fancy work aside. With Ricardo away tending his own ranch this week, she found time lay heavy on her hands. She sighed, missing him. At least they'd made up before he left. After she'd apologized, he'd forgiven her. She smiled, growing warm just thinking about their lovemaking.

Her face turned solemn as she guiltily hoped he never

found out about her dealings with Guillermo. Remembering the foreman's slobbering kisses and pawing hands, she shuddered, finding it hard to believe she'd been desperate enough to use her caresses as a bribe to get Guillermo to hurt Diego. At least she'd had the good sense to call the whole conspiracy off. She was glad Diego hadn't been hurt by the scorpion she'd put in his bed, although he must not have found it anyway.

In spite of his prissy ways, she had a grudging admiration for the way her brother-in-law stood up to her. Not many people did. Peering out the window, she gazed at Elena's wing, wondering if her sister was as lonely as she, since Diego also was absent. Deciding to pay Elena a visit, she glanced in the mirror to check her appearance, then left the room.

She entered Elena's wing and had reached the top of the stairs, when Lupe, screaming, ran toward her. Alarmed, Conception grabbed the maid's arm. "What is the matter? Has something happened to my sister?"

"No!" Her face white, the servant raised a shaking finger and pointed down the hallway. "A stranger! In Don Diego's bed! He is dead!"

Conception shook the hysterical girl. "Are you *loco*?"

Lupe pulled from her grasp and fled down the staircase.

"A dead stranger in Diego's bed! Really!" Shaking her head, Conception picked up her skirts and headed for the room to see for herself. Finding the door partially opened, she pushed it wide and cautiously peered into the room.

There in her brother-in-law's bed lay a dark-haired man. She clamped her hand over her mouth, stifling a scream. *Por Dios!* He did look dead. Her eyes wide, she whirled on her heels and ran to find her father.

*

Unable to match her steps to Juan's long stride, Elena trotted along behind. Tears streamed down her face, blurring her vision. Miguel was very sick. Somehow they had to save him. She panted up the stairs and entered the room to find Juan removing the bandage.

"What are you doing?" she cried, rushing to the bedside.

Juan gave her a swift glance before turning back to the angry red injury. "The wound is infected. If he is to live, we have to drain it. I pray it's not already too late." He handed her the silver pitcher. "We'll need hot water. Send someone for my mother."

Gripping the container, Elena whirled, reaching for the knob when the door suddenly swung inward. Her father stood in the opening.

Elena gasped. The pitcher dropped from her hand and rolled to a stop in front of his feet. She scooped it up. Desperate to shield the man in the bed, she clutched her parent's arm and tried to draw him into the hall. She reached behind her to close the door.

"Elena, what's going on in there?" Her father impatiently pushed her aside and strode into the room. "Conception told me a dead stranger is in Diego's bed."

Frozen with fear, Elena stared at Juan and Miguel.

"What are you doing here?" de Vega roared at Juan. "And who is that man?"

"Someone who needs our help." Juan met Elena's gaze, warning her not to say anything. "Get my mother and the water. Hurry!"

Lifting her skirts, she ran from the room only to meet Conception on the staircase.

"Elena? Who is that man? Is—?"

Elena brushed past her and hurried toward the kitchen. "Lupe, get Consuela!"

*

Trembling, Elena carried the basket of medicinal herbs and followed the older woman up the staircase. She prayed Consuela's knowledge of healing would be enough. Conception, muttering to herself, trailed along behind.

Opening the door, Elena saw Juan and her father bent over the bed. Juan gave her a guarded look. "I told your father that Diego's friend arrived last night. We didn't know he'd been injured until you found him this morning."

Elena nodded, grateful he'd been able to find some explanation for Miguel's presence. "How is he?" she whispered.

Consuela examined the wound and shook her head. "Not good. Everyone but Juan must leave if I am to help him."

"No!" Elena cried. Miguel needed her.

Juan grasped her arms. "Elena! I know you are concerned for your *husband's friend*, but you can do no good here." The expression on his face cautioned her not to protest.

"Of course," she said. Shaken by what she'd almost done, she took Conception's hand and led her curious sister from the room. Her father followed.

"Elena, do you know this man?" he asked.

"Diego has spoken of him often. They are very close, almost like brothers," she said, hoping he would believe her.

"It seems strange he never mentioned him to me," de Vega muttered, shaking his head.

Afraid they wouldn't leave on their own, Elena followed her father and sister down the stairs. The faint squeak of a door made her glance toward the kitchen. Wide-eyed, Lupe peeped through the crack. Elena frantically waved her back. Her heart thudded when the maid withdrew and the door closed. Elena hurried her kin through the salon.

At the door Conception hesitated. "Elena, you look awful. Are you all right?" Her blond sibling frowned at her. "Maybe you should lie down."

"I think I will." Elena opened the door and ushered them through. "If you will both excuse me?" When they finally left, she breathed a sigh of relief. Closing her eyes, she sagged against the facing.

"Señora?"

She raised her lashes to see Lupe staring at her. "We must talk," Elena said, leading the maid back into the kitchen. She gripped the girl's shoulders. "You will not say anything further about the man upstairs," she said sternly. "Do you understand?" When Lupe opened her mouth to protest, Elena glowered at her. "Not a word! If you value your life, *not a word—to anyone!*"

Leaving the chastised Lupe, Elena hurried up the stairs and reentered the room where Consuela and Juan labored to save Miguel's life.

Semiconscious, the wounded man cursed and thrashed wildly, pushing the pair away.

After locking the door, Elena rushed to the bedside and grabbed his hand. "Miguel, it's Elena. Please, lie still and let them help you." She drew his fevered hand to her cheek.

"Elena?" Miguel croaked, his voice weak.

"Yes, my love. I am here," she crooned, brushing a lock of damp hair from his forehead. A rush of icy fear clutched her heart. His skin was so hot.

He moaned, tightening his grip on her hand when Consuela opened the angry wound. A nauseating greenish-yellow mass oozed from the opening and filled the air with its putrid stench.

Feeling faint, Elena closed her eyes. Cold perspiration dotted her forehead. She clenched her teeth, refusing to give in to the weakness. *Miguel needs me. I have to be strong for his sake.* Taking in a deep, calming breath, she forced an encouraging smile to her lips. But when she turned to her husband, he had fainted.

"There. Now it will be better," Consuela said. She handed Juan the basin. "*Hijo,* fetch more hot water and tell Lupe to keep the kettles filled."

"*Sí, Madre.*" Taking the soiled container, Juan hurried from the room.

Elena stepped close to the maid and watched her stir a concoction in a bowl. "What is that?"

Consuela, her brow wrinkled in a worried frown, looked up. "I mixed two measures of powdered slippery elm bark with one measure of crushed, dried comfrey, flaxseed, and cornmeal, then added warm water to make a thick paste. Hold the cloth, Elena, while I smooth this on it."

When Consuela had spread the mixture on the cloth, she placed it over Miguel's wound. She added layers of steaming cloths on top of that. "Before it gets cool, we will add more hot rags. This poultice will draw the infection. After a few hours we will make a fresh mixture."

"How long do we do this?" Elena wanted to know.

"Until the infection and swelling are gone."

"Can I do anything else to help?" Elena asked softly.

The older woman, her face solemn, gazed down at Miguel's unconscious figure. "Pray, *niña.* We have done all we can. The rest is up to a higher power."

Elena closed her eyes and bent her head, praying to the Virgin of Guadalupe to help Miguel.

A few moments later Juan, carrying a large pan of steaming water, came back into the room. Lupe followed, her arms loaded with a pile of clean cloths. After setting the kettle by the bed, Juan raised his gaze from Miguel to Elena. He frowned and came to place his arm around her shoulders. "*Amiga,* you are exhausted. You can do no more here. We will watch over him."

"I can't leave him," she protested.

Juan shook his head, cutting his eyes toward Lupe. He led Elena to the doorway. "You must think of the child. Miguel is Diego's friend," he emphasized the words. "For Diego's sake, you must go."

Blinking back her tears, Elena nodded, telling Juan she understood. By allowing others to see her concern, she would be putting Miguel in danger. But, retreating from the room, she knew leaving him was the hardest thing she had ever done.

Chapter Thirty-one

LATER in the day the sound of horses and voices coming from the courtyard woke Elena from a restless sleep. Going to the window, she peered out and saw her brother-in-law, Ricardo, alight from his carriage and stride toward the house. The salon door opened, and Conception eagerly dashed into her husband's outstretched arms. After a frantic embrace and a long tender kiss, the couple strolled arm in arm to their quarters.

Elena smiled wistfully. If only things could be that simple with herself and Miguel. Anxious to see him, she ran a brush through her tousled hair, then hurried out the door.

When she entered his room, she felt a rush of fear. Miguel tossed restlessly on the bed, mumbling incoherently.

Her face sad, Consuela shook her head. "The wound seems better, but his fever will not break. *Niña,* you stay with him while I go talk with the midwife. Maybe she will know of something more powerful."

Terrified for her husband, Elena hurried the maid on her way. Taking Consuela's place by the sickbed, she squeezed out a cool cloth and wiped Miguel's scorching brow. "*Querido,* it is Elena," she murmured. "Miguel, can you hear me?" But in his fevered state, she could not reach him.

Agitated, in a world of his own, he cried out. *"Vamanos, hombres.* We must hide the gold."

Elena cast a frightened look behind her, grateful that she was alone. Her thankfulness was short-lived, however, for a few minutes later her father walked into the room. Elena held her breath when he approached the bed.

"How is our guest?" he asked, his brow knitted in a concerned frown.

"Not good, Father." Elena bent over the bed and replaced the cloth, praying her body would muffle Miguel's fevered ramblings.

"El Gato—de Vega—gold," the wounded man muttered.

Elena froze. Her breath caught in her throat.

"What?" Her father pushed her aside and leaned over the bed. "What did you say?"

Elena prayed Miguel wouldn't hear him—wouldn't answer.

"No one knows . . . secret."

Realizing she had to do something, Elena clutched her parent's arm. "Pay no mind to his ravings. It is the imaginings of the fever."

Her father shrugged off her hand and leaned closer. "What secret? You can tell me," he urged.

Miguel shook his head. "No. No one knows . . . Diego . . . El-Gat-o."

"What about El Gato?"

Frantic, Elena tugged his arm again. "Father, you must leave. The fever may be catching."

"Be quiet, Elena."

"Elena," a weak voice called. "Can't . . . know—Diego is El Gato."

Elena sucked in a panicked breath. The laugh she attempted came out as a choked sob. "See how he raves? The illness has made him crazed."

Her father locked his gaze on hers. "I'm not so sure." He turned his attention back to the man on the bed. "Diego is El Gato? Who are you?"

Her heart pounding, Elena stared at Miguel. *Dear God, please don't let him answer.*

"Elena?" Miguel opened his eyes. Spying her, he sighed. "I love you, *querida.*" His eyelids drooped, and he drifted back into unconsciousness.

Her father straightened and slowly turned, pinning her with his accusing gaze. "What do you know about this man?"

Elena swallowed and didn't answer. Ignoring his attempt to shove her aside, she stood her ground, placing herself between her father and Miguel.

Giving her a scathing look, the older man walked to the closet and yanked the door open. Muttering something about his gold, he rummaged through the contents. "Ah-hah! Look at this." He held up a group of pillowlike pads that formed a sort of vest. Encouraged by his discovery, he resumed his search. He emerged a moment later with a dark bundle of clothing in his hand.

Recognizing the ebony outfit as El Gato's, Elena's heart lurched. She felt the blood drain from her face. She bit her lip to keep from crying out.

Her father unfolded the slim black pants and shirt. A scrap of silk fell to the floor. He held it up, poking his fingers through the eyeholes of the mask. He switched his attention from the cloth to her. "I thought so." A triumphant look on his face, he strode to the dresser.

Elena trembled, knowing what he would find.

He rifled through the drawer and withdrew a hank of grayish-brown hair. Giving her a contemptuous look, he approached the bed and slapped the wig and lip piece on the unconscious man. "Diego. I scarcely recognized you."

Furious, her father spun toward her. His eyes narrowed accusingly. "You knew, didn't you?"

Elena swallowed. "Knew what?" The quiver in her voice betrayed her.

Without another word, Enrique de Vega stormed out of the room.

Finding her legs too weak to support her, Elena sank into the bedside chair. She lifted Miguel's limp hand and brought it to her lips. "Oh, my love. What will he do to you?" Tortured by her fear, she bent her head and cried.

A short time later Elena heard the door open. Terrified that it might be her father again, she let out a ragged sigh when Juan and Consuela entered the room.

Juan, noticing her tear-stained face, rushed to her side. "Elena, what's wrong?" His gaze went to Miguel. "Is he . . . ?"

"No!" she cried. "It's Father. He knows."

Juan sucked in his breath. "You mean . . . ?"

She nodded. "Miguel was delirious. Father heard him." She raised her hand to caress Miguel's cheek. "He found the clothes and the wig." Her voice broke. "He knows Miguel is El Gato."

"*Por Dios!*"

Consuela gasped and dropped the rag she had removed from the wound. "He is El Gato—the bandit?"

Juan picked up the rag and handed it back to her. "Never mind who he is. He is a good man and my friend. Now, let's see if we can save him." He opened a small bag of powdered herbs and stirred them into a cup of hot water. "Hold his head up, Elena. I'll try to get him to swallow."

"Miguel, wake up. Open your eyes, my love," Elena pleaded.

"*Querida?*" The wounded man raised his eyelids. He frowned at Juan and Consuela.

"Open your mouth, *amigo*," Juan ordered, holding the cup to his lips. "Drink it all."

Miguel shuddered, but obediently swallowed the bitter brew. When the cup was empty, Elena lowered him to the pillow.

"Now sleep, my friend." Juan switched his gaze to Elena. "Let's pray it works."

Elena reached out and anxiously clasped Juan's hand. "Will you stay with us?"

Juan nodded. "I'll be here if either of you needs me."

The night passed slowly with the three of them standing watch by Miguel's bedside. For Elena, the night couldn't last long enough. So far her father hadn't returned. Realizing his hatred for El Gato, she knew with uneasy certainty that for them the calm could not last.

With the arrival of dawn came loud voices and heavy footsteps. The door crashed open. Elena, her mouth dry with fear, saw her father, accompanied by Guillermo and another man, enter the room. She clutched Miguel's hand even tighter. He opened his eyes.

"How touching," her father mocked. He waved a hand toward Miguel. "See how she hovers over the bandit?" His lips thinned. "Get him out of here. Remove the vermin from my house. Lock him in the vault."

"No!" Elena cried, covering her husband's body with her own.

"No, *querida*. Juan, take her away," Miguel said in a faint voice.

"No, I won't let them!" she cried out, clinging to the wooden bedframe. Coarse hands plucked her free and roughly shoved her aside. Other hands, more gentle, reached out to keep her from falling.

Juan held her fast as she struggled to reach her husband. "Elena, we can't fight them."

Her heart breaking, she watched the two men carry Miguel from the room. She twisted away from Juan. "Father, please. I beg you. Don't do this. He will die."

"So he dies." He shrugged, fixing her with a cold stare. "What does it matter? If he lives, I will see him hanged." Following the three men, he stormed out of the room, slamming the door behind him.

Through her tears Elena saw that Ricardo and Conception, obviously drawn by the commotion, had entered the room. She reached out to them. "Please, help me."

Conception curled her lip in contempt. "I can't believe you married El Gato." She shook her head, ignoring Elena's pleas. "Elena, you're behaving like a fool. The man is a thief. I, for one, will enjoy watching him hang."

"No." The vision of Miguel dying at the end of a rope was more than Elena could stand. With a grief-stricken cry, she collapsed in Ricardo's arms and sank into the darkness.

"Now are you happy, Conception?"

Conception shrank away from the blazing anger in her husband's eyes. Her rebellious gaze went to Elena's unconscious figure. It's not my fault, she thought, but seeing the condemnation on Ricardo's face, she swallowed. She'd never seen him this furious. She took a timid step toward him. "Ricardo? Can I help you?"

"You've done enough," Ricardo said, his voice icy. "Open the door. Then get out of my way."

Shaken, Conception opened the door and stepped aside.

"Take her to her room. We will stay with her," Juan said.

Conception trailed behind, waiting while Ricardo lowered her sister to the bed. Elena looked pale as death. "Will she be all right?" she asked, feeling guilty for what she'd done. Even if Elena was a fool, she was still her sister.

Consuela looked at her. "I hope so. I only pray she doesn't lose the child."

"The child?" Ricardo gasped, raising his gaze to Juan.

"Elena is going to have a baby," Juan answered.

"I suppose the child will be El Gato's?" Conception said, wrinkling her nose with disgust.

"The baby will be her husband's, Conception," Ricardo snapped. "Now, before you do any further harm, I suggest you pack."

Conception sucked in her breath. "Pack?"

"We are leaving the Spanish Angel today. I've had enough of your nonsense. If you intend to remain my wife, you will do as I say. If you don't"—Ricardo locked his eyes on hers— "I never want to see you again."

Conception trembled, hearing the cold disdain in his voice. He had to be joking. She stared at him. The look on his face told her he was deadly serious.

"Do you understand?"

Her lip quivering, she bowed her head. "Yes, Ricardo."

"Now, say goodbye to your sister and tell her you are sorry."

"Yes, my love." Conception walked slowly to the bed and knelt by Elena. She lifted her sister's hand and, blinking back tears, gazed into her eyes. "*Hermanita,* I am sorry. Will you forgive me?"

Elena nodded and gave her a weak smile. "Of course, Conception. After all, you are my sister. I pray you and Ricardo will be happy."

Remorse for all the times she'd been mean to Elena rose in a flood of regretful tears. "I'll pray for you, too . . . and your husband," Conception whispered.

Ricardo bent and kissed Elena's cheek. "I, too, little sister." He turned to Juan and Consuela. "Watch over them. Let me know if I am needed." He shook Juan's hand, then walked slowly from the room.

Conception blew Elena a kiss from the doorway. When she looked down the hall, she saw Ricardo waiting at the head of the stairs. He held out his hand. Thanking God she had married this man, Conception ran down the hall to join her husband.

Chapter Thirty-two

TWO days after locking El Gato in the vault, Enrique returned to search his son-in-law's room, hoping he might find some clue as to the whereabouts of the stolen gold. But when he ransacked Diego's possessions, instead of the treasure he sought, Enrique discovered something else—something that shook him to his bones. Clutching his find to his breast, he stumbled to his study and bolted the door.

For hours he'd sat hunched over his desk, an untouched glass of brandy in front of him. He'd remained there until the afternoon faded into darkness and an anemic sliver of moon lit the night sky. Tears of a long-forgotten grief ran and dried in the heavy creases of his cheeks.

His thoughts traveled back through time, unshelving memories that had haunted him over a score of years. The clenched palm of his hand warmed the cold gold of the locket he'd found in a small carved box in Diego's room— the locket with the picture of his beloved Teresa inside.

He'd almost discarded it in his haste to find some clue to his plundered fortune. Something had stayed his hand, made him open it. And when he did, Teresa, young and lovely, a warm smile on her face, had gazed up at him. How often he'd seen that same smile, ever since they had played together as children.

Raised on adjoining small ranches, he'd loved her all

his life. He'd prayed, when they were older, she would be his wife, even though her father frowned on the match because she was pure Castilian and Enrique was of mixed blood. Just when it looked as if Teresa's father would finally approve, Enrique's wealthy, fourth cousin, Victorio Sandoval, stopped by the ranch on his way back from Chihuahua. Only passing through until he'd seen Teresa, Victorio had extended his stay.

Enrique shook his head. How could he, Enrique de Vega with the short, dark looks of his Indian mother, have ever hoped to compete with the tall, dashing Spaniard? Teresa fell in love with Victorio, and later, when the two married, Enrique thought he would die from the pain. From that time onward, he'd hated anything that reminded him of his Indian blood, feeling it was what caused him to lose his beloved.

He'd tried to make up for his shortcomings by learning to read, something very few *hidalgos* knew how to do. It became an obsession, taking the place of any social life he might have had.

Less than ten years later Victorio died after being gored by a bull, leaving Teresa a widow. Now that she was alone, her parents having died of fever, Enrique had dared to hope again. His mouth tightened in a bitter line. That was before old Don Luis Sandoval, Victorio's father, had forbidden him to see her.

Driven to desperation by his love, Enrique had hatched a plan to hold the old man captive and take Teresa away. He was sure once she knew how much he loved her that she would love him in return. He'd thought after he'd kept her long enough to compromise her reputation, to avoid a scandal Don Luis would insist they be wed. Enrique had wanted nothing more than to marry her and raise her young son as his own.

But nothing turned out as he had planned. His hand tightened on the locket. Sobs shook his body as he forced his tortured mind back to that day.

He'd planned it carefully, waiting until the *vaqueros* were absent on a trail drive. But his horse had thrown a shoe, making him late for the rendezvous. When he reached the site where he was to meet Guillermo and the men he'd hired, they were already gone. He trembled, reliving the horror he'd found when he finally reached the hacienda. The dead, mutilated bodies. The women, their legs spread and bloody from the rapes they'd been forced to endure before they'd been killed. The old men, even children.

"No!" he cried into the darkness, remembering how he'd found his lovely Teresa. On the bed in her room she'd taken her own life rather than submit to the degradation. He'd found her small son trampled into the dirt, his jacket the only thing that made his identification possible.

Crazy with grief, he'd hunted Guillermo. But when he'd found him, the young gunman Enrique had thought to be his friend sneered at him. Guillermo said it wasn't his fault. The *vaqueros* at the hacienda had put up a fight. He'd been forced to kill them. He'd pointed out that since the raid had been Enrique's idea, no one would believe the raiders weren't acting under Enrique's orders. He added slyly that no one would believe Enrique de Vega innocent when they found out he was sole heir to the vast Spanish Angel holdings.

After Enrique took possession of the ranch, he bitterly discovered that if one were rich enough, others were happy to overlook his *mestizo* blood. Needing an heir, he'd married Soledad, the daughter of a Spanish nobleman. After their two daughters were born, Guillermo showed up again, demanding to be made majordomo. Enrique had been forced to make him foreman, forced to ignore the atrocities the man had committed since that time. Guillermo continued to blackmail him throughout the years, threatening to tell Soledad, his children, and the authorities that Enrique was responsible for the raid so long ago.

Enrique bowed his head, wishing again, as he had many times through the years, that he'd had the guts to kill Guillermo when he'd had the chance. He'd secretly hoped El Gato or his men would kill the foreman, but Guillermo had managed to avoid any danger. And now, even though he would not be sorry to see the end of El Gato, Enrique knew he was also losing his last hope of getting rid of Guillermo, who'd been a plague to him for so many years.

He opened his hand and gazed down at the locket. How had the bandit gained possession of the necklace? He'd probably stolen it, but when—and from whom? Enrique knew he wouldn't rest until he found out. And the only one who could tell him what he needed to know was El Gato.

Troubled, he rose from the chair and walked around the desk. He hated what he knew he must do. He had to make sure the bandit survived, at least until he had the answers to his questions.

Going into the hall, Enrique searched for the houseboy, but the hour was late. The servant had retired for the night. Enrique shrugged. The bandit was still alive. Morning would be soon enough. Sighing, he trudged up the stairs.

At the top of the staircase he froze, sensing another presence. He raised his head. "No!" he gasped. He shrank back, clutching the banister for support.

A woman in blue stood in front of him. Her face shone pale and condemning in the flickering candlelight of the hall sconces. Tears flowed in silvery trails down her ivory cheeks.

Enrique withered under accusing eyes that bored into him like twin blue fires. "What do you want from me?" he cried.

"You know," the voice whispered. The pain in her cry wrenched his soul. A chill crawled up his spine, leaving him weak and shivering.

"You know," the voice wailed again. The vision faded, then vanished.

Enrique's legs buckled under him and he crumpled onto the top step. "Why won't she leave me be?" he sobbed. "What does she want?" Feeling old and very much alone, he buried his face in his hands.

Juan stood with his mother at the foot of Elena's bed. "How is she?" he asked quietly.

Consuela shook her head. "She does not eat. In two days this is the first time she has slept. I am afraid for her and the child." She raised her head. "Have you been able to see Miguel?"

Juan nodded. "Tonight. I bribed the guard. He let me enter long enough to change the bandage. I repacked the wound. Miguel is better but still very weak. He can think of nothing but Elena and the baby." Juan swallowed and took a deep breath. "He begged me to take her away. He doesn't want her to see him die." Juan swiped at a tear that crept down his cheek. "*Heridas de Cristo,* I must do something to help them."

Consuela placed a hand on his arm. "What can you do, *niño*? You are no match for Guillermo and his men."

Juan's lips thinned. "At least we don't have to worry about the *pistoleros*. If I could find Carlos and El Gato's men, I'm sure we could set Miguel free."

"How could you? Do you know where they are?"

Juan nodded. "Miguel said they are on the—" He broke

off, shaking his head. "Maybe it is better you don't know." He saw the deep-lined worry in her face. "I can tell you that I must leave tonight." He clasped his mother's shoulders and looked into her dark eyes. "Pray for all of us, *Madrecita*. I think we will need it." He let his gaze rest on his sister for a moment, then gave his mother a hug and swiftly left the room.

Early the next morning Enrique left the house and walked swiftly toward the vault where El Gato was being held. When the guard let him in, Enrique blinked, accustoming his eyes to the dim light. He made out the slender figure of his son-in-law sprawled on a crude pallet on the floor.

He knelt and reached out to shake the man awake. He jerked back when El Gato's eyes opened, riveting his with a look of naked hate. "What do you want?" the bandit growled.

Unnerved by the defiance in El Gato's voice, Enrique got to his feet. "I found this in your room." He held out the locket. "I want to know where you got it."

The wounded man let out a roar of rage and staggered to his feet. "Give it to me!" He swayed forward, reaching out to retrieve the necklace.

Frightened, but determined, Enrique closed his hand over the locket and stepped away. "Who is this woman to you?" he demanded.

"Why should I tell you?" El Gato retorted bitterly. "I am going to die anyway."

"Diego, we once were friends. You are married to my daughter. Please, I have to know," Enrique said quietly.

The tall man sagged, the fight leaving him as suddenly as it came. "She was my mother."

"No! Now I know you lie!" Enrique cried.

The bandit's blue eyes blazed. "I do not lie. She was

Teresa Sandoval, my mother. I am Miguel Sandoval."

Enrique stared at the man, suddenly seeing the resemblance to his cousin Victorio. "It can't be true." He stepped closer, gazing into Miguel's eyes—Teresa's eyes stared back. "*Por Dios!*" He shook his head and backed out the door. "No. It can't be true." But even as he heard his words, he knew they were a lie. Suddenly he knew why the angel had haunted him all these years. Tears blurring his vision, he shuffled toward the house.

In spite of the bright sun warming Enrique's shoulders, he shivered as he walked across the wide dusty area and into the manicured courtyard of the hacienda.

He gazed up at the massive adobe structure that for so many years he had called home. Today he felt like a stranger, an unwelcome stranger. Alone and confused, he slumped down on a wooden garden bench.

For the first time in his life he was incapable of making a decision. He stared at the ground. Tears rolled down his cheeks. He raised a shaking hand to wipe them away. If only he knew what to do.

A bitter smile twisted his mouth, remembering how much his friendship with Diego had meant to him. He'd thought of him almost as a son. How ironic that the cherished friendship had all been a sham. Ironic that the boy he'd wanted for a son and buried so long ago should come back from the grave to bring about his destruction.

He knew he could kill Miguel and the secret would die with him. That way he could keep the ranch and everything it represented.

Almost reluctantly he opened the locket and stared into Teresa's trusting face—into eyes that were so like Miguel's. He lifted a trembling finger and wiped a fleck of dust from her beloved cheek. As he did so, he swallowed bitter gall, wondering what kind of man had he become that he could

even consider destroying the only part of her he had left—
her only child.

"The child." He frowned. If the man in the vault was
Miguel Sandoval as he had claimed, then who was the
child they'd buried that day? He got to his feet, knowing
he had to see the bandit again. He had to make sure so that
he could put the past to rest once and for all.

Chapter Thirty-three

GUILLERMO leaned against the shadowy wall and chewed the end of an unlit cigar. A thrill of anticipation heated his blood as he watched Rosita leave her house and carry a small pail toward the goat barn. Curving his lips in a faint smile, he congratulated himself for sending Rodolfo up into the hills to tend the sheep. Ever since she'd had the kid, the man had hung around her like a dog after a bitch in heat. Rodolfo hadn't wanted to go, but a Colt .44 waved under his nose had convinced him he'd better.

Licking his lips, Guillermo moved back into the gloom and waited for Rosita's graceful stride to bring her closer.

The warm morning breeze molded the thin blouse to her full breasts and pushed her skirt tight against her thighs. Tendrils of dark hair escaped her long, shiny braids and curled around her youthful face.

He raked her curves with a lust-filled gaze, finding little to remind him of the skinny virgin he'd dragged into the hay. Heat swelled his loins, making him prideful of the fact she'd born his daughter a bare eight months later. Someday he intended to tell the brat he was her daddy. The kid had a right to know. A bastard son of a whore himself, he'd never known who spawned him. Probably just as well.

He removed his gunbelt and hung it on a nail, then stepped behind the door and waited.

Unsuspecting, Rosita entered the barn and walked toward the small platform where the goat, its bag swollen with milk, stood waiting. After placing her bucket under the doe, Rosita lifted her skirt and sat on the short, three-legged stool.

Eyeing her exposed bare legs, Guillermo unfastened his pants. She was like a mouse in a trap, and he was the cat. Grinning broadly, he silently closed the door and slid the wide wooden bolt. Using the straw-covered floor to muffle his footsteps, he crept toward her.

Sensing another presence, Rosita turned.

He leered at her. "Hello, little mama," he said. "This time I want a boy."

Hitching his pants up, Guillermo left the barn, giving no more than a passing thought to the woman he'd left sobbing in the hay. Women were good for only one thing, unless of course they were Elena de Vega. Along with that prime piece came the Spanish Angel Ranch.

Knowing Elena would soon be a widow, he laughed. He'd have no trouble forcing the weak-willed Enrique to give his blessing to the wedding. Guillermo didn't intend to wait for El Gato's body to get cold, let alone observe the customary year of mourning before he bedded his widow. In fact, he might hump her in front of the vault and let El Gato watch. He grinned.

Deciding to torment the bandit with his plan, Guillermo swaggered toward the strong room. Hearing voices from inside, he frowned at the guard. "Who's in there?"

"Don Enrique," the man answered.

"Give me the key. I'll stand guard while you get your breakfast," he growled. Guillermo waited until the jailer was out of sight, then pressed his ear to the partially opened door. His eyes narrowed.

"No one was supposed to get hurt, but the *vaqueros* returned and started shooting," de Vega said.

"You lie!" El Gato shouted. "The men were gone. They didn't return until after the funerals."

"That can't be. Guillermo said—"

"That bastard was there?" the bandit hissed.

"Yes. Guillermo led the men. I didn't arrive until it was over." Enrique shuddered, remembering. "The dead were everywhere."

"Any dead *vaqueros*?" the bandit asked, his voice filled with sarcasm. "I thought not. If you truly seek the truth, ask El Viejo."

"What would the blind man know of the raid?" de Vega scoffed.

"He was there," El Gato answered. "He'd broken his leg and couldn't go with the rest of the *vaqueros* on the drive. Your men blinded him and left him for dead."

Enrique gasped. "I will talk to him. I must know the truth."

Not wanting de Vega to see him, Guillermo raced away from the vault. He crouched behind the wooden wheel of a *carreta* and waited for his employer to pass. He stared after the man, wondering how anyone could be such a gullible fool. After hiding the truth all those years, Guillermo knew the cat was out of the bag. *Damn it! Why had Enrique told El Gato?* He frowned. How could the bandit know what he did about the raid? He couldn't, unless he'd been there. He shook his head, discarding the idea. The blind man must have told him. Straightening, Guillermo cast a venomous glance toward the village. He'd take care of that matter later. Right now he had to get rid of the bandit.

Knowing he had no time to lose, Guillermo hurried to the vault. The kegs of gunpowder and dynamite he'd set into place were ready, buried in shallow trenches around the outside of the rock-walled building. Damn! He'd hoped to take El Gato away and torture him until he'd revealed where the gold was hidden. He heaved a regretful sigh. Now he'd have to settle for just killing him.

Guillermo fished in his pocket for a match. *Hell. Must have lost them in the goat shed.*

Casting a wary glance toward the study door, Elena rummaged through the drawers of her father's desk again. It wasn't there. She stood, surveying the room. *Somewhere there has to be another key. If it isn't in the desk, then where would it be? Somewhere safe.* Her gaze landed on the gun closet. "Of course."

Trembling with excitement, she retrieved the gun key from the desk and hurried across the room. When she opened the paneled door, a dull gleam of metal caught her eye. *Yes!* She quickly lifted the key from the hook and tucked it into the pocket of her skirt. After relocking the cabinet door, she eyed the desk. Shaking her head, she dropped the second key into her pocket. If her father couldn't open the gun closet, he wouldn't miss the vault key.

She checked the room, making sure things were as she had found them, then turned the knob and peered into the hall. She yanked her head back. Heart pounding, she eased the door shut and leaned against the wall. Just outside the room the houseboy knelt, cleaning the hall floor. She was safe enough, as the boy wasn't allowed to enter the study. Sighing with impatience, she hoped her father stayed away until she had a chance to escape.

Matches in hand, Guillermo left the adobe bunkhouse and strode toward the vault.

"Guillermo! I want to talk to you," de Vega's imperious voice called out.

He turned to see de Vega stalking toward him. "What do you want?" he said contemptuously. "I'm busy."

"You will hear what I have to say." Enrique shook a fist at him. "You lied to me. All these years you've made me live with the guilt of that massacre when it was you who deliberately butchered all those people."

Guillermo sneered, thinking his employer resembled an overwrought banty rooster. "So what if I did?"

"You killed the child, too—?" De Vega's voice broke.

"Yeah. I ran the horse right over the little bastard. Got his pretty jacket all dirty." He laughed. "But then, I guess it held up better than the rest of him."

De Vega's eyes showed his horror. He shuddered. "*Por Dios!* You are a monster. I order you to release Miguel Sandoval from the vault." Enrique shook his head. "I've had enough of killings."

Guillermo raised a brow. *Miguel Sandoval? So that's how he knew about the raid.* Well, it changed nothing. He'd killed the wrong kid, so he'd make up for it now. Reminded of that day, he gave de Vega a sly smile. "Would you like to hear how his pretty mama died?" He watched Enrique grow pale. "When I broke her door down, she ran at me with that little knife. Gave me this," he pointed to a faint scar on his cheek. He snickered. "I knocked it out of her hand. I sent the rest of the men away, then I screwed the hell out of her right there on her own bed." He rubbed his crotch suggestively. "What a woman." He grinned at the older man. "*Amigo,* you don't know what you missed."

"No!" Enrique gave a strangled cry and leapt at him.

Guillermo batted him aside. "I was gonna take her with us, but afterward, when I was pouring myself a drink, she picked up the dagger. I hated to kill her." He shook his head. "Such a waste."

"I'll kill you, you bastard!" Enrique screamed, throwing himself at him.

"Enough. I have no time for this." Guillermo thrust out his hand and held the smaller man at bay. "First, I'm gonna kill the bitch's son, then I intend to have your daughter. After I break her in, I'll marry her—*with* your blessing, old man."

Enrique seemed to shrink inside his skin.

Guillermo laughed. "You know what I say is true, and there's not a thing you can do to stop me."

"Damn you!" De Vega sobbed, struggling to be free.

Doubling his hand into a fist, Guillermo hit the old man, knocking him unconscious into the dust. Glancing around, he dragged him out of sight behind some bushes. "And now for El Gato." He dusted his hands together and, whistling an off-key tune, strode toward the vault.

Elena slipped from the house and ran to the small building that held her husband. Finding the guard absent, she fumbled in her pocket for the key. "Miguel," she whispered. She pressed her face to the bars. She covered her mouth with her hand, stifling a tortured cry. *Santa Maria!* What had happened to him?

Miguel lay unmoving on the ragged blanket, his face swollen and covered with blood.

With trembling fingers, she forced the key into the lock. It wouldn't turn. Sobbing with frustration, she tried again, this time using both hands. It still refused to work. What was wrong? A sinking feeling told her she had the wrong key. Sobbing, she sank to her knees in front of the door. "*La Madama,* please, help me," she pleaded, praying to the angel. She'd already tried everyone else, from God, to the Virgin of Guadalupe, to every saint she'd ever heard of.

A faint flowerlike scent drifted through the small barred window of the vault door. "*I am here,*" a voice as soft as a breeze sighed from inside.

Elena struggled to her feet and pressed her face to the opening. Her eyes widened with wonder as she beheld the vision in blue standing beside Miguel. "*Madre de Dios!*" It was the beautiful lady in the painting. Elena crossed herself. "It is true. You do exist."

The woman smiled.

"If you are able, I beg you, please help us. Miguel is a good man. He doesn't deserve to die."

A rough hand wrapped around her waist. "What the hell are you doing here?"

Crushed against a huge chest, she twisted to see Guillermo. Futilely she grabbed the bars and took another fleeting glance inside before he pulled her away. The angel had vanished. "Let me go!" she cried, kicking backward at his shins.

He tightened his grip, cutting off her breath. "This place is gonna blow any minute. You're coming with me whether you want to or not."

"Blow?" Elena's blood grew cold. "What are you talking about?"

He grinned down at her. "The dynamite. Your pretty bandit will be a permanent part of the Spanish Angel. I bet pieces of him land everywhere." He dragged her backward. "We've got to get out of here before we go up, too."

"No!" Elena screamed, clawing at his arms. "Somebody help me. Please, help me!"

Suddenly the strong hold around her loosened. Guillermo sagged to the ground. A spasm of disbelief contorted his swarthy face. "Rosita?" His incredulous gaze fastened on the small woman standing over him, a sharp bloody knife clutched in her hands. "Why?"

"*Hijo de la chingarra.* You want a son? You should have tried the pigs." She patted her middle. "I already carry a child—Rodolfo's." She spat on him.

"You lie!" he cried, a bloody froth on his lips.

Elena grabbed the girl's arm. "Please, help me find the key." She bent and patted the dying man's clothing. "He must have it in his pocket. He's set dynamite. I have to free my husband."

Rosita's frantic hands joined in the search. The girl held up a long object. "Here!"

Snatching the key, Elena ran the few steps to the building and opened the door. Miguel was still unconscious. "Rosita, help me."

The girl entered and took Miguel's other arm. Together they dragged him free of the building, passing Guillermo, who clawed the dirt in a feeble attempt to crawl to safety.

When they were a short distance away, the dynamite exploded with a deafening roar that knocked them to their knees. The sky above them filled with rocks and flying fragments. A black cloud of smoke and gunpowder spread over the ground, smothering them with an acrid stench.

Elena flattened herself over Miguel, trying to protect him from the falling debris. Rosita did the same. Tightly clutching hands, they murmured a frantic prayer.

Finally the rocks stopped falling, and only the cloud of dust remained. Elena raised her head.

Not a trace of the small building remained. Nor was there any sign of Guillermo.

She shivered, thinking how close to death they'd been. She bowed her head. "Thank you, La Madama," she whispered.

Elena turned to her companion. "And thank you, Rosita." She studied the girl. "How did you know? Did you hear me scream?"

"I was in the barn. Guillermo—" She shook her head. Tears ran in muddy streaks down her cheeks. "After he left, I cried and cried. A hand touched my shoulder. I screamed, afraid he had returned. Then I saw her, a beautiful lady in blue. She told me not to be afraid. She touched me again, and I saw you struggling with Guillermo. When she vanished, I knew what I must do. On my way out of the barn I saw the machete we use to cut the hay. I took it and ran to help."

Elena's eyes filled with tears. They ran down her cheeks and dripped onto Miguel's face.

He opened his eyes. "Elena? Rosita? What has happened?" he asked, noticing their tears.

"Miguel, it was a miracle," Elena said. "Guillermo set off the dynamite. The angel saved you."

He struggled to sit up. His eyes widened as he saw the hole where the vault had been. "*Por Dios!*"

She and Rosita helped him to his feet. When they turned toward the hacienda, Elena gasped. "Father!"

Enrique staggered toward them, his face battered and bruised. Blood flowed from his lip.

"Help him, Rosita!" Elena cried. The girl left them to run to Enrique's side. Drawing the old man's arm over her slender shoulders, she supported his swaying figure.

He gave them a feeble smile. "Elena. Miguel. Thank God, you are all right." He clutched their arms. His tears mixed with the red stain running down his face.

"What happened?" Miguel asked. "The blast?"

"Guillermo." He raised agonized eyes to Miguel. "I know the truth. I told him to free you. He refused. He said he was going to kill you."

Miguel nodded. "He tried. They said the angel saved me, but I think she had a lot of help." Smiling, he squeezed Elena's shoulder. "Whatever happened, I'm grateful." Gazing down, he saw the shadows under his wife's tear-glazed, topaz eyes. "Now, I think we could all use a little doctoring and some rest."

He turned to the bloody, battered man that was her father. "Enrique, let's go home."

Chapter Thirty-four

LATER that afternoon, hearing a knock on their bedroom door, Miguel rose from Elena's side, leaving her to an exhausted slumber. He quietly eased the door open to find his father-in-law standing in the hall. A troubled frown creased Miguel's forehead as he studied the man before him. This was an Enrique de Vega he'd never seen.

Always proud and erect, Enrique looked as if his frame had collapsed, leaving him bent and broken. Deep creases lined his bruised face. His shadowed eyes appeared old and without hope. "Can we talk, Miguel?" he asked humbly.

Miguel nodded. Closing the bedroom door behind him, he motioned for his father-in-law to follow him down the stairs. He led the way into the salon and waved a hand toward a chair. "Please, sit down, Enrique."

The older man slumped into the seat, his head bowed. "Miguel, I have done you a great wrong, and there is no way I can ever make it right." His voice broke. "I would give my life to change it back to the way it was. But I know my worthless being could never be enough to repair the damage I have done to you and your family." He reached into his pocket and took out a faded parchment. His hand trembling, he held it out to Miguel. "This is rightfully yours. I never wanted it, nor did I ever have any right to it."

Puzzled, Miguel opened the ancient paper. It was the land grant, the deed to the Spanish Angel. He looked at his father-in-law. "For many years, since I was a small child, I've lived for one thing . . . revenge. Every day I prayed you wouldn't die so that I might have the pleasure of killing you myself."

Enrique buried his head in his blue-veined hands. His dejected body shook with tormented sobs.

Miguel reached out and gently touched the man's shoulders. "Enrique, now I see that might have been the kindest thing I could have done for you. Never could I have punished you as much as you have punished yourself."

Enrique raised his head. Tears ran from his sunken eyes and trailed down the deep creases of his face. "How could I not? My obsession set the plan into motion. I killed those people as surely as if I had done the butchering myself. Those twisted bodies and tormented faces will haunt me to my grave." He nodded his head. "You were right to seek revenge. Being Miguel Sandoval, you could do nothing else."

Enrique slowly struggled to his feet. "I have packed the few things I could call mine." He held on to the top of the chair for support. "If you would be so kind as to lend me your carriage, I will be gone within the hour."

Miguel got to his feet. He didn't know what to say. He should have felt triumphant. He'd won. He had the Spanish Angel back, and his old enemy was defeated and alone. Everything he'd struggled for all those years had come to pass. But the sadness inside told him his victory was a hollow one.

Looking into Enrique's face, he saw no enemy, only a broken old man who was Elena's father and soon to be the grandfather of their child. He placed his hands on Enrique's shoulders. "The time for vengeance has passed.

I don't want you to leave." He smiled down into the spark of hope lighting the elderly man's eyes. "I want my child to know his grandfather."

"Grandfather?" Enrique's shaking hand clutched Miguel's arm. "Do you mean—?"

Miguel nodded. "Elena and I are going to have a baby."

"A grandbaby." More tears flowed down Enrique's face. But this time they were tears of joy.

Wiping the moisture from his own eyes, Miguel picked up the deed and handed it back. "This belongs to neither of us, my friend. We are only the caretakers. The Angel belongs to the future generations, our children and Conception's children. It is up to us to keep it safe and intact for them."

Miguel gazed out the window, watching the setting sun sink behind pink-rimmed hills. "The past is buried. Now we must band together and be strong. I feel as sure as I'm standing here, someday we will have a battle on our hands. Others will scheme and plot to take all of this away from us." He shook his head. "I don't know how it will turn out. In the meantime, we have a sacred trust."

He looked into Enrique's eyes, seeing the pride and determination return. Miguel smiled. "Now, may I suggest that you unpack? With that mess outside, we have a lot of work to do."

Enrique straightened his shoulders. "I'll see to it right away."

Miguel laughed. "Tomorrow will be soon enough. After breakfast. From now on we will dine together. I think it's time we started behaving like a family, don't you?"

Enrique nodded. "It's all I've ever wanted." Happiness lit his face. "Maybe she'll have a boy." He glanced up at Miguel. "But granddaughters are wonderful, too." He went out the door, murmuring about his plans for the children.

Miguel smiled, hoping that someday Juan would find forgiveness in his heart as well and reveal his secret. He sighed, knowing he had a secret of his own to reveal to Elena.

He turned toward the hallway to find her standing just outside the door, her face stricken and pale as the silken robe she'd slipped over the filmy nightdress. "Elena?"

She raised wounded topaz eyes to his. "You are Miguel Sandoval?" Her voice was filled with pain.

"You heard?"

She nodded. "Everything was part of your plan for revenge, wasn't it? Our marriage"—she bowed her head, placing a hand over her middle—"even our child."

"Yes," he said, slowly walking toward her. "But that was before I fell in love."

"How can you talk of love when you didn't trust me enough to tell the truth?"

Miguel led her into the salon and seated her on the couch. He sat down beside her. "I was afraid. How could I tell you and take the chance of losing you?" He picked up her hand and encased it in his own. "You were part of the plan, but after I took your innocence that night on the mountain, I could think of nothing but you. I fought against it. I thought myself bewitched. Remember, at that time, I thought you were your sister. I couldn't understand how I could feel that way toward Conception. I didn't even like her.

"I was shocked when I discovered you weren't who I thought you were. But my heart knew all the time. Then, when I learned you were to marry Guillermo, I couldn't stand the idea of another man putting his hands on you. Even though you were the daughter of my worst enemy, I knew I had to make you my own."

He gave her a rueful smile. "Do you know what torment I went through on our wedding night? I was crazy with wanting you. What was worse, as your husband, I had the right, but because of my disguise, I couldn't. I was thoroughly tangled in my own deception." He lifted her hand to his lips.

"Did you know I saw you the first night you rode to the pond? When I saw Juan follow, I thought he was your lover. I went insane with jealousy. I hurried away from my men, giving no thought to the gold I had stolen. I only wanted to get back here so I could find out what you were up to. When you weren't home, I knew I had to do something. I stayed up all night waiting for you to come back."

"That was why you behaved so strangely?" she said. "I had never seen you so unkempt. Diego had always been so fastidious about his appearance."

Miguel groaned. "Diego. That was torture in itself. I've always hated fussy things. It was hard to see the revulsion in your eyes when I felt so much love. Then, when I knew Diego had your loyalty and that loyalty would prevent you from being unfaithful, I had to destroy that trust. I had to make you vulnerable, so that as El Gato I could win your heart. Elena—*querida*, will you ever forgive me?"

She gave him a wary look. "What about the baby?"

"The baby?"

"Yes. Did you really want the child, or did you get me pregnant so you could regain control of the ranch?"

"When I learned you were expecting, I was overwhelmed. I knew I had to get you pregnant to get the ranch, but when I found out you were, the ranch was the farthest thing from my mind. I was terrified. I was so proud, so happy knowing I was to be a father, but I couldn't stand the thought of you being alone and unprotected. As El Gato, I knew my life could be forfeit at any time. I realized the ranch was unimportant. You and the child were my whole life."

His eyes pleaded with her to understand. "Elena, *querida*, without you I am nothing. But if you cannot find it in your heart to forgive me, I will leave."

Her face solemn, she studied him. "You didn't trust me. I could forget everything else but that, Miguel. Without trust there is nothing."

Miguel closed his eyes against the pain. He felt as though she had hit him. He'd been so sure their love would win out. Too shaken to answer, he got to his feet and walked toward the door. "If there is ever anything you need, I'll leave an address where you can reach me."

His hand on the knob, he turned for one last look, slowly memorizing everything about her, knowing it would have to last him a lifetime.

Starting with her dainty feet, he followed the slender line of her legs up to her softly rounded stomach, pausing at the enlarged breasts that would soon give nourishment to his child. His gaze caressed her graceful neck and stubborn chin. When he reached her mouth, he blinked. She was smiling!

Shaking her head reproachfully, Elena walked forward. "See, you still didn't trust me. Don't you know I would never let you leave?" She raised her hand and caressed his cheek.

Amazed, he stared down at her. "Elena, what am I ever going to do with you?"

She snuggled into his arms. "Love me, Diego, El Gato, Miguel—whoever you are calling yourself today." Her eyes warm with love, she gazed up at him. "Just love me."

"Oh, *querida*." He bent his head and fastened his lips to hers. *Love her? Por Dios!* That he intended to do every day for the rest of his life.

Epilogue

ELENA leaned back against her husband's arm and watched her father and brother on their hands and knees on the floor. A bevy of small children surrounded them, vying for the chance to ride on their grandfather's and uncle's backs.

Enrique, groaning, gripped the arm of his chair and pulled himself upright. "Juan, my son, I'm leaving them all to you. These old bones aren't up to such rowdiness."

Miguel laughed and pointed across the room at Conception, who was very pregnant with her fourth child. "My friend, it seems we've only just begun." He gazed down into Elena's eyes. "Shall we tell him now or later?"

She grinned up at him. "Now."

He tightened his arm about her shoulder. "We will have a new Christmas present for you, Grandpapa. Could even be two, if we follow Conception and Ricardo's lead."

"That's wonderful!" Enrique shouted, trying to make himself heard over the din. His face wreathed in a smile, he rubbed his forehead. "And to think I yearned for the patter of little feet."

Juan, still a bachelor, grinned. "Sounds more like a stampede to me." He gathered a pair of battling, towheaded twin toddlers into his arms. "Wait until these little devils get old enough to marry. We'll have to clean out the old cannon to keep the boys at bay."

Enrique picked up a dark-haired, blue-eyed girl of three. "We will have lots of practice by then. Miguel and Elena's Angel will give them a run for their money." He ruffled a mop of dark curls.

Elena's eyes filmed with tears as she gazed down at their oldest, five-year-old Victorio who, despite the confusion, slept soundly on a pallet at their feet. His younger brother, taken by fever when only a few months old, lay under a headstone in the Spanish Angel graveyard.

Miguel, sensing her sadness, tightened his arm and tenderly kissed her brow. "Speaking of angels, Enrique, do you see La Madama anymore?"

Enrique shook his head. "Not for years now. I must say it is a relief, but strange as it seems, I miss her."

"Grandpapa, would you get me a drink of water?" four-year-old Marcos, Conception's oldest, pleaded.

"Me, too," Angel added, sliding from Enrique's knee to tug at his hand.

"Again?" He winked at Miguel. "Maybe I should bring the water trough in here, instead." Taking the giggling youngsters by the hand, he led them to the kitchen.

"We had a letter from Carlos," Miguel said. "He's doing a fine job running Billy Storm's ranch in Colorado."

"Billy raised you, didn't he, Miguel?" Ricardo asked.

"Yes. Billy has arthritis so bad it's hard for him to do much anymore. He was grateful when Carlos volunteered to help. Between you and me, I think Carlos had ulterior motives. The old scoundrel took quite a shine to the cook the last time we visited." He shot a sideways glance at Elena. "He's probably warming her tepee right now."

"Miguel!" Elena gasped, blushing.

He gave her a wicked grin. "How about warming my tepee later this evening?" he whispered.

Raising a brow, she gave him a shove. "Your 'tepee' is too warm already. If it gets any hotter, we won't have room for us."

He cuddled her closer. "Then we'll build a bigger one."

"Mama, Papa!" Angel shrieked. "Come quick!"

Frightened, all five adults jumped to their feet and ran toward the kitchen. "What is it?" Elena cried.

"Look!"

All eyes raised to the top of the stairwell. There on the landing, a figure in blue smiled down at them. Along with her presence came a wonderful, comforting fragrance that filled the air with a sense of peace. The angel held out her hands as if to embrace them, then vanished.

"Who was she?" a small voice asked.

Miguel lifted his daughter into his arms. "*La Madama*," he said quietly. "The real Spanish Angel. The spirit of your great grandmother, Angelina. She died long before I was born, when a tile fell from the roof and struck her head. You are named after her."

"Why did she go away?"

"Because right now we don't need her. But I am sure if the time comes that we do, she will return." His eyes caught Elena's. "You see, Angelita, *La Madama* watches over the ones she loves."

"And she loves us?" the little girl asked.

Elena nodded. She gazed up at Miguel, remembering how the angel had answered her prayer and saved his life. "Yes, *niña*, she loves us very much."

When Elena and the rest of the family had returned to the living room, Miguel turned to see his father-in-law staring at the stairwell as if transfixed. "Enrique, are you all right?"

The old man turned tear-bright eyes to meet his. "Miguel, she told me I am forgiven. After all these years, I am forgiven."

Knowing how the elderly man had suffered, Miguel's throat tightened with emotion. "Come on, Grandpapa," he said, his voice husky. "I hear your brood calling." He curved his arm around Enrique's shoulders and gave him a hug, before leading him back to join his family.

Author's Note

DEAR READER,

When I created Miguel Sandoval, the mysterious, black-clad gunman in *Colorado Tempest*, I couldn't resist telling his story and giving him a love of his own. I hope you enjoyed *Bandit's Kiss*.

I had a strange sense of déjà vu when I was doing additional research on the novel and discovered there truly was a Spanish angel. A Franciscan nun, Maria de Jesus de la Conception, appeared many times to the Indians of New Mexico, even though she never left her convent in Spain. When confronted by Friar Alonzo de Benavides, who in 1625 was *custodio* and the first *comisario* of the Holy Office, she confirmed all tales, adding that she had often appeared to Indians three or four times in twenty-four hours. She had flown fifteen or twenty thousand miles on her errands of conversion. Benevides reported: She has a beautiful face, very white, although rosy, with large black eyes. Her habit was coarse gray sackcloth and her cloak was blue; the Indians always described her as garbed in blue. He ended saying he had obtained the very habit in which she made her flights and that "the veil radiates such a fragrance that it is a comfort to the spirit."

As this is only my second book, I would appreciate your comments. Write to me c/o Berkley Publishing, or at

P.O. Box 101, Murphy, Oregon 97533. An SASE, please, if you'd like a reply and news of future works.

Hasta luego, compadres,

Mary Lou Rich

FREE
Romance
(a $4.50 value)

Send in the Coupon Below

To get your FREE historical romance and start saving, fill out the coupon below and mail it today. As soon as we receive it we'll send you your FREE Book along with your first month's selections.

Mail To: **True Value Home Subscription Services, Inc. P.O. Box 5235**
120 Brighton Road, Clifton, New Jersey 07015-5235

YES! I want to start previewing the very best historical romances being published today. Send me my FREE book along with the first month's selections. I understand that I may look them over FREE for 10 days. If I'm not absolutely delighted I may return them and owe nothing. Otherwise I will pay the low price of just $4.00 each: a total $16.00 (at *least* an $18.00 value) and save at least $2.00. Then each month I will receive four brand new novels to preview as soon as they are published for the same low price. I can always return a shipment and I may cancel this subscription at any time with no obligation to buy even a single book. In any event the FREE book is mine to keep regardless.

Name _____

Street Address _____ Apt. No. _____

City _____ State _____ Zip Code _____

Telephone _____

Signature _____
(if under 18 parent or guardian must sign)

842

Terms and prices subject to change. Orders subject
to acceptance by True Value Home Subscription
Services, Inc.

From the acclaimed author of **Frontier Flame**

TENDER VICTORY
Susan Macias —————————————

"A poignant love story. Thoroughly enjoyable!"
—Jill Marie Landis, bestselling author of *Come Spring*

In desperation, Rachel brought her young son to
the ranch of the man she'd always loved. The man
whose heart had turned against her.

Once, Luke loved Rachel only to be betrayed by her.
Her sudden and unexplained marriage had shattered
him; years of unrequited love had hardened his heart.

Now Luke and Rachel face the chance of a lifetime:
to open their hearts to a love that was meant to be. Or
be swept away by the furious passions that divided
them...

___1-55773-862-9/$4.99